'Domestic noir up there with the best of them. Beautiful settings, believable characters, and a moral quandary to keep you reading through the night — *One of Those Mothers* is a page turner in all the right ways.'

— Jacqueline Bublitz, *Before You Knew My Name*

'With stiletto-sharp observation, vibrantly drawn characters and a deeply disturbing secret at its heart, *One of Those Mothers* had me in its grasp from the first chapter. A terrific debut.'

— Charity Norman, *Remember Me*

'Wildly compelling, refreshingly raw exploration of motherhood, friendship and the haunting anxieties of parenthood.'

— Claire Mabey, books editor, *The Spinoff*, former festival director and co-founder of Verb Wellington

'A gloriously claustrophobic and page-turning tale of friendships, relationships and ultimate loyalties. Megan Nicol Reed pins middle-class motherhood to the specimen board and watches it squirm. Compulsory (and cautionary) reading ahead of your next group holiday.'

— Kim Knight, senior writer, *The New Zealand Herald*

'A contemporary tale of complex relationships where loyalties and values are tested. Written by a natural storyteller, it will keep you thinking!'

— Stacey Morrison, television and radio host

'Searing and darkly funny. Megan Nicol Reed cleverly cuts right through to the euphoria and claustrophobia of family and friendship. Extraordinarily gripping.'

— Frances Morton, editor, *Sunday* and *Your Weekend* magazines

One
of
Those
Mothers

Megan Nicol Reed

One of Those Mothers

ALLEN&UNWIN
SYDNEY·MELBOURNE·AUCKLAND·LONDON

Allen & Unwin
Level 2, 10 College Hill, Freemans Bay
Auckland 1011, New Zealand
Phone: (64 9) 377 3800
Email: auckland@allenandunwin.com
Web: www.allenandunwin.co.nz

83 Alexander Street
Crows Nest NSW 2065, Australia
Phone: (61 2) 8425 0100

A catalogue record for this book is available from the
National Library of New Zealand.

ISBN 978 199100 6 295

Cover image: creativephototeam/Alamy Stock Photo
Cover design by Sandy Cull, www.sandycull.com
Internal design by Kate Barraclough
Set in Milona Regular and Minion Pro
Printed and bound in Australia by the Opus Group

10 9 8 7 6 5 4 3 2 1

FSC
www.fsc.org
MIX
Paper | Supporting
responsible forestry
FSC® C001695

For my mothers

Chapter One

October
Friday

The only thing worse than the school holidays was a mother who claimed she couldn't wait for them to start. *Christ*. Bridget took in the sea of chaos that had engulfed her lounge: empty Kinder Surprise wrappers and sticky PlayStation controllers all tangled up in a forsaken blanket fortress.

'This place is a pigsty.'

She was sure she'd spoken aloud, but there was no response from Jackson and Abigail, who were marooned like two small, useless boats upon the debris-strewn shores of the couch, necks tilted unnaturally forward, eyes rooted to their laps.

Who in their right mind enjoyed having to entertain their children for days on end? No, either those mothers were lying or they were deluded. The first time a woman said it to her, Bridget thought she was joking. The second time she'd wondered if it was this weird kind of one-upmanship. *Look at me. Look at what a dedicated mother I am*. Really, Bridget suspected, it was some sort of self-seeking validation. Of justifying their existence, the choice they'd made to be stay-at-home mums. Because, let's face it, no working mother ever declared herself excited at the prospect of juggling childcare with the rest of her commitments.

'We're just shattered,' they'd say. 'We really need a break.' *A break from what*? Bridget always wanted to ask. *The gym? Your coffee catch-ups?* Sometimes they'd elaborate; say what they were really craving was a break from the routine. And, in all fairness, Bridget got that, what mother didn't? But surely the relentlessness of lunchboxes and homework journals was a small price to pay for six hours reprieve from your kids, five days a week.

God, how long had Jackson and Abigail been on those bloody devices? She looked at the microwave. It wasn't even ten-thirty a.m.; they must have already clocked up three hours.

'Okay, screen time's over.'

It was an addiction, she wasn't a fool. And she knew she enabled it, was practically their dealer. It was convenient, that was the trouble. Actual babysitters cost money and didn't clean up after themselves. With screens, though, you knew where your kids were and there was no need to supervise or, worse, participate.

Bridget always envisioned the holidays as a time of great productivity, the children making collages with autumn leaves while she sorted out the linen cupboard. But here they were, holidays almost over, with nothing to show for themselves apart from a bunch of playdates and a big fat mess. A familiar wave of guilt washed over her.

'Right,' she clapped her hands. 'What are we going to do today? Any ideas? How about the museum?'

Jackson groaned. 'Do we have to?'

'No, but we're doing something and, whatever it is, it doesn't involve a screen. In fact, turn them off right now.'

She pulled back the curtains. It was another crappy day. Dull and damp. At least when it properly rained you could legitimately stay inside; light the fire, make scones, play Last Card. This, though, this endless greyness was like living under a constant threat. You felt obliged to leave the house because it wasn't raining, yet when you did, all you could think about was the fact it might piss down on you at any moment.

'Off! Off now! I mean it. Abigail. Jackson. Could you just do what I ask for once?'

Abigail slowly put down her iPad. Jackson reluctantly brought his eyes up to meet hers; his finger hovering, itching to shoot more bad guys. Bad guys who all looked Middle Eastern. 'You know Muslim isn't code for baddie,' she told him at least once a week, unconvinced her feeble lesson in tolerance and international relations was having any effect.

'How about Trampoline Land?'

Bridget loathed the place, but it was about the only activity both her children still agreed on.

'Yay!' said Abigail. 'Can I bring a friend? Can I? Please!'

'No. Just us, eh? You've seen lots of your friends these holidays. It'll be nice for just the three of us to do something.'

It was true, it would be nice, as long as they didn't fight. Bridget had read once that psychologically the optimum gap between siblings was two-and-a-half to three-and-a-half years. She'd thought they'd got it right. Jackson, at twelve already a dead ringer for Greg; Abigail, nine and a half, her very own mini-me: three years, more or less, between them. Ideal age difference or not, though, they were always at each other's throats. Yesterday they'd almost killed each other over who could do a better rendition of some YouTuber's parody of the national anthem. She'd had to physically pull them apart. Comforting and castigating with the same breath. Argh . . . maybe it would be better if they each asked a friend. No, she'd just end up paying. She felt like she'd been paying for other people's children all holidays.

She could call Roz. Paris and Earl had only just turned nine, but the four of them played well together. Actually, thinking about it, Bridget hadn't spoken to Roz in ages. Not since that kids' dinner Roz had hosted the night school broke up.

'Come over early,' she'd said, 'the blokes can join us later. I'll make my famous homemade pizza.' When Bridget and the kids had arrived, two other women were already there, Carol and Lindsay. Mothers from the twins' class; Bridget didn't really know them, but they'd seemed nice enough. By the time the dads had turned up the women were on to their third bottle of Prosecco, with no sign of the famous pizza and the kids running riot.

Always up for a party, Greg had lit a joint and Carol had freaked. 'There are children around,' she'd hissed.

'Simmer down,' Greg had said. When Bridget shot him a look, he'd put it out, but it had thrown a dampener on things and they'd left shortly afterwards.

'Sorry,' Bridget had texted Roz the next day. 'Hope we didn't scare off your new friend.'

'Ha!' Roz had replied. 'Somehow I don't think Carol and I are kindred spirits.'

'How about we invite the twins to come?' Bridget suggested.

'Yay,' cried Abigail.

'Jackson, are you okay if I ask Earl?'

'Whatevs.'

Bridget had known adolescence was coming, though perhaps naively had assumed she still had a good year or so, a year before her baby boy turned into a surly, smelly stranger. But he was metamorphosing before her eyes. She found herself mourning the days her word had been gospel. He hadn't actually verbalised it, that he didn't have to do what she said any more, yet she could sense it coming; his rebellion taking shape, embedding. 'It's inevitable,' said Greg. 'There's no point fighting it. Pick your battles.'

Where was her bloody phone? She could have sworn she'd left it charging on the bedside table. Jackson must have it. He could only text and call on his. He was desperate for his own smartphone, but so far they'd managed to fob him off. *Not until you prove yourself mature enough. Not until you can be trusted to use it sensibly.* Bridget knew this was not good parenting; that according to the literature you were meant to give children firm boundaries, specific consequences, realistic goals.

'Have you got my phone, Jackson?'

He grunted.

'Where is it?'

Pulling it out from under his thigh, he passed it to her. The little battery flashing almost empty. God knows what he was forever downloading, but it swallowed up her data.

She scrolled through her contacts, wondering for the umpteenth time why she didn't have Roz saved to her favourites. After Greg and her parents,

Roz was the person she called the most.

Of course, once Lucy would have been top of that list. But Bridget wasn't going there. She was stopping those thoughts right now. She pictured a balloon sailing away. *Lucy . . . Stop*. She was a bricklayer. She would build a wall. *Stop, stop, stop*.

She clicked on Roz's name. A photo popped up: taken a couple of years ago at this Latin-themed party, plastic fruit spilling off Roz's black hair. One dark eye closed in a wink. Carmen Mirandas had been a dime a dozen that night, but Roz had been the only one puffing on a real cigar. It always made Bridget smile.

'Kia ora,' sang out Roz's voice.

'Hey,' said Bridget.

There was a beep. Shit, she always fell for it. She hung up without leaving a message. Replying promptly to missed calls did not figure highly on Roz's priorities.

Typing 'Trampoline Land' into Google, Bridget tapped on the call option. 'Get with the times, Bridge,' Greg would say if he was there, shaking his once brown, now what he liked to call 'blanched' hair at her. 'Book online, you Luddite.'

But she couldn't help it; she preferred to deal with an actual human.

The boy who answered sounded all of fourteen.

'I'd like to make a booking for one p.m., please.'

'No can do.'

'Well how about two p.m.?'

'Nup.'

'Umm, earlier then?'

'Nah.'

'So, you're fully booked?'

'Nah.'

'Well, when have you got space?'

'Umm . . . eleven-thirty.'

'But you said you didn't have anything earlier.'

'I thought you meant like at twelve or something.'

Jesus. 'Okay. Two kids at eleven-thirty a.m., please.'

If they put their skates on, they should be able to make it.

'We have a special for adults,' he said, suddenly sounding more animated than he had all conversation. 'Half-price for the holidays.'

'Thanks. I think I'll pass.'

The one and only time the kids had convinced her to have a go, her pelvic floor had given way within the first minute of bouncing and she'd spent the rest of the session praying no one noticed the wet patch on her crotch.

'Get dressed, you two. Brush your teeth.'

'Are the twins coming?'

'No, it's just us. Roz didn't answer.'

'Stink!'

'Remember to wear your Trampoline Land socks. I'm not buying more.'

'Have you got your socks?' Bridget asked, pulling into the desolate industrial estate.

Where the Good Times Begin! announced the sign in garish green.

'Abigail,' she groaned, glimpsing her daughter's sheepish face in the rear-vision mirror. 'You're going to have to pay for a new pair out of next week's pocket money.'

'Okay.'

Bridget couldn't stand losing things. Forgetting stuff. She was constantly doing a mental inventory, discreetly running her hand through her bag. Phone? Wallet? Keys? But Abigail couldn't care less. 'Have we spoiled her?' she sometimes asked Greg. 'Raised her with a sense of entitlement?'

'Probably,' he'd say cheerfully. Greg didn't do guilt.

'Can you video us, Mum? Please.'

'Can you get me doing a round-off in slow-motion?'

'Love to.'

Bridget sighed; she'd been anticipating finding a quiet corner with the paper and one of the terrible coffees they served here.

'Mum, you missed it.'

'Over here, Mum. Look at me. Take a picture and send it to Dad.'

She didn't get it. She'd always loathed having her photograph taken;

with this generation, though, it was almost as if they didn't exist unless someone was capturing them on film. She took a few obligatory shots: Abigail, arms and hair akimbo, flying through the air; Jackson rebounding clumsily off a net.

Watching the staff in their foul lime green uniforms half-heartedly trying to organise some little kids into a game of dodgeball, she wondered if a particularly gormless-looking boy was the one from the phone.

The coffee was as awful as she remembered. Still, she seldom got the opportunity to read an actual paper these days, and, as she grabbed the remaining empty booth, she felt a ripple of pleasure at the prospect of a few moments alone.

Discarding the business and sport sections, she scanned the news. The lead story was an MP who'd been abusing his parliamentary perks. She should probably read it. Yawning, she placed a napkin over a gob of old tomato sauce, and flipped to page three.

Identity remains secret
A thirty-nine-year-old Point Heed businessman and father of two convicted for possession and distribution of child pornography has been granted permanent name suppression.

Bridget's throat caught. Point Heed: lovely, leafy Point Heed. Her neighbourhood.

It was only in the briefs. Insulting, almost. Someone, somewhere, must have decided that was the extent of its newsworthiness. But there it was. Two paltry lines sitting below a missing fisherman and above an overturned milk tanker. There was a correction in there, too, languishing at the foot of the narrow column. Something the newspaper had screwed up the previous week. Bridget wondered if anyone would read their *mea culpa*. Whether the paper even cared. Probably not. They were only covering their arses. She'd been told once the real stories of the day were buried in the briefs. You just needed to know where to look.

Porn. As teenagers she and her friends would sometimes hang round the entrance to the X-rated room at the local video store. They'd snigger at the men who slunk in. *Sad lonely bastards!* Now, though, everyone seemed to watch it. Actually, Greg reckoned they always had, it was just these days they felt more comfortable admitting to it.

They'd been at a dinner party a few weeks ago, and somehow the conversation had got on to a clip several of them had seen online. A professor/student scenario, except the professor was a woman with fake tits, who ejaculated like a man ('squirting' they called it) all over the young male student she'd inveigled to go down on her. A guy Bridget didn't know very well had brought it up on his phone, and passed it to her with a smirk. Keeping her face deliberately blank while she watched, Bridget had helped herself to the cheese board. 'So, is it a triumph or a strike against feminism?' she'd asked the table.

Initially it had only been Bridget and a small woman with an unusually husky voice on the 'strike against' side, but in the end they'd won some of them over.

Porn's audience might have changed, Bridget had said, however the statistics haven't. Three-quarters of women working in the sex industry have been sexually abused. She couldn't remember where she'd read that. Some study or other. It was bona fide, though.

The discussion had invigorated her; she'd been positively fizzing when they got in the car. Until Greg had done his best to burst her 'self-righteous bubble' on the way home. Accused her and 'Deep Throat' of getting on their collective soapbox. Of turning playful banter into an ugly scene. 'You know,' he'd said, 'not every man is a misogynist, and not every woman needs to be empowered. Most people just want to be happy.'

Bridget had been quiet, crushed. When they'd climbed into bed, she'd thought he might take her in his arms, like he once would have after a fight. *Never go to sleep on an argument*, they'd promised each other when they were young and stupid with love. 'You need to get over yourself,' he'd said as he rolled away.

The next morning he'd behaved as if nothing was wrong. Kissing her goodbye, even though she was patently ignoring him. Blithely telling her he wouldn't be late home. It pissed her off how he did that. It ran in his family. *Sweep. Sweep. Everything's fine.* Even if you can't walk on the carpet for all the shit underneath. Bridget couldn't remember whether they'd discussed it in the end, or if they'd just moved on. If the pretending everything was fine had eventually made it true.

'Mum! Mum!'

She looked up; Abigail was balancing on top of the highest climbing pole. She knew Abigail was wearing a harness, that, even if she were to slip, a gigantic safety net would catch her, but she felt a terrible hollowness as she imagined that little body crumpled in a heap.

When she'd fallen pregnant with Jackson, she was convinced he'd be born with a hole in his heart. 'I just want him out,' she'd said to her mother, 'so I know he's okay.' 'Oh darling,' her mother had replied, 'this is only the beginning. Irrational fear is the price of parenthood.'

'Wow. How tall are you?' she exclaimed, averting her eyes as Abigail blindly leapt off.

She smoothed out the newspaper lying open in front of her.

No, she thought, *in itself the word 'pornography' isn't shocking any more.* Child. That was the bit that made it repugnant. The sandwiching of those two words together. Child pornography. One did not belong with the other.

She had never shied from the vile. Unlike her girlfriends, Bridget hadn't cowered when those animals had brutally raped Jodie Foster over a pinball machine in *The Accused*. She'd watched. Closely. Taking in every angry thrust.

She was proud of her unflinching curiosity when it came to the underbelly. Her threshold for savagery. Not that she'd ever admit it. Admit she'd happily skip the full-page feature on the US–China trade war, while poring over the story about the street kid who'd scalped the old guy who offered him a bottle of Jack Daniel's in exchange for a blowjob.

Her interest in the seedy didn't exactly sit well with her BA minoring in women's studies, or her Green Party membership. Sometimes she wondered if deep down, in spite of her monthly Oxfam donation, her preference for organic milk, she'd be happier with some tabloid paper and a cheap sausage in nasty white bread. If under her bleeding liberal heart, a redneck lurked.

'I'm gonna fuck your ass up!'

Bridget turned around. What kind of idiot had gangsta rap for their ringtone?

'You motherfucking mofo!'

Shit, it was coming from her bag. A mother with two little girls, all three in matching polar fleece, gave Bridget the evil eye as she desperately tried to make it stop. 'Sorry,' she mouthed. 'Sorry.' Damn Jackson. He was never using her phone again.

It was Roz. She pressed the phone to her ear, avoiding the irate mother's gaze.

'Roz! I take it all back.'

'Take what back, sweetheart?'

'Nothing, I just didn't think you'd return my call.'

'What call?'

'I rang you a little while ago to see if you and the twins wanted to come to Trampoline Land.'

'We're in Sydney. Remember? Jono saw this deal and we decided to surprise the kids. You know how obsessed Paris is with koalas.'

'And there are so many koalas in Sydney . . .' Bridget caught herself. She was being petty. She tried not to be jealous of Roz and Jono's seemingly limitless disposable income. 'I swear you never mentioned it.'

'Really? Anyway, I rang because we're having the best time. The kids are loving it. We took them to a show at the Opera House last night. It made me think, why don't we all plan an overseas trip? Somewhere fabulous. Bali maybe? The kids are old enough now not to be painful on the flight.'

'Hmm . . .' Bridget was determined to start their renovations next year. Besides, group holidays had always meant the three of them: her, Roz, Lucy, their assorted husbands and kids. It wouldn't be the same.

'Did you hear from that new friend?'

'Who?'

'You know. Carol. She spat the dummy when Greg . . .'

'Oh, her. Silly cow. I never picked her as being so uptight. I should have known, though, no one half-normal has arms that bloody toned. Anyway, promise me you'll think about it. We'd have such a riot, Bridge.'

'Promise. Let's talk when you get back.'

Roz would have forgotten by next week. She was an ideas woman, relying on others to actually make things happen.

'Deal! Ciao, darling.'

There was a click. Bridget cursed. She should have asked Roz if she knew anything about the In Brief. About this man who lived among them. Who lived in Point Heed with its precisely trimmed hedges and freshly painted weatherboards. Where every house was either 'done' or a 'do-up'.

Bridget and Greg had a little sweepstake running. Whenever they saw the scaffolding appear, they'd make a bet on whether the owners would go for a black or red front door. She was in the lead by two. She'd known that family with the dog that barked its head off every time you walked past would paint theirs red. 'Duh,' she'd said to Greg. 'It was always going to be red. Haven't you noticed that naff sticker on the side of their bin? As if an image of some jandals under a pōhutukawa tree somehow disguises the fact it's a trash can on wheels.'

There was only one road in to Point Heed. And one road out. Long and busy, the streets spilled off on either side, down towards the water. Most were cul-de-sacs. Every spring, as soon as daylight savings kicked off, the kids were all out there, on their bikes and scooters, playing handball. It was a good area. Tight.

Oh, there were things she didn't like about it. No neighbourhood was perfect. Many of the original residents had been driven out. That sounded dreadful, as though there'd been some sort of Nazi-esque ethnic cleansing. It wasn't like that, but there were definitely fewer brown faces around these days. She guessed it was the opposite of white flight. The pensioners had mostly gone, too. Their rotary washing lines and venetian blinds had died out with them. Replaced with an almost unseemly alacrity by all the cantilevered decks and automatic gates.

Bridget wasn't one of the newcomers, though. She was old school. This was her stomping ground. As a child she'd swum at the beach when a bloated, vitreous-eyed dog had floated past, an oily trail in its wake. She still remembered the full nappies, the used sanitary pads that would come in with the tide.

There was a coffee bar then, but no café; an RSA, but no gastro pub. The supermarket didn't stock quinoa or Peroni either. Actually, it still didn't. It was like some weird last bastion of pre-gentrification. If Bridget were to be completely honest, she would prefer posher groceries — yet she took a perverse kind of pleasure in how much the dearth of culinary options got up the collective nose of the new breed of resident.

She said she pined for the old days, but in truth affluence had brought an ergonomic climbing frame to the playground and an excellent bookshop to the shopping centre. Affluence had even brought new sand to the beach — although it was still an odd excuse for a beach. When you took your fish and chips (and these days they were panko-crumbed and hand-cut) down on a Friday night you didn't stare out to the horizon, but across to the thick traffic on State Highway 5.

She could never decide if she felt embraced by the outlook or hemmed in. The whole peninsula was like that, really. Water, water everywhere, with no sense of the wide-open sea.

At its head you looked across to the vinegar factory, on the other side straight into the landscaped backyards of the next suburb round, with only the mangroves between you.

You might have a sea view, yet half the time it was mud you were admiring. When the tide was out you could walk forever before you got wet past your knees. No, it wasn't the greatest beach in the world. But it felt safe. Good for kids.

'Can I have a Coke?'

Bridget smelt Jackson before she saw him. She smiled at her sweaty son. It might be time to suggest deodorant again.

'How about some water, eh? I'll get you guys a treat after if you're good.'

'I'm thirsty.'

'Then water's the best thing for you.'

He skulked off. Bridget checked the time. There were ten more minutes until the end of the session. Ten more minutes of peace, if she was lucky.

She'd always thought if a child were ever to go missing in their neighbourhood, then she'd know where to look.

There was a man, one street over. Fat with steroids, he wore muscle shirts, peeling protein drink logos plastered across them. His upper arms had to be at least the size of one of her thighs. Her age, late thirties, early forties maybe, he still lived with his parents in their ugly, fake brick-clad house, a rare carryover from the Point's good old days. At some stage someone had concreted over the front lawn, and now a falling-down hurricane fence was the only clue to where their property ended and the footpath began. You never saw the parents; the net curtains were always drawn shut, but he was often out front, tinkering with his souped-up ute.

Bridget had been collecting for the children's hospital once and his father had come to the door. A tiny, frightened-looking man wearing an immaculately pressed flannel shirt, he'd gingerly posted a couple of coins in the slot of her bucket without making contact with its surface. He was already closing the door on her as she was still trying to get his 'I care about kidz!' sticker off the roll, and she'd wondered how this scaredy-cat of a man had produced such a boofhead.

She had been backing out of her driveway the other day, when boofhead son walked by. She'd stopped to let him pass, and he gestured that she should continue. There was something about the way he'd looked at her, though, something that made her momentarily doubt her ability to reverse up her own drive, a manoeuvre she made at least daily. And then he'd winked. A big 'I-know-you-want-it' kind of a wink.

His sleaziness was a running joke among the Point Heed mothers, but she knew she didn't turn him on, that neither she nor any of the other school mums did. If he was getting off on them, it was only at their discomfort.

No, it was her daughter, it was all of their daughters, who filled his fantasies. She'd seen those bulbous eyes taking in the little girls with their smooth-skinned naiveté and quiescent desires, their backpacks bobbing as they walked to and from school. She'd seen how he lingered over the recycling bin as they passed, laughing, oblivious to him.

It had never occurred to her, however, that all along the danger might be even closer to home. Not some bodybuilding freak, some loser who'd never left home, but a father of two, a businessman. It could be any one of the dads at the school.

Two paltry lines.

Chapter Two

January.
Nine Months Earlier
Day One

The boat spewed them out. A baker's dozen. Two families of four. One of five.

'Thank God for that,' said Roz. 'I don't think I could have taken another minute.'

Bridget swallowed back her own nausea; she said nothing. Fortunately Greg didn't appear to have heard Roz over the boat's motor. Or the kids' racket.

'I was first,' yelled Paris.

'No, my foot touched the wood before yours did,' said Abigail.

'No, mine did.'

'Accept it, loser,' said Jackson. 'Paris beat you.'

Abigail launched herself at her brother with a howl.

All Bridget could think about was a shower. Some people felt refreshed after being at sea. She just felt dirty. As if she wore a salty shroud. It was their boat; well, it was Greg's really. A horrible, big old hulk of a thing, disgorging diesel fumes and reeking of burley; it was his pride and joy. Her distaste for being on the water was no secret between them, but what had started out as a joke — the landlubber and the seadog! — was an ulcerated sore after thirteen years of marriage. On a bad day, when everything he did got on her tits, she probed at it. Seeking out its puffy, pallid edges with seemingly innocent questions about the cost of the boat's latest service, or the diminishing fish stocks. Today, though, she bit her tongue. They were on holiday and she was determined it would be happy. A happy holiday. She'd only made two New Year's resolutions and one of them was to try and find the joy.

Bridget looked around her: at their home for the next five nights. It was a horseshoe-shaped bay on the backend of Hine's Island. They'd done well. Actually, Lucy had. Disorganised, useless Lucy, who double-booked her entire life, yet when it came to vacations was oddly on to it. Roz said that was because Lucy was more interested in the good times. That she was all about the play, not so much the work, which was a bit rich, Bridget always thought, coming from Roz.

'It's amazing, Luce,' she said.

Her oldest friend smiled. Bridget noticed how dark the skin around her eyes was. Anyone else would have looked haggard, but somehow the purplish circles added to Lucy's allure.

The two of them had been to Hine's before. On a school trip. What Bridget remembered most about it was how hungry she'd been. A miserable teenager, she'd spent her entire adolescence thinking about her next meal, filling the emptiness with Big Macs and MallowPuffs. She had kidded herself Lucy's diet was equally bad, but while Lucy had remained resolutely delicate, Bridget had grown ever chubbier. On that trip to Hine's though, even her insatiable appetite hadn't been enough to convince her to eat the warm, wet pap of her salad sandwiches, squished in an old bread bag at the bottom of her pack.

Crazy she'd never returned, especially considering it was under an hour by ferry. 'Yes,' she'd said when Lucy had suggested it as their next holiday destination. 'Great idea!' She liked the idea of no cafés or vineyards, no shops or galleries, nowhere she'd feel compelled to tick off. Just beach and bush and more beach. Well, there was one exception: an old mansion. Hopefully she'd be able to convince the others to visit. Bridget loved historic homes, that sense of intimacy interrupted, of frozen domesticity. Someone's most private life preserved. All those rooms with such explicit purposes: libraries and butler's pantries and servants' quarters. Jono, Roz's husband, liked to tease Bridget she had *delusions of grandeur*. But it wasn't that; she just enjoyed being around nice things.

She cast her eye down the length of the long, skinny jetty, already piled high with all their crap, the bags and the boxes and the boogie boards, everything three families would require to survive a week. And there, at the end, was the old farmhouse they'd rented, looking reassuringly exactly like the pictures they'd seen online. And that was it. No one else. Nothing else.

'Mum,' called Abigail. 'Mum, come see.'

The kids were gathered around the top of a barnacled ladder, pointing excitedly at the water. Bridget looked down. A black shape lurked in the shadow of the jetty. She took in its massive girth, the length of its barb, and decided then and there she wouldn't be fulfilling her second resolution — to swim in the sea more — on this holiday.

'I'm not going in there. No way,' said Willow, who at four was the youngest, and, quite possibly, Bridget sometimes disloyally thought, the cutest of them all.

'Don't be silly,' said Skye, forever the responsible older sister. 'Stingrays won't hurt you.'

Actually, thought Bridget, *that's not true*. A stingray had killed Steve Irwin. She'd read how, in only a few seconds, it had struck him several hundred times in the body with its tail spine, piercing his heart. She didn't say anything, though. What was the point in frightening them?

There was a splash. She turned as Zachariah started to lob another stone at the stingray.

'Don't!' she cried. 'Stop!'

It was always Zachariah, their group's firstborn. It was terrible to be repelled by a baby, but she'd been Lucy's support person at his birth and when the midwife finally hauled him out, Bridget had gasped. Quiet yet alert, he was covered in a gauze of black hair. Lucy hadn't seemed in the least concerned, making moon eyes at him as his tight, slippery little mouth searched out her swollen nipple. It was Bridget who'd taken the midwife aside, who had asked if there was something wrong with him. The midwife, who looked younger than them, and as if she knew less about babies than they did, said hastily, 'No, no. It'll probably disappear within a few weeks.'

Zachariah would be thirteen this year and in certain lights Bridget thought she could still detect that dusky chrysalis. She'd heard other people describe him as unique, striking even, but she assumed they were just being kind. It was his eyes she found the most unsettling. Wet and calm, they could hold your gaze with an unnerving deadness. Bridget told Jackson off when he called Zachariah a 'freak', however, at heart, she agreed.

Zachariah brought his arm back down. For a moment Bridget thought he was going to throw the stone at her. But he only laughed.

'Here,' he said, handing it to her.

She tried not to shrink from his touch. *He's your best friend's son*, she reminded herself.

'Thank you,' she said, 'for stopping.'

He shrugged; walking away with that curious lope of his, the gait of an older, bigger man.

The other kids were long gone, racing each other to the house, presumably to bags the best bed. The adults had disappeared, too, ferrying armfuls of gear.

Bridget knew she ought to be helping, but she tarried a moment, admiring her creamy pink nails as she ran her fingers along the rotten railing. They were like small, perfect shells. She'd had them done the day before. Along with her toenails, brow/lash tint, bikini wax and spray tan. Greg and the kids had laughed when she'd arrived home: orange and plucked. 'We're staying at a bach, darling,' Greg had said, 'not a five-star hotel.' 'You look like an orangutan,' said Jackson, Abigail giggling nervously, traitorously, next to him.

Bridget threw the stone onto the sand below, grabbed a banana box of tinned food and stepped awkwardly down onto the lawn. The grass was cracklier underfoot than it had looked from the jetty. For some reason she felt let down by this.

She glanced up at the house. How she hated this bit: the divvying out of bedrooms. While no one would actually voice their desire for the room with the view and the ensuite, beneath the polite veneer they would be tallying up who'd got what on previous holidays, calculating their dues. By her reckoning it was well and truly their turn to have the master bedroom. She'd suggest, though, that Lucy and Tristan take it, seeing as Lucy had found the place. That way Willow could sleep with them, leaving the bunkroom to the six older kids. The website had said there were another two double rooms upstairs, and she was torn between getting in there, staking her claim, or lingering out here, delaying the inevitable discussion that awaited her. Lingering out here next to the border of purple and white agapanthus ('state house flowers' Roz called them); out here on the lawn that rolled down to a horseshoe bay where a stingray lay.

'Happy holiday,' she chanted under her breath, climbing up onto the verandah that wrapped around two sides of the house. 'Happy holiday.'

She counted six sets of French doors. At the other end there was a magnificent bow window. It was a villa, well it would have been originally, but at some point, someone with dubious taste had evidently made some so-called improvements, popping the top to create a second storey. She'd spotted the two ill-proportioned dormer windows from the jetty, one jutting out towards the water, the other towards the scrubby hill that squatted next to the house. Bridget couldn't decide what was more offensive — that the windows didn't line up, or the frames were aluminium.

She walked through the first open set of French doors and into the kitchen, lowering the heavy box onto the bench.

'Give her back,' she heard Abigail cry. 'Jackson!'

'I'm just going to take Emerson for a little swim.'

'Yeah,' said Earl. 'She looks hot.'

'Nooo!' wailed Abigail.

'You're such dicks,' said Paris, every bit her mother's daughter.

There was a loud thud. A sharp scream.

Emerson was the hideous American Girl doll Abigail had insisted she wanted for Christmas. Paris and Skye had got them, too. 'She's so real!' Abigail had exclaimed on unwrapping her. And Bridget supposed she was, if all little girls were white and upper-middle-class, with smooth skin, glossy hair and a seemingly endless line-up of outfits.

Bridget knew she should go in there, sort it out, but she had her own battle brewing. She envied children their honesty. Perhaps it would be easier if adults were more like them, less constrained by good manners. She wished she could just throw herself across the best bed, give anyone who dared try to take it off her a good shove.

'There you are, Bridge,' said Roz from the door of the master bedroom. 'We've brought everything in and sorted the kids. Now we're trying to figure out the adults. I was just saying we might have to send a search party for you.'

Bridget smiled; Roz had probably only carried her own bag in.

'I need you to help me convince Lucy she and Tristan should have this room.'

'No,' Lucy protested, 'Bridget and Greg should. As thanks for transporting us all over.'

Bridget looked around her. The window seat was upholstered in plump, faded sage linen squabs. A garland of lily of the valley and sweet peas was carved around the old wooden bedhead. It was perfect. A perfect room. She imagined waking in here, making love in the half light.

'You have it,' she said to Lucy. 'You're the one who really got us here.'

Roz smiled at her, pleased. Evidently, she'd said the right thing.

Maybe it will be all right, Bridget thought. *Maybe it won't be like last time.*

Chapter
Three

October
Monday

'Come on, you two,' Bridget yelled. 'Up! Time to get up.'

Shit. She'd known this would happen the first day back. Routines, consistency, schedules: all thrown out the window, the kids' body-clocks stuffed by that fleeting aberration that was the school holidays. They were going to be late, dammit.

Last term Jackson's teacher, Miss Smythe, had taken her aside to say his tardiness was unacceptable; the fault, she had implied with every sniff of her scrawny nostrils, obviously lay squarely with Bridget. *Bad mother!*

There was something parched about Miss Smythe. She'd never had children. Probably never had a lover either. Oh Bridget, you *bad feminist!*

The first time they'd met Bridget had called her 'Ms Smith'. Promptly correcting her, Miss Smythe had murmured something about the parallels between a lazy approach to language and modern parenting. The world, in Miss Smythe's view, was going to hell in a handcart. She had no time for chaos or complication. And zero willingness to forgive it in others.

Criticism rooted in truth was always the hardest to swallow. Bridget knew she was a lousy timekeeper. She ran ten minutes late for her entire life. It wasn't that she was slack. She couldn't remember the last time she'd slept in. She'd already been for a run this morning, hung out a load of washing and made muffins for the kids' lunchboxes. It was more that she tried to cram too much in. Greg reckoned she just needed to get the kids up earlier. As if it was that simple. He was usually out the door before they were awake: had only himself to think about.

'Hallelujah,' Bridget said as Jackson staggered out, one hand down his pyjama pants.

Abigail trailed behind him. Even in the morning rush, Bridget couldn't help noticing how lovely they were. Skin pink and warm and soft with sleep. Wild hair.

The thought of something bad happening to them, someone harming them, came over her suddenly, spreading and clutching at her with ugly tentacles. *Stop it. Stop. Stop. Stop!*

'What do you want for breakfast, you two? Something quick. We're late.'

'Pancakes?' asked Abigail.

Bridget snorted. 'I said "quick".'

She got out bowls, dumping a small mountain of Oatie Crisps in the bottom of each, trying not to think about the story on the news the other night. How Oatie Crisps had topped the list of popular cereals for sugar. She sliced up a banana and threw it in. Maybe the potassium would cancel out the crap.

Jackson and Abigail robotically shovelled the brown lumps into their mouths while Bridget got out their lunchboxes, putting a bunch of grapes and a handful of rice crackers into each of the small compartments, a blueberry muffin into the medium part.

'Tuna,' she asked Jackson hopefully. 'Egg?'

Abigail was easy. She only ever wanted Vegemite and cheese. Jackson's sandwich was a daily challenge.

'Avocado and ham?'

'Nooo,' he said, making gagging sounds as if she'd proposed a sandwich of dog poo.

'Well, what? You enjoyed it last term.'

'Meatballs. Like Subway.'

'Jackson, I can't produce meatballs out of thin air.'

Don't scream, she told herself. *Don't scream.* And just when she thought she might, Jackson announced he'd have peanut butter. Bridget looked at the clock. If they had any hope of making it before the bell, the kids had to be dressed, hair brushed, and teeth cleaned in five minutes. *This once*, she silently promised, she'd conveniently forget the school ban on nuts. Cross her fingers there was no one in Jackson's class who would go into anaphylactic shock at the mere whiff of a peanut-butter sandwich.

There was a park right outside the school gate, and Bridget was starting to think she might actually pull this off, when a small silver hatchback nosed in as she indicated to reverse. She beeped. It kept on coming. She put her hand flat on the horn. The driver paid no attention. Rage flooding her chest, Bridget thrust open her door and jumped out into the middle of the morning traffic.

'Mum,' cried Abigail.

A guy in a black BMW flipped her the bird.

'Oh, piss off,' she yelled.

A small gathering of parents and toddlers stared. *Feast your eyes*, she thought, stalking over to the hatchback, and thumping on the driver's window with the heel of her hand.

Bridget reeled back.

Her anger abating as suddenly as it had arisen.

Later, replaying this moment, she would remember it like being punched in the guts.

She hadn't recognised the car. Or the hair. All that long, unkempt hair. Gone. In its place a blunt bob.

Lucy. Her oldest friend. The friend she'd made at Brownies, who hadn't ratted her out for eating all the biscuits they were meant to be selling. The friend she'd protected from the mean girls after they caught her making out with a boy in the year above and named her 'Floozy Lucy'. The friend she'd done her big OE with, who'd shocked their Contiki tour group with her uninhibited ways: skinny-dipping in the Seine, flashing the Queen's Guard. The friend she'd sworn to in a Bavarian beer hall she'd stick by 'srough sick and sin'.

'Lucy,' Bridget said to her oldest friend through the window. Lucy, who hadn't spoken to her since last summer. Since Hine's. Since everything had gone so very, very wrong. 'Lucy. Hi.'

But sweet, dopey Lucy just turned her shorn head.

Bridget thought she might vomit, right there in the street, a bilious torrent outside the school gate.

From the front passenger seat, she could feel Zachariah's oily gaze on her. Skye, who always took her mother's lead, studiously looked the other way. Only little Willow acknowledged her, blithely waggling her fingers from her booster seat.

Funny; Bridget thought she'd managed to quash the hurt and the loss that had plagued her since their island holiday, their *happy holiday*. Had been proud of her supposed resilience. Just like that, though, all the horror and the heartache returned.

Averting her eyes from the parents and toddlers still standing there, still gawking, she stumbled back to the car.

'What's wrong, Mum?' asked Abigail.

'Nothing, honey. Nothing's wrong.'

'Was that Zachariah?' asked Jackson.

'Yeah, I think so.'

'What's he doing here?'

'I'm not sure.'

'How come we never see them any more anyway?'

'No real reason. Just busy, I guess.'

She was certain Jackson knew there was more to it. Abigail, too, probably. After all, they'd been there when it had all exploded, when the holiday had come to its abrupt end, but oddly neither of them had ever said much about it.

'Should we be concerned?' she'd asked Greg. 'What, you mean bothered they don't seem very bothered? Don't go looking for trouble, Bridget,' he'd said. 'They're kids. What they don't know won't hurt them.'

Bridget drove around the block. Once. Twice. On her third circuit she found a park. It was miles away.

Now officially late, she signed Jackson and Abigail in at the office, for the life of her unable to think what she was meant to write in the section asking for your relationship to the student.

The school secretary tapped her foot. Shorter than half the pupils, Mrs Novak ruled the school with an iron hand, as tight-fisted with the sticking plasters as she was with the leave passes. Even Mr Ngata, the principal, cowered in her presence.

'Good start, huh,' Bridget said.

In the absence of any kind of response from Mrs Novak, Bridget laughed; the sound reverberating in her ears.

Opening the office door, she handed the kids an all-too-familiar pink late slip each.

'Bye, sausage. Have a great day. See you after school.'

Her kiss landed on Jackson's ear. He didn't look back as he took off across the courtyard towards the senior block.

Abigail was old enough to go to class by herself, but Bridget wanted to delay being alone.

'Sorry,' she mouthed to Abigail's teacher, who was in her first year on the job and thus, Bridget figured, not brave enough to give her grief.

Ms Snow pointed to a space on the mat where Abigail could squeeze in.

All the little girls were in love with Ms Snow. Half the fathers probably were, too. Not to mention some of the mums. She reminded Bridget of a ballerina; her pretty lips permanently pursed in a small secret smile. Just being around Ms Snow made Bridget feel old and lumpy.

Abigail happily took her seat.

'Miss you already,' said Bridget under her breath.

Terrified of crossing paths with Lucy again, Bridget headed for the bottom gate. What the hell was she doing outside school anyway? They only lived on the other side of the peninsula, but Zachariah and Skye went to this alternative school downtown, called The Imagination Academy, where the kids self-directed their learning and were encouraged to draw on the walls. Initially Lucy had tried home-schooling them, but she had pulled the plug on 'her social experiment', as Greg called it, a few years ago. She'd never really explained why, but Bridget suspected spending day in day out with Zachariah had got the better of her.

As she came around the corner of the field, Bridget saw a group of mothers she vaguely knew blocking the path.

Oh God, the last thing she felt like being subjected to was reports of holidays spent skiing down South or surfing in Bali.

Sina, whose daughter Ivy was one of Abigail's best friends, waved at her. Bridget would just smile and keep walking, pretend she had somewhere to be. Sina was a perfectly nice woman. She was also incapable of talking about anything other than her perfect family.

Although she had never physically met Sina's oldest daughter, Faith, Bridget knew she was excelling at the private girls' school she attended. That she was tossing up between law and music. That while Sina didn't want to stifle her creativity — after all she could be the next Lorde, her singing teacher said she had the same X factor — Sina's husband, a leading barrister, wanted her to get something practical under her belt. Apparently, Faith was burdened with being both highly academic and hugely creative. Poor thing.

It wasn't really a lie anyway; Bridget was busy. Despite her best intentions, she hadn't managed a scrap of work over the holidays. Now she had deadlines coming out her ears. It was, she often thought, one of the major downfalls of working from home. You might be able to determine your own hours, work in your dressing gown if you wanted to, but if you took time off there was no one to pick up the slack.

'Hi. Bye,' she said to Sina, making a jogging motion with her hands to indicate she couldn't stop.

She mentally patted herself on the shoulder. Ruth, that ghastly woman with breasts like boulders and an awful air of officiousness, was holding court, evidently up in arms over something. Again.

'As parents,' Bridget overheard her declare, 'surely we have the right to know.'

Chapter Four

January
Day One

They ate like kings and queens that first night.

They were all of them good cooks, 'foodies'; although the pleasure they took in each other's culinary efforts was inevitably marred by the fear their own offering had been outshone by the next person's. Historically the question of what they would eat on holiday, and how they would prepare it, had proven both divisive and treacherous.

One camping trip, Jono, who had been to Mexico 'myriad times', saw Bridget adding garlic to the guacamole. He had sniggered. 'What?' she'd asked. 'Nothing,' he'd said. 'No, c'mon,' she'd insisted. 'Well,' and as if about to impart the meaning of life, he'd taken a deep breath in. 'You do know in Mexico they never mix garlic and avocado?' 'But,' she'd protested, 'you've always happily eaten my guacamole.' 'I'm not saying it doesn't taste good,' he'd said. 'It's just not particularly authentic.' Roz had called him a 'bloody tosser'. And, though Bridget had felt her face might crack with the effort, she had laughed along with everyone else.

Greg said she couldn't bear to be wrong. But it wasn't that. She just liked to know stuff. To do things properly. Right. All these years she'd been serving up her signature dish, and it turns out it was some kind of mutation.

It wasn't as if Greg could talk anyway. The self-appointed group expert on red meat, he visibly bristled if anyone tried to muscle in on the barbeque. Every time he fired it up Bridget waited for the same tiresome old scenario to play out.

Someone would ask if they could put their steak back on for a minute. 'I thought you liked it medium-rare,' Greg would mutter, picking up the offending piece of meat and slapping it on the grill, a bloody trail in his wake. 'There you go,' he'd say a few minutes later, whacking it down on their plate, his face all pissy. 'One overdone steak.' And he'd hack into his own meat with a kind of testy gusto.

It would be almost comical if it wasn't so unpleasant.

And then there was Roz, the permanently unhappy owner of ten extra kilos, forever evangelising about her latest diet. They'd once gone away for a long weekend when Roz had been on Atkins and she'd lectured them endlessly about the evils of carbs, all the while gazing longingly at their bowls of ravioli. Worse had been her raw phase. She'd nicknamed the outdoor pizza oven at the place they'd rented 'the crematorium', banging on about the correlation between char-grilled food and colorectal cancers every time they'd used it.

Bridget walked to the edge of the lawn. She closed her eyes for a moment and breathed in the sea air, forcing herself to enjoy the stillness.

Of the six of them, Tristan was the only one who wasn't precious about what he ate or how it was cooked. As if he didn't really get what all the fuss was about. But then he'd always been the most laidback.

Bridget looked over at him now. He was pretending to be asleep while the girls took it in turns to sneak up on him, tickling his feet, blowing on his face, until he leapt up with sudden ferocity and wrestled them to the ground.

'I've got you now,' he growled, grabbing one of Abigail's wriggly thighs. 'You can't get away from me!'

'Stop it. Noooo! Don't touch me. Stop it,' her daughter screamed, breaking free and running madly for the 'crocodile-free' safety zone of the verandah.

Caught deliciously between delight and terror, the other girls urged her on.

How lucky they were, thought Bridget, growing up around adults who cared for them like their own, who'd known them since they were born. Adults they could trust.

It was Greg who'd introduced Tristan and Lucy.

When Bridget graduated from university she and Greg had moved to the UK, and Lucy had followed, dossing on the couch in their tiny Brixton flat while she found her feet.

Greg had been fortunate to get a job with a well-known landscape designer, who specialised in Georgian walled kitchen gardens and working his young employees to the bone. After a few weeks Greg had said he never wanted to see another espaliered lemon tree as long as he lived. But he'd sucked it up because the money was good and he liked the other guy he worked with. One night the two of them had gone to the pub and his workmate had missed the last tube home.

'Girls, this is Tristan,' Greg had announced, staggering in through the front door, his arm around an astoundingly good-looking man, eyes the iciest blue. 'Tristan, this is the girls.'

'Where will he sleep?' Bridget had hissed.

'Oh, don't worry about me,' Lucy had said, scooping up her long, honeyed mane with one hand, patting the cushion next to her with the other. 'It's plenty big enough for two.' *For two Norse gods*, Bridget had thought, tucking her own dun-brown hair self-consciously behind one ear.

That night she'd scarcely slept for the moaning, and when she got home from work the next day there'd been a sunflower poked into an old wine bottle and a note pinned to the fridge. *Thanks for the couch*, it said in Lucy's reckless scrawl. *I guess I won't be needing it any more! Love L xoxo*

Lucy and Tristan had lasted seven months. Until Lucy's mother was diagnosed with terminal cancer, and Lucy's father had asked her to come home and help him care for her. It took three long, horrible months for her mother to die, and afterwards Lucy went on an extended bender.

In spite of the thousands of kilometres that separated them, by piecing together the odd rambling email from Lucy, and Roz's increasingly hysterical phone calls, Bridget was able to track her best friend's downward spiral: the drugs, the sex with strangers, the blackouts. And while Lucy had no idea who the father was, Bridget had no doubt getting pregnant with Zachariah had saved her from some worse fate — finding out she was going to have a baby the metaphorical equivalent of a slap to the face.

Zachariah was two when Tristan got back in touch with Greg, saying he was planning a trip to New Zealand and that it'd be great to catch up. Of course, they'd asked him to stay and on his second night Bridget had suggested they invite Lucy over. The next day Tristan had moved in with her and Zachariah.

And ten years later, here they were: a sixsome. They'd had their ups and downs, their sicks and sins, but that first night on Hine's it was as if all their past grievances, the petty hurts and tiny brutalities, were forgiven, forgotten.

'You must be knackered from all that skippering. I can do it,' Tristan said.

At the barbeque Greg hesitated.

'Actually, you'd be doing me a favour. Keep the girls off me.'

And though Bridget knew Greg would rather eat his arm than give up the tongs, he passed them over.

While the other adults got dinner sorted, Jono played Swingball with the kids, his T-shirt riding up over his jiggling belly.

'That's it,' he shouted encouragingly to Willow as her bat connected with the ball. 'Atta girl!'

The older kids cheered her on, and though there were still the predictable claims of cheating, the endless accusations of bad losing, no one packed a sad. And when they tired of smacking a small yellow sphere around a pole, no one whined about being hungry, about where dinner was.

Inside Roz chopped tomatoes and parsley for the tabbouleh, while Lucy peeled carrots and cucumber for the kids.

'Anyone for a G&T?' asked Bridget.

'Does a bear shit in the woods?' said Roz.

Bridget laughed. 'Jono is sweating up a storm out there.'

'Yeah, what's got into that husband of yours?' said Lucy. 'I want some of what he's having.'

'I reckon you're going to see some action tonight,' said Bridget.

'God save me!' Roz choked on her drink, spraying Bridget with a fine mist of gin. 'Sorry, darling. No, the silly bugger will probably give himself a heart attack first.'

Bridget could tell Roz didn't mean it. That she was quietly chuffed. Bridget felt pleased for her. Pleased and relieved. Past experience had taught her marital harmony was crucial for a successful group holiday.

They fed the kids on an old rug in the middle of the lawn. And even Paris, the fussiest eater of the lot, didn't complain that the bread her sausage was wrapped in had seeds in it, or the cucumber was cut long ways not in rounds.

The adults ate on the deck and Bridget held her breath when the lamb was served and it was more brown than pink.

'Delicious meat, thanks Greg,' said Lucy.

'The credit is all your husband's,' said Greg, and Bridget smiled at him, unable to detect a single note of sarcasm in his voice.

'Let's deal to the dishes in the morning,' suggested Jono.

'Hear, hear,' said Greg.

And so, they stayed there, Jono fetching blankets, Baileys and the dense Christmas cake his mother baked every year, while Tristan tasked the kids with finding sticks to skewer and toast their marshmallows on, until long after they should have all been in bed.

Fortified by the alcohol, and a sense of peace she didn't often allow herself, Bridget cast her mind back to their previous holiday in a rumpty old schoolhouse on a wild West Coast beach. To how awful it had been. How it had rained incessantly and the kids had squabbled, their arguments subsequently playing out between the adults in less childish, yet equally disagreeable ways, under the thin pretence they weren't merely taking their own child's side. How the nose on the Operation guy had stopped buzzing, and Jono had refused to let the twins play Monopoly because it glorified capitalism, and how they'd run out of family-friendly DVDs within the first forty-eight hours.

And how every day, Roz had started drinking before lunch. ('Elevenses,' she'd say, as though there was nothing odd about a mid-morning chardonnay.) Belligerent and loud, she'd offered up a stream of how-to-live-your-best-life advice no one had asked for, and everyone had tried to ignore her, except Greg, who'd made an aggressive kind of sport out of goading Roz's ill humour.

And every night, in the privacy of their bedroom, Bridget and Greg had fought bitterly. 'Why can't you just tune her out?' she'd say in a hushed, furious voice. 'Like Tristan does.'

'And why can't you just get off my case?' he'd respond.

Bridget had spent the entire week walking on eggshells. She'd sworn that was it, no more group holidays. And yet here they all were . . .

Looking across the bay at the listing yachts' flickering lamps and around the table at her dearest friends, taking in their warm murmurs and the crickets, which almost, but didn't quite, drown out the children's over-tired screams, she made a vow to herself.

This holiday would not be like the last. Neither the last, nor any of the ones before. It would not be one of those holidays from which she returned home feeling as brittle and fragmented as stained glass. She wouldn't let it.

Chapter Five

October
Monday

Shutting the front door behind her, Bridget leant back against it with a deep shudder. She ran her hands through her hair. What a morning!

Her plan today was to tackle her most demanding client: Rosie Thear, an interior designer for ladies who lunched. But even the mere thought of coming up with fresh content for Rosie's website was unbearable. If she had to find yet another synonym for soft furnishings, Bridget feared she might just slit her wrists.

Contemplating Mount Laundry, she considered getting stuck into the housework instead. Absentmindedly, she picked up one of the kid's crusts, still sitting on the bench from when she'd cut them off their sandwiches earlier. She wiped it around the sides of the peanut butter jar, downing it quickly, almost reluctantly. She repeated the action. Again, and again. Until there were no crusts left.

It was an old coping mechanism. Bridget supposed it was comfort eating, except it never felt particularly comforting.

Oh, she made a show of starting work, of cleaning the house. She pulled out her laptop from under the pile of junk mail that had accumulated on her desk, removed a mouldy orange from the fruit bowl and wiped away the dusty green residue. But, like a rabid dog let off its leash, her dirty little habit reared its voracious head.

A couple of crackers, she promised herself. *Just while you do your emails.* Before she knew it, the entire box was gone, along with the better part of a block of cheese. 'Enough,' she said, through a mouthful of the chips she kept in the cupboard for the Friday night drinks she never quite got around to organising. She crammed in handfuls of pretzels — she didn't even like pretzels — washed them down with chocolate milk, glugging it straight from the bottle. She took the strawberry swirl cheesecake Abigail had talked her into buying out of the freezer. Hacking off great cold, fatty chunks, she didn't bother waiting for it to thaw.

What the hell had Lucy been doing outside the school? How could she just ignore her? Bridget would never turn her back on Lucy like that. No matter what had happened between them, no matter what had been said. Thirty-five years of friendship and she couldn't even fucking acknowledge her?

Over and over, she worked it through; darting from one unsatisfactory explanation to another. Zachariah had been expelled from his free-loving, everyone-is-welcome school. Shy little Skye needed a more structured environment. Tristan's trust fund had dried up and Lucy was applying for a job as a teacher's aide.

Around and around Bridget went, circling, circling, always coming back to the only real conclusion she could draw: that she no longer had any idea what was going on in Lucy's life, that she no longer knew her former best friend.

Standing at the fridge door, she stuffed olives and gherkins and pickled onions into her mouth, the bittersweet brine dripping down her arm. She gripped the soft flesh around her middle with one hand and reached for a packet of malt biscuits with the other. Sandwiching solid wedges of butter between two biscuits at a time, she slowly demolished the packet.

Eventually she stopped. Not because of any physiological imperative. Not because she ran out of food. No, she was stopped, quite literally, by the bell. When the wind was blowing the right way, you could hear the school bell for miles.

Shit! Late to drop off, late to pick up. Shit!

Bridget was filled with self-loathing. She'd put everything on hold during the holidays. And now here she was, at the end of the first day of term, having achieved nothing.

'Sorry,' she said. 'Sorry,' pushing her way against the oncoming tide of small children, scooters, parents, bikes, nannies, dogs, pushchairs, trying to calm her breathing. To appear in control, sorted. She wasn't neurotic. She might be late, but she was cool. Kept her own time, marched to her own beat. And then that mother she'd had a ridiculous run-in with at the last bake sale over whether it made more financial sense to sell a banana cake as a whole or by the slice, the one Roz reckoned wore a Hi-Vis vest to bed, said in a big, loud voice: 'Watch out, children! There's a mum coming through. Mum coming through!'

Bridget was just considering whether she could get away with tripping her up, when she spotted Moana shepherding her three boys through the crowd. Moana rolled her eyes in Hi-Vis's direction.

'We need to catch up!' she mouthed.

Bridget gave her the thumbs up.

She picked up her pace. She wasn't worried about Jackson and Abigail — they were used to her being late — it was Miss Smythe and her disdainful frown she could do without right now. Miraculously, though, there her children were; playing happily on the monkey bars, not a grumpy teacher to be seen.

'Watch me, Mum!' called Abigail.

'Hi, darlings.'

'Hey,' said Jackson, doing chin-ups.

'Can we stay a bit? Please, Mum, please?'

'Five minutes,' she said, smiling at her daughter's lack of modesty as she hung upside down, sweatshirt bunched under her chin, pancake chest exposed.

Bridget sat on the edge of a wooden planter, her jeans straining painfully around her waist. *God, that's right*, she thought, flooding with shame. No dinner for her tonight.

The weird thing about her random bingeing was she never felt sick, let alone full. She pictured any potential nausea running scared in the face of all that hateful gluttony; a blob of vomit, its sticky cartoon legs pumping, fleeing an insatiable beast.

Ha! It was almost funny.

She looked at the sad little collection of plants behind her: a few lacy-leaved lettuces, a couple of droopy tomato plants. There'd been a young student teacher last term, bursting with enthusiasm for a kitchen garden project. Jackson had come home with reports of the delicious carrot fritters they'd made, but without exception the entire class had baulked at the borscht. The student teacher had tried to sell it to them as the food of tsars, but when you're twelve years old, apparently cold beetroot soup is cold beetroot soup.

Bridget noticed a tight knot of parents, huddled together on the other side of the playground, talking intently. There were four of them. Junior school parents, she guessed, by the age of the only other children on the jungle gym.

Casually attempting to re-stake one of the tomato plants, she strained to make out what they were talking about. It was no good, she was too far away. She stood up.

'Two minutes, kids,' she called, sidling closer.

'*Something, something . . .*'

She tried to decipher what they were saying.

'Could live next . . . Can't believe it . . . *something, something* . . . Normally such a *something, something*,' said a woman with long, thin hair and a long, thin voice to match.

There was a hum of agreement, and then, quite audibly, the sole man in the group said, 'Bloody paedophile! I'd skin him alive if I got the chance.'

The story in the paper last week. The brief. It had to be.

The last few days of the holidays had flown by in an attempt to squeeze in everything she'd promised they'd do: shopping for summer clothes, making bath bombs with Abigail, clearing a bookshelf for Jackson to store his PlayStation games.

She'd forgotten about the child pornographer in their midst. She'd meant to ask Roz, font of all knowledge, if she knew anything when she got back from Sydney but it had slipped her mind.

She hadn't even given the kids the stranger danger talk. She'd meant to remind them that, even if it was an adult they knew, they were allowed to say no if they felt uncomfortable, remind them of the difference between good touching and bad touching. *Bad mother!*

There was a wail. Bridget looked over to see Abigail catapulting off the parallel bars and onto that spongy stuff they surfaced playgrounds with these days.

'It's all right, pumpkin,' she said, gathering her up. 'C'mon. Let's go get some afternoon tea.'

'Mum,' said Jackson. 'Guess who's in my class?'

'Who?' asked Bridget, picking flecks of rubber out of Abigail's bloodied knee; another pair of leggings ruined.

'Zachariah.'

Chapter Six

January
Day Two

They were so pack-like, children. They'd only been on the island twenty-four hours and already there was something feral to them. It was like this every holiday, and yet it never ceased to amaze Bridget. It was as if those poor sheltered city kids couldn't wait to shed their urban skins. As if shoes and socks, shampoo and soap, all those essential underpinnings of civilised life, were but fakery. Here were their true selves. Faces freckly and begrimed; hair thick with salt.

She was intrigued, too, by how instinctively, how quickly, the pecking order established itself, although it was more fluid, murkier, than *Lord of the Flies* would have had it; lines sometimes drawn according to age, other times gender.

And then there was Zachariah: even when he wasn't disappearing off, somehow always apart. There but not. Never seeming to quite get it: sneering; refusing to partake in the other kids' games; or making new rules; pushing past the fun; taking things to an uncomfortable place.

Several times, Bridget had been on the phone, talking freely, under the assumption she was alone, when she had sensed something, someone, and there he was, lurking on the edge of her personal space.

'How does Tristan put up with it?' she'd asked Greg one day after they'd found Zachariah systematically pulling each and every flower off their gardenia. 'With what?' asked Greg, who could be irritatingly obtuse when he chose to be. 'With that little shit,' she'd replied.

'You know Tristan,' he'd said, 'he's always had blinkers on when it comes to Lucy.'

'I guess,' she'd said, but mulling it over later it occurred to her Greg hadn't really answered her question.

It wasn't as if Tristan only tolerated Zachariah either; he actually engaged with his hobbies. Taking him along to the organised battles for a fantasy warfare game he was obsessed with. Helping him construct and paint the fiddly model soldiers and weapons.

'Ugh,' she'd said to Tristan. 'Jackson made me take him to a session once. To this odd, smelly room filled with odd, smelly guys. I couldn't get out of there fast enough!' Tristan had just laughed. Said it was 'all a bit of humour.'

That first morning in the farmhouse Bridget slept in, coming downstairs to find the children had made themselves breakfast — a trail of milk, rice bubbles and jammy crumbs from one end of the table to the other — and were now nowhere to be seen.

'Where're the kids?'

Roz, busy slathering butter and avocado on sourdough doorstoppers, evidently not eschewing gluten or dairy this holiday, shrugged. 'They said something about going up the hill.' She pointed vaguely out the window with a greasy finger. 'I'm praying they don't return in a hurry!' She laughed loudly, sloshing her coffee across the table.

Bridget shrank back.

She should go get the novel her mother had given her for Christmas, find a sunny spot on the verandah. But while she claimed to love how much freedom the children had when they were all away together like this, their unstructured play, their independence, in truth it made her uneasy.

As far as she knew, none of the adults had checked out what lay beyond the property yet, and she was willing to bet none of the kids would have thought to wear sunblock or hats.

She started gathering up the dirty dishes. Carrying them to the bench, she wrung out the dishcloth and wiped around Roz.

'Bridget, we're on holiday. You're making me feel guilty.'

'I know. You're right. Sorry.'

'Here,' Roz said. 'You sit down. I'll put the kettle on again.'

At Roz's small, unexpected kindness, Bridget felt her eyes beginning to well up. She was wondering how she was going to explain what was wrong, given she didn't even know what it was herself, when the men barrelled through the door. Grateful to have escaped one of Roz's well-intentioned, albeit gruelling, interrogations, Bridget rubbed her eyes on her sleeve.

'Boom,' said Jono.

'Boom,' said Tristan.

'Boom! Boom! And boom,' crowed Greg.

Apparently, the snapper had been practically jumping into the boat on their dawn fishing trip. From the flush in Greg's cheeks Bridget suspected there'd been more than just coffee in the Thermos he was brandishing.

The kitchen suddenly felt very cramped. It wasn't just that men occupied more space physically, thought Bridget. It was everything. Their voices were bigger, their body language more strident.

When entering a room, or joining a conversation, most women erred on the side of diffidence, assessing the situation before making themselves known.

Was it innate? A question of survival; always alert to predators. Or was it learned? An awareness of one's place.

Greg started getting bacon and eggs out of the fridge.

'I'm a little concerned about where the kids have got to. Would one of you have a look for them before you sit down to breakfast?'

Bridget could tell by the set of Greg's shoulders she was spoiling their fun. She supposed she was. No one else appeared remotely worried over the children's whereabouts. Busying themselves at the table, Tristan and Jono seemed to have found an urgent sense of purpose, and Roz had conveniently taken herself off.

Conscious she looked a fright — hair ratty, breasts loose under the T-shirt she'd slept in — Bridget decided to get changed. She'd look for the kids herself.

Passing the master bedroom, she spied Lucy sitting up in bed, reading.

'Morning,' she called through the door.

'Oh, hello, petal. Come talk to me.'

'How do you always look so luscious?'

Lucy reminded her of a ripe peach, somehow managing to be both soft and firm all at once. Bridget wasn't attracted to women — she'd tried it once, just to be sure — but something about Lucy always made her think of sex.

'Good on you, having a lie-in. I wish I could.'

'I didn't sleep very well. Willow ended up in our bed and then spent half the night kicking me.'

Both Bridget and Roz were of the view Lucy and Tristan's kids needed some firmer boundaries around their parents' bed. Christ, Zachariah was probably still sleeping with them. But they never said anything; Lucy might radiate a dreamy kind of calm, however she was quick to lose it if anyone dared question her parenting.

Lucy patted the bed, drawing Bridget down beside her.

'Did you sleep okay, petal? You don't look too rested yourself.'

'You know me,' Bridget said, wondering whether Lucy and Tristan had had sex last night, and whether that explained the slight dampness of the tangled sheets beneath her. 'I never sleep well in a strange place. Too many noises. First it was the waves — I kept thinking there was going to be a tsunami. Then it was the moreporks. Plus, there's this big pōhutukawa right outside our window. Every time the wind blew it rattled against the glass.'

'Bloody nature!' said Lucy.

Impulsively, Bridget brought Lucy's hand to her mouth, lightly kissing the back of it. Lucy smiled at her.

'Where are the kids? It's awfully quiet out there.'

'Apparently they've gone up the hill.'

Bridget was keen to appear nonchalant. You could never tell how Lucy would react to signs of autonomy or, for that matter, defiance in her children. Once, angry at being made to have a bath, Zachariah had taken a staple gun to Skye's Barbie dolls. Bridget had been shocked at the destructiveness, the underlying brutality, but Lucy had hardly blinked an eye. And then, that same afternoon, she'd gone apeshit when she'd caught

Skye eating a lollipop she'd been told she wasn't allowed.

'Hmm, have they?' Lucy said drowsily. 'That's nice.'

'I wasn't sure how you'd feel about Willow going off . . .'

'Willow? No, I saw her when I got up to go to the toilet before. She was playing in the living room.'

'She might have been. She's not now, though. I'll tell you what, you stay there and I'll go check on them. I feel like a walk.'

'Would you? Thanks, Bridge. You're a trooper.'

Bridget hurried upstairs. Entrusted with a job, she felt her unease flower into panic. They must have been gone over an hour by now.

She pulled on some tights, scrabbling awkwardly to fasten her bra. She'd have happily gone in her pyjamas, but didn't want the others to think she was completely mad.

'Just going for a walk,' she called, ducking out the French doors. 'Work off last night's feast!'

No one looked up. Greg was regaling them with some fishing tale, and even Roz, who had reclaimed her seat at the table, looked spellbound. Roz had zero interest in fishing, but she was one of those people who was always present, always able to enjoy the moment, whatever it was.

Picking her way over the trail of boogie boards strewn across the lawn, wishing she could be more like that, more unhampered, less fretful, Bridget heard a scream.

A child's scream.

Chapter
Seven

October
Monday

'Are you sure?' Bridget asked Jackson, the uneasiness that had lurked in her chest since encountering Lucy lodging at the base of her throat. 'I mean I know we saw them this morning, but it can't be Zachariah. Lucy wouldn't send him here. She's always been so anti mainstream schools.'

'What's a mainstream school?' asked Abigail.

'Duh, Mum. Like I think I'd know whether Zachariah was in my class or not.'

'Did you talk to him?'

'Course. Why wouldn't I?'

'I don't know. I guess you haven't seen each other in a while.'

'Nah, he was cool. He seemed different.'

'How?'

'I dunno. Not so weird.'

'So, is Skye there, too?' Bridget was conscious her attempt at striking a relaxed note was failing miserably.

'Yeah,' said Abigail. 'She played tag with us at lunchtime.'

'Oh . . . did you ask why she and Zachariah have changed schools?'

'No. Skye's such a fast runner. I really like her leggings. They have cupcakes on them. Can I get some?'

Bridget had almost managed to convince herself that seeing Lucy outside school this morning had just been a coincidence. That she was enquiring about the gym classes they ran in the school hall after-hours. Or dropping something off at a house across the street.

But not this, please God, no. Not fellow school mums.

She had tried to make contact with Lucy after their disastrous holiday. Of course she had. Once the anger had waned, she'd attempted to get in touch. Lucy was her best friend. It was unimaginable they wouldn't be in each other's lives in some shape or form. No matter how many messages she'd left, though, how many texts and emails she'd sent, Lucy had steadfastly refused to speak to her.

They'd been back from Hine's a few months when Bridget had summoned up the courage to go over there, to have it out in person. She knew Lucy would be home. Lucy was always home. She hadn't really worked since Tristan had re-entered her life all those years ago. Hadn't needed to.

Apparently, the landscape gardening had just been a distraction. A brief rebellion. Not only were Tristan's parents loaded, but Tristan was some kind of mathematical whiz, an Oxford graduate. Bridget had never really understood what he did. Something to do with foreign markets. With money. Making lots of money. Enough so that Lucy, having never settled at anything anyway, had been able to embrace full-time motherhood as if it was her calling. Her *raison d'être*.

In a suburb of bungalows, brick and tiles, and ex-state houses, Lucy and Tristan had somehow managed to find a villa. And that day, standing in front of Lucy's beautiful leadlight front door, stomach in a ropy knot, Bridget had knocked and knocked but no one had come.

She had cast her mind back to Boxing Day, the last time she'd been at their house before everything had turned to crap. The last time before Hine's. They had stuffed themselves silly on thick slices of ham and pineapple fried in butter, had got drunk on a punch of puréed strawberries and the dregs of the Christmas day bubbly. They'd been so happy. Excitedly planning their trip, innocent of what was to come.

Looking around their porch, Bridget had wondered at how it was as if nothing had changed: the same dusty jumble of gumboots, running shoes and jandals, the broken Nerf gun, the flat *Dora the Explorer* ball. She didn't know why she was surprised — housekeeping had never been high on Lucy and Tristan's priorities — but somehow that pile of rejected footwear and toys had stung more than Lucy's refusal to answer the door. So much had happened since she was last here, it seemed wrong anything could still be the same.

For a moment Bridget had contemplated fighting her way down the side of the house, through the feijoa trees, to the French doors around the back. It was only a sense of self-preservation that had stopped her. She could have taken being yelled at, the door slammed in her face, but not being blanked, not this nothingness.

It was as if Lucy had decided she didn't exist. It wasn't just Bridget either. They'd all been cut off. Roz and Jono. Greg. He didn't really talk about it, yet Bridget could see how hurt he was. Greg might have plenty of friends, but it was Tristan he'd always confided in.

All through February, all March and April long, Bridget had barely functioned. She'd kept going. She hadn't had a choice. The kids, work, Greg: it wasn't as if she could just pull the covers over her head.

But negotiating daily life without Lucy in it had been excruciating; the regular phone calls about nothing in particular, the comfort afforded by a history shared. It was worse than when she'd broken up with her first boyfriend. Worse than when her grandmother had died. There'd been an inevitability to those shitty times that had softened the blow. Her grandmother had been old; her boyfriend a waster.

There was nothing inevitable about losing Lucy, however. The possibility had simply never occurred to her.

Eventually Bridget had decided the only thing she could do, the only way she could go on, was to pretend Lucy had died. So she'd taken some tacky mementoes from their Big OE down to the beach and made a little funeral pyre out of them.

The pain had been different afterwards. Not so raw, so punishing. Less like someone was sandpapering her heart. More just gently wringing it out from time to time. And gradually she'd begun to feel lighter. Joy had started to peek through again. On a good day she'd even begun to appreciate the extra headspace she had without Lucy to fill it. She'd started to think she was better, that she might be over it.

Stupid fool!

Time might heal, but while nine months was long enough to grow a baby, it was evidently no match for years and years of friendship or, for that matter, one horrific day.

Somehow, she got through the afternoon.

Cheese, crackers and apple quarters for afternoon tea. Drop Abigail to ballet. Drop Jackson to guitar. Pick up Abigail. Pick up Jackson. Do homework. Battle with Jackson over spelling. Battle with Abigail and Jackson over screen time. Peel potatoes for dinner. Crumb fish. Make salad.

And all the while thinking about how it would be. At the school picnic, seeing Lucy and Tristan under the trees. At swimming sports, spotting them on the bleachers through the chlorine fug. At the school gate for drop-off and pick-up. Oh Jesus, the daily hell of the school gate.

She desperately wanted to talk to Greg. Have him tell her it would be okay.

He was in the middle of a stressful project at work, though; some fancy new gourmet supermarket car park the clients were adamant they wanted bordered with edelweiss. 'We're not in the Alps,' she'd heard him telling them over the phone last week. 'We live in a subtropical climate.'

No, she wouldn't bother him. She would wait. Tell him in person tonight.

But when he finally staggered in the door the kids threw themselves at him and there wasn't a chance to say hello properly, let alone talk privately.

Bridget almost felt jealous of Jackson and Abigail sometimes; like she was in competition with her own children for her husband's attention. They were so free with their love. Occasionally she'd go to hug him and something would hold her back. That she hadn't cleaned her teeth, or she would remember he had snapped at her that morning when she'd asked if they could go over their life insurance policy later on. The kids would never second-guess his affection.

'Dinner,' she called. 'Wash your hands.'

'Could you wait until I've sat down?' she said, as she put the fish on the table and Greg grabbed at a fillet.

'Mmmm,' he said through a mouthful. 'So, sproglings, how was your first day back at school? I want a blow-by-blow account. Anyone get a mohawk in the holidays? Anyone break their legs skydiving?'

Abigail and Jackson laughed as if it was the funniest thing they'd ever heard.

'Zachariah's in my class,' Jackson said, upending the tomato sauce over his plate.

'I think that's enough,' said Bridget, grabbing at the bottle.

'Zachariah?' repeated Greg.

Bridget busied herself tossing the salad, aware of Greg's eyes on her, his face one big question mark.

'Yeah, and I played with Skye.'

This time Bridget met Greg's gaze. *Later*, she signalled, raising her eyebrows and tilting her neck. *We'll talk later*.

Jackson flicked an olive on to Abigail's fish.

'Gross! I'm not eating that.' She pushed her fish away with her fork. 'It's contaminated now.'

'Eat it,' said Bridget. 'More?' she asked Greg, pushing fish and salad onto his plate before he'd had a chance to respond.

She picked at the last lonely potato. *Fuck it*. She'd been going to skip dinner altogether. Tomorrow. Tomorrow, she'd start afresh.

After they'd cleaned their teeth, the kids announced they were still hungry. Bridget made them peanut butter on toast, and reminded them to do their teeth, again.

Greg read to them while she made a feeble attempt to tackle the pile of washing. It was almost nine p.m. when, kids finally down, Greg reappeared.

'Any chance of a matching pair of socks?' he asked, starting to dig along Mount Laundry's northern flank.

Bridget laughed. 'May the force be with you!'

She pulled out a pair of Jackson's underpants: fraying at the elastic, they weren't long for this earth.

'Do you want a cup of tea?' she asked. 'There's a bit of dark chocolate in the fridge.'

'No thanks, hon. I think I'll hit the sack. I'm bushed.'

'Really? There's so much to talk about, though . . .'

But Greg was already heading down the hall.

By the time Bridget had emptied the dishwasher, spread the kids' lunchboxes out to dry on the bench so they were all set to go in the morning, washed her face, and applied the serum the woman at the pharmacy had sworn would take ten years off her, he was sound asleep.

Christ, it was only half past nine. It was like being married to a child. Or, worse, an old man.

She picked up the phone.

Roz would still be awake.

Chapter Eight

January
Day Two

Bridget ran. Across the lawn, behind the shed, grabbing at the long grass to propel herself up the hill.

She knew that scream. Would know it anywhere. In a crowd of thousands. It was the same piercing noise her daughter had made on entering the world, a small, bloody force of nature, shooting out of Bridget into the astonished midwife's hands.

'Abigail! Abigail!'

The sheep grazing on the hillside stared at her.

Bridget wasn't convinced sheep were as dumb as everyone said. She reckoned that vacuity was just a ploy to trick humans into thinking they were harmless. That one day they'd take revenge for all their slaughtered babies and severed coats. Greg had laughed uproariously when she'd shared her theory with him. 'Only a city slicker could come up with mumbo jumbo like that,' he'd said.

She wondered how she appeared to the sheep; this almost forty-year-old woman clutching great handfuls of grass, chest heaving. They probably thought she was bonkers. Most likely she was. The kids were no doubt having some awesome adventure. And where were the other adults? Back at the house relaxing, that's where, while she hysterically speculated about the inner life of sheep.

She nearly laughed out loud. Except it would have required too much effort.

Christ! It was steeper than it looked, and she was unfitter than she'd thought. Her twice-weekly runs around Point Heed obviously weren't cutting the mustard.

She was contemplating giving up when she recalled the particular pitch of Abigail's scream; the unmistakable sound of pain.

Taking a gulp of dry air, she committed to the hill with fresh resolve.

Finally, the ground levelled out.

If Bridget had turned around just then she would have been struck by the view.

She would have taken in that immense expanse of water and fancied she could see all the way to Australia.

And if she'd just paused a moment on that hilltop, if she'd just looked back, she'd have seen something: something going on behind their farmhouse with the beautiful big bay and the two ugly dormer windows, something that would have changed everything.

Bridget didn't turn, though. She was too busy trying to make sense of what lay before her.

She guessed it was normally a pond, but with no rain for weeks it was as parched as a desert, great fissures marring its surface. And dotted around its edges, framing all that aridity, lay dozens of beehives.

Bridget had always liked beehives, they reminded her of liquorice allsorts with their multi-coloured layers. It killed her to think bees were teetering on the edge of extinction. These bees obviously hadn't got the memo, though. She could almost feel their humming, like a slight vibration glancing off her skin, their productivity only serving to highlight the barrenness of their environs.

But it was what lay on the pond's far side that seized her attention. There, beside one of the tallest hives, were the children, gathered in a semi-circle around Abigail.

Abigail and a man.

A strange man who was cradling her daughter's foot in his lap.

'Hey!' Bridget's voice reverberated around the shallow crater.

She began to jog, halfway across tripping on a rock and landing heavily on the baked clay. Ignoring the tenderness in her shin, she clambered to her feet. The man stood, too.

'Are you all right?' He moved towards her.

'I'm fine.' She avoided the hand he offered. 'What's going on? Abigail, are you okay?'

'Mum, your leg is bleeding.'

Bridget waved Jackson away. 'What's going on? Who are you?'

'I'm Don,' said the man. 'Don Davies? I manage the farm.' He gestured expansively around him.

'A bee stinged me, Mum.' Abigail held up a filthy foot as proof.

'Oh, my poor darling. Here, let me have a look.' She crouched down, grimacing as her calf seized up. 'No one mentioned a manager.'

'The letting agent must have forgotten. I live in the valley down there. Keep an eye on the livestock. Air the place out from time to time. She's going to be fine, anyway. I managed to get the sting. You're a brave girl, aren't you, Abigail?'

Bridget flinched at the familiarity with which he used her daughter's name.

'Right, well, thanks for your help. C'mon kids. We'd better let the manager get back to his work.'

'I don't mind. Glad to be of service. It's pretty quiet out here.'

'Can we still come see your horses?' Paris asked.

'Can we? Can we?' asked Willow.

'Don said we can have a ride,' said Earl.

'And he said he's got heaps of other cool stuff, too,' said Paris.

'Sure. You kids are welcome any time.'

'We'll see,' Bridget said.

'I'll help you get Abigail down the hill if you like.'

'That's okay. We can cope.'

It was only as they were hobbling away, with Abigail hanging off her shoulder, moaning theatrically, that Bridget registered Zachariah wasn't with them.

'Where's your brother?' she asked Skye.

'I'm not sure.'

'Did he come up the hill with you?'

'Nah,' said Earl. 'He went off somewhere after breakfast.'

'Yeah,' said Jackson, 'somewhere seeecreeet.'

He and Earl high-fived.

'Bruh.'

'Bruh.'

Chapter Nine

October
Monday

'Bridgey,' Roz bellowed down the phone. 'How are you, darling?'

'Have you heard?'

Bridget found it best to cut straight to the chase with Roz before the actual reason for your call was buried under a deluge of titillating, yet ultimately irrelevant information.

'Heard what? Do you mean have I heard Julie's given that slut of a husband the boot? Apparently when she finally got up the guts to do it, he tried to tell her she and the kids would have to move out. Because, get this, she was the one breaking up the marriage! She was only leaving him because he'd given her freakin' chlamydia from all his whoring around!'

'God, poor Julie. What a wanker. I hope she sticks to her guns this time. But listen, that isn't what I wanted to talk to you about.'

There was a small clunk.

'Roz?'

'Hey, Bridget. How's Greg?'

'Oh, hi Jono. He's fine. A bit tired and grumpy, you know what it's like. Am I on speaker phone?'

'Uh-huh.'

Bridget could hear the Insinkerator roaring into action.

'Sorry to be rude, Jono, but I really need to talk to Roz.'

'What was that? Can't hear you over all the bloody noise.'

'Roz,' Bridget yelled. 'I need to talk to her. Is she still there?'

'Umm . . . she was. She's disappeared off somewhere. Hang on a tick.'

Bridget listened to her friends' dinner scraps being pulverised.

'Sorry about that. I was busting for a wee. And these days when I gotta go, I gotta go. Right, I'm all ears, darling.'

Bridget exhaled. Now she had Roz's attention, she knew it would be undivided.

Lucy had been the one to discover Roz.

After dropping out of a half-hearted BA in psychology, Lucy had made ends meet waiting tables at this swanky Italian restaurant. On the rare occasion Bridget's student allowance had stretched to a bowl of their over-priced fettuccine, she'd always been too intimidated to enjoy it. The ubiquitous sun-dried tomato garnish had been the sole colour in that arctic room with its sharp metal chairs and angular plates. The tomatoes, and Roz, the maître d'.

Back then Bridget and Lucy had been desperately channelling Kate Moss's heroin chic — bias-cut satin slips, black velvet chokers garrotting their necks — but Roz hadn't been channelling anyone, bar, perhaps, herself. She'd dressed exclusively in op shop 'finds': one day wearing an oversized men's suit jacket with nothing else except for a pair of bovver boots and a bowler hat; the next, a tutu, fishnets and pillbox. The only constant, her impressively deep, permanently on-display cleavage and fire-engine red lips.

Filling in time until Lucy finished her shift, Bridget would nurse a cappuccino and watch all the posturing. Watch the ad agency bigwigs and the property developers merrily flexing their wallets and swinging their dicks about. Watch when her best friend placed some guy's veal masala down in front of him, and was pulled onto his lap. *Chauvinist pigs*, she'd mouth sympathetically if she could catch Lucy's eye. Accustomed to being the object of men's desire, Lucy dealt with the succession of drunken suits in her normal, slightly disinterested way; her breezy brush-off merely serving to stoke their lust. If ever one went too far, however, all it took was a look from Roz.

In her mid-twenties, Roz was only a few years older than Bridget and Lucy, but a million times more worldly. She hadn't enjoyed the secure, comfortable Point Heed childhoods they had. Roz's parents had been abusive alcoholics, their state house always freezing, the fridge always empty. She'd grown up tough. 'I had to,' she'd say if ever they complimented her grit. 'Didn't have a choice, did I?' And Bridget would chastise herself. For sounding so patronising. For sounding so privileged.

Once Bridget saw her physically remove a man from the restaurant. 'Cunt!' he'd yelled when she deposited him on the footpath. Roz hadn't even turned around, just marched straight back in to a standing ovation.

Later that same night, halfway through her third frozen margarita at the backpackers' bar all the hospo crowd drank at, Roz told them she'd had an 'uncle' who used to call her 'My little cunt'. That he'd wait until her parents were safely passed out on the couch before slipping into her room. Roz had swept aside their shocked sympathy. 'Let's dance,' she'd said, striding onto the dance floor, elbowing young German tourists out of her way.

Jono was the manager of the backpackers'. With his pierced ears and braids (done in 'deepest Peru') he fitted right in. In spite of his vanilla upbringing (bank manager father, housewife mother), or perhaps because of it, Jono had been into 'finding himself'; heading off to Varanasi to track down some swami, returning with a head full of New Age psychobabble. But when he found Roz, he seemed to lose the urge to keep looking.

Physically, Bridget would never have put one with the other; where Roz was swarthy, Amazonian, Jono was pale and squat, freckly and ginger-haired. He was the only one, though, who could talk Roz down from one of her tequila-fuelled frenzies, putting her in a booth with a chamomile tea and instructions not to move until he'd finished up and could drive her home.

Roz told Bridget and Lucy she would invite him in to her flat, more out of gratitude than any real desire, but he never took her up on it. Until one day she showed up at the backpackers' in the cold light of day, and told him she thought she might be in love with him. They'd done it right there, on the bar. And afterwards, telling them about it, Roz had said she never thought she'd be capable of sober sex.

Greg and Jono bonded over their love of fishing; the two couples, plus Lucy, a gang of sorts. Sunday lunches, a ritual that quickly turned competitive: Yorkshire pudding-offs, crockpot challenges. It had seemed harmless back then, funnier.

One wet afternoon, stuffed with rendang and roti, the men smoking a joint while they did the dishes, Roz had confided she would never have children. 'You guys would make great parents,' Bridget and Lucy had protested. 'Nah, shitty parenting might be hereditary,' Roz had said. 'Don't be silly,' they'd laughed. 'I'm not,' she'd said. 'I've never been more serious.' Hugging her, they'd told her she was nothing like her parents. 'Maybe,' she'd replied, 'but even the good parents can't always protect their kids.'

The gang had lasted a year and a half or so, until Bridget and Greg, followed shortly by Lucy, ruined things by moving to London. Jono and Roz had sent care packages, saying they gave them two years, tops. At the time it had annoyed Bridget and she'd been determined to prove them wrong. But after returning to the UK from her trip home for Zachariah's birth, she'd missed her friends and her mum and dad so desperately that Greg had gone out and bought them two one-way tickets home.

Apart from the addition of Zachariah, carted around everywhere by Lucy in a Moses basket, at first it was like nothing had changed. Until Bridget and Greg, who said they weren't in any rush to have kids, got married and promptly fell pregnant. Poor Roz and Jono did their best; trying to be understanding when Sunday lunch was cut short because Zachariah or Jackson was losing the plot. But then Tristan turned up. For a while the gang limped along, the gaps between their once weekly catch-ups growing longer and longer, and although Bridget was sad, she was also relieved when things fizzled out completely. With two young children and a new business, there wasn't much room for anything else.

Then, one day, out of the blue, Roz and Jono got in touch to suggest a reunion. Over laksa at their old favourite restaurant, Roz had announced she was pregnant, with twins. Everyone was thrilled; no one more so than Jono, well into his late thirties by then and balding. Greg had slapped him on the back and said he'd put money on him having no hair whatsoever by the time the babies were six months old. They'd all laughed and Jono looked like the cat that got the cream.

And so, without recrimination about the dearth of contact, without finger pointing, they'd slotted into each other's lives again.

'Did Earl or Paris mention anything about Zachariah and Skye today?' she asked Roz now.

'Zachariah and Skye? No. Why would they?'

Bridget paused.

'Spit it out, Bridge.'

'They've started at Point Heed.'

'Stop the bus!'

'It's true. I saw Lucy pulling up outside the school this morning. In fact, she stole my park. I got such a shock. I assumed she was just running an errand or something. Then when I picked up the kids this afternoon, Jackson told me Zachariah was in his class.'

'Did she acknowledge you?'

'No. She actively ignored me. It was horrible. I'd hoped I was over it, but I don't know, seeing her just brought it all back.'

'Bloody hell. How does she think she's going to keep avoiding us if her kids are at the same school as ours?'

'I've no idea. I mean what are they even doing there in the first place? Lucy used to be so dismissive of Point Heed School. Like it was too ordinary for her kids or something. Like it might be okay for the rest of us, but her kids were too fucking special . . .'

Bridget reined herself in. Regardless of everything, it felt disloyal to talk about Lucy like that.

Mind you, if there was anyone she could diss Lucy to, it was Roz. Bridget might have loved Lucy the most, but Roz had been a close second.

'God, wait till I tell Jono. He's still pissed at them for how badly they dealt with everything. What did Greg say?'

'I haven't had a chance to talk to him about it. The kids brought it up at dinner tonight but I didn't want to discuss it in front of them. And now the bastard's asleep.'

'That's men for you . . . useless! Hey, there was something I wanted to ask you, actually. I had a coffee with a few of the mums after drop-off, and all they could talk about was some news story on a kiddy fiddler in the 'hood.'

'I saw it, too. I'd forgotten about it until these parents were freaking out at school today. I was hoping you might know something.'

'Nah, this morning was the first I'd heard of it.'

'I think kiddy fiddler might be over-egging it. It said he'd been dealing in child pornography.'

'Same diff. Why don't you hit up some of your old media mates? See if any of them knows anything.'

'He's got name suppression, Roz. No one's going to just tell me.'

'Ha! What's the name of that guy you used to work with? You know, you used to invite him to those curry nights? Glasses? Unlucky in love?'

'Oh, you mean Darren. Darren Peters.'

'Yeah, him. Wasn't he a court reporter or something? He was always blabbing about the cases he was covering. That guy couldn't keep his mouth shut if he tried.'

Chapter Ten

January
Day Two

If Bridget had been expecting an anxious reception back at the house, or some acknowledgement, at least, of the rescue mission she'd undertaken, then she was bitterly disappointed.

Dozing in a deckchair, a trashy magazine splayed across her face, Roz was happily oblivious to their return. Over by the smokehouse Greg and Jono scarcely looked up from the task at hand: to their left an open chilly bin, silver snapper sitting prettily on the salted ice; to their right, a pulpy pile of guts. As for Lucy and Tristan, they appeared to have vanished.

Bridget wondered whether she ought to go and look for Zachariah. Bugger it. He was twelve, old enough to take care of himself. Surely she'd fulfilled her quota of worrying about other people's children.

Stepping into the cool dimness, Bridget discovered the kitchen was in even more of a mess than when she'd left.

A pan of bacon fat lay congealing on the stove; a fat fly crawled slowly, rapturously, over it. Greg reckoned if the bees died out, they were going to need flies for their pollination skills, but she found it impossible to summon up any affection for them.

She forced herself to look away. She was going to tend to the cut on her leg and then have a nap. Approaching the stairs, she heard a low moan coming from Lucy and Tristan's room.

Unbelievable.

She should have known. She and Greg had once tried to count the number of times they'd overheard Lucy and Tristan having sex, but they'd given up. That first night in their flat in Brixton had set the tone for every group holiday, every time they'd crashed at one another's houses, too plastered to drive home. There was, they'd agreed, nothing even remotely sexy about listening to other people doing it.

Putting her hand on the balustrade, Bridget turned slightly in order to squeeze past the heap of togs, sunglasses and caps on the bottom step. As she did, she realised the door to the master bedroom was ajar. It took her a moment to register what she was looking at: Tristan, kneeling on the bed, utterly naked, the headboard behind him, lily of the valley sprouting from his shoulders like whimsical wings. Beneath him Lucy. As Tristan stroked himself, Lucy's hand moved furiously between her bare thighs, her mouth opening hungrily, the tip of her tongue grazing the ridged base of his balls.

Taking the stairs two at a time, Bridget rushed up to the second floor. She shut the door behind her, pulled the curtains together, and threw herself on the bed, earlier lethargy supplanted by a sensation of raciness. She rolled onto her side, trying to still her breath. When she was younger, she might have masturbated, maybe tried to lure Greg away for a quickie.

She picked up her book, *The Uninhabitable Earth: Life After Warming*.

Argh! She didn't know if she could deal with the coming apocalypse right now. She closed her eyes. That was worse; Lucy and Tristan's glittering flesh filled her head.

She got up. A nap was obviously out of the question. She may as well head down to the beach. She shoved her book and some block into a basket, grabbed her straw hat and slipped on a pair of jandals.

Downstairs all was quiet. Deserted even.

She hurried out the French doors.

At the beach, Greg had manoeuvred the boat away from the jetty and the kids were jumping off the top deck into the water.

God, I can be contrary, she thought, lowering herself onto her towel, mindful of her sore leg. Desperate to be alone. Unable to bear her own company.

She looked down at her stomach. Her spray tan was coming off already. It was darkest around her tummy button, as if all the colour had been propelled there by some centripetal force. Maybe it was something to do with having an innie. Hers was particularly deep. Greg called it 'The Abyss'. She spread it apart with her fingers, flattening out the crêpey skin around it. One of her nails was chipped, too. Two days ago, she'd been perfect, or at least as near to it as she got, but the decaying process was quicker to set in now.

She manipulated her belly. Tighten. Release. It was a little like a withered balloon. No number of crunchies was ever going to make it smooth again. She could still feel the slight gap where her abdominal muscles hadn't properly knitted back together after Abigail.

There was a shriek of laughter.

'Watch out,' screamed one of the boys.

A huge splash.

'Wahoo!'

She put her hand up to her eyes, the glare making her squint.

Willow's tiny frame teetered on the edge of the bow, her arms and legs poking out from her life jacket like a stickperson's. Squealing, the little girl plunged into the water, laughing as Greg hauled her straight out again, wriggling like a fish he'd hooked.

Bridget watched his big, strong back arching as he threw the kids overboard. Desire flooded her groin.

That was better. Lust for her husband: that she could do something about.

At first Bridget had been attracted to Greg's hedonism, his appetite for fun, but it was his underlying sense of responsibility that had persuaded her he was the one.

She'd been with other men; it had been so long, though, she could scarcely remember their names, let alone what it felt like to actually share her bed with another man, to truly reveal herself.

She'd met Greg during Orientation. She and Lucy had been attempting to play pool in the campus bar when a couple of guys had asked if they could join them. The shorter of the two had introduced himself as Blake, explaining he was doing a BCom, and that his dumb friend was visiting from down the line.

Bridget had looked at the dumb friend. Tall and built, he'd made Blake seem like a kid. The kind of man you would want by your side in a natural disaster.

And even as she had been thinking this, she was writing him off. Out of her league. The type who'd only have eyes for Lucy. So, she had resigned herself to shrimpy, smart-arse Blake, but when Greg went up to the bar, Blake had zeroed in on Lucy. *Great*, Bridget had thought, *even the boy-child is going to try his luck with my best friend.*

She'd been sitting there, filled with pity at the inevitability of her rejection, at the unfairness of it all, when Greg had reappeared with a round of drinks. And as he'd stretched across her to put the jug down, his forearm had brushed the side of her breast. He'd blushed, slopping the beer over the table. 'Sorry,' he'd said. 'That's okay,' Bridget had replied, before adding — and to this day she couldn't believe she'd been so bold — 'it felt quite nice, actually'. Greg had looked at her, startled, and right then Bridget had known she could have him if she wanted him.

Occasionally Blake or Lucy had wandered over to see what they were talking about, and Bridget had held her breath, waiting for Greg to come to his senses, to realise his mistake, but he hadn't budged from her side. She'd regaled him with her best witticisms, with the astuteness of her observations of university life, and he'd laughed and laughed. Girls where he was from didn't talk like her, he'd said.

Later they'd slipped away, Lucy winking at Bridget as she grabbed her denim jacket from under the pool table. Greg took her hand as they walked downtown. They'd shared a dripping cheese and sweet corn toastie and marvelled at how they both thought spearmint left all other milkshake flavours for dead. And then, because he was bunking down at Blake's, Bridget still lived at home, and neither of them had enough money for a room, they'd made out for hours on a park bench.

They'd finally pried themselves apart as the sun was rising and he'd walked her the whole eight kilometres back to Point Heed. But even when he'd kissed her tenderly goodbye, even when he'd asked for her number, she had told herself she'd never hear from him again. Not to hold out much hope. That it had been an incredible night, however, that was all it was, one night.

Two torturously long days later, he'd rung. Her mother had answered, and, clutching the receiver to her chest, she'd said: 'It's him! It's him!'

'Hi,' he'd said when Bridget picked up, 'it's him.' And although she'd wanted to die a thousand deaths, not to mention kill her mother a million times over, she'd just laughed, and so had he. And she hadn't needed to explain.

The son of a farmer, he was expected to take over the family farm eventually. But, while he had no desire to work in an office, neither did he want to farm. He just hadn't figured out how to tell his parents.

It was Bridget's dad who'd introduced Greg to a mate of his with a landscape-gardening business. When he'd offered him an apprenticeship, Greg had said yes on the spot. His parents had been furious.

Two decades and two grandchildren later, Bridget suspected they still hadn't forgiven her for taking their boy away.

She was hungry, Bridget realised, rousing herself.

Shaking the sand from her body, she rolled up her towel. If she hurried, she'd get a head start on the kids; they must be starving.

But when she got back to the house, she was pleasantly surprised to find the dishes done and Roz and Lucy busy buttering bread and slicing cheese.

'Hey,' she said. 'Sorry, I lost track of time.'

'We thought we'd just cut up a bunch of stuff and everyone can make their own,' said Lucy. 'Select-a-sandwich style.'

They smiled at each other.

Bridget had put herself through university working lunchtimes at a select-a-sandwich bar. She'd been paid per sandwich and the owner had liked to boast she was 'faster than my own daughter!' She could still remember the spiel. Wholemeal or white? Butter, mayo, or both? Salt and pepper? Horseradish with your roast beef? Any extras? Alfalfa sprouts, cottage cheese, crushed pineapple . . .

'Hello, ladies,' said Tristan, coming in the back door.

An image of his swollen cock rushed unbidden into Bridget's head. She looked away, mortified.

'Did you find Zachi?' asked Lucy.

Chapter
Eleven

October
Tuesday

Like papier mâché, thought Bridget, lurching unhappily between states, neither asleep nor awake. Like a balloon someone had plastered over with newspaper, layer upon layer, this monstrous orb gummed together with a gelatinous paste of flour and water: that's what her head felt like.

All night she had tossed and turned, unable to leave the events of the day alone: manipulating them, recasting them, desperate to make sense of it all.

Locals often talked about Point Heed being a village. And it was true: someone would tell you if you had left your headlights on, your window open; you could pop next door to borrow a cup of sugar, nick a lemon off your neighbour's tree. But in reality, it was a sizable suburb; its residents able to go about their daily lives, conduct their business, with a degree of anonymity.

Of course, Bridget had known it was unavoidable that one day she'd bump into Lucy. However, she had assumed it would be from a manageable distance. That, pausing in the chilled aisle of the supermarket to compare the apricot yoghurt's nutrition panel with the chocolate dairy food's, she might glimpse Lucy dithering over the mozzarella. That she'd have the opportunity to beat a hasty retreat to the butchery department.

Not this though, not this sudden incursion of her turf. Rendered all the more unsettling by the certainty of future encounters.

It must have been after four a.m. when she'd finally dropped off, and now she was being dragged from the blessed dullness, from the welcome suspension of consciousness, by a tugging on her shoulder.

'Whaaa . . .' she tried to open her mouth, found it stuck fast, a sour thickness cementing tongue to palate.

'Mum,' said Jackson. 'Mum, wake up. I'm hungry and Abigail's crying.'

'Where's . . .' she searched for the word. 'Where's Dad?'

'I don't know, but can you just get up?'

Bridget reached for her phone, knocking a pile of books to the floor with the charger cord. *Shit!* It was 8.07 a.m. She threw back the duvet, and half rolled, half fell, out of bed.

'What's that? Ewww. Gross!'

Great. She had leaked in the night, a reddy-brown crescent, right where she'd lain. Right across her best fitted sheet.

'Mum, it's all over you.'

'It's just blood.'

Bridget wiped ineffectually at the rusty stain rimming her underpants, tracking down her thighs.

'All night long!' That's what the ad for those new maxi-pads promised. *All night long. My arse!*

Impatient to check on Abigail, and yet keen to avoid another outburst of disgust from Jackson, she grabbed a wet facecloth from the bathroom vanity, rubbing at her hands and dragging it roughly over her legs.

She wrapped her dressing gown around her, ears attuned to the whimper coming from the direction of the lounge.

Coming from Abigail, a small ball of pity curled into the couch.

'Darling. Abigail, darling. What is it?' She stroked her daughter's thin arm.

'Where were you, Mum? I had the worst sleep. I called and called and you never came. And then you weren't in the kitchen this morning like usual.'

Even after all these years of mothering, Bridget could still be taken aback by just how much these two small people she had created depended on her, on her very there-ness.

'Oh sweetheart, I'm sorry. I didn't hear you. Was it the nightmare? Did you have it again?'

For months now Abigail had been having this awful dream. She hadn't been able to tell them what it was exactly that woke her in the wee hours, what it was that gripped her little body with such a terrible terror. Once she'd said it had eyes, yellow eyes and a face so big you couldn't see its edges. Another time she'd described it as dark and scratchy. Mostly she just said it was bad. That it was really bad.

Abigail had a notebook with a pink fluffy cover she liked to doodle in. Tidying her room one day, Bridget had flicked through it: what she wanted for Christmas, her favourite chocolate bars scored out of ten, drawings of flowers and balloons and birthday cakes. She had been about to put it away when she'd glimpsed a page covered in dense scrawl.

You know how you shouldn't never ever let a baby play with a plastic bag, Abigail had written. *In case it puts it over its head and it can't breathe. Well, it's like that. Like you're in this plastic bag and it's sticking to your face and it's in your mouth, and you can't see what, but you know something is watching you suffocate, and it's smiling. Not a good smile, a bad smile.*

Bridget wanted to take her to a child psychologist. Perhaps something had happened to her. Perhaps she was too scared to tell them. Greg said Bridget was being ridiculous, that she was over-reacting. 'It's just another stage,' he'd said. '*Night terrors III.* She'll grow out of it. Just like she did when she was eighteen months, and just like she did when she was five and a half. Abigail's always been dramatic.'

'Why didn't you come into Mummy and Daddy's room?'

'I don't know. I thought no one was here.'

'We would never leave you home alone, Abigail. You know that. Daddy must have gone to work early and I was so deeply asleep I didn't hear you. C'mon, let's get you both something to eat.'

'Finally,' groaned Jackson. 'I thought I was going to starve to death.'

'Jackson, there is about as much chance of you starving to death as there is of me becoming a supermodel. Anyway, you could have got yourself some food. You're plenty old enough.'

'I opened the fridge, but I couldn't see anything that looked like breakfast.'

'You eejit!'

Pulling him into her chest with one arm, she gathered Abigail up with the other.

'Do you know how much I love you two?'

For a moment, her children safe in her embrace, Bridget felt that maybe everything would be okay. That she would get on top of the house and her deadlines, that she and Greg would get on better, Lucy would get over last summer, and they'd all be friends again. That everything would work out.

Remarkably, in spite of her wreck of a night and sluggish start, she got the kids to school just as the bell went.

She had read somewhere once that if you told yourself you were well-rested your body would respond accordingly.

She'd first tried it when Abigail was a baby. In the depths of those dark, lonely nights, woken yet again by her daughter's plaintive cry, Bridget thought sleep deprivation would be the death of her, but come morning she would jolly herself along, and, somehow, she'd get through the day. She guessed it was habit now.

As she was turning into their driveway, Greg rang.

'You left early,' she said, aware her tone was more than a little accusatory.

'I know. I woke up and decided just to get going rather than lie there stressing about everything I had to do. I gave you a kiss, but you didn't even stir.'

'I slept really badly.'

'Sorry, Bridge. I know you wanted to talk last night, I was bushed. Tonight. We'll get the kids down early, and you can fill me in on everything.'

'Okay, I'm going to hold you to that.'

'I love you, you know.'

'I know. Me too.'

Inside, she stripped the bloodied sheet off the bed.

She was lucky. Greg, the children, their home: there had to be some truth to all that guff about counting your blessings, etc.

She put the lid back on the honey.

Recalling yesterday's gluttony, she threw Abigail's leftover crumpet in the bin. Why had she made such a fucking pig of herself? She felt the regret return.

No, what was done was done. Besides, she had such a heavy period. Her body must have needed it. Well, perhaps not a half-frozen strawberry swirl cheesecake, but extra sustenance at least.

She started on her inbox. By noon she'd cleared all seventy-three unread emails. Dealing with the one or two urgent ones, skimming over and deleting the school notices and real estate newsletters, shifting everything else to her to-do file.

While she waited for the jug to boil, she resolved she would tackle Rosie Thear next, that she wouldn't stop for lunch until she had sorted the damn soft furnishings page.

With a groan, she sat back down in front of her computer.

Two new emails. One from Tatiana, who was apparently horny and could go all night long. *Yeah, you and my maxi-pad*, thought Bridget, sending Tatiana straight to the junk folder.

The other was from Amanda Williams.

God, she hadn't heard from Amanda in ages.

When Bridget had graduated from university with a BA in English Literature, she'd been at a loss over what to do. With visions of red carpets and war zones, she'd enrolled in a journalism course.

She'd met Amanda on the first day. A small-town girl from a wealthy Catholic family, she was not someone Bridget would have ever imagined being friends with.

Sent to the same provincial paper for their mandatory two-week internship, where the chief reporter had tried to force Bridget into digging up some dirt on the district rugby coach. Spotted holding hands with a man in the park, apparently he was a 'bloody fag'. When Bridget had nervously refused, Amanda had backed her up. 'Even if he is,' she'd said, 'he's not hurting anyone.' Later, over chips and cider at their freezing youth hostel, Bridget had thanked her. 'I assumed you'd be on the chief reporter's side,' she'd admitted. 'What, because I'm Catholic?' Amanda had snorted. 'I can't stand bullies.'

They'd kept in touch, and when she and Greg came home from London with a couple of maxed-out credit cards and a wedding to pay for, Amanda, by then a high-flying journalist at one of the major papers, had helped her get a foot in the door. It had been a fairly junior role, but just as Bridget was starting to make herself known to the features editor, she'd fallen pregnant.

She'd returned part-time, once Jackson was weaned. Then Abigail had come along and heading off to an office had felt impossible. Serendipitously, a colleague of Greg's had asked her to rewrite his website content, and eight years later, here she was: full-time mother, part-time online content producer. Her regret at what might have been only occasionally rearing its head; usually when she came across Amanda's byline attached to some big hard-hitting investigative piece.

They caught up now and then, always saying they must do it more often, but Bridget was conscious it was probably more a lack of common ground than opportunity stopping them.

It would have been a good ten or eleven months since they'd last spoken. Just before Hine's, Bridget thought: pre-Lucy, her eternal calendar reference point these days.

HELP, read the subject line of Amanda's email.

Chapter
Twelve

January
Day Two

'He hadn't gone far,' said Tristan. 'He was just in the flax bushes behind the house. Messing about. You know how Zachariah does.'

He laughed.

It was a small, hollow sound, and as she reached into the cupboard for a pile of plates, Bridget observed a kind of grimness to Tristan's expression. She saw, too, that he was staring at Lucy. But Lucy didn't seem particularly interested in her husband now he'd done what she had asked, and, picking up the tomato she'd been slicing, she turned her back.

Counting how many plates short she was, Bridget registered her discomfort, and how, weirdly, this exchange between husband and wife felt almost more intimate than the scene she'd witnessed earlier from the stairs.

Bridget wasn't sure whether or not Roz had picked up on the thin snake of tension that had slithered into the room, but either way she was thankful when Roz announced: 'Lunch is ready!'

When there was no sound of anyone approaching, Roz turned to Tristan. 'Make yourself useful, will you, buddy? Go round up the troops.'

'I think it might be rosé o'clock,' said Lucy.

'On it already,' said Roz, brandishing a corkscrew.

Maybe she had imagined any hostility, Bridget thought, balancing a roll of paper towels on top of a bowl of nectarines and following Tristan down the verandah steps, forcing herself not to dwell on the way his calf muscles contracted as he walked.

As she was making her second trip, this time bearing a jug of icy lemon water, Tristan reappeared: little arms and legs marching in sandy unison behind him. The Pied Piper of Hine's.

'Right,' Bridget said, springing to action. 'Wash your feet in the bucket. Then go get yourself a sandwich.'

'Yes, sir,' said Jackson.

'Yes, sir,' chimed the other kids.

'Yes, sir,' said Greg, grabbing her around the waist.

Instinctively Bridget sucked her belly in. 'Careful!' she said as the jug teetered. But, oblivious to the water sloshing up her arm, Greg just nuzzled her neck.

'Yuck,' said Jackson.

'Yuck,' repeated the other kids. 'Yuck!'

'Oi,' said Greg. 'Enough of that nonsense from you lot!' He was laughing, though, as he said it, and, as Bridget turned to go, he patted her on the arse.

Oh God, the little wife, she thought, cringing, and yet conversely, thrilled.

'Mum, have you seen Emerson?'

'No, I don't think so, honey.'

'Skye and Paris can't find Kendall and Courtney, either.'

'I'm sure they'll be somewhere, girls. I'll help you look after lunch.'

They spread mats across the lawn and dragged every cushion and beanbag they could find under the shade of the big old tītoki tree.

Bridget sank down next to Abigail, dripping mayonnaise on her head as she bit into her overstuffed sandwich.

'Whoops! Sorry, sweetness.' She wiped at her daughter's matted hair with her thumb.

'It doesn't matter, Mum. I'm going swimming again after lunch.'

Bridget smiled at her, kissing her sandy brow.

It was like a painting, she thought, looking at her friends sprawled around her. Like Manet's *Le Déjeuner sur l'herbe*, if you discounted the fact there were no naked women and added seven kids, unusually and mercifully quiet as they hungrily shovelled food into their waiting mouths.

It made her happy to see Roz and Greg chatting companionably, about fermentation of all things, Jono whittling away at a stick. It was his thing; he'd even been known to bring out his Leatherman at dinner parties. It drove Roz nuts, but Bridget found it oddly endearing. He'd presented her with a miniature duck once. Because, he'd said, she always accused him of ducking her questions. She still had it. On top of her chest of drawers.

It sat next to an enamel snuff box she'd picked up in a junk shop one day, wagging school with Lucy. They had fought over it, both claiming to have spotted it first. Usually, Bridget was the first to give in; this time, though, she'd stood her ground.

It seemed crazy now. She didn't even like it that much.

But at the time it had seemed symbolic, a shift in their relationship. And so she'd held on to it all these years.

Bridget looked over at Lucy, lying between Tristan's legs, a beer in one hand, a hunk of ham in the other, and she marvelled at her ability to turn even the act of swigging beer and gnawing meat into such an intensely feminine gesture, into something almost sexual.

There was no sign of the animosity she'd detected between Lucy and Tristan earlier. If only she wasn't so hypersensitive to other's moods Bridget thought, rearranging her sarong; she was like a frickin' sponge.

'Can we?' asked Abigail, interrupting her self-flagellation. 'Please?'

'Can you what?'

'Go see Don?'

'I thought you were going swimming.'

'After that. Remember, he said he'd show us his horses. That maybe we could ride them. Can we? Can we?'

'Who's Don?' asked Jono.

'He's the farm manager,' said Earl.

'Yeah, he's really nice,' said Paris. 'We met him this morning by the beehives. A bee stung Abigail's foot and he helped her.'

The adults all looked at Bridget.

'It's true,' she said. 'There's a dried-up old pond on top of the hill. It's the strangest place. Almost otherworldly. Anyway, this guy Don keeps a bunch of hives there. I was going to tell you about it when I got back, but everyone was . . . um, otherwise engaged.'

'Actually, I do remember the letting agent mentioning something about a manager, now that I think about it,' said Lucy. 'That he'd keep to himself, but if we had any problems, he should be able to sort it out for us.'

'I saw his place,' said Zachariah.

'When?' asked Lucy.

'This morning. I went for a walk.'

'I thought you were mucking around behind the house?'

'Before that. There's a dead sheep. Maggots crawling out its mouth. And this real skinny dog. Looked like it was starving. Like a skeleton. It barked its head off. Didn't see no horses, though. I reckon he was lying.'

'Don's not like that,' said Paris. 'He's cool.'

'Yeah, Thackawire,' said Willow, who, much to her brother's disgust, had never been able to say his name. 'Don's cool.'

'Maybe later I'll take you to see Don and his imaginary horses,' said Jono. 'But you're not to go on your own.'

'They're not imaginary,' Abigail muttered. 'They're real.'

Greg stood up. 'First one to take their plate inside gets first go in the kayak.'

There was a sudden scramble and they were gone. Lucy yawned languorously.

'You took the words right out of my mouth,' said Roz. 'Nap or swim? Swim or nap?'

Jono patted her thigh fondly. 'Why don't we leave all this,' he suggested. 'Take care of it later. Let's head down to the beach. Have a dip and then a kip on the sand.' He laughed as he said it, pleased, presumably, with his rhyme.

The afternoon stretched exquisitely before them; adults taking it in turns to play lifeguard while the kids happily paddled around in the kayak, never tiring of tipping each other out.

'Don't you want to play with the others?' Bridget asked Zachariah, who was kicking at the sand with his heels.

He was like an insect, she thought, this peripheral irritation marring the idyll.

'Nah,' he said. 'Can I have your phone, Mum?'

'Zachariah,' Bridget couldn't help herself. 'Beaches are for swimming. For sandcastles. Not screens.'

He gave her a withering look. 'Sandcastles!'

'Actually, he's not *just* on a screen,' said Lucy. 'He's downloaded this editing app. You're my budding filmmaker, aren't you, Zachi?' She ruffled his hair. 'He got into it at school. That's one of the things I love about The Imagination Academy. Rather than fixating on reading and writing, they encourage them to discover their passions.'

Behind Lucy, Roz rolled her eyes.

It had been a good day, Bridget thought, lying in bed that night. *Mostly*.

Fortunately, the kids hadn't mentioned visiting Don again. With any luck they'd just forget about him. He was probably harmless. Harmless and lonely; living out here all by himself. Even so, she wasn't about to let her children fulfil a middle-aged man's need for company.

Swatting listlessly at a persistent mosquito, she picked up her book. Bridget regretted not bringing something lighter: something escapist, not a confrontation with the end of life on earth as we know it. She berated herself for being such a pretentious idiot, preferring to be seen reading something edifying, literary, rather than the latest bestseller. As if anyone would have cared.

Slap! She opened her hands, a tell-tale black smear on one palm.

Suddenly unbearably hot, she pushed away the sheet she'd been hiding under, looking down at her naked body with a critical eye.

She was examining her bikini line for ingrown hairs when Greg opened their bedroom door, a waft of dope and bourbon following him into the room.

'Where've you been?' she asked, pulling up the sheet to conceal her self-grooming.

After twenty years together there wasn't much mystery left, yet there were certain acts your partner did not need to witness.

'Tristan and I did a bit of tidying, then had a nightcap on the deck.'

'Smells like more than a nightcap,' she said.

He lay down heavily beside her. The mattress sank in the middle, throwing Bridget against him.

'Hmmm,' he said, 'I've been thinking about this all day.'

'So have I,' she said, stamping out the little spark of guilt that flared in her chest.

She still enjoyed sex, still fancied her husband and occasionally, after a rare wild night out, they would surprise each other with their raunchiness, but mainly there was a predictability to their sex life. It didn't bother her particularly; she knew they both drew a certain comfort from knowing which position brought each of them to the quickest, most mutually satisfying orgasm.

For her it was more about the scenarios she conjured up in her mind, anyway. She'd always assumed it was the same for Greg, but he said he never thought about anything specific during sex. That he didn't need to. That just the sensation of being inside her was enough.

Not that she'd have really cared if he was picturing another woman spread across the bed in front of him. God knows, there'd been enough times she'd pretended he was Lenny Kravitz.

But tonight, as her husband mounted her and the image of Tristan and his carved wings filled her head, it felt wrong.

It felt like betrayal.

Chapter Thirteen

October
Tuesday

While the beans and tortillas were heating, Bridget grated carrot and cheese, chopped tomato and avocado, tore the foil lid off the sour cream. Banging and clattering, she slid plates and glasses along the table, dumped an assortment of cutlery.

'Great,' said Greg. 'Wraps.'

'Yum,' said Abigail. 'My favourite!'

'It's all I had time for,' said Bridget, passing Greg the jalapeños, damned if she'd apologise. 'I completely forgot I've got a bloody Parents' Association meeting tonight.'

'I thought you wanted to catch up.'

'I know, but I shouldn't be late. Talk when I get back, huh?'

She touched him on the shoulder, questioningly, hopefully. He shrugged, non-committal. It was a little power game he played. He knew she liked certainty.

Bridget brushed her teeth, spat. With one hand she splashed water up the basin sides, sluicing it clean. She doused herself in perfume; applied foundation, bronzer, brow pencil, mascara, gloss. She slapped and smudged and swept instinctively.

In the kitchen the kids were at the bench doing their homework. Greg was bent over, loading the dishwasher. She blew them a kiss.

'Bye, darlings. Be good for Dad.'

'Are you meant to be a tiger or something?' asked Jackson.

'What do you mean?'

'Ah, you might want to check the mirror,' said Greg. 'You've got these sort of orange stripes.' He painted lines in the air with his forefingers.

She rubbed at her cheeks with the heels of her hands. *Faark.*

'Thanks.' On impulse she wrapped an arm about his waist, pressing her forehead into his shoulder. 'Try and wait up for me, honey.'

Shifting his weight, he leant back into her, so fleeting she might have imagined it. 'I'll do my best.'

Bridget drove past the school. Around the block. It was as bad as drop-off. She should have got Roz to swing by en route.

A park!

Hopping out, she checked her position; front tyres slightly encroaching on a driveway. She wasn't blocking it, but . . . she weighed up her options. The house had lace curtains, the glow of a TV. Someone elderly probably lived there; it was unlikely they'd be going anywhere at this time of night.

Jogging up the hill, feet sliding uncomfortably in her loafers, Bridget suddenly realised Lucy might be at the meeting. Panic grabbed her. No, surely not. Zachariah and Skye had only just started. Lucy had never been one for committees. Never been particularly predictable either. Oh God.

As she edged open the staffroom door, Bridget tried to make herself as insignificant as possible. Awkwardly she scanned the room. No Lucy. Roz waved her over, she'd saved her a place. Sinking into the seat, Bridget squeezed her friend's hand.

At the front of the room, Marcia, their chairwoman, was outlining the evening's agenda.

'I'm just wondering whether it would be better to send out more than one newsletter each term,' a mother interrupted.

Bridget didn't know who she was but she'd seen her around. Seen her berating her son at the school gate for getting mud on his jeans.

'Fortnightly, even. I just think communication is key, you know.'

'By all means,' said Marcia. 'If you're keen to take it on.' She looked at

Lesley, the Parents' Association secretary.

Lesley nodded enthusiastically. 'I'd be only too happy to hand it over.'

'Well,' said the mother. 'It was just a thought . . .'

It was always like this. A bunch of women all puffed up with their *thoughts*. Scant intention of actually putting in the hard yards.

Marcia was a doer, though. They weren't friends exactly, but Bridget liked her. Liked that she wasn't a typical Point Heed mother. Liked that Marcia drove a plain, sensible car. That she, her husband, and their three children wore plain, sensible clothes. Even had matching no-nonsense haircuts, as though they'd got a group discount at Hair 4 Less, the salon at the mall that didn't require appointments.

The first time Bridget had met Marcia, she'd mentally written her off: too straitlaced. And then at a school disco one night, while the other parents milled about the edges of the hall, talking up the merits of a private education, the need to focus on maths, on what really mattered in life, Marcia had taken to the dance floor. She'd danced freely, wildly, like there was no tomorrow, and the kids had flocked around her.

Bridget had been transfixed.

'You should get yourself one,' mouthed Roz, gesturing to the open bottles of wine on the table.

As if to lend support to her suggestion, Roz took a loud slurp from her own very full glass.

'I can wait,' Bridget whispered, not wishing to draw any more attention to herself than she already had with her late arrival.

She looked around the room. Of course, Ruth, with the boulders for breasts, was there. And Hi-Vis Mum.

The mother of a friend of Jackson's gave her a small wave. Bridget smiled. She could never remember her name. She recalled guiltily she owed her son a sleepover.

On the other side of her was a group of younger women she didn't recognise. She tried not to stare at the taut, tanned thigh poking through the slit in one woman's skirt, at another's painfully thin bra strap, T-shirt sliding artfully off one shoulder. Bridget glanced down at her own linen shirt and chinos.

'Okay,' said Marcia, 'best we get on with it, I think. We've got a lot to cover off with Fright Night fast approaching.'

Fright Night was the school's Halloween fundraiser. It was the main reason Bridget and Roz were here tonight. More fun than the spell-a-thon, they'd figured, when they'd signed up a few years back.

'Has everyone got a copy of the list of jobs requiring names against them?' asked Lesley.

'Actually, before we start, I had an idea that might change things up a bit.'

It was one of the young mothers. As everyone turned to look at her, she flicked her hair away from her face self-consciously. Bridget admired how immaculately tousled it was. She knew the effect was meant to be that you'd rolled out of bed looking like that, not spent half an hour in front of a mirror with a pair of tongs.

Marcia sighed. 'Yes?'

'Well, I thought it could be super cute to have a "vintage" theme. You know, bobbing for apples, pin the tail on the donkey, that sort of thing.'

Next to Bridget, Roz groaned.

'Amazing,' said the one with the tanned thighs. 'That kind of old-fashioned, wholesome vibe would tie in nicely with something I wanted to raise. Last year was Wolf's first Fright Night and we were really shocked at the amount of junk food on offer. I'd like to look at how we can reduce sugar this time.'

'Fuck me,' muttered Roz. 'Bunting and bliss balls!'

'And a smoothie bowl stand!' Bridget couldn't help herself. 'Oh, and cornets of kale chips. They'll go down a treat.'

Roz snorted.

As if their momentary lawlessness had enabled others, around them the meeting dissolved, bedlam briefly taking hold. Hi-Vis Mum looked at Bridget and Roz with the sort of ill-concealed disappointment you'd usually only bring out for an unmannerly child.

Marcia clapped twice, sharply. 'Okay ladies, if we could get back to the agenda. We can return to the matters of, er, theme and nutrition later. For now, there's a more important issue we need to attend to. Apparently, there's been some discussion about the zombie-wrestling stand. Whether it's appropriate.'

'What do you mean?' asked Bridget. 'There have never been any problems in the past. Why the sudden concern?'

'A few of us have been unhappy about it for a while now,' said Ruth, her voice a decibel or two louder than necessary. 'In fact, I wouldn't let Timothy and Joshua participate last year. It just didn't feel right. Some man they didn't know, roughing them up. It felt like it was undoing all the hard work my husband and I had put in about stranger danger.'

'But,' said Bridget, 'they're just school dads. Hardly strangers. And you can stand right there if you want, keeping an eye. Plus, there are teachers everywhere. Other parents. What could happen?'

'It wouldn't be so bad if you could see their faces. If you knew who they were,' said another woman.

Bridget didn't know her name. She'd seen her hanging around Ruth before. One of Ruth's minions, as Roz called them.

'If you could see their faces,' said Bridget, trying to keep it light, 'if you knew it was Sam's dad, or Toby's dad, or Mr Ngata, then it wouldn't be scary. They have to be in disguise. They're zombies, for goodness' sake.'

Ruth's bosom quivered indignantly. 'Well, in my house we're taking extra precautions. Given recent events, Jeremy and I have decided to ban trick or treating this Halloween.'

'What recent events?' asked one of the young mothers, whose boots Bridget had been quietly coveting across the room.

There was the sound of women shifting in their seats.

'Until . . .' Ruth began.

The word hung in the air. Bridget had to give her credit. Ruth knew how to work an audience.

'Until we know who in this community is depraved enough to deal in child pornography, then as far as I'm concerned none of our children are safe. None.'

Evidently the young mothers hadn't heard the news; in almost perfect unison they reeled back in horror.

Bet that wasn't what you signed up for when you bought into the Point, thought Bridget.

Gazing around the room at the ripples her declaration had generated, Ruth looked as if she might explode with satisfaction.

It wasn't that Bridget disagreed with her — after all, what parent wanted to live alongside a paedophile? — but something about Ruth's sanctimonious way of viewing the world made Bridget feel like taking an axe to the moral high ground she'd so smugly built her nest atop.

Chapter Fourteen

January
Day Three

They were in to the swing of it now, thought Bridget as she came downstairs; it always took a day or two, a couple of sleeps. No one was ever quite able to switch off at the beginning, exhausted from what it had taken just to get there, drinking too much in a bid to have a good time, to be seen to be having a good time.

You might catch up regularly over the course of the year, but you were never really prepared for the onslaught of each other on holiday, the relentlessness of all that rubbing along together. And then, towards the end, any sense of novelty to the communal living, any delight in one another's foibles, had likely dissipated, to be replaced instead with a hankering for the routine of home, for the very thing you had been so desperate to escape only days earlier.

No, the middle of a vacation, this bit, was always the best, the cream, the Promised Land.

Under her bare feet the hallway floor was sticky, and while this would usually repulse her, she observed instead how the house seemed to glow with the light of a new day, how there was a headiness to the warm air.

In the days ahead, Bridget would wonder at how easily she'd been seduced by the brightness, the hopefulness of that morning. Could she really have been that stupid, that desperate, for everything to be all right that she'd failed to see, to really see, what lay before her: the incipient behaviours, the burgeoning situation?

Right now, though, innocent of what was to come, she reminded herself she had a choice, that happiness was a choice.

In the kitchen, elbow-deep in dishes, Greg and Tristan were doing a surprisingly good rendition of Bill Withers' 'Lovely Day'. The kids, a human chain, passed crockery and cutlery down the line from bench to cupboard, where Jono stood waiting, a hulking beast, quieted only when fed. He rubbed his belly, one of those middle-aged men who had retained the scrawniness of youth everywhere else except for his impressive gut.

'Dishes,' he intoned, 'I need dishes,' clamping on as soon as Willow, littlest and thus last in line, placed them in his great mitts. 'More dishes,' he roared at the slightest lull in production, and the children shrieked.

'Has anyone had breakfast?' Bridget whispered to Greg, loath to interrupt the hilarity.

'Nope, that's why we're washing up. There was nothing clean to eat off.' He nibbled on her ear.

He had nibbled on her ear last night, as they were having sex, and the memory made her blush. She eased out of her husband's reach.

'Who wants pancakes?'

'Yay,' the kids cheered.

'With maple syrup, please.'

'I want lemon and sugar!'

'Nutella!'

'You bet,' she said, mentally calculating how much mixture she'd need.

'Are you sure?' asked Greg. 'You complain what a performance it is making pancakes for the four of us.'

'I'm in the mood for a mission. Mind you, I'm going to need some help. Where are Roz and Lucy anyway? Bet they're in bed, lazy things.'

'They went for a walk,' said Jono. 'About half an hour ago.'

It was silly to be hurt. In their shoes, though, Bridget would have waited.

They were both so impulsive. They didn't mean to be unkind, but neither of them thought things through like she did; always going with whatever felt good in that moment.

She remembered how once, bursting with excitement, they told her they'd booked themselves a four-night package to Fiji. Apparently, they'd been at lunch, and, stumbling out of the restaurant after several bottles of wine, they'd 'practically fallen over' this travel agent, who was 'practically giving away' these trips. It didn't seem to occur to them Bridget might have felt left out, and when she'd said, doing her best to banish the bitterness from her voice, that it would have been nice if they'd thought to ask her, they'd been genuinely taken aback. 'But,' they'd said, 'we know you're on a budget with the renovation, and how busy you always are with everything, we just assumed you wouldn't be able to.'

She wasn't one of those women who'd held on to that teenage girl trait of thinking everyone had to do everything together. In fact, it had been a relief to leave all that suffocating inseparability of the schoolyard behind. Nonetheless, a threesome was problematic. One usually on the outer.

It didn't seem to be such an issue with men, perhaps because of the slight distance at which they tended to hold each other. Women, though, were like plaits, entwining the strands of their lives in and out, around and around, lovingly strangling each other.

Bridget already saw it playing out among Abigail and her friends. The crushing triangles; the endless little cycles of exclusion.

She got out flour and salt from the pantry, eggs and milk from the fridge.

'Who can tell me how much milk I'll need if the recipe uses three-quarters of a cup, and I'm making four times that?'

'I know, I know,' said Abigail. 'It's two-and-a-half cups.'

'Remember your strategy for working . . .'

'Duh,' Zachariah interrupted. 'It's three cups.'

Bridget gritted her teeth, the calm she'd felt earlier slipping even further from her grasp.

'Yes, you're right, Zachariah, however Abigail's younger than you, and she was trying her best.'

She could sense Greg's eyes on her. She knew what he was thinking.

Years ago, at one of those hideous indoor playgrounds, an older boy had deliberately body-slammed into Jackson, and Greg had bailed the boy up in a corner of the bouncy castle. The father had come over, fists at the ready, and the staff had threatened to call the police.

On more than one occasion she'd had to remind Greg of that day, remind him it was never a good idea to reprimand another parent's child in front of them.

Hypocrite!

Still, regardless of the fact Tristan was standing right there, she didn't regret speaking to Zachariah like that. Little shit.

'Sorry, Abigail,' Zachariah said suddenly. 'You're not dumb.'

It took Bridget by surprise, and, automatically, she checked for the smirk, the rolled eyes, something to negate his words. But there was only contrition on Zachariah's face, and she recalled a true crime show she'd seen once; apparently the mark of a sociopath was their ability to disarm you by never behaving according to expectation.

'That's okay,' said Abigail, who seemed less bothered than Bridget by the whole thing.

Under his breath, Greg hummed the 'Lovely Day' chorus.

Jono pretended to whip a squealing Willow with the tea towel.

'Coffee?' asked Tristan.

She smiled gratefully. Bridget assumed Tristan felt something for Zachariah; he'd been there since he was a toddler, after all. Yet, while Greg was probably right about Tristan's blindness when it came to Lucy and anything connected to her, surely, deep down, he didn't really share her wilful ignorance regarding Zachariah.

Her wilful ignorance, or her lioness's instinct to protect him.

Bridget was wondering if she had time to leave the batter to chill in the fridge, when she heard Roz and Lucy. Well, she heard Roz, groaning as she staggered up the steps. Exercise was a necessary evil for Roz; innately sedentary, she took no pleasure in exerting herself.

The kids crowded around the walkers.

'Bridget's making pancakes.'

'With anything you want.'

'Oooh,' said Lucy. 'I see what you mean about that old pond, B.' She balanced effortlessly on one leg, drawing the other foot up and pulling her trainer off. 'It's so alien.'

'We found this crazy beach, too,' said Roz. 'Over the other side of the hill. Like something out of a bloody magazine. A kind of natural lagoon. White sand. Turquoise water. You should have come, Bridge.'

Bridget tried to smile. *Happy holiday*, she told herself. *Happy holiday*.

'Right, shower time,' said Roz.

Standing over the stove, Bridget felt hot and frazzled.

'How long?' the children whined.

'Not long.'

'We're starving,' they moaned.

'Have an apple.'

'Greg,' she yelled. 'Greg!'

'What?'

'Do you think I could have some help here?'

'It was your mad idea to make pancakes.'

'I know and I could kick myself. But right now, please just give me a hand.'

He yanked the cutlery drawer open.

'Mum?'

'Abigail! Stop hassling me. The pancakes will be ready soon.'

'It's not that. We still can't find Emerson and Courtney and Kendall.'

'What? Since yesterday?'

'Yeah.'

Bridget was about to say something dismissive when she saw how agitated Abigail and Paris were, how close to tears Skye looked.

'That's strange. Don't worry, girls. We'll find them after breakfast.'

'Wait,' said Greg. 'Are you talking about those dolls? I think I saw them this morning. Now where was it? Oh yeah, that's right. They were at the back door. Made me laugh. Sitting there, like they'd been locked out.'

With a squeal of relief the girls skipped off.

Bridget was scraping the last of the batter into the pan when Roz and Lucy resurfaced. She noticed they'd both put make-up on.

'Right,' said Roz, 'give us a job.'

'Umm, it's a bit late for that. It's ready.'

Bridget wiped a lank strand of hair from her face, clocking the awkwardness that laced the air. She knew she'd caused it and a part of her was glad.

Breakfast was demolished in a fraction of the time it had taken to make. While the kids fought over how to split the last three pancakes, Bridget fantasised about being somewhere far away, somewhere clean and peaceful with no one to bother her.

Lucy clapped her hands.

'I don't know what you guys were thinking today but I thought we could head over to that amazing beach Roz and I saw. Pack a picnic?'

'Is it far?' asked Paris, who had inherited her mother's lack of enthusiasm for moving more than necessary.

'You'll be fine,' said Jono, tousling his daughter's hair.

'I could whip up a couple of bacon and egg pies,' suggested Roz.

Bridget knew the olive branch was hers for the taking. She started gathering the dirty plates.

'I'll clean up,' said Lucy.

Trying to unpack what she was feeling Bridget kept piling the dishes on the bench.

So often in relationships she let other people take control, let their mood set the tone, tempering her own accordingly.

She could sense the whole table's eyes on her, as if, somehow, she was personally responsible for the success of everyone's day. Bridget was intrigued to discover she kind of liked it; that she wasn't quite ready to let them off the hook. She was putting the plug in the sink when there was a decisive knock on the French doors.

Chapter
Fifteen

October
Tuesday

'Where are you parked?' asked Roz.

'Miles away. Halfway down Albury.'

Bridget shivered. She'd been overly ambitious thinking one thin layer would suffice. In spite of Marcia's best efforts, the meeting had dragged on and it was properly dark now.

'What a pack of killjoys,' said Roz.

Having reached a stalemate on whether there'd be zombie wrestling at this year's Fright Night, the committee had decided the principal would make the call, which probably meant, for the first time in the history of Fright Night, there'd be no zombie-wrestling stand. Mr Ngata would roll over in the face of Ruth's indignance; biding his time until retirement, he no longer had any appetite for a battle.

It was a widely held view among Point Heed parents that a less jaded principal was required. A leader befitting their school. The only inner-city school to run from kindergarten through to year eight, it was special.

In spite of Point Heed's farms having long ago been carved up into residential lots, there was something pastoral to the school, something old-fashioned, the littlies and the big kids all in together. It added to the locals' illusion they lived in a village and were therefore somehow apart. A law unto themselves.

'It's funny,' said Bridget. 'You assume being cool goes hand-in-hand with an open mind. Under their fashion-forward outfits, though, I reckon those new mothers are more uptight than Ruth and her minions.'

'Ha! Jono calls them "Junior Tories". That hipster front, everything organic, but really, they're hell-bent on turning us all into free-market apostles. We get them at work constantly. Does my head in. Sometimes we charge them a premium just for being such precious fucking tits.'

Bridget laughed. Roz and Jono ran a successful event management business. A few months ago, they'd wangled her and Greg an invitation to this party some lifestyle magazine was throwing for fellow aesthetes. Bridget had been blown away by what her crazy friends had pulled off. The party was held on a train, and each carriage was themed around the work of a famous artist: daiquiris and ceviche tacos in Frida Kahlo's carriage, a house DJ playing and vodka served out of diamante skulls in Damien Hirst's.

The party had been overflowing with women just like the young mothers at tonight's meeting. Bridget had tried making conversation with a couple of them, and been struck by how unworldly they were beneath the sophisticated veneer.

They'd stood there, tottering in their inhumane heels, discussing how 'now' Central American food was, and when Bridget had said she'd love to visit, they'd looked at her as if she was a complete lunatic.

'But it's meant to be so dangerous,' they'd bleated.

Later, waiting for the loo, Bridget had clocked them coming out of a cubicle together, all wild-eyed. The blonder of the two had passed the shorter one a rolled-up banknote.

'Thanks, hon,' she'd said. 'I'll need that for the babysitter.'

And they'd both shrieked with laughter.

They reached Roz's car. Bridget quickly kissed her goodbye, she wanted to catch Greg before he turned in.

'Thanks for keeping a seat for me. I was terrified Lucy would be there.'

'Nah, she knows you and I are on the Parents' Association. She'll be avoiding it like the plague. Hey, did you try getting in touch with what's-his-name, that guy you used to work with?'

'Darren? No, I mean it's been so long; it felt a bit weird, just making contact out of the blue. But, funnily enough, Amanda emailed me today.'

'Oh?'

Roz had never been keen on Amanda.

At a dinner party once, they'd had a blazing row. Bridget couldn't recall exactly what the argument had been about now, some political hot potato, however it had set the tone for all future interactions between them. Roz raising the issue of, say, child poverty, and then dismissively rubbishing whatever Amanda said on the subject, intimating that someone who'd had such a privileged upbringing couldn't possibly comprehend hardship. For some reason she forgave Bridget and Lucy their happy childhoods, but something about Amanda's moneyed, white-picket-fence fairy tale riled her.

'She's doing some big story on the real estate bubble and is looking to use Point Heed as a case study. Said she wants to pick my brains. We're going to have lunch. I thought I might ask her if she knew anything about our local pervert.'

'Keep me posted, doll,' said Roz, clambering up into her ridiculously large Land Rover.

Greg was fast asleep when Bridget got home.

She sighed. She couldn't really be cross. It must be exhausting; physical work all day, every day.

She contemplated putting on an episode of this Nordic noir series she was addicted to; attacking Mount Laundry. But she wasn't really in the mood for all those bleak landscapes and depressed detectives drowning their sorrows in rollmops and aquavit.

As quietly as possible, she got ready for bed, too drained to dwell any further on the events of the past few days.

The first to wake, Bridget basked in the calm; the silent joy of feeling the morning was hers alone for a few moments. Compared to the torture of the previous night, she'd slept surprisingly well.

Next to her, Greg stirred.

Normally he leapt out of bed as soon as he opened his eyes; even on the weekend, heading off fishing or just out to the lounge to watch sports. For once, though, despite it being a Wednesday, he didn't seem in a hurry.

'Morning, wife.'

'Good morning, husband. Aren't you going to work?'

'This new job is only down the road. And the client would rather we didn't kick off until she's dropped the kids at school.'

'That's odd. Who is it?'

'Apparently her kids are late risers and their bedrooms are right where we need to gain access with the digger. I don't mind. It makes a change from the usual sparrow's fart starts. Her name's Kate Crichton. That big place on Spur Street? You know, the one you reckon looks like a bunker.'

'Oh right. What do they need you for? That garden is immaculate.'

'They "did" the front when they renovated. To maintain the "street appeal", he wiggled his fingers in the air in the shape of inverted commas. 'Then ran out of money to "do" the back.'

Bridget looked at her watch. She didn't need to get the kids up yet. 'So does that mean you've got time to talk?'

'Uh-huh. I'm all ears.'

Bridget loved Greg best like this, patient and willing. When her initial lust, her astonishment this big, handsome guy actually fancied her, had subsided, his listening skills were what she'd fallen for.

And so, she told him about Lucy blanking her. How ill she'd felt on discovering Zachariah and Skye were enrolled at Point Heed School.

'Did Crackpot College turn out not to be so *aaamaaazing* after all?'

'The Imagination Academy. Don't be so judgemental, honey. Not everyone is cut from the same cloth.'

'It just seems a bit rich. It was like Lucy always thought her kids were better than ours. Too unique to learn the same way as the rest of the kids in the neighbourhood. Man, that's going to be fun when we see them at school functions.'

'I know. I can't stop thinking about it.'

'Did Roz have any idea?'

'No, it was news to her, too. I keep going over and over it in my head. I just can't figure out why.'

'Who knows, love. Once I would have said I knew those guys like the back of my hand. But they may as well be strangers now.'

Greg drew her down onto his chest and they lay like that for a while, drawing comfort from the familiarity. Normally this kind of intimate moment would lead to sex; Bridget was relieved when Greg seemed content with a cuddle.

Later, after Abigail had crawled into bed with them, Bridget remembered she hadn't told him about the local guy being done for child pornography, how there'd been a bit of a stink about it at the meeting last night, and as a result they'd probably be dropping the zombie-wrestling stand.

Greg would be bummed. He'd always volunteered for it. Sometimes Bridget had wondered who was getting more of a thrill: the kids lining up, clutching their gold coin in anticipatory terror, or her husband.

Chapter
Sixteen

January
Day Three

Don let himself in: an invader in the space they had already claimed their own.

The kids crowded around him as if he was some YouTube sensation, when in truth he was just a middle-aged man in gumboots.

The only adult who'd met him, Bridget reluctantly made the introductions.

'This is my husband, Greg. Our friends: Lucy and Tristan, Jono and Roz. Everybody, this is Don Davies, the property manager.'

'Pleased to meet you, folks. Sorry to bother you, I was just checking on some stock over this side and thought I'd pop in, say gidday, see how Abigail's foot is.'

Bridget watched him seek out her daughter as he spoke.

'It's fine, thanks,' she said shyly.

'Not too itchy? Get Mum to put some vinegar on it if it is. Best thing for it. Everything else okay?' he addressed the adults. 'Things to your liking?'

'Yes, everything's fine, thanks,' said Bridget.

'Can I get you a coffee?' asked Greg.

Bridget could have kicked him.

Don pulled out a chair and sat down. 'Bonza, mate. I've been up since the crack of dawn. So, when are you kids going to come meet my horses then, eh?'

'Can we? Can we now?' they clamoured.

'Fine by me,' said Don, heaping sugar into the mug Greg passed him. 'I was heading back home after this.'

'Maybe not today,' said Bridget. 'We've already made plans to go on a picnic.'

Roz looked at her with a raised eyebrow.

'Mum,' grumbled Jackson. 'You always ruin everything.'

'Where's your picnic?' asked Don.

'Some beach,' said Earl.

'Yeah,' said Paris, 'Some sucky beach over the hill.'

'You mean Mermaids' Cove,' said Don.

'Is that what it's called?' asked Skye. 'Are there real mermaids?'

'Yep. Seen them meself. Beautiful maidens. At dusk, when the tide's right, if you're lucky you might spot one combing her hair, perched on a rock next to the lagoon.'

'He's just pulling your leg,' scoffed Zachariah. 'Mermaids aren't real.'

The girls, who'd been hanging off Don's every word, looked crushed. For once Bridget was thankful for Zachariah's antagonism.

'You're not lying, are you Don?' pleaded Abigail. 'The mermaids are real, aren't they?'

'Well, I guess it's like all magic,' he winked at the adults. 'You gotta believe.'

'Yeah, like the Easter Bunny,' muttered Zachariah.

'You're a strange chook,' said Don. 'Next, you'll be telling me there's no such thing as Father Christmas!'

'Zachariah has never been into childish stuff,' said Lucy.

'Well, you're one out of the box, mate, I'll give you that,' said Don.

'I'd think we'd best let Don get back to his work,' said Bridget quickly.

Lucy was starting to get that look she got when she thought someone was maligning Zachariah.

'But what about the horses?' whined Jackson.

Bridget made a silent promise to throttle her son when she got him on his own.

'Actually, my place isn't far from your picnic spot,' said Don. 'You kids could come with me if you like. I can bring them down to the beach after they've had a look at the horses. Meet you lot there.'

'That could work,' said Roz. 'Get them out of our hair for a bit anyway, while we get organised. If you're sure it's no trouble.'

Bridget stared at her. Was this the same woman who'd said she wouldn't have children all those years ago because you couldn't protect them? About to happily let them go off with some guy they didn't know from a bar of soap?

'Yay!' chorused the kids.

'Perhaps another adult could go, too?' Bridget said. 'They can be a bit of a handful, all of them together.'

'Whatever you say, Boss,' said Don.

'I'm happy to go,' said Jono. 'See a bit more of the island.'

'Sorted,' said Don.

Chaos ensued as seven children tried to find a hat and walking shoes.

Don leant back in his chair, front legs suspended, drumming out a beat on the tabletop. Intermittently he hummed.

It sounded suspiciously like Bill Withers and Bridget wondered if it was just coincidence she was hearing his music for the second time that day. She considered Don, his hefty forearms and ruddy face. For a man who had chosen such a solitary life, he seemed remarkably comfortable among their unwieldy group. When Lucy accidentally squirted him with sunblock he laughed. Using his hand as a spatula, he wiped it off his thigh and smeared it on Willow's nose. The little girl giggled.

Watching them all troop off up the hill, Bridget felt a sense of urgency.

'Honey,' she said to Greg as he headed over to the fish smoker. 'Can we just focus on getting the picnic ready?'

'What's wrong?'

'Nothing. Nothing's wrong. I just don't want to be late for Jono and the kids.'

'They'll be fine, Bridget.'

'It's not that, it's just . . .'

'What?'

'There's something about him I don't trust.'

'Who? Jono?'

'No. Not Jono, you idiot. The farm manager, Don.'

'You're being a bit harsh, aren't you?'

'No, I think he's overly familiar with the kids. I mean we don't know the first thing about him.'

'He seemed harmless enough. Give the guy a break. Christ, he's willingly taken the kids off our hands. We should be thanking him.'

Unable to shake her need to get moving, Bridget put hummus, crackers and a block of cheddar into a backpack. On top she placed a bag of grapes and a jar of olives. She got the container of banana and chocolate chip muffins she'd brought from home out of the freezer, found an old tablecloth in the tea towel drawer, and slipped them into a supermarket bag, along with some knives, plastic glasses and a handful of napkins. It would have to do. There wasn't time for Roz's pies.

'Can you organise drinks?' she asked Greg.

When Roz wandered back into the kitchen, Bridget explained she'd made an executive decision on the food.

'Fine by me,' said Roz.

Bridget had known Roz's inherent idleness would trump her conflicting desire to be in charge.

'I'll just get my things,' she said, hurrying upstairs.

Bridget had pictured herself in a sundress: her new navy one, with the shoulder ties, but it needed ironing. Instead, she grabbed shorts and a T-shirt from the floor, and pulled a cap over her bed hair.

Coming down a few minutes later, she was relieved to see Lucy and Tristan ready to go; Tristan carrying several large folded rugs, Lucy, a wine cooler bag.

Bridget and Lucy walked together, Greg and Tristan up ahead, their long legs making short work of the climb. Puffing and panting, Roz brought up the rear.

As they crested the hill, Bridget was once more blown away by the singularity of the landscape. Somehow its unexpectedness made her feel laid bare.

'Look,' said Lucy, shielding her eyes with one hand and pointing at a white shape on the horizon with the other. 'I've always wanted to sail off like that.'

'Have you?' said Bridget, who couldn't think of anything worse. 'You've never told me that before.'

'Oh, I don't know . . . it's just as the kids get older, and life gets more complicated, the idea of setting out across the ocean, away from all the distractions, from other people's judgements . . . something about it's very appealing.'

There was a wistfulness to her best friend's voice Bridget hadn't heard in a long time.

'Is everything okay, Lucy Lu?'

'Yes, why?'

'You seem kind of distant. I don't mean now especially, but in general.'

Bridget watched her friend draw her lovely face together. For a moment it had felt like Lucy might open up, properly, like the old days, when they had each been the axis around which the other had spun.

'Not all the time . . . just . . .'

'I'm fine. A bit tired, maybe. But what about you? You seem pretty on edge yourself.'

'You know what an old worrywart I am. I'm okay, just want to get there so I can see the kids are all right.'

'What's this about the kids?' asked Roz, coming up behind them.

They slowed their pace to match hers.

Bridget knew Lucy hadn't necessarily been talking about her current mood either, and she was relieved not to have to try and explain her self further.

What would she say? *I'm anxious about whether everyone is getting on. Your son gives me the shits. Greg and I are always at each other. I'm having these intensely sexual urges around your husband.* 'Nothing,' said Bridget. 'I just want to make sure they're okay.'

'What could be wrong? Jono's with them.'

'Thank God. I wasn't at all keen on them going off alone with Don.'

'I quite liked him,' said Roz.

'Would you guys have let them go off with him by themselves?'

'Yeah,' said Roz. 'Safety in numbers.'

'Zachariah's almost a teenager, too,' said Lucy, as they reached the cliff's edge. 'He's really starting to show a sense of responsibility, to be mindful of others.'

Bridget looked down to the beach below. Zachariah would be more likely to push you off than move you out of harm's way.

Chapter
Seventeen

October
Wednesday

With Greg there to help, the morning had been a breeze. She'd got the kids to school on time, almost finished Rosie Thear's job, lunched on a virtuous salad and green tea.

And now at bell time she was actually waiting on the courts: the designated collection point. Bridget got why the teachers had made the rule. It must drive them nuts when parents hung around the classroom door, peering through the windows, trying to catch a glimpse of their prodigy. But, with everyone out here, pacing, scrolling through their phone, it did feel rather like a holding pen.

When the doors finally opened and the children all poured out, it took Bridget a moment to spot Abigail, another moment to register she was tugging a girl along behind her. A little girl almost as familiar to Bridget as her own daughter.

'Mum, can Skye come for a play? Please? Please?'

Bridget searched for a reason why, no, Skye couldn't come for a play. Not today, not next week, probably not ever.

Skye stood slightly away from Abigail, sucking on a scraggly strand of hair, eyes cast down. She'd always been shy, but Bridget didn't remember her cowering. Or needing a good wash.

This wasn't just the dirt of a day spent running around the playground, either. This had an air of neglect.

Lucy and Tristan had never been big on hair being brushed or socks matching, and yet as a family they had always radiated a golden kind of wellbeing. Apart from Zachariah, of course, but then his cave-dwelling appearance had only served as a foil to the rest of them.

Bridget tried to stifle her concern. Lucy and Tristan had made it painfully clear they wanted nothing to do with any of them. It was not her place to worry.

'Hi, Skye. Nice to see you, sweetie. I'm sorry, though, girls. No playdates today.'

'Why not?' Abigail demanded. 'It's Wednesday. We don't have anything on Wednesdays.'

Bridget scrambled for a reason. 'You've got homework to do,' she said, already kicking herself as the words came out of her mouth.

'Homework! I never do homework straight after school.'

Ignoring her daughter, Bridget asked Skye how she was getting home. It had occurred to her Lucy might be arriving any second.

'With Zachariah.'

Abigail was now stamping her feet and wailing.

'Hi, honey.' Bridget gave Jackson a distracted smile as he approached, a look of disdain on his face.

'I could hear you from the senior block,' he said to his sister. 'You're such a baby.'

'No, I'm not. Mum's mean. She says Skye can't come over. She says I have to do homework.'

'Heavy.'

'C'mon, guys,' said Bridget, deciding she would only fuel Abigail's meltdown by acknowledging it. 'Bye, Skye.'

She grabbed Abigail by the hand and half dragged her out the school gate. She had no desire to cross paths with Zachariah.

As they passed the shop, Abigail's cries magically abated.

'Dairy day?'

'No, only people who behave get treats.'

The wailing started back up, this time even louder.

'Oh, all right. One thing. That's it.'

It wasn't the girls' fault their parents weren't talking.

The dairy was owned by an elderly Korean couple. They were very sweet but Bridget avoided going in if she could. The smell of kimchi and fried meat that seeped through the bead curtain separating the shop from their living quarters always made her crave salty, oily things: salty, oily deliciousness she didn't need.

Her eyes took a few seconds to adjust to the fluorescent strip lighting. She blinked. Marcia was at the counter, several bags of orange, cheese-flavoured snacks in front of her.

'I told the kids they couldn't have lollies because we're cutting back on sugar,' she said, laughing, not remotely defensive.

The fact Marcia was buying MSG-loaded chips for her children's afternoon tea made Bridget like her even more.

'As a matter of fact I'm pleased I've bumped into you,' said Marcia. 'I've just had a meeting with Mr Ngata about Fright Night.'

'How was that? Unfruitful?'

'Quite the opposite, actually. He got all riled up. Reckons modern children need more rough and tumble, not less. I think his exact words were: "We're not having any of this PC nonsense. Not on my watch."'

'Go, Mr Ngata.'

Usually it pissed Bridget off when something was dismissed as being too PC — most so-called political correctness was just good manners — but she wasn't about to look a gift horse in the mouth.

'Wish me luck breaking it to Ruth,' said Marcia over her shoulder as she escaped out into the fresh air.

Bridget found a spot as far away as she could from the small horde of children dithering over which lollies to choose. Poor Mr Lee, standing there, tongs poised above the sour snakes; the man had the forbearance of a saint.

Bridget got out her phone.

'You won't believe it,' she texted Roz. 'Mr Ngata is on our side! xxx'.

Seeing Abigail still hovering indecisively in front of the freezer, Bridget handed her a ten-dollar note. 'Go find your brother, honey. I'm going to wait outside. Remember, one thing each. Don't forget the change.'

Eventually they emerged, Abigail holding a packet of M&Ms, Jackson, a bag of bhuja mix.

'What?' he said at his mother's quizzical look. 'My tastes are changing.'

'Evidently,' said Bridget, trying not to laugh.

When Abigail willingly shared one of her M&Ms with her, Bridget gauged it safe to broach the subject of Skye and why they couldn't have playdates.

'You know how you fall out with your friends sometimes? And you don't want to play with them? Well, that happens to adults, too. And sadly, that's what's happened with Mummy and Daddy and Skye's parents.'

'But that doesn't mean Skye and I can't be friends.'

'No, you're right. Of course, it doesn't. Unfortunately, it makes it tricky, though.'

'It's because of what happened, isn't it? On the island?' asked Jackson.

He'd danced around the edges before, but he had never been this pointed.

Bridget didn't want to lie to her son, but she didn't know if she was ready to explain it to him yet either. Didn't know if she had the right words.

'It's a long story,' she said lamely.

She couldn't stave him off forever.

They turned the corner onto Alders Avenue.

Parked on the side of the road was an old bus, the hefty, square kind she remembered from her childhood. The kind she and Lucy would catch into town after school on a Friday; fourteen years old and in a hurry for their lives to begin, trying to apply eyeliner as the bus juddered along, desperate for the boys in the back to talk to them, and yet terrified that they would.

Those buses were yellow, though, this one was black: inside and out, top to bottom, even the windows. Spray-painted in crude lettering along one side: The Roach Coach.

'Whoa,' said Jackson. 'Cool!'

Bridget didn't think it looked cool. She thought it looked like you might get on and never get off.

But she was grateful for the distraction. She wondered what it was doing here, parked up on a quiet residential street.

'Do you think someone lives in it?' asked Jackson.

'Maybe.'

Her phone dinged: it was a text from Roz. 'Love it! Hopefully zombie wrestling will be his swansong!!! xxx'.

She'd heard an interview on the radio recently with a digital communication expert, who'd claimed excessive use of exclamation marks and kissy 'x' sign-offs was an instant giveaway the sender was a middle-aged, middle-class woman. Bridget knew he — of course, it was a he — was probably right but whenever she tried to leave them off, her messages sounded so terse she ended up reinstating them.

After arriving home, she headed to the kitchen to cut up fruit for the kids' afternoon tea: rockmelon for Jackson, banana for Abigail.

She wondered if it was emblematic of her love; the way she continuously revised and updated her knowledge of their culinary likes and dislikes. In her mental filing cabinet, she also maintained a list of Greg's favourite and least favourite foods, her wider family's, and close friends'. More likely it was a sign of an obsessive personality, she thought. Or, she winced, recalling Monday's bingeing, an eating disorder.

'Empty your bags,' she called. 'Bring me your lunchboxes and any notices.'

Silence.

She looked out the window. Abigail was practising flick-flacks on the trampoline. Jackson was probably in his room, engrossed in one of his magazines.

She gathered up their belongings from where they'd dumped them on the hall floor and was pleased to see lunchboxes more or less cleaned out. Fishing a piece of scrunched-up paper from the bottom of Jackson's bag, her heart sank. It was a permission slip for a class trip to the museum.

She got out a pen to circle, 'Yes, I can attend as a parent helper', reminding herself this was why she worked from home: so she could be part of her children's lives.

'Fruit,' she called, tapping on the window. 'Abigail. Jackson.'

The front door banged. Greg. Bridget's heart sang.

'This is a nice surprise.'

He kissed her. Properly, on the lips.

'Look at this, Dad,' said Jackson, coming out of his room, magazine open at a picture of some guy sticking paper clips up his nose.

Like most men Bridget knew, Jackson seemed to be endlessly fascinated by other males doing crazy, dumb shit.

'Awesome,' said Greg, ruffling his hair.

'Remember, though,' they chimed in unison. 'Don't try it at home!'

'We got as far as we could,' said Greg over Jackson's head. 'We're laying pavers and there was no point carrying on until the cement had set. Hey, my client, Kate, was telling me someone on the Point has been done for child . . .'

Bridget glared at him.

'Child what?' asked Jackson.

Chapter Eighteen

January Day Three

There were no mermaids, but in every other respect the cove lived up to its reputation.

It was like the beaches you saw on travel brochures, Bridget thought from her precarious lookout halfway down the steep slope. Actually, it was better than that. There was a standardisation to those palm tree-lined stretches of white sand, a feeling that if you looked closely, you might spot the rake marks left behind by the local guy paid a pittance to keep the beach pristine for the rich tourists. Mermaids' Cove was pristine, too, in the way of nature untouched by humans — no discarded Doritos bag glittering among the shells, no tangled fishing line encircling the driftwood. Pure yet untrammelled, she decided, taking in the asymmetry of the lagoon, the deep-rooted trees, boughs hanging low and heavy over the sand, the waves slightly bigger than was comfortable.

Greg and Lucy were already down on the beach. Bloody mountain goats.

Knowing how much he would be loving this place, Bridget felt the need to be by her husband's side. To experience it with him.

She braced the foot of her good leg against a rock, calculating whether she could risk jumping the final metre or two, but it dislodged and the ground slipped away beneath her. As she opened her mouth to scream, a strong arm grabbed her.

'Crisis averted,' Tristan said.

Bridget blushed. 'What an idiot.'

Walking around the lip of the lagoon, Bridget observed the sea anemones, undulating so gracefully in the gentle current. She rubbed her thumb cautiously along her arm, a burning absence where Tristan's hand had been. She could hear Greg and Lucy arguing playfully about where best to put the picnic blanket.

'Why don't we set up here?' she called out to them. 'There's shade, but no branches for the kids to jump off on to us.'

'Done,' said Lucy.

'Fine,' said Greg, pulling a face Lucy was supposed to see.

Lucy laughed, deliberately shaking the blanket over him as she spread it out.

It was a source of relief to Bridget that her husband and best friend got on so well. They hadn't always.

The lead-up to Bridget and Greg's wedding had been particularly fraught. Bridget wanted a party in a gallery or a warehouse, somewhere cool and sophisticated, while Greg, keen to please his parents for once, was set on getting married at the family farm. In a fit of loyalty, Lucy had told him he was marrying her best friend, not his parents. 'I'm not marrying you either,' Greg had said. 'And thank fucking God for that.'

Bridget and Greg had hardly spoken for weeks. At the department store, supposedly selecting gifts for their register, they'd barely been able to look at each other.

Eventually they'd reached an uneasy compromise: a vineyard near where he'd grown up.

When the canapés were brought out, Greg's mother sniffily remarked to one of her many sisters that, personally, she would have been happier with a nice lamb on a spit. For the sake of future relations with her in-laws, Bridget had managed to hold her tongue.

Later in the evening, she'd overheard Greg, swaying at the bar, apologise to Lucy for, 'only doing your duty as maid of honour'.

Having always felt eclipsed by Lucy, the not-so-pretty one next to her best friend's gloriousness, Bridget had feared it would be no different on her wedding day. She needn't have worried. While she glowed with joy in all the photos, Lucy looked wan, a pale imitation of herself.

Exhausted from feeding Zachariah on demand 24/7, it was the first time she'd left him, and as the speeches were about to start, she'd leaked, great milky stains spreading along the front of her silk bodice.

One of Greg's aunts had found them in the loos, Lucy in her undies, milk dripping from her nipples, Bridget holding the sodden dress up to the hand drier, both crying with laughter.

Bridget checked the time on her phone: midday.

'I wonder where the kids and Jono are? I thought they'd be here by now.'

'Who cares?' said Roz, throwing herself across the rug, flicking all of them with sand. 'Isn't this heaven!'

Bridget tensed, expecting Greg to react, but he was preoccupied with separating the plastic glasses.

'How about it?' he said, holding up a bottle of rosé.

Bridget didn't want to drink wine; she wanted to discuss whether they should be concerned the kids hadn't arrived yet. She forced herself to take the others' lead, though, to sit, relax. The children would be here soon enough, and she'd kick herself for not having made more of the momentary peace and quiet.

She chose a spot away from Tristan. Could she really be attracted to him? Now? After all these years? Sure, she'd admired his good looks before, but only in the way you might a classic car: from a distance, casually. He wasn't even her type. She liked masculine men. Strapping. With his slightly too long hair and slim hips, there was still something of the boy to him. He was blond, too. She'd never fancied blonds.

He turned her way, and she felt her face grow suddenly hot. *He has no idea*, she reminded herself, toying with the frayed edges of a hole in the blanket.

'Bridge?' Greg was looking at her questioningly.

'Sorry, I was away with the fairies.'

'What was that place in Greece? You know, the one we thought would be like this. Private little bays, olives, ouzo. What was the name of it again?'

'Kos.'

'Kos! That's right. We'd imagined old ladies in headscarves, tending their sheep; instead, the place was overrun with whingeing Poms on package holidays, cramming their gobs with souvlaki and chips.'

'Mum. Mum!' Earl's stocky little body charged down the beach towards them.

Roz clambered up. 'Are you okay, bubs?'

'Yeah. It was so cool at Don's. I got to shoot a gun.'

'A gun?'

'Yeah, Dad said it was okay.'

'Did he just?'

Roz's tone was grim, but before she could quiz him further the girls arrived, breathlessly recounting how Don had a horse called Thunder and another called Missy, and a short, fat one called Pies, who'd tried to eat their clothes.

Jackson trailed sullenly behind the girls.

'What's wrong, sausage?' Bridget asked. 'Didn't you have a good time?'

'Nah, it was okay.'

'Where's Jono?' she asked.

'Dad's coming,' said Paris.

'With Don,' said Abigail. 'Don came too, so he could show us a shortcut. He's so nice. Can we ask him to stay for the picnic?'

'I'm sure he's got work to—' Bridget started, but before she could finish, Jono and Don were upon them, a bulky shadow across the blanket.

'Don was just telling me how he used to be a roadie. It's amazing, he's toured with some of the greatest bands of all time. The Rolling Stones, U2...'

Bridget looked at Don's chunky thighs, the grubby singlet that barely contained his gut.

'Wow,' said Greg. 'The Stones!'

Even Roz, usually not easily impressed, seemed awestruck, the matter of the gun apparently forgotten. Everyone scooched around the blanket, making room for the newcomers. Greg handed Don a glass, apologising for its flimsiness.

'Looks good to me,' said Don, plonking down next to Tristan, legs spread wide enough Bridget could see the mat of coarse dark hair protruding from his shorts.

At the others' urging he happily launched into a story about how he'd once procured one thousand pink lilies for Alison Moyet with only twenty minutes' notice.

'God, I loved Alison Moyet,' said Roz. 'Remember how you used to tell me I reminded you of her, honey?'

'You did,' said Jono. 'Practically her doppelgänger.'

'And then there was the time I managed to find someone to restring Sting's favourite guitar just as he was about to go on stage,' said Don airily.

The anecdotes streamed from him, uncensored and unchecked. The groupies. ('Mate, we were always happy to mop up the overflow.') The drugs. ('We'd snort it off anything. You name it. Toilet seats, tits, top hats.')

'The kids,' cautioned Bridget during one particularly smutty account.

'Oh they're not listening,' said Jono, waving carelessly towards where they were playing on a rope swing that was looped around one of the bigger trees.

'So how come you ended up here then?' Bridget asked. 'If you were having such a ball, I mean.'

For the first time Don seemed unsure of himself, at a loss for words.

'There's nothing to tell really. I won't bore you with that.'

'Please,' said Bridget. 'We're all ears.'

'Maybe another time, eh,' said Don, looking away.

Chapter
Nineteen

October
Wednesday

'Child-minding,' said Bridget quickly. 'Someone has been done for overcharging to look after kids.'

'Done?'

'Caught. You know, honey, in trouble with the law.'

'Oh,' Jackson said, but he had already lost interest, eyes drifting back to his magazine.

Honestly, Greg could be so dense sometimes. Bridget opened the fridge. What to make for dinner? She checked the use-by date on a packet of ravioli. Her phone rang.

Damn. It was her mother-in-law.

'Hello, Sue. How are you?'

'Now, Bridget, a couple of things. I wanted to check you'd remembered Aunty Joan's birthday is next week. It would be nice if you sent her a little card.'

Bridget clenched her fists. When Greg's mother rang, she never asked if it was a good time. Always just launched straight in. Assumed you'd drop everything. Bridget wanted to say: she's not my aunt, tell Greg to send *Aunty* Joan a *little* card. But her mother-in-law was of that generation that believed it was a wife's role to keep track of family goings-on.

And to be fair, it *was* Bridget who bought the gifts, sent out the invitations, wrote the thank-you emails. All Greg had to worry about was her: birthday, Christmas, wedding anniversary. And she usually told him what she wanted. Although last birthday, as an experiment, she hadn't.

He'd given her a voucher for their local mall. There hadn't been a card. Just her name after the 'To', his after the 'From'. Not even a 'Love'.

'Sorry,' he'd said, when he presented her with it, 'I've just been so busy this week.' *Actually*, she'd thought to herself, *you've only had all fucking year*.

'Now, Bridget.'

Sue began a lot of her sentences like this, as if she was about to reprimand her.

'On the subject of birthdays, I was wondering what Jackson would like for his? It's coming up.'

'Well, he's getting to that age where he really just wants money.'

'Money? I was thinking of a surprise. A new toy, perhaps.'

Another of her mother-in-law's annoying traits: asking questions when she patently had no interest in the answer.

'Jackson doesn't really play with toys any more.'

'Well, I never! What sort of a boy doesn't play with toys . . . I suppose you know best, though, Bridget. How about a nice tracksuit then?'

Sue loved a 'nice tracksuit'. At the back of Greg's wardrobe were half a dozen in matching grey polyester. He never wore them, but he wouldn't throw them away either. Bridget could never figure out if it stemmed from some complicated sense of loyalty towards his mother, or if it was just to piss her off. Probably both.

'Jackson's got quite set ideas about what he wants to wear these days.'

Down the line Bridget could sense Sue's indignation.

'Would you like to speak to Greg? He's home early today.'

She passed her phone over before Sue could respond. Greg sighed.

'Hi, Mum.'

He walked towards their bedroom. He always hid from her when he talked to his mother. Bridget guessed she couldn't blame him for not wanting to fuel her aversion. It must be awful to feel caught between your wife and your mother.

Once Bridget had sounded off about Sue to her own mother. 'Have a little compassion, Bridget,' she'd chided. 'How would you feel if Jackson grew up to reject everything you stood for?'

'Greg hasn't though,' she'd said. 'Sue raised a good man. And he's still a good man.'

'Yes,' her mother had said, 'but the life he's chosen is not the life she wanted for him.'

Greg handed back her phone; he looked miserable. Bridget could imagine the conversation. Sue would have laid on the guilt about his father's health, the pressures of running a farm at his age. She decided to eschew her usual probing.

'Glass of wine, darling?'

He smiled gratefully.

Abigail came in from outside, throwing herself at her father. He closed his eyes as she babbled on about school and flick-flacks and the watermelon pencil case she really, desperately needed, and Bridget knew he was willing away his mother's words, bringing himself back to them, to home.

Perhaps picking up on their father's mood, in a rare show of amenability the kids did their homework without any great drama, and ate their spinach and ricotta ravioli without needing to be threatened with the retraction of screen privileges if they didn't.

'Can you read to Abigail, darling? I've got to tidy up this bombsite of a kitchen.'

The kitchen did need seeing to, but Bridget was always happy to get out of reading to Abigail. No sooner had you picked up the book than Abigail would start rolling around her bed and endlessly interrupting, and when, finally, you reached the end of the chapter she would complain you hadn't read enough and whine for more. Greg didn't exactly look enthralled at the prospect himself; however he put on a brave face.

'Chase you to your room!'

Squealing, Abigail took off down the hall, her father making roaring sounds behind her.

Bridget smiled as she scrubbed the pot she'd cooked, and burned, the tomato sauce in. If they could get the kids in bed by nine p.m., they might actually get to blob on the couch together.

She picked Jackson's shoes up from where he'd discarded them on the dining room floor.

'I feel like a broken record. Please put your shoes away when you take them off. I don't know how many times I've asked you.'

Jackson was curled up on his bed with the blanket he'd had since he was a baby. He was so big now, almost taller than her, but sometimes he still seemed like such a little boy. Her irritation abated.

'Don't you want to read, sweetheart?'

'Nah.'

'What's wrong?'

'Nothing.'

She sat down next to him, brushing his thick hair away from his forehead.

'Mum?'

'Yes, darling?'

'It's kinda strange having Zachariah in my class.'

'I can imagine. I thought you said he was different to how he used to be, though?'

'I thought he was, but I think it was just 'cos I hadn't seen him in a while. He's still weird.'

'In what way?'

'I dunno. He doesn't really talk. And he stares.'

'At who?'

'Everyone, I guess. I heard some of the girls saying he gives them the creeps. Sam and Gus keep hassling me.'

'Why?'

'They said he's a vampire and that 'cos I know him and stuff I must be too.'

Bridget couldn't help herself: she laughed.

'Oh Jackson, you know there's no such thing as vampires. Zachariah's not a vampire. He's just different. You tell Sam and Gus they're the crazy ones if they believe in vampires.'

'They want to put garlic in his bag, see what he does. They reckon if he reacts it'll prove he really is a vampire. They said if I want to prove I'm not like him then I should do it.'

'That's bullying, Jackson. They're trying to bully you into bullying Zachariah. You tell them you won't, and that if they carry on, you're going to tell Miss Smythe.'

Jackson pushed his face further into his blanket.

'Promise me, Jackson. Dad and I didn't bring you up to treat other people badly.'

He nodded. She kissed his warm cheek.

'Try not to worry, sweetheart. It's just because he's new. It'll all blow over. I guarantee it.'

She was wrong, though. Wrong about everything.

Greg was already on the couch; a bottle of red wine open next to him, a cake of dark chocolate on his lap.

She sat down, leaning in. He passed her his glass, and she took a long sip. She told him what Jackson had said about Zachariah, how Abigail had wanted Skye to come home for a play.

'Maybe it's time to try and make contact again.'

'What, with Lucy and Tristan?'

'Yeah, see if we can't build a bridge.'

'I don't think I can put myself through the rejection. The trying almost killed me last time. Surely, it's up to them to make the first move. I don't know that we're the villains in this.'

'You've changed your tune.'

'I just don't think it's fair, that somehow it all ended up being our fault.'

'You're all talk, Bridge. I bet if they knocked at our door now, you'd be a quivering, apologetic mess.'

She broke off a square of chocolate.

'Hmm . . . you're probably right.'

She took another sip of his wine.

'Oi, get your own!'

'Sorry, no more. Promise. Hey, that was dumb this afternoon. Saying that in front of Jackson.'

'I forget about those flapping ears. Still, he's old enough that we should be talking to him about this stuff. Better he hears about it from us than some kid at school.'

'I know. I guess I just want to protect his innocence a little longer.'

'I'm not sure he's as innocent as you think. I'd be surprised if he hadn't already stumbled across porn, the amount of time he spends on the internet. How come you hadn't told me about the local perv anyway?'

'I've been meaning to, but the kids have either been around or you've conked out so early. I read something about it in the paper over the holidays. I'd more or less forgotten about it until I overheard some parents talking at school this week. And then at the meeting last night everyone was up in arms about whether zombie wrestling is such a good idea.'

'That's nuts. What's one got to do with the other?'

'Yeah, I thought it was a stretch. Apparently, Mr Ngata is on our side, so hopefully it'll still go ahead.'

'Man, I almost feel sorry for the guy.'

'Who? Mr Ngata?'

'No, the perv. Imagine having the Point Heed mothers after you. You'd be better off taking your chances with the crims in prison.'

'How do you know he's not in prison? I've been keeping an eye out, but I haven't seen anything about what he got, sentence-wise.'

'I don't. But this new client, Kate, her husband's a lawyer, and he reckons he would have got home detention.'

Chapter
Twenty

January
Day Three

Don stood up, crushing his plastic glass in a beefy fist.

'Thanks for the hospitality, folks. I'd best be getting back to it.'

They watched as he struck off down the beach, a solitary, solid figure.

'Nice one, Bridge,' said Greg. 'How to make a guy feel welcome.'

'Don't tell me you bought all that "me-and-my-superstar-mates" crap. He's clearly deluded.'

Bridget looked around the rug for allies. No one met her eye. There was little sign of the bonhomie of a few moments earlier.

'So, what was this about you letting Earl shoot a gun?' Roz said to Jono.

'It was just a BB gun. He was a pretty good shot, actually. Don was impressed.'

Roz's ire visibly dissipated at the mention of a hitherto unknown talent in her son, and deftly, Jono kept the conversation moving.

'It's some set-up old Don's got there. He's quite the survivalist. This big outdoor oven made out of rocks he's collected from around the island that he bakes his own bread in. Meat drying in one corner. Sort of a jerky. Flavours it with this native plant. It wasn't bad, actually. All these possums he's skinning in the other corner. Sends their fur off when he's got enough. Reckons he makes a bit of money from it. I tell you what, nothing goes to waste. All his tools hanging off these wishbone hooks, everything in its place. Living the sustainable dream, he is.'

Lucy looked spellbound.

'How cool. I love how simple it is. Nothing extraneous. No distractions. You could pretend the outside world didn't exist. Let's move to the country, honey.' She took hold of Tristan's hand. 'Somewhere super remote.'

Bridget thought Don's place sounded like something out of *Deliverance*. Even less appealing than Lucy's earlier fantasy of living on a boat.

'I reckon he's had some trauma, though,' said Jono.

'Like what?' Bridget asked.

'He didn't say. But I got the feeling this isn't the life he would have chosen for himself.'

'Do you mean like he's hiding something? Don't you think it's odd he wouldn't tell us how he ended up here?'

'Poor bloke's probably just not used to being interrogated by the Gestapo!'

Greg poked her in the ribs, so she smiled, and, on seeing this, everyone else, judging it safe, laughed. But his joke had stung. They'd always vowed they would never be one of those couples who put one another down in front of other people, that they'd air their furies and frustrations in private. Lately, though, Greg always seemed to be having a crack at her 'idiosyncrasies'. Code, she knew, for personal failings.

When she'd brought it up with Lucy and Roz, they'd told her she was being overly sensitive, that his teasing obviously came from a place of love. She wasn't convinced. He might know her best, but didn't familiarity breed contempt?

Jono pulled another bottle out of the bag. After sloshing wine into a glass, he clumsily hacked off a lump of cheese. Lucy was steadily working her way through the grapes, popping them succulently into her mouth, every so often pausing to feed Tristan one.

'I'm going to take some food to the kids,' said Bridget, grabbing the crackers and hummus. 'Before you lot scarf it all.'

Over at the swing there was an elaborate turn system going on. Apparently once you'd had your go (five pushes strictly regulated by the others), you nominated the next person, who couldn't be your sibling or anyone you'd already picked. Given there were only seven of them from three families, they had already struck some glitches.

'Who's hungry?' she asked brightly.

They ignored her.

Unable to face returning to the adults, Bridget leant back against a rock.

At times children could be very useful: the perfect excuse to get you out of doing something or going somewhere; the fail-safe pretext for leaving a party early; the ultimate reason to hide behind.

Jackson, clearly over whatever was bothering him earlier, had nominated himself chief pusher, and was taking great pleasure in causing the swinger to shriek in terror as he adroitly shoved them at just the right angle to narrowly miss colliding with the tree.

Perched high up in the branches above, Zachariah was randomly raining leaves and bark down; when he timed it right, coating whoever was on the swing in debris.

Abigail's go was coming to an end when she announced: 'Mum's turn.'

'No way, Jose.'

'Bridget! Bridget!' chanted the kids.

Jackson held out the rope.

'I'll go easy on you, Mum. Promise.'

'Oh, what the heck. Why not. But Zachariah . . .' She searched him out. 'No confetti, thanks.'

He gave her a mock salute. 'No, ma'am.'

As she climbed on, the branch gave a little. What the hell was she doing?

Before she could change her mind, though, Jackson took hold of the rope and swung her out over the sand in a large arc. The kids cheered. Laughter escaped from Bridget's mouth in small joyous bubbles. Jackson grunted, throwing all his weight behind every push.

She waved at the adults. *Look*, she wanted to call out. *Look how carefree I am. See what fun I can be!*

From her bird's eye view, she admired how Lucy and Roz's hair, one light, one dark, caught the sun. How Greg's long legs splayed across the sand in front of him. Sometimes it was easier to love from a distance.

She didn't want it to end, but Jackson was tiring, the pauses between pushes lengthening. Her feet brushed the sand, once, twice, three times. She stayed where she was, swaying softly, until, finally, she came to a stop.

The girls rushed to her side, helping her off, chattering, giggling.

'That was wonderful,' she said, stroking Abigail's ponytail, smiling at her sweaty, red-faced son.

Feeling magnanimous, she looked up. 'I appreciate you respecting my wishes, Zachariah.'

He nodded, opening his fist; a handful of ground-up foliage finely showering the ground beside her.

'Who you going to pick? Who you going to pick?' asked Willow in her funny wee voice.

'Why you, of course,' said Bridget, swooping her wriggly body up and on to the swing. Jackson gave Willow a push.

'Hold on!' he called.

Willow squealed. It gladdened Bridget to see how gently Jackson placed his hands on her.

'Phew, she's a bit lighter than you, Mum.'

She cuffed him around the ears.

'Bridget,' called Willow. 'Look at me! Look at me!'

'Wow! Watch you go,' she said, clapping her hands.

There was a sickening thunk.

Bridget watched in horror as a branch bounced off Willow's slender back. She flew through the air, hitting the ground with disturbingly little sound.

'Willow. Willow, are you all right, darling?' Bridget hurried to where she lay.

She was crying softly, a raised, red welt already forming under the strap of her togs. When Bridget brushed the sand from her tiny face Willow started to bawl properly.

Bridget peered into the tree. Zachariah was still there, in his leafy roost. She hoped to see remorse on his face, concern. Fear, at the very least.

But, as she said to Greg in bed later that night, there was nothing.

His baby sister seriously hurt. By his hand. And his expression was blank.

Chapter
Twenty-one

October
Thursday

Bridget awoke with a start; a wild beast thrashing in her chest.

Was it Abigail?

She trained her ear, alert to a cry. But all was calm; all was well in their little house.

Or was it?

Next to her the sheet moved. And then the bed itself. The slightest motion.

She lay there, quiet as a church mouse, absorbing her husband's desperate rhythm in the stillness of the dark.

She thought about turning on the bedside lamp. About reaching across, taking him in hand, finishing the job.

No, it would be over soon.

She steadied her breath, slowed it to the cadence of sleep, and counted.

One Mississippi, two Mississippi . . .

At thirty-seven Mississippi she felt the shudder of his climax. Fifty-nine Mississippi he wiped himself quickly. She hoped it was with whatever piece of clothing he'd discarded on the floor last night and not the sheet. By one hundred and fourteen Mississippi she sensed him sinking into slumber.

Bridget looked at her phone: 5:02 a.m., the day had as good as begun. She wrapped her dressing gown around her middle, the floorboards frigid underfoot.

When they renovated, she was definitely getting carpet in the bedrooms.

The house she'd grown up in, where her parents still lived, had old tongue and groove floors and teetering piles of books everywhere. The walls were hung with protest posters; Nelson Mandela staring down at you when you were on the loo, his face curling around the edges, fly dirt sullying his cheek. People forever *popping* in. Her mother *popping* the kettle on. Her father *popping* open a bottle of his explosive ginger beer.

Recently Bridget had suggested it might be time to do up the kitchen. 'Why?' her father had asked, genuinely puzzled. 'Because,' she'd said, pointing to the monstrously ugly mug tree that was a permanent fixture on the end of the bench, 'I made that in form one woodwork class.' 'Exactly,' he'd said, as if all along her intent had been to prove his point.

Bridget's friends adored her parents. Roz, in particular, was drawn to them. Saw their bohemian habits as the ultimate embodiment of culture, of 'authenticity'.

But just as Roz had spurned her cruelly neglectful upbringing, Bridget, too, in her own way had rebelled. Politically her apple hadn't fallen far from her parents' liberal tree, yet materially she hankered after the up-to-date, after minimalism and matching wine glasses, a house of bare surfaces.

She had envied Lucy her store-bought biscuits. Her bank manager father and housewife mother. Their annual holidays to the Sunshine Coast. The afternoon teas of orange cordial and triangles of foil-wrapped cheese. The late-night shopping on a Thursday to buy five-packs of new undies, a mince pie for dinner at the coffee bar, everyone with their own miniature sachet of tomato sauce.

Lucy said it had been stifling, unbearable. Bridget had thought it perfect.

Softly now, she opened the bedroom door.

Tiptoeing down the hall, she checked on Abigail. She'd kicked her duvet off. Chook, her threadbare rabbit, was face-planted on the floor. She tucked Abigail back in, reinstated Chook to his rightful position beside his owner's head.

In the bathroom Bridget relieved herself, expelling a night's worth of urine in a powerful stream. It was surprisingly satisfying. Peeing like that always made her feel like a man.

She put the plug in the bath. Turned on the hot tap. Measured out a capful of the rose essential oil Roz had given her.

Roz was obsessed with baths. As a child she'd moved house constantly. The rare times they'd had a tub it was usually cracked and discoloured, with a bathroom door that didn't shut properly so you could never relax, could never trust who was going to come in. Roz's shoulders had visibly tensed when she'd told Bridget that, and Bridget had seen not the bolshie woman she knew, but a small, vulnerable girl.

Roz and Jono's bath was ivory porcelain; it had claw feet, and was deep enough to fully submerge yourself in. When they'd chosen it, Jono had posted a photo on Facebook of a fully-clothed Roz trying out a display model at the bathroom design store. 'She's not in the ghetto now,' he'd captioned it. And while Bridget knew Jono wasn't trying to be offensive, the implication behind his words, that he had somehow rescued his wife, had made her blench.

Standing in front of the mirror, she ran her fingers in a circle around her upper lip and chin, searching for the stray woody hairs that sprouted there now, grabbing and yanking with a pair of tweezers when she struck one. Stubborn little bastards.

Those young mothers last night, their sleek hair and shapely brows, had made her realise how much she'd let things slide lately.

She took a pair of nail scissors out of the drawer and cut her nails, both fingers and toes, and then, catching it with a cupped hand as it fell, she trimmed her pubic hair. She collected it all up, her body's detritus, and brushed it decisively into the bin.

Bridget felt lighter, reduced somehow; brave enough for the scales. Holding her stomach in, she stepped on: 64.2 kilos. It could be worse.

She lit a cheap vanilla candle her mother-in-law had given her for her birthday, and lowered herself into the steaming water, allowing her mind to drift.

Why hadn't Greg woken her for sex? Because she would have been grumpy, that's why, resentful he thought his urges more important than her sleep. What had turned him on so much he'd wanted to jerk off, anyway? Nothing, probably. It was just a tool. Like a baby sucking its thumb. It was how he self-settled. Bridget stifled a laugh.

Hearing the rest of the house starting to stir, she sighed.

A day of work and domesticity spun out before her. The joys of getting across town and back again in rush hour traffic to drop Jackson at water polo and pick Abigail up from jazz ballet. And bloody drinks with the parents from Abigail's class this evening. Which reminded her, she needed to confirm with the babysitter.

Jackson staggered into the bathroom.

'Morning, sausage. Sleep well?'

Yawning, he pulled down his pyjama pants and plonked himself on the toilet seat.

'Jesus, Jackson!'

The stench of faeces flooding her nostrils, Bridget scrambled out of the tub.

'Gross, Mum! I don't want to see your fanny.'

'I do,' said Greg, rubbing his eyes.

'Ewww, that's disgusting,' Jackson protested.

'I want an ensuite,' said Bridget.

'Next year, honey. Next year.'

Greg made the kids porridge while she packed their lunches.

'Let's all walk up to school,' he suggested.

She could get used to this, she thought, him starting late.

Somehow Greg being there turned the school run into an excursion. He waved to Mrs Gillies, who lived across the road and hadn't got the memo that filling milk bottles with water and scattering them about your front lawn to stop dogs pooing on it was just an urban myth. At number 117, he made them all stop and smell the jasmine vine choking the fence.

'I love you,' she said.

He smiled at her.

'What's a roach, Mum?' asked Jackson.

She'd hoped that bloody bus would have gone by now. But there it was, as squat and ugly as yesterday, somehow even more menacing in the thin morning sun.

She shuddered as they passed. It didn't belong here.

'A roach?'

'It's short for cockroach, buddy.'

Bridget shot Greg a look of gratitude; she wasn't in the mood for explaining the technicalities of dope-smoking.

'Freaky,' said Jackson, darting ahead.

'We'll leave you here, okay?' she said, as they reached the gate.

'I thought Dad was coming in,' said Abigail. 'He promised.'

Greg laughed. 'No, I didn't.'

'Not today, darling. Daddy and I have to get to work.'

'But Dad,' whined Abigail. 'I was going to read my story to you.'

Bridget's heart sank. She knew what that meant. With Abigail 'a' story meant every single story she'd written all year. They were never going to get out of here.

While she waited for Greg, Bridget looked around Abigail's classroom. There were three laminated lists tacked to the wall: Takahe, Tuatara, Tarakihi. Abigail's name was halfway down the Takahe. Bridget tried to figure out what that meant. Probably nothing, but then again Ruby was on the list, too, and she always won the speech competition.

Over in the reading corner, Greg and Abigail were laughing together at something in Abigail's exercise book, Greg's long frame doubled up in a child-sized chair. Bridget's heart expanded.

The bell rang, and a wave of children descended upon the mat in front of where Ms Snow sat beside the whiteboard. Bridget observed her husband's sidelong glances. On anyone else, Ms Snow's prim floral dress would have looked dowdy, but on her it was like the ultimate girl-next-door fantasy come to life.

C'mon, she mouthed at Greg.

Outside, on the court, Greg took her hand.

'This is nice,' he said, smiling at her.

'It is,' she said, trying to banish any thoughts of what he'd been doing with that hand a few hours earlier.

He was right, though: it was nice.

'What if we see her?' she asked suddenly.

'See who?'

'Lucy. What do we do if we see Lucy?'

'We say hello.'

'What if she ignores us?'

'Well then at least we've been the bigger ones.'

'You make it sound so simple.'

'It can be.'

On Alders, *The Roach Coach* hadn't moved. Without the kids to shepherd quickly past, Bridget paused.

Globules of paint ran down from each letter: obviously not a professional job. It reminded her of the trespass notices the kids pinned on the door at Halloween: 'Ghosts Welcome! Goblins Keep Out!'

Presumably the signwriter wasn't referring to insects, but as Bridget took in the broken rear-vision mirror, the missing hubcaps, it wasn't hard to imagine it being home to both some old pothead and a marauding army of cockroaches.

'That was quick thinking,' she said.

'About what?'

'Before, with Jackson. Roaches.'

'Thought I'd better make up for last night's foot-in-mouth.'

Bridget squeezed his hand.

'It's funny, actually,' said Greg.

'What is?'

'That bus; it takes me back. This crazy night. I hadn't thought about it for years. I came to the city with a couple of mates for a ZZ Top concert.'

'ZZ Top! You bogans.'

'Through and through. We hitched a ride. No plans where we were going to stay. Anyway, we hooked up with some chicks who invited us back to this house bus after the show. Said we could crash there. We were naive as fuck, never even smoked weed before, but this guy on the bus offers us acid and so we took it. Didn't want to look like country bumpkins. It was the worst fucking night of my life.'

'Poor darling. How old were you?'

'I dunno. Fifteen? Sixteen, maybe. I was convinced that bus was alive. I remember pressing my ear to the cracked vinyl, sure I could hear the seats breathing. "Just go with it," one of the girls said. "Just flow, man." When I woke up the next morning, the girls were gone and so was my wallet.'

'That's a terrible story!'

'Ah, it's not so bad. I lived to tell the tale.'

'But imagine, you were only a few years older than Jackson . . .'

'Yup, we've got all that to look forward to.'

'Don't . . . I can't bear it.'

Bridget reached out to pat the cat sunning itself on the low wall in front of number 91. It drew away, hackles up.

'You haven't forgotten we've got class drinks tonight, have you?'

Greg groaned. 'You're kidding. Do we have to go?'

'Yip, you got out of the last ones. I'm not going alone again.'

'At least there'll be something to talk about other than which private school they're going to send their child genius to. A nonce in the neighbourhood. That'll put a cat among the fucking pigeons.'

'Most of them are actually all right if you give them a chance. Promise me you won't be a shit-stirrer. Not tonight.'

He winked.

Maybe it would be better if she did go without him. More than once she'd put the hard yards in with some mother, only to have Greg undo all her work with an incendiary comment.

To be honest, Bridget probably wouldn't normally choose to befriend many of them herself, but these people were their community. And you never knew when you'd need to ask a favour. Not just a cup of sugar, but a real favour, like picking your kids up after school and keeping them for dinner because you were at a long liquid lunch that had ended up being far longer and more liquid than planned.

She was reminded of her lunch date with Amanda next week and made a mental note to watch the booze. Lunch with Amanda was always fun, but last time they'd got properly trashed, and Bridget had to put herself to bed afterwards.

'Who's babysitting?' asked Greg.

'When?'

'Tonight.'

'Oh, right. Laura.'

'Is she the one Jackson claims is super strict? Makes him go to bed at the same time as his sister?'

'Yeah, but Abigail seems to like her.'

'What happened to that boy? Josh? Was that his name? He was cool. They both liked him.'

'You mean Joel. Nothing happened to him. I just didn't know if it was such a good idea to use him any more.'

'Why not?'

'I read this article about the sexual impulses of teenage boys, and how you couldn't fully trust them around younger children.'

'That sounds pretty bloody sexist to me. So, what are you saying? That in a year or two we won't be able to leave Jackson alone with Abigail?'

'No, of course not. I'm probably being stupid. I just figured it was better to be safe than sorry.'

Chapter
Twenty-two

January
Day Three

'Touched by the devil, that one.'

Watching Zachariah's unnaturally upright posture as he headed off along the sand, the words slipped out of Bridget's mouth.

She hadn't meant to say it aloud. She looked around. No one appeared to have heard. Everyone caught up in their own thoughts.

The picnic had come to an abrupt end after the accident. Not that it had been a goddamned accident, but that's how Lucy was referring to it: just a terrible accident. So that's what it was.

Even the kids had been quiet when they were told to pack up.

Bridget had wanted to shake Lucy. To scream at her. Sort your fucking son out!

And more than anything she had wanted to hurt Zachariah. To cause that little shit some serious pain.

Roz had once said there was a pitbull inside of her, just waiting to get out. 'Takes one to know one,' Bridget had retorted. She wasn't sure whether she liked the idea or not: some interior mutt, straining at its leash.

When they'd all crowded around, Bridget had stepped aside so that Lucy and Tristan could take her place next to Willow. Roz had clocked her tightly clenched fists and shot her a look: *Easy girl*. Bridget didn't need to be told, though. She was used to keeping a lid on her anger.

As they followed the shoreline ahead of her, Bridget considered their motley crew. How Jono held Paris's hand and Roz had a protective arm across Earl's shoulders. How Abigail and Jackson flanked Greg, and Tristan cradled Willow. Homeward bound, the air of happy anticipation that had heralded their arrival was long gone.

Lucy, meanwhile, was already halfway down the beach, presumably trying to catch up to Zachariah.

Bridget would love to know what was going on in that beautiful head of hers. Unlike Roz, who wore not just her heart, but her guts on her sleeve, you could never second guess Lucy. Sometimes what came out of her mouth was so unexpected, so unforeseen, it could literally stop you in your tracks.

Bridget looked back. Skye was shadowing her.

'You all right, sweetie?'

To Bridget it seemed like Skye could never quite get her parents' full attention, couldn't compete with her troubled older brother, or her impossibly cute little sister. Another child might have acted out, but Skye never did.

'Do you think she's okay?'

'Willow will be fine, sweetheart. She probably got more of a fright than anything. Bet you by the time we get back to the house she'll be running around like normal.'

'No, I meant Mum. She hates it when people think bad things about Zachariah and everyone will hate him now.'

Not wanting to lie, Bridget said nothing.

'Look,' she said after a moment, reaching down and picking up a perfectly intact, miniature kina shell from the sand.

Carefully, she passed it to Skye, who pushed it around her palm a couple of times, and then, forming a fist around the tiny carapace, crushed it.

They watched the pale green dust fall to the sand and Bridget felt a pang of something like loss.

By the time Bridget and Skye made it back, the men had disappeared, no doubt to the safety of the boat, while the twins were playing a half-hearted game of Swingball against Jackson and Abigail, and Roz was pouring herself a rum and Coke.

'Do you want one?' she asked.

'No thanks, think I'll give the alcohol a miss tonight. I might scramble the kids some eggs. They've hardly eaten since breakfast. Then get them off to bed early, huh?'

'Good idea. Reckon I'll turn in pretty early myself. I'm knackered.'

'Where's Mum?' asked Skye.

'I think she's putting Willow . . .' Roz began.

'I'm here,' said Lucy, walking into the room. 'Why?'

'Um, I was just wondering where you were.'

'Where'd you think I'd be, Skye?'

Lucy started pulling the remains of their picnic out of the backpack. Bridget noticed the cheddar was embedded with grains of sand: like blackheads, she thought, repulsed. Skye hovered a little longer, but when her mother didn't say anything else, she trudged outside.

'How's Willow?' asked Roz.

'Fine,' said Lucy, not looking up. 'She's fine. Just a little tired.'

'What a relief,' said Bridget. 'I was imagining having to call the rescue helicopter out.'

'Oh, for God's sake, Bridget. Do you always have to be so dramatic? She fell off a swing.'

Bridget's hand trembled as she tried to steady the egg she was holding against the rim of the bowl.

'C'mon, Luce, she didn't just fall off it,' said Roz. 'Her brother threw a bloody branch at her!'

'So? That's what kids do. Dumb stuff. Kids do dumb stuff all the time. And she's fine now. I don't know why you're both making out like it was such a big deal.'

'We were worried,' said Bridget. 'So was Skye. It was scary.'

'Can I get any of you ladies an apéritif?' asked Jono, coming through the door, followed by Greg and Tristan. 'I thought I'd whip up some mules . . .' he trailed off.

'Everything okay?' asked Greg.

'Everything's great,' said Lucy, her eyes on Tristan.

Gathering an armful of towels, she pushed one of the French doors open with her foot and strode out onto the verandah.

'Whoa,' said Jono. 'What did we miss?'

'Nothing,' said Roz. 'You didn't miss anything, you idiot.'

'I'll go check on her,' said Bridget.

'No, it's all right,' said Tristan. 'I'll go.'

'Take these, while you're at it, would you?' said Roz, holding up the sandy picnic blankets. But he'd already gone. Shaking her head, she got a couple of cans of baked beans from the cupboard.

'Let's get the kids fed, eh? Greg, you're on toast. Jono, you bring them in. Make sure they wash their hands.'

Thank God for Roz, thought Bridget, dishing out the eggs.

As she served Zachariah, she imagined giving him a good hiding with the wooden spoon. She slopped his eggs down, hard enough that a glob splashed onto his face.

'Sorry,' she said.

He licked the skin below his lower lip clean.

Bridget noticed how whiskery his chin appeared in the last of the day's sun. *Why, he's not far off shaving*, she thought with a small jolt of surprise.

'No worries,' he said, his odd eyes on hers.

Chapter
Twenty-three

October
Thursday

There was a knock. Bridget waited for the sound of one of the kids making their way to the door.

Nothing. Just the distant tat-tat-tat of gunfire from Jackson's room.

'Someone's here,' she called.

Another knock.

'Could somebody please get the door?'

She may as well be talking to herself. Drying her hands on a tea towel, she marched down the hall.

'Oh! Laura . . .'

'Hello Bridget.'

The adolescent girl on the porch smiled brightly at her. Teeth gleaming, hair shining.

Bridget tried not to stare at her breasts. Pert and round. No sign of a bra.

'Uh . . . come in. You're early, aren't you? What time is it?'

Bridget followed Laura's gaze downward. Great, there was bolognaise on her top. She scraped it off with the edge of her little finger. Considered eating it. No, Laura probably already thought she was a slovenly old hag.

'You said seven p.m., didn't you?'

'Yes, but . . .' Bridget looked at her watch.

Shit, it was 6.59 p.m. She could have sworn she still had twenty minutes up her sleeve. And where was bloody Greg? He'd rung earlier to say he was going to take a couple of his workers for a beer. Promised he'd be back in time for the class drinks.

'Goodness, so it is. I completely lost track of time. I was just about to put Abigail in the bath.'

'No worries. You go get ready. I'll sort out Abigail.'

'Okay,' said Bridget, wondering how it was that she felt like the subordinate in this situation.

She texted Greg with one hand while dragging a brush through her hair with the other: 'Where are you?'

She didn't finish with her usual x. That would show him!

What was she going to wear? Her green dress? She tried to remember if she'd worn it to a school event before. Where was it? Shit, that's right: she hadn't got around to ironing it yet. Cashmere pants? Grey marle, super comfortable. Greg said they reminded him of his mother's ubiquitous gifts.

She pulled them on. *Too bad.*

Her phone rang.

'Hey, sweetheart.'

'Greg, it's after seven. You promised you'd be home half an hour ago.'

'I know, but the guys wanted to talk work and I didn't feel like I could leave. Sorry, sweetheart.'

Greg was good at blaming 'the guys' whenever he got waylaid at the pub. Bridget could tell by the way his words ran a tiny bit into one another that he was already half-cut. Fantastic. Just what she felt like: managing a drunk Greg around the school mums.

'I guess I'll see you there then,' she said, hanging up, and tugging on a blazer as she poked her head into Jackson's room.

'Only twenty minutes more, okay honey? Go to bed when Laura tells you to. You need to read your book.'

He fired at someone in a flak jacket.

'Jackson, it's rude not to acknowledge someone when they're talking to you.'

'Huh?'

'I said to go to bed when Laura tells you to.'

'What? Laura! You didn't tell me she was babysitting. She sucks.'

'Shhh! She'll hear you. Yes, I did. Dad and I are going out. We've got Abigail's class drinks. And she doesn't suck. Abigail likes her.'

'She would. Goody two shoes.'

He threw a grenade at a Jeep full of soldiers.

In the bathroom Laura was massaging conditioner into her daughter's head, Abigail's little body taut with the pleasure of it.

'See, Abi, that's not so bad, is it?'

Abigail sighed rapturously. She usually hated having her hair washed, screaming it was in her eyes before Bridget even had the lid off the bottle. *Traitor.*

'Bye, darling. Be a good girl for Laura.'

'She always is.'

Yeah, thought Bridget, *she's good for you because you're pretty and fun and she sees you for half an hour once in a blue moon.*

'Thanks, Laura. Eight-thirty bedtime for Abigail. She might like you to read her a chapter of *Harry Potter*. Nine p.m. for Jackson. No screens in bed. Lights out at nine and nine-thirty. Make sure they clean their teeth. There should be some biscuits for you in the tin. None for them, though.'

'Got it. We'll be fine. Have a good time.'

The drinks were at the bar up the road.

Bridget had lost count of how many class drinks she'd been to there over the years. She'd been so thrilled the first time. As if she'd gained entrée to some proper grown-up club. Now it felt like Groundhog Day. Something to be endured. Like so much of parenting. Still, at least it wasn't far to go.

She searched the dimly lit room for a familiar face.

Given the affluence of Point Heed, it probably wasn't particularly surprising most of the women here tonight were what Roz would call 'classic clingers-on': foreheads as smooth and round as boiled eggs, hair professionally highlighted to within an inch of its life. Roz reckoned there were two kinds of women at their age: those who'd already given up and those who were still holding fast. Women's mags made out that ageing was a decision, but Bridget figured it was probably determined more by your financial means than anything else.

She felt exhausted just looking at all the worked-on bodies and microbladed brows. It was almost a relief to spot the odd quitter — stoutly clad in tunics and leggings, flesh bulging around bra straps.

She adjusted her blazer. Surely there had to be a happy medium.

'Pinot gris?'

It was Moana, a bottle and a glass in her outstretched hands.

'Is the Pope Catholic?'

'Atta girl! Come join the troops.'

Bridget looked over to where she was pointing: Therese and Sophie were standing in the far corner.

'Did you hear the latest?' asked Therese as they approached. 'Ruth has proposed that any parent manning a stand at Fright Night should be vetted by the police.'

Bridget kissed her proffered cheek. There was a bowl of salted peanuts on the leaner in front of them. She picked out a couple.

'That's insane! What next? Security guards patrolling the school grounds?'

'I know,' said Moana. 'But you've got to admit it's kind of scary. I mean all we've got to go on is that there's some paedophile in the area. Abigail could be invited to a sleepover and you'd have no idea her friend's dad was the guy.'

'You know I'd be the first to out him if I knew who he was. I just don't see what it's got to do with zombie wrestling and pumpkin carving,' said Bridget, scooping up a handful of the peanuts.

'I heard it was pretty bad,' said Sophie in her whispery voice.

Sophie could always be relied on to have the most salacious gossip. Bridget wondered if it was because her voice persuaded people she was harmless, so they divulged all to her.

'Oh God,' said Moana. 'In what way?'

'Apparently what he was caught with was as bad as it gets: hundreds and thousands of images of full-on rape and everything. Little kids. Babies, even.'

Moana made a retching sound.

'Who told you that?' asked Therese.

'These mothers were talking about it at the girls' dance class on Tuesday. They weren't even from Point Heed. Their kids are at East Bay.'

'Oh, it just makes me so mad,' said Moana. 'We live in this world where everyone overshares on social media, and yet, weirdly, personal privacy has become like this inviolable right. Why should he be allowed to retain his privacy when those poor children have lost all right to theirs?'

Bridget felt a hand on her bum, a warm current of breath down her neck. She whirled around.

'Oh, hey,' she said, pressing her lips tightly together as Greg planted a beery kiss on her mouth.

'And how are we this evening, ladies?'

'Good thanks, Greg. You?' said Sophie.

'Fucking awesome.'

'Greg's already three sheets to the wind,' said Bridget with a small apologetic laugh.

'Ben's over at the bar,' said Moana. 'I'm sure he'd love to see you.'

'That would make one person,' said Greg, stumbling slightly as he turned away.

'Thanks,' Bridget said to Moana when he'd gone. 'Bloody men.' She helped herself to more nuts.

The other women smiled sympathetically.

'So, what do we do about him?' asked Therese.

'About Greg?' Bridget almost choked on a peanut.

'No, you wombat,' said Therese, hitting her on the back. 'The paedophile.'

'Oh right,' said Bridget. 'Him. I don't think we can do anything, can we?'

'Not if we don't want to get done for breaking the law,' said Moana. 'They've been really coming down on people who flout name suppression orders. I think everyone has this idea that because it's only Facebook or Twitter or whatever, somehow it doesn't count.'

Moana was a lawyer. Well, she used to be. Now she drove her boys to extracurricular activities five days a week and reminisced about when she'd been paid to use her brain. Bridget couldn't understand why she didn't just go back to work.

'Where would we even start looking for his name?' asked Sophie, her whispery voice rising in excitement.

'If anyone could find out, Sophie, it would be you,' said Therese.

They all laughed.

'I wonder if Mr Ngata knows,' said Moana. 'Whether the police have alerted him.'

Bridget briefly considered mentioning her plan to ask Amanda about it over lunch next week, but decided against it. Eventually their conversation moved on: to summer holiday plans and a recipe for keto sourdough. Bridget yawned. She glanced at her watch: 9:20 p.m.

'Bed's calling, darlings,' she said, blowing a round of kisses.

Over at the bar Greg was holding court among a circle of dads.

'C'mon,' she said. 'Home time.'

'Lemme finish my drink.'

Bridget sighed.

'Moana says you guys are thinking of taking the kids out of school next year,' she said to Ben. 'Travelling around Europe in a motorhome?'

'Yeah, he's got to get out of town,' said Rob archly. Rob had the campest affectations of any straight man Bridget knew. 'Heat's getting too much for Benny Boy.'

Ben grinned awkwardly. 'Fuck off, mate.'

'Ooooo,' jeered Rob.

'What do you mean?' asked Bridget.

'It's all right, Ben,' said the father Bridget had mentally dubbed Handsy, after an unfortunate encounter at a quiz night. 'You're among friends. No one's judging you for your schoolgirl fetish.'

Bridget looked at Ben, finally twigging, her eyes wide.

'They're just pulling your leg, Bridge,' said Greg.

'You don't need to worry about me, Bridget,' said Ben. 'I'm as happily married as they come.'

'Yeah, wives: thirty-five and over. Ultimate fantasy: only sixteen and under need apply.' Handsy whooped at his own wit.

'Ugh! I can't believe you guys are joking about it.' Bridget shuddered.

'My wife's not joking about it,' said Rob. 'She reckons if she caught me doing anything like that, she'd slice off my balls, fry them up in butter and feed them to the neighbour's dog.'

He did a funny little jig, as if in anticipation of his potential forthcoming castration.

'You're not worried about the kids missing all that school,' Bridget asked Ben, 'if you go travelling?'

'Nah, not at this age. We figure now's the time to do it. Before we send them off to Saint Patrick's.'

St Patrick's cost twenty-five thousand per annum. Ben was an old boy. He liked to pass himself off as progressive, but Bridget suspected his privileged, conservative upbringing still lurked very close to the surface. Greg had told her that when Ben was drunk, he referred to Moana as his 'dusky maiden'.

'Where's Jackson going?' Ben asked.

'Oh, you know, just the local.'

Bridget was annoyed at herself for sounding embarrassed to be sending her child to the perfectly good, only a short bus ride away, state high school.

'You ready?' she asked Greg.

He nodded.

At the door she shivered as a cold wind caught the edge of her jacket. She wrapped her arms around her waist.

'See you at home,' said Greg, walking out past her.

'Don't tell me you drove?'

'It was only down the road.'

'It doesn't matter. Jesus, Greg, you know better than that. What are you? Twelve?'

'Give it a break, Bridge. I ordered a couple of platters for the guys. I'd eaten. I was fine to drive.'

'Well, you're not fine now. Leave your truck here. You can walk up in the morning and get it.'

For a moment she thought he was going to ignore her. But he put his keys back in his pocket.

'Okay, boss.'

'Exactly how many beers have you had anyway?' she asked, unlocking her door.

'Christ! You never let up, do you?'

An unpleasant silence descended upon them.

'Sorry,' she said, a few minutes later, pulling into their driveway. 'I don't want to fight.'

'I don't either,' he said. 'C'mon, it's fucking freezing.'

As they opened the front door, Laura appeared in the hallway. She had knotted her T-shirt behind her so that it rode up over her flat stomach and hugged her perfect breasts. She looked, thought Bridget glumly, spectacular. She sensed Greg do a double-take.

'You know Laura, don't you?' she said.

'Yeah. Hey, Laura. You've gone and got all grown-up.'

'Greg!' Bridget cringed.

'What? She has.'

'Sorry, Laura. Ignore him,' said Bridget, aware her outrage was tinged with more than a hint of jealousy. She handed the girl a fifty-dollar note. 'I think that's about right. I hope the kids were good?'

'Angels,' said Laura. 'Abigail is so cute. Did you have fun?'

'Um, I don't know if I'd call it fun. Are you all right to get home?'

'Yes, I've got my licence now.'

'Oh right, that's great.'

She walked her to the door. 'Thanks again. I'll be in touch.'

In their room Greg was already pulling back the duvet, clothes in a pile on the floor.

'That was really inappropriate.'

'What?'

'What you said to Laura.'

'It was an observation, that's all. She had grown since the last time she babysat. It must be a year.'

'You were patently referring to her breasts.'

'What!? No, I wasn't.'

'Don't pretend you didn't notice them.'

'I'm not blind. But I'm not stupid either. She's a bloody kid.'

'According to your mates, isn't sixteen and under the optimum? The rest of us ready for the scrapheap?'

'Don't try and tar me with that brush, Bridget.'

'I just think you should be a little more careful, that's all. Particularly at the moment.'

Chapter Twenty-four

January Day Four

Bridget opened her eyes in their room among the trees to find Greg's face inches from hers, snoring softly, his breath warm on her skin.

She appraised her husband: uncomplicated, solid, there. When he stirred, she kissed him. He tasted like toothpaste. Drawing her lips away from his, she was reminded of Velcro. Greg never shaved on holiday; it only took him a day or two to sport a full face of stubble.

'How come your breath smells so good? Have you been downstairs already?'

'I heard the kids so I went to check they weren't getting up to any trouble. I must have nodded off again. Do you know how beautiful you are when you sleep? Even when you dribble.'

She shoved him in the chest, pleased.

'And were they?'

'What?'

'Getting up to trouble?'

'Nah, well I guess it depends how you define trouble. They're playing that stupid Operation game. I don't think it'll work for much longer. They've squished banana around the little plastic bits you're meant to surgically remove. To make it harder.'

'Seriously? That's disgusting.'

'I thought it was kind of ingenious.'

'You would. God, what are they like? This will be the second one they've trashed. Remember last year on the West Coast when his nose stopped buzzing? Hey, was there any sign of the others?'

'Nope.'

'That was hideous yesterday. I couldn't believe Lucy trying to turn the situation back on us.'

'People are always defensive when they're embarrassed.'

'That's no excuse, though. It wasn't her in the wrong anyway. It was Zachariah.'

'Aren't you the one who's always saying our children are an extension of ourselves?'

'True, but if Zachariah's an extension of Lucy, then she's not who I thought she was.'

'I know you've got him pegged as some sort of psycho in the making, Bridge, but he's just a bully. Someone needs to cut him down to size, that's all. Put him in his place.'

'Well, I wish someone would hurry up and do it. I keep thinking about how apoplectic Lucy was when his kindergarten teacher suggested she take him to a child psychiatrist. Remember? He was soiling himself and hiding his dirty undies in the other kids' cubbyholes. Lucy said she refused to have him "labelled". At the time I kind of admired her having her boy's back like that.'

Bridget picked at a downy feather poking through the duvet.

'Most kids can be little shites when they're younger, go through a bit of a weird phase. But Zachariah's quirks have only become more pronounced. You can't put it down to immaturity any more. The way he behaves, it's not normal. You know, I'm almost of a mind to tell Lucy what's what. Pull the wool from her eyes.'

'You big brave thing, you!'

Bridget kissed her husband again and felt his cock stiffening against her belly. She pushed him gently aside.

'Not now, honey. I need to see Lucy.'

'Wow, you really are going to strike while the iron's hot.'

'What? Oh . . . no, it's not the right time. I'm going to try and smooth things over. I don't want to ruin the holiday.'

Jumping out of bed before he could guilt-trip her in to a quickie, she grabbed her sarong.

Downstairs, Lucy was grinding coffee beans.

'Mmm . . . I love that smell.'

Lucy didn't turn around.

Bridget's stomach tightened.

So, it was going to be like that.

She reached for the dishcloth, wiping it in short, fast strokes across the smeary table. She was deliberating whether to say something or carry on like nothing was wrong, when Lucy spoke.

'I'm sorry. For what I said yesterday, when we got back to the house, I mean. I guess it was just all too much.'

Bridget felt the vice encircling her tummy ease.

'That's okay. I was only worried about Willow. But you know me. Water off a duck's back.'

'Yeah, sure.'

They both laughed and Bridget wrapped her arms around her best friend.

'I was worried about her, too,' said Lucy, her head resting lightly on Bridget's shoulder. 'I knew she was okay, though. She's tough. It's Zachariah. He's complex, you know. People don't appreciate him the way I do. He's so bright. It makes him sensitive.'

How thin Lucy was, thought Bridget, hands resting on the knobs of her spine. Too thin.

She would try harder with Zachariah, she resolved. Maybe Lucy was right. Maybe he was simply misunderstood.

'Sorry, Luce, I don't want to cut you short, but I'm suddenly busting for the loo.'

'Go, go.'

In her haste to pull her pants down, Bridget almost stood in a pool of urine on the floor. *Gross.* Mopping up the tiles around the foot of the bowl with a wad of toilet paper, she tried not to think about who might be responsible for the mess. Your own child's wees was one thing, but . . .

At the basin she scrubbed her hands while studying her reflection. She shrugged her shoulders up to her ears, rolled them back and down. If Roz could make her peace, too, then hopefully they could get back to enjoying the holiday.

In the kitchen Roz was straddling a chair the wrong way, her eyes following Lucy as she busied herself at the coffee machine. Bridget felt her body stiffening again. Roz yawned and stretched her arms above her head.

'Morning, Bridgey-Boo.'

Lucy placed a mug down in front of Roz.

'Do you want one, B? My special almond milk latte.'

'Yes, please, that sounds like just what the doctor ordered. Hey, Roz.'

Bridget smiled at them both. Relieved. Lucy must have apologised to Roz, too.

The men took charge of breakfast; frying up a pig's worth of bacon on the barbeque.

When it was done, they laid down thick slices of white bread, and cooked it in the hot grease. They didn't bother with plates, passing around a roll of paper towels and a bottle of tomato sauce.

'Jesus,' said Roz, who had eaten her own sandwich and was now finishing off Paris's. 'It's a heart attack on a plate.'

'Ugh, I know,' said Bridget. 'I feel disgusting.'

She fumbled to loosen the sarong she had tied so ambitiously firmly around her middle when she first got up, her stomach empty after skipping dinner the night before.

'How can something that tastes so good make you feel so bad?'

'Scientists have discovered cured meat's a killer,' said Roz. 'Apparently you knock half an hour off your life with every sausage you eat.'

'Nonsense. A brisk walk up the hill and you'll be right. Convert those extra calories into muscle before they turn to fat.'

'Sod off, Greg,' said Roz, her voice muffled by the towel she now lay face-down on. 'A snooze is more like it.'

Bridget tore a small strip of skin from her cuticle.

'How about us men take the kids to the beach,' said Jono. 'Maybe play some volleyball. Leave you ladies to relax. Then later we might go for a fish and you're in charge.'

'Deal,' said Roz.

'Sure,' said Lucy, before wandering off in the direction of the house, her long, filmy dress trailing behind her.

'Make sure the kids are sunblocked,' Bridget called to their already retreating backs.

'I'm sorry,' she said, swiping at an ant crawling along her calf.

'For what?' asked Roz.

'For Greg.'

'It's not your fault he can be a dick sometimes.'

'He gets it from his mother. That superior attitude.'

'I don't know how you put up with her.'

'Yeah, I definitely bombed out on the in-law front.'

'Greg struck frickin' gold with your parents. Geoff and Claire are great. You're so lucky, Bridge. What I can never figure out, is how I had such a fucked childhood, and yet look at me now: sorted. But you, showered with love, and you came out a basket case!'

'Thanks!'

'Only joshing you. Look, Bridge, I adore Greg. I know my bolshiness pisses him off. He pisses me off when he's a pompous twat, but it's just how we roll. I've known Greg as long as I've known Jono, and you guys and Lucy, well, you're the closest thing I've got to family.'

Lying on the beach that afternoon, Bridget squinted up at the sky. It was still stinking hot, but the sun was sitting lower now. Grey clouds hung fatly overhead. The men had taken off on the boat the moment they'd been released from duty. They'd been gone a while. It must be well after three p.m.

The back of her legs stuck to the plastic weave of the lounger she'd carted down from the verandah; her thighs pushing through the gaps between the slats like a cheese toastie squeezed in a sandwich press.

She'd been trying to read a *Marie Claire*. It was too heavy to hold while lying down, though, and if she sat up, the back of the lounger collapsed on her. *Argh*.

Perspiration pooled in the cups of her bathing suit. *So slimming*, the woman in the shop had enthused, fussing with the girdle-like ruching across her stomach. It was meant to make you appear a size smaller, but Bridget just felt matronly.

She looked over at Lucy. Tied together with a few bits of string and doing some fancy-pants yoga pose. *Whoosh*. Each exhalation was loud, deliberate.

'Could you not?' groaned Roz, opening her eyes. 'I'm trying to sleep.'

'Yeah,' said Bridget. 'Do you have to rub our faces in your body beautiful? I swear it feels like someone plastered the walls of my stomach with pig fat.'

Lucy studied them serenely. 'Why don't you join me? I guarantee you'll feel better.'

Roz threw a jandal at her.

Whoosh. Lucy exhaled.

'This is infuriating,' said Bridget.

'I know,' said Roz. 'Just ignore her and maybe she'll go away.'

'No, this,' said Bridget. 'I'm fully armed with everything I could possibly require for a session of idleness and I can't get comfortable.'

'That,' said Roz, 'is because you have no idea how to chill out.'

'There is one thing you're missing,' said Lucy, her exquisitely toned buttocks flexing as she lunged a lithe leg behind her along the sand.

'Please,' said Bridget. 'Not a sun salutation. You must be mad doing yoga in this humidity.'

'It's perfect for yoga,' said Lucy. 'We could be in India.'

'No, we couldn't,' said Roz. 'If we were in India there'd be a man offering to make us a gin and tonic.'

'Well,' said Lucy, 'if you'd let me finish, that's what I was going to suggest. Not a gin and tonic necessarily. But a cold alcoholic beverage of some description.'

'Now you're talking my kind of language,' said Roz. 'I could murder a beer.'

'Me too, Luce. I'll give you a hand.'

'I can manage. You sit there and practise doing nothing.'

'Watch me. It's easy . . .' Roz picked up the *Marie Claire*. 'God, I love Brad Pitt!' She held up a full-page photo of the star. 'If I wasn't a grown woman, I reckon my walls would still be covered in posters of him.'

'Give me Angelina any day,' said Lucy over her shoulder as she walked away. 'She's number one in my wank bank.'

Bridget and Roz looked at each other.

'Did she really just say that?' Bridget spluttered.

'Yup,' said Roz. 'She really did. You know, sometimes I think that woman is crazier than the two of us put together. And that's saying something.'

'Jesus, it's hot,' Bridget said, pushing herself up again.

The kids were doing the only sensible thing you could in this weather: staying wet. The girls star-fishing in the shallows, the boys . . .

Actually, what were the boys doing? Bridget peered down the beach.

Packing their boardies with sand, they appeared to be competing to see who could keep his shorts on the longest; their huge, distended crotches dragging everything south. God! Males and their bloody penises!

How long was it since any of them had been sunblocked?

'Hey!' she called. 'Time to slip, slap, slop.'

'Good luck with that,' snorted Roz.

Retrieving the tube from the bottom of her bag, Bridget wandered down to the water's edge.

'Block-time, everyone.'

A lump of sand walloped her thigh.

'Ouch!' Another caught her in the chest. 'That hurt.'

Jackson grinned.

'Right, you're in for it now, boyo,' she whooped, chucking the sunblock behind her onto the sand. 'Raaaaahhhh!' she charged through the choppy waves, drawing her breath in sharply as the water hit her belly.

She threw herself on Jackson, the two of them tussling in the surf as Abigail leapt on her back. Shrieking with excitement, Paris launched herself at Earl. He was too quick, though; slipping out of his sister's reach, he caught hold of Zachariah's foot.

Don't spoil it, Bridget prayed. But when Zachariah surfaced, he was laughing. He grabbed Skye and tossed her into the air. Observing the breadth of his shoulders, Bridget was struck once more by how he'd filled out.

Abigail came at her again and they fell backwards, cushioned by the sea.

'Enough,' said Bridget, choking on salt water.

'Do this, Mum. Try this.' Abigail shook her head in an arc, a spray of water fanning around her.

Bridget copied her. *Just like a Coke ad*, she thought . . . *not*.

'Who's yo' Mama now?' she taunted Jackson.

He smiled at her, and the innocent delight on his face reminded Bridget of a time when she was still his entire world. A small sense of loss coursed through her.

Her reverie was interrupted by a wolf whistle, and she turned to see Greg, Jono and Tristan at the bow of the boat, giving her the thumbs up.

Blushing, Bridget dove under, letting the current carry her out a little. She felt weightless. *Happy holiday, happy holiday* . . . It rolled off her tongue like a mantra.

Perhaps she really could start afresh with Zachariah. Perhaps he was just a slightly peculiar kid. What did her mother always say? *It takes all sorts* . . .

She ducked down, holding her breath until her tummy dragged along the bottom.

On the beach, she pulled her togs out of her bum as gracefully as possible, as she bent to pick up the tube of block.

Lucy was back with a chilly bin of ice and Coronas, a zip-lock bag of lime quarters and a packet of corn chips. Bridget wrapped a towel around herself, and Lucy passed her a beer. They watched their husbands wading through the water towards them like Bedouin women: dry bags balanced on their heads.

'How does a bonfire on the beach sound, ladies?' asked Jono. 'Fresh snapper fillets pan-fried in a little butter, potatoes baked in the embers . . .'

'Truly terrible,' laughed Lucy. 'Can't think of anything worse.'

'Is the plan still to visit the mansion tomorrow?' asked Bridget.

'Bridget, Bridget,' said Jono, 'always thinking ahead. You need to learn to live in the moment, my friend, and I've got just the thing.'

He winked.

Chapter
Twenty-five

October
Friday

Greg didn't kiss her goodbye in the morning. Although to be fair, Bridget didn't kiss him either. She would text him later. She didn't want to start the weekend off on a sour note.

Not that the kids were helping with her mood. Needling each other, looking for a rise. Abigail had finished the last of the strawberry jam, and Jackson was filthy on her.

'Abigail, there was enough left in the jar for at least three bagels. That was selfish. Here, look Jackson, I can scrape some onto yours.'

'Noooo!'

'Don't be ridiculous, Abigail.'

'I'm not touching it anyway. She's probably goobed all over it.'

Abigail pinched her brother's arm.

'Jackson,' Bridget cautioned as he started to rock Abigail's chair. She reached out to grab his arm, but she was too late.

Abigail slid off sideways, beginning to howl before she even hit the ground. Pretty sure the damage was minor, Bridget picked her up, patted her perfunctorily on the back.

'Jackson! You're old enough to know better. That was completely unnecessary. In fact, you're both behaving appallingly. You can get your own way to school and home today. I've got too much to do.'

The day passed in a vaguely disagreeable blur. Bridget wasn't unproductive, but she laboured under a general kind of malaise.

Still, it was a relief not to have to switch off her laptop at 2.45 p.m. Dodging the school run had probably gained her an hour. She ought to lay down the law more often.

Her phone dinged. It was a text from Sina.

'Hi! Hope you're good. Girls keen to hang out. Can Abigail come for a play?'

'Sure,' she replied. 'What time should I pick her up?'

'Five-ish?'

'Perfect. See you then.'

Double bonus. Jackson would be only too happy to make himself two-minute noodles and entertain himself while she kept working.

She knocked off five-hundred words for a client with an online wedding registry business, and was just starting to wonder what time Greg would be home, whether they should have takeaways for dinner, when her phone dinged again. Sina.

'Girls pleading for Abigail to stay. Fine with me if it's okay with you?'

Bridget hesitated. *Abigail could be invited to a sleepover and you'd have no idea her friend's dad was the guy.* Like a premonition, Moana's words ran through her mind.

'So kind,' she texted back, 'but don't think it will work tonight. I'll be there shortly.'

Sina lived on the best side of the so-called 'best' street in Point Heed.

Right on the water, Marine View Road had always been desirable. However while you'd once been able to glimpse slivers of sea in between the original residences, those modest abodes had long since been replaced by great, unwieldy structures. In keeping with its neighbours, Sina's house sat heavily behind a fortress of a fence.

Bridget pressed the intercom.

'Just push,' sang out Sina.

The house was super-modern — a small box on top of a bigger box —

the garden incongruously French country. Topiaries and lavender; it gave Greg heart palpitations.

'Hello?'

'Out the back,' Sina called.

Bridget made her way down the hall. Stretched across a massive canvas as if it was priceless art was a posed black and white family studio portrait. She blinked at their frozen expressions, her gaze drawn, instead, to a faded photo in a frame, half-hidden behind a phalaenopsis orchid taking up most of the narrow console. Bridget peered closer. It was of an elderly Pasifika couple, standing in front of a large palm tree and a small, humble house. She wondered what they made of their daughter's life.

'I hope you don't mind but the girls are in the pool. We haven't even turned the heating on yet. Crazy things! Got time for a cheeky sav?'

Sina was standing at the long granite kitchen island, slicing raw chicken. She took a slug from a goldfish bowl of wine.

'Thanks,' said Bridget. 'Maybe a small one.'

'Do you mind getting it?' Sina held up her hands. They were slick with meat juice. She gestured towards an enormous, multi-doored fridge with her elbow.

'How old were you when you moved here?' Bridget asked, taking a punt and opening the door closest to her.

'What? Oh, from the islands? No, I was born here, thank God. My parents moved back when they retired. I mean it's fine for a holiday, but I couldn't live there.'

From Sina's tone, Bridget judged it best to change the subject. 'I think I've got fridge-envy,' she said, admiring the symmetrical array of sauces, the deep fruit and vegetable crisper, a half-empty bottle of sauvignon blanc lined up alongside a selection of kombucha and craft beers, everything exactly in its place.

'Isn't it the best?' said Sina. 'Honestly, every time I get out the milk, I feel so grateful.'

'Mum!'

Bridget looked outside to where Abigail was balanced on the edge of the pool.

'Watch this flip.'

She held her breath as Abigail's tiny body arched and then with a sudden jerk went back over into the water, her head narrowly missing the pool's unforgiving edge.

'Wow!'

She turned to Sina. 'I can hardly bear to watch.'

'I know, but you can't spend your time worrying about what might happen, huh? Dry off before you come inside, girls. There are clean towels in the pool house.'

'Did you bring my overnight bag, Mum?'

'No, honey. I've come to pick you up.'

'What? But we were going to have a sleepover.'

'Yeah,' said Ivy. 'Mum said it was fine.'

'It's all organised,' said Abigail. 'We're having chicken tacos and we're going to watch a movie and eat popcorn.'

'Not tonight, okay.'

'You always spoil everything,' cried Abigail, running off down the hall, Ivy trailing behind her.

Sina smiled sympathetically. 'Are you going out?'

'Ahhh . . . not exactly. I guess sleepovers just don't seem like such a great idea at the moment. You know, with what's going on and everything.'

Sina stared at her: 'I'm not sure I understand what you're trying to say, Bridget.'

Chapter
Twenty-six

January
Day Four

The flames surged into the night sky. High, so high. Bridget's face burned; beneath her the sand was bitter, rasping her bare thighs. She should go and get some track pants. The house was so far away though. So, so far. Too far. Maybe Greg would get them. Hang on, where was Greg? There was Lucy, there was Jono . . .

'Greg?'

The kids cavorted around the bonfire's edges. Round-and-round-the-merry-go-round. They were making her dizzy. Were they getting too close? And what was it they were chanting?

Oy, lyoll lee lyoll lee, lyah ah, lee ee, lyoll lee lyoll lee, dah rah.

At least that's what it sounded like. She gave up. Lay down. The sand was so cold.

She should go and get some track pants. The house was so far away though. So, so far. Too far. Maybe Greg would get them. Hang on, where was Greg? There was Lucy, there was Jono . . .

'Greg?'

Bridget had been reluctant to take the E Jono had produced out of his 'magic bag of tricks'.

'C'mon,' the others had pressed. 'We're on an island. What can go wrong?'

'Maybe later,' she'd said. 'After the kids are in bed.'

'Nah,' said Jono. 'It'll be too late. We want to do it as the sun goes down.'

'Just a quarter,' Roz had counselled. 'Micro-dosing, that's the key. And then later, if you're feeling good, you can have more. Nail another quarter.'

Bridget had relented, of course. She didn't want to be seen as a stick in the mud. A handbrake on the others' fun. And who knew? Maybe it would be a laugh. Just because she hadn't particularly enjoyed it previously; had hated the comedown that went on and on for days. Maybe she hadn't been in the right frame of mind. And look around — they were in paradise, as Roz and Jono kept reminding her. Proclaiming it as such a given — *Isn't this paradise!* — that not only would it be churlish to disagree, clearly, you'd be wrong.

Where better to do it, when better, than here, now, surrounded by her bestest friends in the whole wide world? That was another declaration Roz and Jono liked to make at regular intervals. And even though it was true, even though they were all one another's best friends, the repeated saying of it sometimes made Bridget want it not to be true. *How do you know?* a small treasonous part of her wanted to retort. *How do you know I don't have all these other friends I love just as much?*

Zigg ra yoov hurr roh vudd da ya woo mee loh vuh vorr rut.

Survivor! It came to her suddenly. That's what it was. They were singing the theme song to *Survivor*.

She sat back up.

The children weren't just going round and round. They were conducting a tribal council and Zachariah was the host.

One by one, they solemnly approached him, placing something in the bucket he was holding out in front of him.

Oh God, it was an elimination ceremony. This game was going to end in tears.

She should nip it in the bud now, but it was as if someone had poured cement down her throat. Legs like lead weights, jaw grinding, she was rooted to the spot.

Helplessly, she observed as Zachariah pulled each 'vote' out of the bucket.

'Jackson,' he intoned. 'Earl. Jackson. Jackson.'

Evidently a stick meant Earl. A shell, Jackson.

'Earl.'

Relishing the high drama of the moment, Zachariah took his sweet time revealing the deciding vote.

Bridget held her breath.

'Jackson,' he pronounced, keeping his fist tightly clenched around the object.

Bridget's heart slumped. Why did it have to be her boy?

She looked over at Jackson, a consolatory smile at the ready, and, as she did, she caught the shift in his expression. In a flash of blue T-shirt and yellow boardies, he dove at Zachariah, knocking him to the ground, the two of them narrowly missing a red-hot log.

Do something, Bridget told herself. *Do something, for fuck's sake.*

And still she sat, fixed in place. With her eyes the only part of her she seemed to have any control of, she tried to signal through the flames to the other adults — who were all happily oblivious to the fracas taking place on the other side of the bonfire.

Bridget could but watch as Zachariah reached out and grabbed hold of a stick, one end alight, the other yet to catch. Straddling Jackson's hips, he raised the weapon above his head, poised to strike, when Abigail screamed.

'No! Stop! Dad!'

As if someone had doused them with icy water, all at once Zachariah threw his burning stick back into the fire, Jackson shoved him off, and the other parents leapt to their feet.

'What's going on?' demanded Greg.

'Nothing,' said the older boys.

'Jackson started it,' said Abigail. 'But then Zachariah was going to kill him.'

'No, he wasn't,' said Earl. 'Don't exaggerate, blabbermouth.'

'That's enough of that, thank you, Earl,' said Roz.

'Is that true?' asked Greg. 'Jackson? Zachariah?'

Neither boy said anything, Jackson staring at the ground, Zachariah at his mother.

'What was the fight about?' asked Greg.

'We were playing *Survivor*. Zachariah said Jackson had been voted off but he can't have been because . . .'

'Shut up, Abigail,' said Jackson.

'Well, it sounds like a big misunderstanding to me,' said Lucy.

'Hmm . . . I think we have some seriously over-tired children here,' said Jono. 'Bed, you lot.'

'Agreed,' said Greg, bending down. 'Jump on, Willow. I'll give you a piggyback up to the house.'

Surprisingly, the children allowed themselves to be corralled.

'Say goodnight,' instructed Jono.

'Nite,' they called. 'Nite.'

As the two men and children trooped off, Bridget glanced around the fire at the remaining adults. Would they take their offspring's side? She steeled herself for the argument to continue, for the small, underhand snipes.

'Whoa,' said Roz, 'that was full-on. I was trying to keep it together but it felt like my face was going to fall off.'

Tristan and Lucy laughed.

'It takes a special kind of skill to parent while you're off your face, huh?' said Lucy.

'Yeah,' agreed Tristan. 'It's like you're in this altered state of consciousness and they're kind of entering it and exiting it and it's like, who are you again? Oh, that's right . . .'

Bridget laughed. It was a laugh of relief but it came out like a honk.

'What are you doing over there by yourself, Bridge?' said Roz. 'Come join us.'

'Mmmmm.'

'Are you okay, pumpkin?'

'Kinda hard to talk . . .'

'You're okay. Don't fight it.'

'Mmmmm . . . trying . . .'

'Here,' said Lucy, pulling Bridget to her feet, 'you need company.'

Tristan shifted over on the blanket, and Lucy drew her down between them.

'You should drink this.'

Bridget felt Lucy's hand on hers as she passed over a bottle of water, felt the coolness of the glass, the heat of the fire.

'Are you getting that?' Bridget asked.

'What?' asked Lucy.

'That. Your skin and the air. Like simultaneous silk and velvet tides. Juxtaposed universes.'

'Ooh,' said Roz, 'she can talk. Poetry and everything. You are on a trip, darling.'

The three of them laughed. Were they laughing at her? It didn't matter. Bridget was floating. Their laughter but a ripple on an endless ocean. Her head started to spin. Round-and-round-the-merry-go-round. She groaned.

'Here,' said Tristan, placing a gentle hand on the back of her head and guiding it down between her knees. 'Close your eyes, and take a deep, slow breath.'

Bridget swayed, if that was possible while sitting, but did as he said. She felt herself calming. She lay back and looked up at the stars. So beautiful. So many. Too many. She felt sick. Constricted. Maybe she should take off her clothes? She began to wriggle out of her shorts.

An arm tugged on hers.

'I don't know if you want to be doing that. Why don't you dance? Try that. It feels good.'

'I . . . uh, I don't think I can,' said Bridget, opening her eyes and immediately closing them again.

Tristan's handsome face was right there, peering at hers with concern. Or was it lust? She opened her eyes again. His eyes were so pretty. Such pretty eyes. Bedroom eyes.

'Where is everyone?'

'Dancing. Everyone's dancing.'

Bridget struggled to her feet. So they were. Greg, Lucy, Jono, Roz.

Everyone was dancing. A wave of nausea hit her. She fell forward onto her knees, her head hanging like a millstone.

'Come on,' said Tristan, his hands clasping her hips from behind. 'Let's get you upright.'

It was like they were doing it doggy style, thought Bridget, and she burst out laughing, her knees sliding out from under her so that both she and Tristan collapsed in a messy heap.

'What?' he said. 'What's so funny?'

'Nothing,' she said. 'Nothing.'

'Go on,' he said. 'Tell me.'

'It was just such a compromising position,' she said, starting to laugh again.

He drew himself up on to his forearms so that he hovered above her chest.

Oh God, was he coming on to her? She was certain the air between them was thrumming with desire. She couldn't be imagining it, could she? It was so loud. Surely everyone could tell.

On the other side of the bonfire there was a joyous whooping.

Jumping up, Tristan shook himself.

Feeling a confusion of longing, shame and regret, Bridget watched him join the dancers.

Chapter Twenty-seven

October Saturday

Over huevos rancheros they nutted out a plan of attack for the day.

Saturday mornings meant soccer in their house. The season had felt interminable this year. Still, it was almost over and at least both kids had home games today. Small mercies, Bridget reminded herself.

'What time is Abigail's?' asked Greg, reaching for the jalapeños.

'Nine-thirty a.m. The coach wants them there for warm-up by ten past, though. Jackson's is at ten a.m. Field eleven. I think it's over by the Point Heed Road entry. We should be able to tag team. Watch a bit of each.'

'Why do we never get to play on the artificial turf?' complained Jackson. 'It's always the stupid little kids.'

'You're stupid,' said Abigail.

'Am not.'

'Are so.'

'Stop it. Both of you. Could we just enjoy breakfast without the bickering? It hasn't rained for at least a week, Jackson. The field should be fine to play on.'

Bridget dug into her dressing-gown pocket for her phone. She clicked on the weather app.

Checking the forecast had become something of a habit lately. She found it reassuring to know what lay ahead. She liked being able to drop into the conversation that the weekend was going to be wet or they had five days of clear, sunny skies in store. It always made her feel faintly superior when someone was genuinely surprised. As if she had insider knowledge somehow, that she alone was privy to the vagaries of the meteorological system.

'Yip, no sign of rain whatsoever. Should we do a barbeque tonight, honey?'

Bridget had imagined they would discuss their argument when Greg got home on Friday, but by the time they'd put the kids to bed, Abigail still sulking about her thwarted sleepover, Thursday's fight seemed a long time ago. And when she had sat down next to Greg on the couch and he'd picked up her foot and ran his thumb across it, she read it as an apology and decided to let the Laura comment and the subject of his drinking slide.

'Greg,' she prompted him now. 'What do you reckon? Is October too early for a barbeque?'

'Huh?' he said, looking up from his plate, a drip of yolk on his chin. 'What's happening tonight? I thought we had a quiet weekend.'

'Honestly, honey. We discussed it last week. Roz and Jono and the twins are coming over. It's just casual. We haven't caught up properly in ages.'

'Oh right, right. Sorry, it's been a big week.'

Bridget wasn't sure how it worked in gay relationships but she didn't know of a single straight couple in which the woman wasn't the social secretary in the household. The holder, controller and initiator of everyone's engagements and schedules. It was exhausting.

'So, what do you think? A barbeque?'

'Nah, once that sun goes down, it's bloody cold. Maybe a big pasta?'

'Good idea. Let's take the car to soccer. You guys can walk home and I'll nip to the supermarket. Get supplies for tonight.'

'Go, boy!' yelled a well-worn woman, pacing along the sidelines of the pitch. 'Go!'

She was wearing a scarf in the colours of the opposing team: purple and gold; royal hues. When translated into nasty polyester stripes, though, the effect was more bogan than regal.

'Oh, for God's sake! Un-fucking-believable,' the woman cursed loudly under her breath.

After seven solid years spectating at her children's soccer games, Bridget still struggled to grasp anything other than the most rudimentary of rules, but even she could see that the scrawny midfielder, who she assumed was the woman's son, was seriously talented, and that the chubby girl he'd just passed the ball to had screwed up an easy goal. When the boys in the team all groaned loudly, the girl looked like she might cry.

This was Abigail's last year playing in a mixed team and Bridget was relieved. Initially she'd liked it, all the little boys and girls bumbling along together. But at some point, an awareness of gender seemed to take hold, their camaraderie supplanted by something less good-natured, less open. Exactly the same thing had happened with Jackson's team. Greg said it was instinctive, primal. To Bridget it felt like the opposite of consciousness-raising, a corruption of their natural non-bias.

A cheer erupted from the parents on their side. Bridget looked up.

'You little beauty!' Greg was practically levitating on the spot. 'Yes!' He high-fived one of the other dads on the team.

Bugger, what had she missed?

'Did you see it? Did you see my goal, Mum?' Abigail called out across the field.

Bridget gave her a big thumbs up.

'Fantastic, darling.'

'Liar,' said Greg, who was used to his wife's lack of enthusiasm for sport, even her own children's.

'Don't you dare tell her.'

The mother of one of the boys in Abigail's team smiled at her sympathetically. Bridget didn't really know her, but she always imagined they might be friends, if only she could summon up the energy.

'How were the holidays?' Bridget asked. She should make more of an effort.

'Um, let's just say I'm thankful they're over,' the mother laughed.

She had a lovely laugh, almost musical. God, what was her name? Jane? Something beginning with J. June, that's right.

'You?'

'Ditto!'

They were grinning guiltily at each other when Bridget sensed someone behind her.

'Bridget, I was hoping I'd see you here.'

'Oh, hello Ruth.'

'I wanted to talk to you about this whole situation,' said Ruth, somehow managing to insert herself between Bridget and June. 'I mean it's just ridiculous if you ask me.'

No, thought Bridget. *No, I wasn't asking you, and I have zero desire to talk to you about it.* She decided to play dumb.

'What situation is that?'

'Zombie wrestling, of course,' Ruth spluttered, her tone growing more strident by the second. 'And how ludicrous, no, dangerous, how dangerously irresponsible it is that as a community we're allowing it to proceed.'

If there was a line delineating her personal space, thought Bridget, then Ruth had well and truly stepped over it. She found herself fixating on Ruth's mouth: a furious slash of bright coral lipstick; strings of spittle stretching and contracting with each new word formed. Alongside her, she felt June withdrawing.

'Look Ruth, it's not up to me, but I really don't see what the problem is.'

'What the problem is? Instead of helping us to protect our children, when we have no idea who this appalling degenerate even is, the school and the wider parent body are proposing to let them be manhandled by . . . by strange men!'

Greg cleared his throat.

The last thing Bridget needed was Greg wading into this with his two cents' worth. It would be like striking a match next to a leaky gas connection.

'Sorry, Ruth,' she said, backing away. 'I'd be happy to talk about this another time, but I need to get to Jackson's game.'

'I thought I was . . .'

Bridget cut Greg off: 'I promised him I'd watch him in goal for the first half.'

'Liar, liar, pants on fire,' Greg murmured.

Bridget couldn't spy a single woman among Jackson's team's supporters. She hesitated, unsure where to put herself in this throng of fathers.

'Howdy,' said Angus's dad, making room for her. 'Good to see Jackson back in goal. That boy of yours has great organisation skills in the box.'

Bridget smiled, utterly clueless what he was on about. She waved at Jackson, who studiously ignored her.

'Don't be distracting our goalie now,' said a dad in a white adidas hoody.

Bridget girded her loins; the sideline chat at Jackson's games was always all stats and on-field analysis.

'Anyway,' adidas-hoody said, turning back to Angus's dad, 'as I was saying, if that was me and I'd been found with that stuff, I'd have expected her to have turfed me out on my ear!'

Dear God, thought Bridget, soccer stats suddenly seeming surprisingly attractive, *was there no escaping it?*

'It depends on what it was, really, doesn't it?' said Angus's dad. 'I mean if it was adolescent girls, you know like fifteen, illegal, but only just, then that's one thing. But if it was like little kids and bestiality and shit . . . A guy at work was telling me about this guy they nabbed in Oz who was videoing his toddler all dressed up in full bondage and discipline gear and then selling it online to perverts. I mean that's seriously fucked.'

'What the hell?' said adidas-hoody. 'Where would you even get something like that? Imagine going into the local adult shop, "Uh, I'll have a dominatrix outfit in size three, please."'

They erupted into laughter. Bridget recoiled.

'Excuse us,' said Angus's dad. 'We forgot we were in polite company.'

'You can get anything you want on the dark web,' said another father, joining in their conversation.

Bridget had seen him around before but they'd never actually talked. The awkward way he'd spoken just now, though, like he couldn't get his words out fast enough, confirmed what she'd always assumed about him: a geek, probably worked in IT. 'You can't generalise like that,' Greg had protested when she'd told him. 'Just because the poor guy wears his phone clipped to his belt.'

But journalism had taught Bridget that stereotypes were often borne out of small truths. The problem with stereotypes wasn't that they were wrong, rather that they were lacking — only painting a partial picture, telling a version of the story.

'Do you think that's how they caught the bastard?' asked Angus's dad. 'Set a trap for him on the dark web?'

'Probably,' said adidas-hoody. 'The cops have got feelers everywhere these days. They have to. Interpol, the FBI, they're all working together. The KGB, MI5, they'll be all over it, too.'

'I'm not so sure about that,' said IT dad. 'I don't think some bloke distributing kiddie porn in little old New Zealand is on the Russians' radar somehow.'

Bridget snorted. She might have to revise her assumptions about IT dad.

'Hey,' he said, 'have you heard about that Facebook page someone has started up? Urging Point Heed dads to declare it's not them. I guess the idea is if enough of us confirm "it's not me", the culprit will eventually be revealed through a process of elimination.'

'I can't see how that will achieve anything,' said adidas-hoody. 'I mean, if you were the perp, wouldn't you just add your name?'

'Nah,' said IT dad. 'There's no way he'll be allowed access to the internet.'

Standing with these men she didn't really know, and despite the open field, the big skies above, Bridget had a feeling of claustrophobia.

She inhaled sharply.

Angus's dad gave her a funny look.

'I might do that,' he said. 'Out myself as not being the paedo. I'm no Snow White, but right now we're all being tarred with the same dirty fucking brush.'

Chapter
Twenty-eight

January
Day Five

What was it they used to say, those ancient mariners?

Bridget stretched her arms above her head, gaze returning to the pink crease of the horizon.

'Hey, Greg,' she called, 'you're an ancient mariner, aren't you?'

She laughed, pleased at her joke, but there was no response from her husband. Snoring gently, he was rolled up in a blanket like a sandy burrito.

Pink eye? No, she chuckled to herself, she was pretty sure those crusty old sailors weren't talking about conjunctivitis. Pink sky? Red, that was it. Red sky at night, sailor's delight. Red sky at morning, sailor's warning. Got it! She pumped her fist. But was it night or was it morning? She laughed. Who would know?

This was nice. She was sooooo relaxed. It was so quiet. And peaceful. No kids to . . . *Shit!* She scrambled to her feet. Where were the kids?

'Greg!' She shook him. 'The kids! Greg, where are the kids?'

Greg mumbled something and turned over.

Actually, thought Bridget, looking around her properly for the first time, *where was everyone*? Apart from the two of them, the bonfire remains, a bunch of empties and some wet towels, the beach was empty. She tried shaking Greg again, but he didn't rouse at all.

Bridget wrapped her arms around herself. She was freezing. Dragging the sleeves of her sweater down over her knuckles, she decided to leave

Greg to sleep it off. There was little chance of him being washed away.

As she picked her way along the jetty, the rough, barnacled planks brutal on her bare, ice-block feet, bits of the night came back to her.

Greg and Jono taking the kids off to bed, Lucy and Tristan looking after her, she and Tristan . . . oh, God . . . She and Tristan, what?

Nothing, she told herself. *Nothing happened*. There was no she and Tristan.

'Ouch,' she exclaimed, stepping on a frosty prickle. The lawn was almost more merciless than the jetty.

'Are you all right?'

It was Roz. Sitting on the verandah, a rug around her shoulders, a mug of something steaming in her hand.

'I'm fine, just stood on something. Where is everyone?'

'Bed. I'm still so wired. I can't imagine going to sleep.'

'Me, neither. Feel like company?'

'Course. Wow, what a night, huh?'

'Yeah, half of it's a blur.'

'You were pretty wild there for a bit, Bridge.'

'Argh, don't remind me.'

'It was good. Good to see you cut loose.'

'If only you knew,' she said, irked to be reminded, once again, that apparently, she didn't know how to have fun.

'What do you mean?'

'Nothing. I'm just being stupid.'

'No, c'mon, you can't do that. Hint at something salacious and then not deliver.'

'It's probably nothing . . .'

'In my experience nothing is usually something.'

And so, Bridget told Roz. About this attraction for Tristan that had arisen out of nowhere. About how she'd thought it was all in her head but last night there'd been something. Something intense between them. Something she couldn't explain.

Roz was quiet. And then she laughed.

'I can explain it, Bridge. You're bored. You've been with Greg since you were a fucking kid. You've got two children, a satisfying-ish job, a nice house in the 'burbs, your life is fine, but there's no excitement.'

'Thanks a lot! My life's not that dull. But even if you're right, why Tristan? Why now?'

'What is it they say about proximity? Tristan is there. And in a weird kind of a way it's safer to fantasise about him than some stranger. Because you know you'll never act on it. Plus, Tristan is hot. He doesn't do much for me, too fucking pretty, however there's no denying he's well above average in the looks department.'

'But, last night . . .' Bridget trailed off, not sure why she was defending something she didn't even want to acknowledge had happened, or, she reframed it, could have happened.

'Last night, Bridge, last night was called being out of your mind on E. It makes everyone horny. I was pashing Lucy, for God's sake.'

'Were you? I didn't see that.'

'Yeah, well it was a long night. And you were off on your own little psychedelic journey for a good part of it.'

'It felt like minutes.'

'More like hours. Anyway, Bridge, I think you can put that one out of your head. Go get yourself a vibrator or something to spice things up with Greg. Seriously, you've got a good man there. You don't want to screw that up for some imagined frisson between you and that dodgy toff. You're playing with fire there, girlfriend.'

'What do you mean? Tristan's not dodgy.'

'Maybe it's because I wasn't there when you guys met him, but he's always kinda felt like an interloper to me. Or maybe it's because after he moved out here the gang disbanded. I know it wasn't his fault, but some part of me can't help but blame him.'

'We regrouped, though. It was just a phase. A stage of life we were all at. Are you sure you're not just jealous?'

'Jealous! Of what?'

'His fancy upbringing. All that old money. That his parents are landed gentry or something.'

None of them had ever met Tristan's parents. Bridget always pictured this tweed-clad couple lording it over the serfs, a couple of small dogs yapping at their heels.

'Nah, but it's possible that explains his reserve. That stiff upper-lip thing.'

'I don't find him particularly reserved.'

'It's probably not the right word, but don't you feel there's this sort of unknowable quality to him? Somehow, he always makes me want to hold something back, too.'

'You?' Bridget choked. 'Bless you, Roz, but when did you ever hold anything back?'

'Lots, actually,' said Roz a little peevishly.

'Like what?'

'Like, you know how Jono and I went round and round in circles about getting carpet in the bedrooms? How I held out for floorboards? I told everyone it was because carpet was naff, but that wasn't the real reason. When I think of carpet in bedrooms, all I can see is the stained carpets of my childhood. So fucking threadbare the only purpose they served was to muffle a man's footsteps in the night.'

Roz shivered and Bridget saw once more that scared little girl who had grown up to become her stout-hearted friend.

'Oh God, Roz,' she said, wrapping an arm around her. 'That's terrible. You're always so gutsy, I guess I assume you've put that stuff behind you.'

'Nah, I just put on a brave face.'

'Have you ever thought about getting counselling?'

'No. I'd never risk losing how far I've come by picking the top off that scab.'

'What scab?'

'The scab that grew over my childhood. Open that baby up and I don't reckon you'd ever staunch the pus.'

Bridget didn't know what to say, but it was like Roz couldn't stop.

'That's probably why I was so batshit on our last holiday.'

'Were you?' said Bridget, feigning ignorance.

'Yeah, you remember, Jono and I were fighting all the time.'

'Kind of.'

'I could hardly bring myself to look at him. I should have told you and

Lucy what was going on but I just couldn't bring myself to voice it out loud.'

'To be fair, they were challenging circumstances. The accommodation wasn't one of Lucy's better finds. On paper that old school house sounded charming, in reality, though, there was nowhere to escape each other.'

'Yeah, but I could have been at a five-star resort and I would have still been miserable.'

'So, what was it?' prodded Bridget, properly curious now.

'It's a long story.'

'I'm not going anywhere.'

Roz breathed out slowly.

'When I first met Jono, he was upfront about the fact he liked porn. And I liked that he didn't make a secret of it, that he wanted me to watch with him. It seemed harmless enough. An occasional hobby. You know, on a wet Saturday afternoon at the counter of Videos-R-Us he'd slip a copy of *Girls' Night Out XXXX* under the new release blockbuster we'd picked out together. And he'd turn to me and wink.

'So, I tried. Tried to get into it, too. God knows, I'm no prude. But, you know, sex has always been confusing enough for me, without the added complication of wondering what's playing out in my lover's mind while he's watching other people doing it. I guess, when you boil it down, I'm distrustful of sex.'

'Well, that's hardly surprising.'

'In order to enjoy it, I need it to be as simple as possible. Just me and him. No implements, no artifice. Lights out. No positions that lessen my sense of control. No dirty talk. Nothing to suggest the balance of power is anything but equally shared. When I watch porn, I'm never able to suspend my sense of belief for long enough to buy into the actors' pleasure. I'm always worried whether everyone is fully consenting, and feeling worried isn't exactly a turn on.'

Roz sat up straighter, causing Bridget's hand to slide off her shoulder.

'Anyway, I'd always assumed Jono's interest in pornography would naturally peter out. You know, a young man's game, yada yada . . . And for a while it did. When we had the twins, he told me he wanted for nothing. And when he seemed less interested in the bedroom department, I didn't look for reasons why. To be honest I welcomed the reprieve. I thought it was because we were middle-aged now. But last year, packing to go away, I was searching through some files on the computer, trying to find this document I'd put together for housesitters explaining how to turn the automatic watering system on, etcetera, when I stumbled across his secret stash.

'I'll tell you what: my heart was in my mouth. I was terrified I was going to discover my husband got off on watching women being fucked by horses or worse . . . But it was all fairly innocuous. Amateur porn, I think they call it. Some guy with a hairy back plundering his wife's ample arse on a nasty pink bedspread. You know the kind of thing.'

Bridget nodded, not sure she did exactly.

'Why didn't you talk to us?'

'I couldn't. It wasn't that I didn't trust you, I just couldn't bear for you to think less of Jono. To feel sorry for me. I was more disappointed in him than anything. And I felt like a fool. How could I have not known? There was so much of the stuff. Clip after clip.'

'Did you confront him?'

'Nope, I didn't know what to say. I just took it out on him instead.'

Him, and everyone else, thought Bridget.

'I knew I was being a right bitch. If I was Jono, I would have spat the dummy, but he always just waits me out. Anyway, eventually I couldn't bear it any longer, so, on the car trip home, Paris and Earl dozing in the back seat, Hall and bloody Oates playing on the only radio station we could tune into, I go: "Don't you want to know what you've done?" "Not particularly," he replies, cool as a bloody cucumber. "But I'm guessing you're going to tell me."'

'Argh, that's just how Greg would have reacted!'

It was as if Bridget wasn't even there, though. Maybe it was the MDMA, maybe it was the relief of confession, but whatever it was, the words that had begun with such a reluctant trickle were now an unstoppable torrent.

'So, I told him. Laid it all out, exactly what I'd found. Told him how let down I felt. To his credit he didn't try to deny it. Or laugh it off. He seemed more surprised I was so upset than anything. Said I'd always known he enjoyed porn. That he couldn't see what had changed. And when I said, yes, but it hadn't been something secret then, that we'd always promised no secrets, he said, that while he had no desire to be with anyone else, he'd grown weary of his advances being spurned. That he'd thought this was a workable compromise.'

'Oh darling, I'm so sorry. I had no idea.'

'No one did.'

Roz stood up, throwing whatever was left in her mug onto the lawn.

'Anyway, driving back along those treacherous coast roads, I felt my anger seep away. I felt sad, sad but determined, you know. I resolved to try harder. To not turn from his touch. To suggest now and again we try something different. I prayed it would be enough.'

'And was it?'

'I think so. At least I hope so.'

Chapter Twenty-nine

October Saturday

Why did she do it?

She'd intended to grab a few things for tonight — wine, a nice cheese, cream to go with the orange cake — but somehow, she'd turned it into a shop for the week.

'Greg,' she yelled from the driveway. 'Jackson, Abigail, come help carry in bags.'

'Have you invited half the neighbourhood round?' asked Greg, contemplating the boot full of groceries. 'I thought you were just getting supplies for Roz and Jono coming over.'

'I know, I know, it saves me going back Monday, though.'

She had been nursing fantasies of returning to a tidy house: dishwasher cycling, table polished, dirty uniforms dealt to — but the house was in even more of a state than when they'd left for soccer earlier.

'What time are they due?'

'Five-thirty. While I get these groceries unpacked, would you clean the bi-folds?'

Greg rolled his eyes. 'I thought you said this was a casual thing.'

'It is, but I still want the house nice, and I'm sick to death of looking at those greasy handprints.'

'I was hoping for a bit of couch time. Catch up on some sport.'

'Please, darling. I promise you can have as much couch time as you want tomorrow.'

It would never cross Bridget's mind to turn on the television during the day; TV was an evening activity. But she'd realised early on in their relationship she was going to have to accept Greg's daytime TV habit. Accept it or sign up for a lifetime of acrimony.

'The kids have had lunch,' said Greg, reaching under the sink for the paper towels.

'Great,' said Bridget, crossing that off her mental list of tasks.

Only the groceries to put away then, the house to clean, the cake to bake, the sauce to make. She counted backward from their anticipated arrival time; it was doable, just.

At 5.23 p.m., she was jumping out of the shower, hair dripping wet, praying, *please be ten minutes late, please be ten minutes late*, when she heard a commotion.

'What is it?' she asked, coming out of the bedroom.

Potting mix and broken pieces of terracotta fanned out across the hall runner. Abigail had a guilty look on her face; angry tears coursed down Jackson's cheeks.

'Jesus Christ!'

'She ruined it,' sobbed Jackson. 'She ruined my pollination experiment.'

'I just wanted to have a look at it,' Abigail cried. 'It was an accident.'

Bridget took a deep breath.

'Okay, right now the only thing I'm interested in is cleaning this up. Abigail, go and get me the vacuum cleaner. Jackson, I'll take you to the plant centre next week, promise. It'll be coming out of your pocket money, Abigail.'

Bridget was still clad in a towel, hoovering up the last of the dirt, when there was a knock. *Fuck!*

'Greg,' she called, 'Greg, can you answer it?'

As Roz, Jono and the twins excitedly spilled through the front door, she shoved the vacuum into the broom cupboard and ducked into the bedroom. She yanked a kimono top off its hanger. Having people over always seemed like such a good idea at the time.

'Hello, hello,' she said, walking into the living area a few minutes later, a trickle of cold water from the low ponytail she had hurriedly scraped her hair into running down her back.

There was always a transition phase, a readjusting, when people first arrived, she thought, taking in the bags dumped on the throw she'd placed so artfully on the sofa, the children grabbing handfuls of cashews and smearing the freshly cleaned bi-folds as they went out to the tramp.

'I told you not to bring anything,' she protested as Roz shoved aside food on the carefully arranged platter to make room for a fillet of smoked salmon.

'Nonsense,' said Roz.

Snap out of it, Bridget told herself, taking a sip of the pinot gris Greg passed her. These were their friends. This was their life: messy and loud, like life should be.

'So, there we were, right,' said Jono. 'In the middle of a bowling alley, surrounded by millennials chugging back craft beer.'

'Hang on, wait,' said Bridget. 'When was this?'

'Last night,' said Roz. 'At the launch party for this new salt and vinegar-flavoured beer.'

'Salt and vinegar,' snorted Greg. 'I thought it was bad enough when they started putting chocolate in beer!'

'Yeah,' said Jono, 'it's the brainchild of this bunch of twenty-something-year-old guys. Apparently, they had the idea one night cramming for a chemistry exam, washing down their favourite snack with a few quiet ones. I suspect they hit up the bank of Mummy and Daddy.'

'They've been a pain in the arse to deal with from the word go,' said Roz. 'We warned them there was a test match on last night and they might not get the turn-out. When they refused to budge on the date, Jono suggested they have the launch at a sports bar. "Uh … brand cringe," goes one.'

'And then, get this,' said Jono. 'They have the audacity to send us an email this morning expressing their "disappointment".'

They were like a well-oiled machine, thought Bridget, listening to them build on the story as she washed rocket for a salad. She wondered whether she and Greg ever presented such a united front. Not that Roz and Jono had always been so simpatico.

'I wanted to reply, "What, disappointed because your mutual masturbation session clashed with a test match?"'

Uninvited and unwelcome, an image of Jono hunched over a computer screen flashed into Bridget's head. Flinching, she recalled her heart-to-heart on Hine's with Roz, and she marvelled at the contrast between that crushed, burdened version of her friend, and this one — feisty as all hell.

'You didn't,' said Greg, choking on his wine.

'No, I stopped her,' said Jono, fondly patting his wife's thigh.

'But, get this,' cried Roz around a mouthful of brie and cracker. 'It was genius, if I do say so myself. For decorations we made lanterns out of hundreds of bags of salt and vinegar chips. It took frickin' hours.'

'What did you do with all the chips?' Bridget gasped. 'Surely, you didn't eat them!'

'Nah.' Jono grinned. 'There're only so many salt and vinegar chips one family can consume. We dropped them off at the homeless shelter. Not exactly nutritious fare but . . . Actually it was a win-win from a tax point of view. We can write the chips off, because they were for a job, and then I reckon we'll be able to claim a tax credit on them too.'

'I'm not sure I follow,' said Bridget.

'Cos they were a donation, see,' Jono explained.

'Oh,' said Bridget, not certain she did, but cognisant that if there was a way to work the system in his favour, then Jono would be all over it. Legal shmegal.

'You know, I was thinking last night how much I miss Lucy,' said Roz suddenly.

'Why?' asked Bridget, surprised. 'I mean, not that I don't, too. What was special about last night, though?'

'I don't know . . . maybe because it was such a bitch of an event, but something about it made me hanker after the early days, you know, before Lucy had the girls, and she used to help us out. She would have had those weedy boys wrapped around her little finger. I miss just being able to call her up, you know. She was always my go-to good-time friend.'

Bridget knew she'd never been anyone's party girl, but, still, it hurt to have it spelt out.

'We all miss them, luvvie,' said Jono, putting his arm around Roz. 'Have to say, though, I don't miss the drama.'

Bridget would have argued Roz and Jono, always such big presences, were the ones most likely to bring the drama to a situation.

'I know what you mean,' said Greg. 'I loved those guys just as much as anyone, but I always used to wonder what minefield I'd be walking into this time.'

'Did you?' exclaimed Bridget. 'You never told me that.'

'Yes, I did,' he said. 'You just never wanted to listen. There was always a scene with one of the kids. And it used to do my head in seeing Lucy pull Tristan's strings. Like he was some kind of freakin' puppet.'

'Yeah, can't say I miss Zachariah, either,' said Jono.

Bridget knew he was expecting her to agree with him. But, even now, she couldn't bring herself to be that openly disloyal to Lucy.

'This is nice, though, huh?' said Jono. 'Us four.'

'Uh-huh,' said Roz. 'And without Lucy always in the middle, complicating everything, you and I are definitely closer, Bridge.'

'True.' Bridget squeezed her hand.

Typical Roz: took the wind out of your sails one minute, and then love-bombed you the next.

'I'm just so terrified of bumping into her.'

'C'mon, B,' said Jono. 'Grow a pair. You don't have anything to feel bad about. No one here was to blame for it all going tits up on Hine's.'

'Weren't we? I don't know what to think any more.'

The others looked at her with consternation. Bridget was aware her words upset the unofficially sanctioned version of events. She hadn't even known she was going to say it, but it was the truth: she didn't know what to think. Picturing Skye's sad, grubby little face in the playground the other day, she was reminded of the incident at Mermaids' Cove, how dismissive Lucy had been of Skye afterwards, how defensive. And sitting there, in her living room, with her husband and friends, the memories of their pear-shaped holiday chafed at her.

Chapter Thirty

January
Day Five

'Has anyone seen my husband?' Roz asked, entering. No, Bridget corrected herself, *making an entrance* into the kitchen.

Roz was wearing some kind of tasselled orange robe, a hot pink terry-towelling turban on her head. Bridget couldn't decide whether she looked marvellous or insane. She was in awe that even after all these years, Roz could still be relied on to rock out the most over-the-top looks. Only now, instead of thrifting, Roz shopped at eye-wateringly expensive boutiques.

From the top of the antiquated stepladder she was perched on, Bridget watched as the dust motes Roz's arrival had stirred up gradually resettled.

'Uh-uh,' said Lucy, slowly shaking her head. Contrary to the explosion of noise and colour that was Roz, Lucy seemed to be moving in infuriatingly slow motion. Mindfulness in action, figured Bridget.

'I like your . . . er . . .' said Tristan, who was standing at the foot of the ladder, holding it steady.

'Muumuu. It's called a muumuu. And thanks, I'll take that.' Roz rubbed her eyes with the back of her hand. 'That light's brutal.'

'It's always brightest in here around now,' said Bridget. 'Just before lunch.'

'Fuck me. It can't be that time already. I swear I've only had an hour's sleep.'

'I haven't even been to bed yet,' Bridget admitted.

'Seriously,' said Roz, 'what time did I peel off?'

'Seven a.m., maybe.'

'I don't know how you're still standing! What are you two doing anyway?'

'Nothing,' said Bridget quickly, already regretting having confided in Roz last night about her attraction for Tristan.

On tiptoes she reached for the old-fashioned kitchen scales, wedged in behind some Agee jars on the top shelf of the pantry.

'We thought we'd try making pizza on the barbeque,' explained Tristan.

Bridget passed the scales to him, skipping the last couple of rungs and landing, with what she hoped was a balletic thud, in front of him.

'Wow,' he said, holding up a black finger. 'These can't have been used any time this century.'

'I'm going to get the dough under way,' Bridget told Roz. 'And then we thought we'd head to the mansion.'

'How can you think about going anywhere?' groaned Roz. 'In fact, how can you think about anything?'

'You know me,' said Bridget. 'Action stations.'

As if for confirmation, she looked to Tristan, but he'd already wandered outside. Through the French doors, Bridget watched him mirror Lucy's eagle pose, leaning in for a kiss as he balanced on one leg.

'What a pair of show-offs,' said Roz. 'So, you've got no idea where Jono is? The kids want to go to the beach and I can't face it.'

'No, I haven't seen Greg either. After you went to bed my conscience got the better of me and I went down to the beach to wake him. I know he made it back to the house but after that I'm not sure. I assume he's still sleeping it off somewhere. Jono, too, probably.'

'So, what do you reckon, Rozzy,' asked Lucy, coming though the French doors, Tristan following. 'We're keen for an excursion.'

Bridget looked at Roz. 'C'mon. Time's running out on our holiday.'

'All right, all right. You win.'

'Great, we'll go get ready,' said Lucy, taking Tristan's hand.

Roz rolled her eyes. 'My arse, that's what they're off to do.'

Bridget pretended not to hear her. 'Thanks. For agreeing, I mean. I know it's the last thing you fancy, but it feels like we need to resurrect the holiday somehow.'

'You worry too much, Bridge,' said Roz, gently kneading her shoulder.

Bridget had actually thought she was quite relaxed but under the insistent pressure she became aware of a tight band running down either side of her neck.

'Now, where are those husbands of ours?' Roz stopped the massage as abruptly as she'd started it. 'I'll be buggered if I'm going to do everything while they get off scot-free.'

Muumuu swirling behind her, she strode out the French doors.

Bridget measured out the yeast. She was mixing in the olive oil when Roz reappeared.

'Found them! They were passed out on a couple of bean bags round the front of the house. Sort of hidden behind that big pōhutukawa. It was the noise that gave them away. Like a couple of freight trains bearing down on you. I was going to wake the bastards. But I decided to leave them be.'

Bridget smiled. 'That's not like you.'

'Tell me about it. Self-sacrifice is usually more your style. Don't you worry, though, I'm already planning how I'm going to redeem the brownie points.'

'Well, you haven't actually done anything yet.'

Roz seemed momentarily affronted and then burst out laughing.

'True! Quick, gimme a job before I change my mind.'

'I know the kids should organise their own stuff but it would be so much faster and simpler if you and I just do it.'

'Lead the way.'

Bridget hadn't actually ventured into the bunkroom for the last couple of days. She looked around with disgust.

It was as if someone had tossed the place. Towels and togs lay in wet, sandy piles. Sticky bowls bore the traces of old cereal, dried rock hard now. Not one bed even close to what you'd describe as made. A box of Lego had been upturned across the middle of the floor.

Bridget cursed as she trod on Darth Vader's small masked head. She bent to pick up a clump of dry, yellowy crumbs. They were everywhere. She'd assumed it was food of some description, but it smelt too chemical. In the far corner of the room an old couch had been turned into a kind of hut; the stuffing from the squabs spilling out. That must be what it was. With a shudder, she flicked the couch innards onto the floor.

'What a fucking pigsty,' said Roz from behind her.

'Yup.'

Bridget nudged a damp towel with her foot, revealing the sunblock, lid missing, a goopy trail right through Abigail's bag. She added it to the growing list of things in her head to deal with later. Putting the lid back on, she thought she detected a slight movement under the duvet heaped on the furthest top bunk.

'Who's there?' she said, throwing it back.

Huddled underneath was Zachariah, a look of disquiet on his face.

'What are you doing hiding under here? You must be cooking!'

He slid his hand between the mattress and his belly.

'What have you got there, Zachariah?' asked Roz.

'Nothing.'

He rolled away from them towards the wall.

'I'm sure he was doing something he wasn't supposed to be,' Bridget said to Roz, once they were out of earshot.

'Probably, but there's not much we can do about it, is there? No way am I saying anything to Lucy. Not after the other day.'

'I guess so,' said Bridget, unable to shake the sense they had caught Zachariah *in flagrante*.

'Anyway, let's get this show on the road, eh? Before I change my mind!'

Roz handed Bridget a drink bottle. She was turning on the tap to fill it up when the girls traipsed in.

'Can we go for a swim?' asked Paris.

'Please,' echoed Abigail. 'Please, Mum.'

'No,' said Roz. 'We're getting ready to visit the mansion.'

'We could go by ourselves,' said Paris. 'At swimming lessons, I can do ten laps without stopping.'

'I can do eleven,' said Abigail. 'How many can you do, Skye?'

'I'm not sure,' said Skye, looking at the floor.

'No,' said Roz. 'Don't even think about it.'

'Not fair,' whined Paris. 'You're always saying what good swimmers we are.'

'Not good enough to swim without an adult watching.'

Chapter
Thirty-one

October
Sunday

Bridget fumbled her way down the hall, caught in that soupy wilderness between sleep and wakefulness.

I'm coming, my darling. Mummy's coming.

Like a closed circuit, the words ran through her brain on repeat.

The trick was to get to Abigail before she fully woke up; before her screams woke the rest of the house.

From the dim glow of that ridiculous llama nightlight, Bridget saw she hadn't been quick enough. Abigail was sitting up, bed covers in a heap on the floor, her body wracked with sobs.

'It's all right, sweetheart. Mummy's here now.'

She picked up the duvet, draping it over the small, shaking form, and sat on the edge of the bed. Looking down at her naked breasts, hanging heavy and free, she wished she'd grabbed a dressing gown. Silly, given her only audience was Abigail, but she felt exposed.

'You were probably just cold, hey. It can wake you up, give you a fright.'

'No,' wept Abigail. 'It wasn't that. It was the dream. The bad dream. I had it again. I couldn't breathe.'

'Oh, darling. That's no good. You poor thing. Poor little sausage. C'mon, close your eyes, sweetheart. The best thing is to try and get back to sleep.'

'No! No, I don't want to close my eyes. It might come back.'

'What might come back?'

'The thing in my dream. The thing that watches me when I can't breathe.'

Bridget sighed. This was not going to be a quick resettle. She stood up.

'No, don't go! Don't leave me!'

'I'm not. I'm not going anywhere. I'm just making room.'

Lifting Abigail's head up with one hand, she pulled the bottom pillow out with the other.

'Scoot over.'

Hardly enough space for a nine-year-old girl, let alone a middle-aged woman, thought Bridget, her face in Abigail's hair.

God, she'd better not have nits. She hadn't checked in a while.

'Ssh now, darling, Mummy's here. Try to go back to sleep.'

As Bridget waited for the sobs to subside, she fought off her own somnolence. Each time she judged it safe to move, though, Abigail flinched.

Finally, inhalations deepened to the snuffles of sleep, and, painstaking inch by painstaking inch, Bridget was able to extricate herself.

It was kind of like the meditation at the end of a yoga class, Bridget thought, lowering the toes of her left foot to the ground, this piecemeal restoration of life to each body part.

Back in her own bed, Greg reached a clumsy hand across her chest.

'S'everything all right?' he asked groggily.

'It is now,' said Bridget, trying not to sound resentful. What was the point? She had always been the one to get up when the kids called out in the night. 'One of her dreams. I'll tell you about it in the morning.'

Lying there, Bridget listened to all the noises you were never aware of amid the life and activity of the day: the hum of the fridge, the creak of the wooden joinery, the scuttling of small, unwanted creatures. It was such a lonely time, everything scarier, more worrisome in the dark. No wonder children panicked when they stirred in the small hours.

Almost as if to deliberately torture herself, Bridget made a mental inventory of what was amiss: Abigail's nightmares (disturbing), house (a mess, again), work (still behind), marriage (okay, not great), Lucy (disastrous). She let her mind run wider: child pornographer (concerning but she was keen not to buy into the hysteria). And then wider again: climate change (utterly terrifying).

Bridget didn't like to think of herself as a pessimist, but in truth she was more glass half empty than glass half full. And the bitch about having a brain that plagued you with worst-case scenarios was you always had to consider the possibility things might play out as feared.

The next morning, she awoke with a feeling of surprise. She couldn't even recall falling asleep. She rubbed her eyes. Beside her Greg scrolled through his phone.

'Any news?'

'Just the same depressing shit,' he said. 'Basically, humankind's headed for disaster.'

'Don't. I was awake half the night, tormenting myself with what-ifs. What do we do if the bees die out? What do we do if the world runs out of water?'

'Personally, I find counting sheep more conducive to a good night's rest than apocalypses and dystopias.'

Bridget laughed. 'I think Abigail's nightmare sent me down a grim path.'

'Not another one.'

'Don't you remember? I was up with her for a good hour.'

'What do you reckon it's about?'

'I don't know. I keep thinking maybe something happened . . .'

'Like what?'

'I don't know. I might try and talk to her again.'

'I still think it's a phase,' said Greg, drawing the curtains open. 'You don't want to go putting ideas in her head. Wow, what a pearler of a day. I bet it's a millpond out there.'

Bridget sighed inwardly. She knew what was coming next.

'Perfect for a fish . . .'

Bridget didn't say anything. She was buggered if she was going to make it easy for him.

'Would you mind, Bridge? I haven't been out for ages.'

'That's not true, you went in the holidays. Oh, I guess it doesn't matter. We haven't got anything on. What time would you be back?'

'Lemme check the wind and tide.'

In the end Greg took Jackson, too.

'We'll be home by five. With fish for dinner!'

'This is nice, isn't it?' Bridget stroked Abigail's head as the door slammed. 'Just us girls. What should we do?'

'We could have lunch at the mall. Get our nails done.'

'Abigail,' Bridget laughed. 'When have you ever had your nails done?'

'That's what they always do in the movies, on girls' days out.'

'Oh my God, you've been brainwashed by Hollywood. How did I let this happen? If that's what you really want to do, sweetheart . . . it's such a beautiful day, though. It seems a waste to be inside when the sun is shining.'

They reached a compromise: a walk on the beach, then back to make scones with cream and jam for lunch, followed by a home pampering session.

Down by the water, as Abigail danced with the waves, Bridget chastised herself. Ahead of her lay a lovely day with her baby, a delicious family dinner, and yet, try as she might, she couldn't shake this sense of unease. It clung to her like a limp anorak.

Abigail slowed to draw something in the sand with a stick she'd found.

'What is it, honey?'

'My dream,' said Abigail, perfectly matter of fact.

'Oh.'

Bridget had been trying to work her way round to the subject without being too obvious about it and now Abigail had delivered it right into her lap. She looked more closely at the crude sketch.

'So,' she said, pointing with her foot to what appeared to be a face, 'this is you, and . . .'

'No, silly,' laughed Abigail. 'That's him.'

'Who?' asked Bridget, careful not to let her anxiety colour the question, mindful of Greg's words. 'Who's him?'

'The thing. You know, that watches me.'

'How do you know it's a him?'

'I dunno. I just do.'

'Is it someone you know?' *Gently, gently*, Bridget cautioned herself.

'No, Mum. I don't know any actual monsters.'

Bridget let her breath out. 'No, course not. So where are you then?'

'Here,' Abigail said, placing the stick on what looked like a bunch of scribble.

'Right . . .' said Bridget, none the wiser.

'There's something over my head, 'member. I can't breathe.' Giggling, Abigail threw the stick away, and took off running down the beach.

Taking one last look at the big, round face, the furious scratching out next to it, Bridget only wished she felt as carefree.

Thanks to Abigail's zealous mixing, the scones resembled small bricks.

Bridget scrubbed at the lumps of gluey flour that were now stuck, concrete-like, to the bench and floor. Cooking with children might sound like fun, but in practice, *yeah, not so great.*

She was just wondering what chaos was afoot in the bathroom, where Abigail was assembling everything they needed for their 'beauty salon', when her phone rang.

'Hello,' she said, tapping the receiver button with her elbow without looking at the caller's name. 'Hang on.' She pushed the speaker button with the side of her little finger. 'Sorry, my hands are all mucky.'

'Hello, Bridget, it's Sina.'

There was an echo-iness and Bridget pictured Sina standing in her vast kitchen with its immaculate granite island.

'Oh, hi Sina, sorry about that. How are you?'

'I'm okay. I wanted to talk to you about something, actually.'

Bridget had hoped the coolness she'd detected in Sina's voice was just the line, but at those words she felt her heart sink.

'Sure, is everything all right?'

'Not really. I haven't been able to stop thinking about what you said. How basically you accused my husband of being a paedophile.'

'What? No, I didn't.'

'That's effectively what you were saying.'

'I'm so sorry you took it like that. That wasn't my intention. I suppose I just feel like we all have to play it safe at the moment.'

'My husband would never touch a child. He's a partner in a major law firm, for God's sake. How would you feel if I refused to let Ivy stay at yours?'

'I guess I'd be sad, but I would hope that in the current climate I'd understand, too. I'm sorry, Sina, it's just I've never even met your husband.'

'Well, if you had, you'd know he'd be incapable of such a despicable thing.'

'I'm sure he's . . . Look, this is just a big misunderstanding.'

'The thing is, Bridget, I'm not sure I can be friends with someone who goes around defiling my husband's reputation like that.'

'Hold on, Sina, I haven't been going around doing anything.'

'You need to watch yourself, Bridget.'

There was a click.

Rattled, Bridget berated herself for not having tread more carefully. She should have known Sina would lose it at the merest suggestion her perfect family could be anything but.

God, the list of people she had to avoid at school was growing by the day. Maybe she should drop some flowers around by way of apology.

Picking up the bowl of cream, she spooned some into her mouth, before grabbing the jam and tipping it all over the top.

It looks like blood splatter, she thought, taking a spatula and dragging it through the mixture.

She licked it clean, then dragged it through again.

Chapter Thirty-two

January Day Five

While everyone else went on ahead, Bridget stopped at the sign.

It took her a moment to decipher the cursive text.

Apparently, the mansion had been built in 1833 by James Thomas, a missionary who'd gotten the local chief's daughter pregnant. After the church shunned him, Thomas took up whaling to support his new family, his success on the ships eventually funding this grand building.

Tragically, however, a mad sealer, jealous of Thomas' good fortune, clubbed his wife and daughter, Hine, to death when he was away at sea. Never remarrying or returning to the church, evidently Thomas cut a sad and lonely figure, rattling around his vast family home until his eventual death, aged eighty-three.

'So, that's how it came to be known as Hine's,' murmured Bridget.

'Huh?'

Bridget whirled around. Tristan was leaning against one of the colonnades lining the path to the front door. She blushed. Had he been watching her?

'Sorry, just talking to myself.'

'No need to be sorry. What did you find out?'

'Oh, it's a heartbreaking story. The man who built this place lost everyone who mattered to him.'

'I guess that explains it then.'

'Explains what?'

He shrugged. 'The eerie feeling. I had to get out of there. Get some fresh air.'

Bridget wished she could shake this newfound awkwardness she felt whenever she was in Tristan's vicinity. To have known someone all this time and suddenly see them in a completely different light, and not just anyone, her husband's best friend, her best friend's husband. She knew it was wrong, but at the same time she felt more vital than she had in years; aflutter with the possibility her lust might be reciprocal.

She wanted to say: *Tell me to follow you down to the beach. Tell me all the ways in which you'll take me. Here against this pillar. There on the ground behind that shrub. Ask me if I want it, too.*

What she said was: 'I haven't even made it inside yet.'

But Tristan had already turned away, towards Willow, tearing out through the front door.

'Dad, Dad, Daddy! I bored. I can't find any the big kids. Dad, Dad, Daddy, I need to go wee-wees.'

'Do you now?'

'I suppose I'll check it out then,' Bridget said to Tristan's already retreating back, Willow thrown over his shoulder, wriggling and giggling. 'The mansion, I mean . . .'

In the gloom of the foyer, Bridget blinked. She wiped at her eyes, waiting for them to adjust.

Slowly the heavy velvet drapes and richly coloured tapestries lining the vast space took shape. She stood still, digesting the sweeping staircase, the dense oils in gilt frames.

It all seemed so incongruous, so far removed from modern interpretations of beach-life — the nautical blue and white, the shell-themed art. Incongruous, she thought, but no less a folly.

Bridget could hear voices from the next floor. The howl of Roz's laughter.

She tracked the sound upstairs to the master bedroom. The main bedroom, she corrected herself. Such a sexist term. As if it was a man's domain alone, when in most heterosexual couples the bedroom was primarily the woman's turf; she who picked out the bed linen, she whose clothes and shoes monopolised the closet.

And then there was the master–slave relationship. *Yes, Massa. No, Massa.* Bridget, who had watched her share of films set in America's southern states in the eighteenth and nineteenth centuries, winced at the image.

Usually in historic homes the rooms were roped off, viewable only from the doorway. But Roz and Lucy were actually lying on the four-poster bed, writhing with hilarity, while Greg and Jono put on a kind of peekaboo show, jumping in and out from behind the large chinoiserie screen in the corner.

'What on earth are they doing?'

'God knows,' said Lucy, tears rolling down her cheeks.

'How rude,' said Greg in a ridiculous falsetto. 'Isn't it obvious? We're seducing you.'

'Yes,' said Jono, trailing a silk cord across his stout trunk. 'We're the most beautiful courtesans for miles around. Our waists . . .' and he paused to do a little shimmy, 'are the tiniest in all the land.'

'Stop, stop,' cried Lucy. 'I'm going to wet myself.'

Bridget smiled. It was never easy to join in on the end of a joke.

'This place is something else, huh?'

'Too ostentatious for my tastes,' said Jono. 'I'm just a simple guy.'

'My arse, you are,' Roz snorted. 'More like a pretentious twat.'

Jono advanced on his wife, spinning the cord lasso-style. 'Watch it, *mon amour.*'

'Where are the kids?' Bridget asked.

'They were here a minute ago,' said Greg.

'I think the high-class act was a little too much for them,' Lucy laughed.

'I saw Willow outside with Tristan,' said Bridget. 'But I haven't heard boo from the others since we arrived.'

She wandered into the hall, checking each of the bedrooms. What must it have been like to live here? Seeing out your days in this hulking monument to a family that almost was.

With no sign of life on the first floor, she headed back downstairs. Off to the right of the foyer was a room with the highest stud she'd ever seen; a table big enough to seat two dozen at its centre. Bridget was admiring the wallpaper when she heard a faint *thump, thump,* coming from the direction of what she assumed was the kitchen.

Thump, thump. Louder now.

She looked around. Copper pots and kettles hung from butcher's hooks above the range. On the other side of the large weathered work table was a door. She guessed it led to a butler's pantry.

'Hello,' she called, trying the handle.

She felt pressure from the other side and stepped back just in time to avoid being knocked over by a furious ball of boyish energy.

'Where is she? I'm going to get her,' fumed Jackson. 'That little bitch!'

'Hey, don't talk about your sister like that.'

'It's true, though,' said Jackson. 'It was her idea to shut us in there.'

'Yeah,' said Earl. 'They locked the door and then they took off.'

'There you are,' said Lucy, putting an arm round Zachariah.

The other adults pressed in next to her.

'Where are the girls?' asked Roz.

'No one seems to know,' said Bridget. 'They were playing some kind of game of hide and seek . . .'

'No, we weren't,' interrupted Jackson.

'Yeah,' said Earl. 'We were exploring and they thought it would be funny to trap us.'

'Maybe they're with Tristan,' said Greg.

Outside, on the front lawn, Tristan was whirling Willow around by her hands.

'Have you seen the girls, hon?' Lucy asked.

'What was that?' he said, coming to a stop. 'Wow, I forgot how dizzy that can make you. Especially after a night . . .'

'The girls,' said Roz. 'We can't find the girls.'

'Nope, I've only seen Bridget and Willow since I came out here.'

'They must be hiding inside somewhere,' said Bridget.

'I'll check the formal garden out back,' said Greg.

'Abigail!'

'Skye!'

'Paris!'

Their calls resounded about the house.

Bridget returned upstairs. Looking under beds, in wardrobes, behind curtains.

Through a window at the end of the hall, she spotted Greg, his hands forming a peak across his forehead, scanning the neat rows of box-hedging.

'Anything?' she asked, meeting up with Jono in the foyer.

'Nada.'

'Where could they be?' Bridget felt the panic start to kick in, as if it was only ever just in abeyance, lying dormant until the time was ripe.

'Search me,' he said.

'I don't think they're here,' she said. 'We need to split up.'

'Hang on, love,' said Greg, coming back inside. 'They're probably just . . .'

'Greg, no one even really knows how long they've been gone.'

'We're on an island, Bridget, they can't have gone far.'

'Exactly, Greg, an island, there are dangers everywhere.'

'I'm with you, Bridge,' said Roz. 'They're probably up a tree or something but the sooner we find them the better.'

Bridget gave her a grateful smile.

The women decided to make their way to the farmhouse, while Greg and Jono took the clifftop path beyond the mansion, and Tristan stayed put with the boys and Willow in case the girls turned up.

'Keep in radio contact,' Bridget called to the men. As soon as they were gone, she turned to Lucy and Roz: 'I know exactly where we need to head.'

'Aren't we going back to the house?' asked Lucy.

'They won't be there,' said Bridget. 'I reckon they'll have made a beeline for Don's. It's like he's got some sort of weird hold over them.'

'Honestly, Bridge,' said Lucy. 'I think you're the one who's obsessed.'

Bridget ignored her. 'Abigail! Skye! Paris!' she shouted into the silence.

The only response was a gull, high up in the sky. *Huoh, huoh.*

It seemed to hover above them for a moment.

Chapter
Thirty-three

October
Monday

As usual the café near the school was full of school mums.

There was the odd father, but most would be grabbing a coffee to go, having dropped their kids en route to some bland office building in the CBD.

Considering what it cost to buy a house on the Point these days, it never ceased to amaze Bridget how many women could afford not to work. Of course, there were plenty who held down full-time jobs, but they were the ones who double-parked on the yellow lines in front of the school gate, already indicating to pull back out into the traffic before their offspring had even shut the door.

As for those with a nanny or an au pair, you didn't see them at all, until they popped up at some school fundraiser, bidding two grand for a weekend at someone's poxy bach. Guilt money, she'd heard a mother on the Parents' Association sneeringly call it.

'A trim flat white, please,' she said to the barista. 'Oh, and two stamps.'

A look of irritation crossed his face.

'You forgot last week,' she said, handing him her coffee card. Arrogant little twat.

She was relieved to see the others had managed to nab their usual table in the corner, well away from the toy box where the younger mothers with their rowdy, sticky-fingered toddlers congregated.

It was a standing appointment: every second Monday after drop-off, she, Moana, Therese and Sophie met for coffee. Having only just caught up at class drinks on Thursday, today's gathering felt less than pressing. Still, they'd known each other since their eldest were in year zero, and while it was a friendship that had been borne out of circumstance, it was now sustained by a genuine fondness for each other.

It never failed to amaze Bridget how the shared act of motherhood could be such a unifying force, and yet conversely, she thought, recalling her unpleasant encounter with Sina, so divisive.

Pulling out a chair, she felt a pair of hands clasp her around the waist.

She smelt Roz before she saw her. Roz had been wearing the same heady perfume, her 'signature scent', for as long as Bridget had known her. It could be overwhelming first thing in the morning.

'Hey Roz,' said Moana, shuffling around the table. 'Join us for a coffee?'

'I'm meant to be getting a green smoothie on the run,' said Roz. 'But, all right then, twist my arm. You know me, never had any willpower, not when it comes to the four Cs: coffee, chardonnay, chocolate . . .' she paused for effect, 'cocaine.'

Everyone shrieked with laughter.

Oh God, thought Bridget, *Roz is in one of her show-offy moods.*

'Great,' said Therese. 'Now you two are here, maybe we can talk about something else. I can't bear to think about the situation with this father any more.'

'I know what you mean,' said Bridget. 'I felt like I was going mad at soccer on Saturday.'

'It's getting a bit like that, huh,' said Moana. 'Roz, I bet you got up to something more exciting over the weekend. Regale us poor plebs with your tales of A-list parties.'

Bridget was used to people being fascinated by what Roz and Jono did for a living. She couldn't blame them; the way Roz talked about it you'd think they were basically being paid to large it up night after night.

Having heard how Friday's event had really panned out, Bridget wasn't surprised when Roz conveniently glossed over the bratty clients, the hundreds of salt and vinegar chip packets they'd fashioned into lanterns.

Roz never saw the need to disabuse anyone of their inflated notion of how glamorous it all was.

'Oooh, who was there?' asked Sophie. 'Anybody famous?'

'Let me see,' said Roz, 'where do I start?'

Bridget knew none of the invited big names had made an appearance, but Roz managed to dredge up a few titbits that satisfied the others' thirst for celebrity gossip.

'I want your life,' said Moana.

'You're welcome to it,' Roz chortled. 'I'm knackered.'

'So, Bridget,' Moana asked, 'how was your weekend? Apart from Saturday morning soccer misery?'

'It was okay. Actually, I wanted to ask you guys your advice about something. I know we're not meant to be talking about what's going on around here at the moment, but . . .'

'We're listening,' said Therese, sitting up straighter.

Therese was studying to be a counsellor; Bridget wondered if this was her professional stance.

She told them how Abigail had been invited for a sleepover at Ivy's and she'd said no.

'I tried not to make a big deal of it. I just said I didn't think sleepovers were such a good idea at the moment. Then, yesterday, Ivy's mum, Sina, rings me. Terribly upset. Accusing me of besmirching her husband's name.'

'Remind me who Sina is again?' said Roz.

'You know,' said Sophie, 'the flash one. Drives a Porsche Cayenne.'

'Did I do the right thing?' asked Bridget. 'I feel awful.'

'You absolutely made the right call,' said Moana.

'I mean you don't want to deliberately upset anyone,' said Therese. 'But we all have to put our children first.'

'Yeah, I don't envy you, though,' said Sophie. 'I wouldn't want to get on that lot's bad side.'

'Which lot?' asked Moana.

'That group of mothers with the fake boobs,' replied Sophie.

'Now I know who you're talking about.' Roz clapped her hands. 'The Real Housewives of Point Heed!'

'If it makes you feel any better, I think I put my foot in it this morning,' said Moana. 'You know Sebastian's mums, Kath and Liz? Well, we were talking about the pornographer and how dreadful it was and I said, at least you don't have to worry about your partner. I thought they'd laugh, but they just looked at me like I'd said something totally inappropriate. It does make you think twice, though, doesn't it? Somewhere in Point Heed some poor woman has to wrap her head around the fact that the father of her children gets his thrills from watching kiddy porn. I can't even begin to fathom what I'd do if I ever found out Ben was into that shit.'

'Do you think it would make a difference,' asked Sophie, 'if it was boys or girls? Or how young they were?'

'I don't think in the end it would really matter,' said Bridget. 'Regardless of the details, I don't know how you'd ever get past the picture of your husband sitting at his laptop, wanking over children.'

'Oh, don't,' said Therese. 'It doesn't bear thinking about. Hey, make sure you get your menfolk to put their names on that Facebook page.'

'Yeah, some dads were talking about it at soccer,' said Bridget.

'Have you looked at it?' asked Sophie. 'It's only been up a few days and there must already be a couple of hundred names on there. I'll tell you who isn't, though . . .'

'Who?' asked Bridget. 'I don't know if Greg even knows about it yet. So, I doubt he's on there.'

'Yes,' said Sophie, 'but we all know Greg's straight-up. No, that Frank guy.'

'Frank guy?'

'Yeah, you know. Wears his pants so high they kinda flap about his ankles?'

'Oh, I know him,' said Moana. 'His daughter's in Kahu's class. He's okay.'

'I'm not so sure,' Sophie said, and she dropped her whispery voice even lower. 'He's the only dad that ever volunteers for the parent-reading programme.'

'Maybe he just likes reading,' said Bridget.

Roz stood up. 'Right, I'm going to have to love you and leave you, ladies. Places to be, people to see, yada yada.'

She blew them all a kiss.

'God, she's a riot,' said Moana.

'Hmm . . .' said Bridget, watching her old friend hustle out the door, as hastily as if something, or someone, was on her tail.

Chapter
Thirty-four

January
Day Five

Bridget was no artist, but if you'd asked her to draw a picture of how she imagined Don's house, she'd have selected a piece of charcoal and sketched the dark outlines of a derelict cottage. Somewhere the beast in the fairy tale might call home. Somewhere neglected, evil even.

Jono had said Don's house was located at the end of the valley, and, as they descended into it, Bridget readied herself for what they would find.

'Abigail! Skye! Paris!'

Like some kind of terrible chorus, every few seconds one of them took up the cry.

Bridget's voice was growing hoarse and her knees ached. They always did on the downs. There was a tightness in her hips. She drove her knuckles into the muscle around the bone, the pain momentarily offsetting the panic.

Please, she prayed, *don't let him have hurt them. I promise . . .* she searched for what she could offer some higher being in return for the girls' safety. *Do with me what you will. Take me instead! Give them back to us in one piece and I'll dedicate the rest of my life to charitable acts.*

So certain was Bridget that they would find ugliness at Don's, it took her a spell to notice the change in their surrounds.

Where the land had felt dehydrated at the valley's entrance, the foliage scraggly, now there was a lushness. Native flowers sprouted prettily from rocks that appeared to have been almost artistically placed alongside a small cheery stream. Little birds dipped and dove above them, feasting on the rich insect life. And behind a cluster of graceful palms, lay Don's house. Like something from a storybook, yes, but not the hovel where the baddie dwells.

Low and unassuming, the white weatherboards were the perfect foil to the red tin of the roof, the orange brick of the chimney. Although it boasted neither the grandeur of the mansion, nor the solidness of the farmhouse, of the three it was quite the loveliest.

Everywhere Bridget looked it was evident this was the residence of someone immensely house-proud: a pair of boots neatly lined up at the front door; window boxes planted with sweet williams; a wicker rocking chair on the porch.

She recalled Zachariah's description: *dead sheep, maggots, skeleton.*

It was funny, she usually mistrusted everything to come out his mouth, and yet, on this, she'd been happy to swallow his account, hook, line and sinker.

That's because it fitted better with the narrative you'd constructed, a little voice in her head said. *Perhaps*, countered her eternal Doubting Thomas, *but just because Don has good taste doesn't mean his moral compass points due north.*

Pushing past Lucy and Roz, Bridget knocked loudly on the door, the setting of her engagement ring pressing uncomfortably into her clenched fist.

From inside there was the sound of a chair being slowly pushed back, of heavy steps approaching.

Bridget steeled herself as the door swung open.

'Ladies,' said Don, a look of surprise on his face. 'To what do I owe the pleasure?'

Before Bridget could say anything, Lucy spoke: 'Sorry to bother you, Don. We've lost the girls. We thought you might have seen them?'

'The girls?'

'Yes,' said Bridget. 'Abigail? Skye? Paris? Are they here?'

'The girls,' he repeated. 'Here?'

He gripped the handle of the door as if to steady himself.

'Are you all right?' asked Lucy. 'You look a little faint.'

'I'm okay. I just have these peculiar turns from time to time. Sorry, ladies, I don't think I can help you. I haven't actually left the house this afternoon. I'm pretty sure I haven't seen the girls since the other day at Mermaids' Cove.'

'Okay, thanks anyway,' said Lucy, starting to turn away.

'Actually, do you mind if we come in?' asked Roz. 'Just to be sure. Check the girls aren't hiding somewhere.'

Bridget mentally high-fived Roz.

Don didn't seem entirely thrilled at the prospect but he stepped to one side.

'As you can see,' he said, gesturing around with a fleshy arm, 'there aren't exactly many places to hide.'

The cottage was essentially a large room, a potbelly stove in one corner, an immaculately made divan that presumably doubled as a bed in the other. There was a mug, a bowl and a spoon draining on the bench, a cast-iron pan of something savoury simmering on the stove. In the middle of the table was a jam jar with a bunch of the wild flowers they'd spotted growing in the valley poking out of it.

Considering the humbleness of its environs, the turntable sitting on the shelf above the old dresser seemed incongruously hi-tech. The shelf also held a large collection of LPs. Tacked to the wall behind were a bunch of concert posters, a map of the States detailing Route 66, and a creased black and white photo of a woman cuddling a young child.

Overall, the effect was charming and yet utterly lonely.

'How long did you say they've been missing?' asked Don. His eyes, initially foggy, now alert.

'We didn't,' said Bridget.

'A good hour. Maybe two,' said Lucy. 'We were visiting the mansion and everyone just figured they were off exploring somewhere.'

'An hour . . . that's not good.'

It was almost as if he were talking to himself.

'We thought they might have made their way here,' said Roz. 'They're infatuated with your horses.'

'Have you checked the farmhouse?' he asked, pulling on a pair of tramping boots.

'No,' said Bridget. 'We thought it made more sense to come here first.'

Don gave her a look she couldn't decipher.

'Okay,' he said, grabbing some binoculars and a cap from a hook on the back of the door, 'you three head for the farmhouse. I'll meet you there.'

He strode outside. They watched as he cut across the stream and made for the hills to their left.

Bridget's phone rang. Greg.

'Tell me you've found them,' she said.

'No,' he said. 'I take it you haven't either?'

She didn't bother answering.

'We retraced our steps to the mansion. The kids are hungry. They're getting scratchy. Tristan and I are going to bring them back.'

'What about the girls, though?'

'Jono will stay. Just in case. But we've scoured the area. They're not here. We'll see you soon.'

Bridget relayed what Greg had said. Neither Lucy nor Roz responded.

What was there to say?

Chapter Thirty-five

October Monday

Straight to work! Bridget beat out the words with her feet. *No tidying. No social media. Straight to work!* Number 43, number 45. Almost home.

My husband would never touch a child. Number 57, 59. *Stop that train. You need to watch yourself. Push Sina away. Shoo. Shoo. Shoo. Oh no you don't, the train's just getting started. Lucy. Lucy. Choo-choo. God, now you're talking in rhyme!*

She put the key in the door. Her phone pinged. The profile shot showed the familiar bowl of fruit, the fat cigar. 'Fancy a walk?' read the text.

Weird. They'd only just caught up. Roz would never suggest a walk for fun. Had Bridget said something to upset her? She racked her brain.

'Of course. When? xx'

'After school? Faith's babysitting 'cos I'm meant to be working. The kids can all hang out.'

'Perfect. See you at yours.'

The train was getting longer by the minute. Something else to torment herself with.

No, she would build a wall over the top of this new worry. *Brick, brick* . . . Roz didn't sound upset in her texts. She would tie a balloon to it. *Float, float away* . . . Maybe Roz genuinely felt like a walk . . .

Straight to work! Straight to work!

Abigail raced ahead up Roz's drive.

'Paris! Paris!' she yelled, pushing open the door without knocking.

It comforted Bridget to see her daughter so at ease in their friends' home.

'C'mon,' she said to Jackson, who'd been less enthusiastic when she'd told him the plan. 'You and Earl always have fun together.'

'Hello,' she called out.

'Down here.'

At the kitchen bench Roz was heating milk; the sound impossibly loud.

'Just doing hot chocolates. Bloody Faith hasn't turned up yet. Do you want a coffee?'

Greg said Roz and Jono's espresso machine was bigger than the engine of a small car. 'We don't do capsules here. Old-skool styles,' Jono had a habit of saying whenever he started it up. Sometimes he created images in the froth. *Actually, it's the crema.* Greg liked to mimic him. We all have our own little pretensions, she would remind him. *Barbeque, anyone?*

'You know me, no coffee after midday or I'll be up all night.'

'I'm up all night these days anyway. Bloody peri-menopause!'

'Don't, I'm dreading it.'

'Yeah, sweaty tits and a dry fanny, it's a riot!'

As Roz came out from behind the island, Bridget properly registered her outfit: a green satin jumpsuit and purple platform hi-top sneakers.

'Is that what you're wearing walking?'

'Why? What's wrong with it?'

'Nothing, it's just . . .'

'You know me, Bridge, I wouldn't be seen dead in fucking active wear. Not like those women who get around all day in a pair of leggings.'

Bridget looked down at her own attire: cotton drawstring pants and a stripy long-sleeved tee. It wasn't Lycra but it wasn't far off either.

'Can't you find Earl, Jacks?'

Bridget hadn't realised Jackson was still there. Amazing he hadn't made himself scarce at the mere mention of menstruation.

'Earl,' Roz called. 'Jacks is here.'

'Sorry, kiddo,' she said when there was no response. 'He's around here somewhere.'

She disappeared down the hall. Something fierce in her stride.

'What's wrong?' Bridget asked Jackson.

'Nothing,' he said.

'Why are you being so sullen?'

'I'm not.'

'Off,' they heard Roz yelling. 'You've got company. Get off.'

She marched back into the kitchen, a controller in her hand.

'Mum,' said Earl, stomping his feet behind her. 'I hadn't finished my game.'

'I don't care,' said Roz. 'You know the rules.'

'But I was just finishing my round.'

'I don't care, Earl. It's super rude. You have a guest.'

'I was winning and you made me kill myself.'

'Good! I'm glad.'

Earl burst into tears. He swiped at them angrily. Bridget was shocked to see Roz looked on the verge of tears herself. Roz never cried.

'I think both you boys need cheering up, huh? Jackson's been a sad sack the whole way here. If they promise to go kick a ball afterwards, Roz, how about we let them have thirty minutes on the PlayStation?'

When Roz didn't say anything, Bridget took the controller gently from her and passed it to Earl.

'Sorry, sorry,' said Faith, a flurry of long hair and friendship bracelets, her arrival circumventing any further discussion.

Bridget noticed Faith's bare feet were in need of a good scrub. She'd been working off and on for Roz and Jono since the twins were babies. Bridget found her a little flaky but Roz was surprisingly tolerant of her many quirks.

'I was in town and there was the most incredible busker. This guy was juggling watermelons. Watermelons! Have you ever picked one up? They're like seriously heavy.'

'No worries,' Roz said, kissing her on the cheek. 'Bridget and I were going to go for a walk. Are you all right to keep an eye on the four of them?'

'Course. More the merrier. Hi, Bridget.'

Bridget smiled at the young woman. She meant well.

'Sorry about before,' said Roz once they were outside. 'For losing it like that.'

'You don't need to apologise.'

'I don't know what's wrong with me. I never imagined I'd be that kind of a mother.'

'What, the normal kind? It's okay for your children to see you having a bad day. I'm worried about you, though. Is everything okay?'

'You know me, box of birds.'

'When you suggested a walk, I thought maybe I'd done something.'

'God, Bridget, it's not always about you.'

Bridget flinched. 'I know, I just . . .'

'Sorry, I didn't mean it like that.'

'It's fine.'

They were both quiet as they crossed Alders Avenue.

Bridget looked up the hill. There was the bus. Was it really menacing? At the café this morning the others had laughed, said she must have a very vivid imagination when she'd shared her unease about it.

'Actually, Bridge, there is something. I'm just not sure I know how to say it.'

'You can tell me, petal. What's the saying, a problem shared is a . . .'

'Problem halved, I know, I know. But nobody really wants to deal with anyone else's dirty laundry, do they?'

'Our friendship is bigger than that, Roz.'

Roz threw her shoulders back. 'You're right. Remember what I told you on Hine's, about Jono's, um, hobby? Well, he's up to his old tricks again. I thought we were good. An enclave of normality amidst the madness, you know. But ever since I first found out last year, I've been keeping an eye on his search history. Anyway, I checked yesterday and he's back at it.'

'Oh Roz. How long?'

'I dunno. Three weeks maybe.'

'It's not . . .' Bridget couldn't bring herself to say it.

'No. God, no. Just the same harmless shit. It's more that I'd thought we'd moved on.'

Harmless shit. Was it, though? Soft, hardcore; humans, animals;

women, kids: pornography didn't exist in a vacuum. And where exactly would she draw the line, if it was Greg? If it was her husband downloading 'harmless shit'?

'Oh honey, what are you going to do?'

'Christ knows.' Roz laughed. It was a mirthless sound, almost a bark.

'Are you going to confront him?'

'I want to. You know me; I'm hardly one for holding my tongue. But it obviously didn't change anything last time. In some ways I can't really blame him. I'm so not interested in sex these days. I tried for a while, but the truth is I just can't be arsed. Maybe it's better this way. At least he's not going anywhere else for it. Brothels. Tinder. Getting his end off making sexy talk with some poor Filipino woman for a dollar ninety-nine a minute.'

'Are you sure you can live with the dishonesty, though? I don't know if I could bear it.'

'That's how I felt initially. But it's kind of like his whittling. I wish he didn't feel the need, but as long as he keeps it under control, then I suppose I can cope.'

'Well, if you put it like that, then on a scale of husbandly misdemeanours it seems fairly minor.'

'Thanks Bridge.' Roz squeezed her hand. 'I guess I just needed someone to tell me I'm not bloody crazy.'

'Never.'

'There was something else I wanted to talk to you about, too. After I left you guys this morning, I saw Lucy.'

Bridget wondered if she would ever again reach a point where Lucy's name didn't precipitate such dread.

'You did? Where? Did you speak to her?'

'A couple of blocks from the café. Crossing the road. I tried to. I called out her name but she didn't look up. She was far enough away that she might not have heard me but I'm almost positive she did.'

'God, how long's she going to keep avoiding us?'

'Search me. I'll tell you what, though, you know how she used to glide around the place like a fucking ballerina, all erect. Well, this Lucy . . . I dunno, it's like she's broken.'

Chapter
Thirty-six

January
Day Five

'Abigail!'

'Skye!'

'Paris!'

By the time they reached the farmhouse's crackly lawn, they'd ditched any pretence of giving equal weight to the missing girls. Like a broken record stuck on the most harrowing lyric, each could only call her own daughter's name.

Over and over. Again and again.

Somehow Bridget knew they weren't there, but she took the steps to the verandah two at a time anyway, hoping against hope she'd find them huddled around the dining table, three chocolatey faces looking ruefully up at her.

But the kitchen was as they'd left it several hours earlier, and at the sight of the towel Bridget had asked Abigail to put away before they left, still damply draped over the back of a chair, she started to cry.

'Hey,' said Lucy, 'No tears. We'll find them.'

She wrapped her arm around Bridget's waist; it seemed selfish to take comfort when Lucy was in the same situation.

'They're not here,' said Roz. 'I've checked up and down.'

Bridget watched her put a trembling hand on the wall. It was as if Roz had aged in the short time the girls had been missing. Seeing her usually robust and bold friend so rattled shook Bridget out of her own state of helplessness.

'Here,' she said to Roz, pulling her out a chair. 'You sit down. Lucy, why don't you make Roz a cup of tea. Strong with lots of milk and sugar. I'm going to go check the beach. They can't have just disappeared into thin air.'

Bridget jogged along the jetty, willing them to be there, building a castle, three sandy faces turning remorsefully towards her.

However, the bay that had seemed so safe, had been the scene of such fun over the past few days, felt desolate now. And although it was obvious there was no one here, that she was wasting her vocal cords, Bridget returned again to that desperate chorus:

'Abigail! Skye! Paris!'

Looking down at her goosebumpy arms, Bridget saw the weather was changing. While before there had only been relentless blue, now ominous clouds scudded across the sky.

Where are you, my darling? Where are you?

Making her way back over the grass, she heard voices.

Please. Please. Oh God, please.

But it was just the men and the other children.

She ran to Greg, collapsing into his chest, her bravado deserting her as speedily as it had appeared.

'It's okay,' he murmured into her hair.

'How can you say that?' she cried, pulling away from him. 'We've looked everywhere. He must have stashed them someplace. We need to call the police. Before it's too late.'

'Who?' asked Tristan. 'Who's stashed them?'

'Don,' said Lucy, joining them on the verandah. 'Bridget is convinced Don has taken the girls.'

'He must have,' said Bridget. 'He's been after them since that day Abigail got stung by a bee.'

'You need to calm down, honey,' said Greg, taking her by the arm. 'Those are some pretty big accusations you're making.'

'You weren't there. None of you were. But I saw, I saw the way he looked at them.'

Bridget was aware she sounded like a crazy woman, that Tristan was looking at her peculiarly; she was beyond caring, though.

'Are you all blind?' she cried. 'Tell them, Roz. Tell them. I know you've got your suspicions, too.'

Roz shook her head. 'I don't know, Bridge. He didn't seem like a guilty man to me.'

'Jesus Christ, he's got you fooled, too.'

Willow started to cry.

'Skye,' she wailed. 'Want Skye.'

Tristan picked her up.

'I'm with you on the police, though,' said Roz. 'It's been almost three hours now.'

'What do you think, love?' Tristan asked, looking at Lucy. 'Do we call the police?'

'They'll have to send a chopper over,' said Greg. 'I reckon I take the boat round the island first. Check all the different bays.'

'And while you're playing at Coastguard, Greg, he could be . . .'

'Look!'

Almost in unison, they turned to look where Jackson was pointing, pointing at the distant figures of Don and three small girls, heading down the hill towards them.

Bridget reached them first.

'Abigail. My baby. My sweet darling.'

The relief was overwhelming at first, but, as she clasped her daughter to her chest, she registered the dripping hair; observed how Paris's T-shirt clung wetly to her belly; saw the seaweed caught in the sodden cuff of Skye's shorts.

Everyone was talking over the top of each other, clamouring to be heard. 'Where were you?' 'We were worried sick.' 'You're in so much trouble!'

Greg turned to where Don was standing, off to one side. 'Where'd you find them, mate?'

'I had an inkling I might find three mermaids swimming at the cove.'

'What!' Roz roared. 'I expressly forbade you to go swimming!'

'We only swam in the lagoon,' said Paris.

'Yeah, where it was safe,' Abigail added.

'I can't believe you'd be so naughty, Skye,' Lucy castigated, grabbing her by the elbow.

Taking in the fury on her friends' faces, Bridget started to laugh.

Lucy and Roz looked at her as if, this time, she really had lost the plot.

'Sorry,' she gulped for air. 'It's just . . .' But the more she tried to stop, the more hysterical she got. Tears streamed down her face.

'Thank God,' she finally managed to get out. 'Oh, thank God.'

Struggling to compose herself, she turned to Don: 'I owe you an apology. An apology and my eternal gratitude.'

'No thanks necessary. I'm just stoked they're all right. I couldn't bear to lose another little girl. Not on my watch.'

Bridget noticed Don didn't ask what she needed to say sorry for. She hoped that meant he hadn't picked up on her suspicions.

'Do you have plans for dinner, Don? I'm sure I speak for everyone when I say we'd love you to join us.'

She could feel the others looking at her in astonishment, and refused to give them the satisfaction of meeting their gazes.

'Yes, yes, can you, can you?' the children pleaded. 'Please!'

'I don't want anyone going to any bother on my account . . .'

'We've got plenty to go around. Besides, it's the least we can do to thank you for finding the girls.'

'Let me check my busy social calendar.' He mimed flipping through the pages. 'Nope, free as a bird, unless you count beans on toast as plans.' He gave a gentle laugh, and Bridget wondered how she had misjudged him so badly.

'Great, that's settled then. You'll be our guest of honour.'

With a whoop, the kids took off across the lawn.

'Uh-uh. Not so fast, girls,' said Roz. 'Back here.'

Reluctantly, Abigail, Paris and Skye turned around.

'You're not getting off that lightly. Do you have any idea what you put us all through? What you did was extremely naughty, but more importantly it was super dangerous. Imagine if one of you had got into trouble in the water.'

'Whose idea was it anyway?' asked Lucy.

There was an uncomfortable silence.

The girls looked every which way but at each other; Bridget was struck by their loyalty.

'How about we decide on their punishment,' she suggested, 'and then leave it at that? I think we've all been through enough, and I, for one, could do with a stiff drink.'

'Now you're talking,' said Greg. 'What can I get you, Don?'

'Cheers, mate. What's on offer?'

'We've got some excellent craft beers. Or something stronger? Gin? Rum?'

'A craft beer would hit the spot nicely.'

'Why don't you come check out the selection?' Greg led Don into the kitchen.

'Right,' said Roz, 'what's it going to be then? No swimming tomorrow?'

'That seems a shame,' said Bridget, 'when tomorrow's our last day.'

'How about they do all the dishes tonight,' proposed Lucy.

'Nooo!' Paris wailed. 'There'll be millions!'

'Dishes it is,' said Roz.

'It's so unfair,' complained Abigail. 'I bet the boys wouldn't even have got told off.'

'Hey,' said Lucy, 'I'd make myself scarce if I was you, before we change our minds.'

'Shit,' said Roz. 'I'd better let Jono know the girls have been found.'

In the kitchen, Lucy and Bridget got the pizzas under way; slicing salami and mushrooms, dividing the dough into fist-sized balls.

Outside, Tristan had the kids help him lug the ancient picnic table onto the deck, pushing it up against the other table, while Greg simultaneously stoked the barbeque and enlightened Don on the nuances of the can of craft beer he was clutching.

In the bottom of a drawer filled with random tea towels and placemats, Bridget unearthed a long narrow piece of red fabric.

'What do you reckon?' she asked Lucy, unfurling it. 'I'm thinking a runner.'

'Perfect.'

There was just enough material to do the two tables. Bridget snipped some hibiscus, their soft petals almost ready to retire for the night, and placed them in a chipped yellow vase she found in the sideboard. She filled a glass jug with water and plenty of limes and mint.

'Nice,' said Don, coming up the steps. 'Very festive.'

'Thanks.' Bridget stood back, admiring her handiwork.

'You guys make a pretty good team, huh?'

She looked around, everyone busy in their unspoken role. Roz and Greg even had a mini assembly line going; Roz rolling out the dough for Greg to top with sauce.

'Yeah, we do, don't we?' She felt oddly proud.

Later, buoyed up by booze and the conversation, which had warmly traversed subjects far and wide, Bridget turned to Don.

'What did you mean,' she asked, handing him a glass of Jono's homemade limoncello, 'when you said, "another little girl"?'

The silence around the table brought the other sounds of the evening into stark relief: the children's increasingly fierce game of stuck in the mud, the crickets' ceaseless verse.

'It was a long time ago,' Don said eventually.

'You don't need to tell us, mate,' said Jono.

'Nah, that's okay. I don't mind.'

He drained his drink.

'She was seven. Seven years old; as pretty as a flower. We were driving home from a party. I'd had one or two but nothing major. I wasn't over the limit or anything.'

He looked up, seeking eye contact, as if to ensure they believed him.

'My wife was in the front seat. We were arguing. She reckoned I'd been flirting with this chick, this stupid groupie, at the party. I wasn't, but she'd always been jealous. It's hard, you know, on a marriage, the touring life.

Anyway, one minute I'm turning to look at her, next she's screaming, and there's these massive headlights bearing down on us. That's the last thing I remember. This awful scream, the worst sound I've ever heard in my life, and these lights, these fucking lights burning through me.

'When I came to this poor bloody doctor, a young guy, hardly out of med school, draws the short straw and has to break it to me that they're gone. Both of them. Just like that. Never stood a chance.'

'Oh God, Don, I'm sorry. That's terrible,' said Bridget.

'It probably does me good in a funny kind of a way, to talk about it, you know, to acknowledge them.'

'So, is that why you moved out here?' asked Jono.

'Yeah, I couldn't go back to my old life. Even if I'd wanted to, I wasn't medically fit. That's why I have those spells I mentioned to you ladies. Apparently, I took quite the knock to the old noggin.' He tapped his fingertips against his temples.

'Living here feels like a kind of penance. Like I'm doing some good, looking after things, planting, growing. And no one I can hurt.'

'Well, I think you're an inspiration,' Lucy said.

'Hear, hear.'

'To Don.' They charged their glasses.

'My advice,' he said, 'is to make the most of every day 'cos you never know what life's gonna throw at you.'

By this time tomorrow their friendship would lie in tatters around them, and Bridget would wonder at just how prescient his words had been.

Chapter Thirty-seven

October
Tuesday

'She's not your problem,' Greg had whispered into her ear last night as they'd been dropping off to sleep, his hand hot and heavy on her hip.

She's not your problem, Bridget had repeated as she'd hauled herself around the Point a few hours earlier, her breathing unattractively ragged. 'She's not your problem,' she said to herself now, as she hurried home from school drop-off.

Not your problem, not your problem, not your problem.

On the corner of Alders Avenue, Bridget stopped. At home, work and chores were piling up, urgent, dull, all requiring her attention. She wavered a moment and then turned around. She needed to talk to her mother.

Bridget knew she was lucky to be so close to her parents, to live a stone's throw from her childhood home, but she couldn't help feeling there was something almost shamefully parochial about it, too. She had always imagined a big life for herself; now she feared the way she lived actually meant small horizons, a narrow field of vision.

Opening the gate to her parents' ramshackle property, she noticed the path was strewn with even more cabbage tree leaves than the last time she'd been here. Her parents had always been of the mindset that nature knew best, but these days their front garden could pass for a jungle. She made a mental note to have Greg send one of his guys around when they had some down time between jobs.

Briefly she wondered if she should have called first. No, unlike their daughter, her parents loved a popper-inner.

As she'd known it would, the door gave when she pushed. She stifled her irritation. It was pointless. She had been telling them for years they needed to keep it locked. They weren't about to suddenly change. 'If they can find something worth stealing, then they probably need it more than I do,' her father always said.

'Hello,' she called out. 'Mum? Dad?'

'Bridget!' Her father stepped into the hall, joy on his face.

'Hi, Dad.'

Bridget went to him. He smelt of ginger and yeast, and she breathed in the comforting familiarity of him.

'Is Mum here?'

'Hmm,' he said distractedly, nudging his smeary glasses back up his nose. 'Let me see, she was a minute ago.'

'Claire,' he called. 'Claire, we've got a surprise guest.'

'What have you been doing, Dad?' asked Bridget, taking in the ladder leaning precariously against the overflowing bookshelf.

'Jim asked if he could borrow this book, on indigenous cave art. I know it's here somewhere.'

'You need to be careful. That ladder isn't stable . . .'

'Just what I've been trying to tell the silly old bugger,' said Bridget's mother coming into the room, a massive cauliflower in her hands, soil still clinging to its roots. 'Hello, darling. This is a lovely surprise.'

'Mum, you're dropping dirt.'

'Am I? Ah well, a bit of dirt never killed anyone. Here, let me put the kettle on. Have you got time for a cup of tea?'

'Um . . .'

'Of course you do.'

'A-ha,' said Bridget's father.

He clambered back down the wobbly ladder and triumphantly thrust a book in front of Bridget's face.

'Come talk to me while I get it ready, lovey,' Bridget's mother called from the kitchen.

Bridget smiled apologetically at her father, but he was already engrossed in a world of cave art.

At the bench, Bridget's mother scooped three heaped spoonfuls of loose-leaf tea into the battered old teapot.

'You're in luck,' she said, getting a tin out of the cupboard. 'I just made flapjacks. How have you been anyway, darling? Feels like ages since I saw you. Are the kids good? Greg?'

'I know, sorry Mum. Time seems to have flown since the holidays. Everyone's fine. We need to have you and Dad over for dinner.'

'We'd love that, darling. I know how busy you are, though.'

Bridget watched her mother pull a stained tea cosy over the stout body of the teapot. She had knitted it when Bridget was a child, and Bridget both loved it for its history and was repulsed by it for the very same reason.

'That's better,' said her mother, sitting down with a whoosh of breath. 'I needed to put my feet up a minute. Now, it's not that I'm not thrilled to see you, but I'm guessing your visit isn't purely for the pleasure of seeing your old mum.'

'Why do you say that?'

'Well, my darling, you're not usually one to spontaneously call round in the middle of the day.'

Bridget sighed. 'Sorry Mum, you're right. I did want to talk to you about something.'

'I'm listening.'

'It's about Lucy.'

'Oh dear, I wondered when she'd rear her head again.'

'What do you mean?'

'I know you thought you'd dealt with things but you can't be friends with someone your entire life and have it end that neatly.'

'I'd hardly call it a *neat* ending. That day on Hine's was one of the worst . . . Even just thinking about it now makes me feel nauseous.'

'Trauma has a long tail, huh?'

'It was just so shocking, and Lucy was so . . . hateful, she was so hateful.'

'Yes, well Lucy's always had that capacity.'

'Has she? I thought you adored Lucy.'

'I did. I do. But that doesn't mean I didn't recognise a certain callousness in her. When I'd watch you playing as little girls, it was obvious she was a compartmentaliser. One time she broke your favourite doll. It was an accident, but you were beside yourself and she just turned her back.'

'I don't remember that at all.'

'It's almost a skill, really. To be able to harden your heart like that. When you called him out in front of everyone . . .'

Bridget watched as her mother took a bite of her flapjack. She waited for her to continue what she was saying, but first she licked her finger, pressing it on each oat, each seed that had fallen to the table, and one by one placed them in her mouth. *Waste not, want not.*

'Lucy would have seen it as a clear choice: him or you. She's always been one-eyed like that. I'm afraid you never stood a chance, darling.'

'God, it's all so bloody complicated. Do you think I did the wrong thing?'

'I think mostly we can only ever be who we are. And that situation between you two had been brewing for a long time. It's just a shame it had to come to a head in such a public, damaging way.'

'How did you get so wise, Mum?'

'You don't get to be my age, darling, without having figured out a thing or two. But what I want to know is what's happened to bring it all up now?'

'Lucy's moved her kids to Point Heed School.'

'Oh dear, that does make things tricky. Why's she gone and done that?'

'I don't know, that's the thing. I can't stop thinking about it, though. Worrying about when we're going to cross paths again. I ran into her last week outside the school and she refused to acknowledge me. She was in her car but she definitely saw me. She looked so different. Roz has seen her, too, and she reckons she's a pale shadow of her former self. This image of her keeps popping into my head; she was so pitiful, so alone. And it's not only Lucy, either. Abigail tried to bring Skye home for a playdate the other day.'

'What did you do?'

'I said, no, of course. Gave some ridiculous excuse.'

'Oh, Bridget, you should never punish a child for the sins of their parents.'

'I know that, Mum, but there was no way I was about to contact Lucy, ask if it was okay. The thing is, I would have liked to bring Skye home. Shown her some love. There was something so forlorn about her. So uncared for. In a funny kind of a way, even though it hurt like hell, it was easier to shut them all out when I pictured them how they used to be: gorgeous, shining; carrying on their charmed lives without me.'

'That's because you're a compassionate person, darling. But you also have an overly anxious disposition, coupled with a very vivid imagination. You spend a lot of time interpreting others' actions, and then angsting over them, without actually verifying the story you've written in your head.'

'So, what are you saying? That I should talk to Lucy?'

'Not necessarily. But, like it or not, to some extent your lives are still entwined. And one way or another you have to find some peace around that.'

Chapter
Thirty-eight

January
Day Six

Months later, rehashing it, trying once more to make sense of it all, Bridget would return again and again to the sex.

To the sex she'd had with her husband on that final morning, up high in their room with the ugly dormer windows.

Not that it hadn't been enjoyable, but when she'd brought herself to orgasm, efficiently, confidently, with the tip of her middle finger, in her mind it hadn't been Greg taking her from behind, but Tristan, her husband's best friend, her best friend's husband.

And she hadn't been able to shake the notion that somehow through her betrayal, her double betrayal, she had set in motion everything that followed.

After Don left and they'd got the kids to bed, Jono put Fleetwood Mac on the stereo and they'd tackled the dishes while they discussed the next day.

Well, Bridget had tried to: the others had shut her down. 'Don't think about it,' they'd said. 'Don't spoil things with talk of what we need to do.' 'You're right,' Bridget conceded, chastened.

But now, lying in their sandy, tangled sheets, her groin clammy with Greg's semen, Bridget wished there was a plan.

On the last day of a holiday, she just wanted to get going, head off, clear out, and although she already felt exhausted at the very thought of the cleaning and tidying, the packing and unpacking, she saw no reason to prolong the inevitable.

She knew, however, that she would be alone in thinking like this.

It had almost become a badge of honour among the rest of them to eke every last second of pleasure out of the holiday. Who gave a fuck if it meant arriving home in the dark — too late to get a load of washing on, no milk for breakfast — they were going to enjoy themselves, goddammit!

Half-sprawled across her, Greg had nodded off. His penis, so rod-like moments earlier, now lay vulnerable. If she were to touch it, she knew it would feel as cottony as her babies' bottoms once had.

A wave of remorse washed over her.

She slid out from under the solid length of his thigh, solicitous not to wake him.

But only to a point. He needed to rise and shine. They all did.

There was shit to do.

Downstairs, even though all week long the kids had insisted on getting up with the sparrows, contrarily they, too, seemed to have decided that this morning they would sleep in.

Caught between her own need for action and the others' perversely determined inaction, Bridget opened the fridge door.

She contemplated what was left. On the last day it had become their tradition to put everything out, for their 'Final Feast', as it had come to be known; to make sandwiches with the smidgen of mayonnaise and the two remaining eggs, a spread with the cream cheese and the scraps of smoked salmon, a salad with the cold roast vegetables.

When the kids were younger, she and Greg had gone away with some new friends, and she'd been gobsmacked by the lettuce leaves tossed thanks to the slightest edge of brown; the packets of crackers put away half-open to go limp; the partial bottle of milk left behind because no one could be bothered carting it home.

She stepped outside. Christ, it was stifling already. She retreated to the relative coolness of the kitchen.

May as well start on the stove. Usually, they stumped up for the cleaning fee, but there'd been no option with the farmhouse. Don's responsibilities obviously didn't stretch to scrubbing toilets.

She was attacking the grill when she heard the first rustlings of the rest of the house. She put down the scouring pad.

'Who's the idiot that left this on the stairs?' Jono demanded, holding up a Swingball racket. 'I just about broke my bloody neck!'

'Morning, darling,' Bridget said to Abigail when she hobbled into the room, trailing her favourite blanket along the filthy floor. 'How did you sleep?'

'My foot hurts.'

At breakfast the marmalade ran dry and then the honey.

'Watch it,' Lucy snapped when Skye dropped the butter.

'Excuse me,' muttered Greg when Roz reached across him for the plunger.

Was it just an unwillingness to return to normal life, to alcohol-free days and remembering what week to put the recycling out, or had everyone just got out of the wrong side of bed this morning?

Bridget felt jumpy. Like something was coming: a tempest, a woe.

She should move pre-emptively, she thought; stack the sandbags, batten down the hatches. Get off the island; make for home.

Before it struck.

After they'd eaten everyone drifted outside.

Greg and Jono sat on the steps sharpening knives. The blades coruscated in the harsh sunlight.

On the front lawn the kids lethargically kicked a ball.

Under the sparse shade of the kōwhai tree Lucy appeared to be in some kind of meditative state. Tristan sat beside her, running his fingertips up and down her arm.

Bridget shivered.

Wrap it up, she wanted to say. *We need to go. Now!*

She forced herself to sit.

Abigail flopped across Bridget, her little body moist and heavy.

'Eww, get off me!'

When she didn't budge, Bridget hoisted herself up instead; her inner thighs making an unattractive noise as they peeled apart, her right knee giving way slightly, causing her to stumble forward so that her breasts jiggled up and out of her ill-fitting bikini top. As she corralled the flesh back into its enclosure, she met Tristan's eye, and, blushing, turned the other way.

Zachariah gave her a knowing grin.

'Nice suntan,' he said.

Bridget looked down; a line of fire-engine red rimmed her cups, and between her breasts the final, unnaturally orange, vestiges of her spray tan.

He'd spoken quite loudly and there was a small pause before everyone laughed.

The way he'd said it, so boldly, made her wonder if it was something he'd overheard. Oh God, had Lucy and Tristan been laughing about her?

Well, fuck them.

All of them.

If they wanted to finish their vacation with a last-minute panic, then they were welcome to it.

In the lounge, Bridget picked up an iPad that was sticking out from between two of the sofa squabs.

Idly, she browsed through the photos. For every decent shot there were dozens of rubbish ones; heads summarily decapitated, bodies a mere blur.

As she swiped at the screen, she felt herself softening, already reminiscing about their holiday. She smiled at a photo of the boys bombing off the side of the boat, drops of water exploding around their curved forms. There they all were, lolling around the picnic blanket, not a care in the world. One of Greg, manning the barbeque, a massive grin on his face. A rare photo of her, Roz, and Lucy that flattered them all.

Bridget was about to scroll past a picture of lawn, when the image moved.

A video.

She tapped on it, filling the screen.

At first there was just grass, the omnipresent soundtrack of crickets.

Bridget's finger hovered over the trash icon. No point having a video of grass hogging up storage space.

And then, from left of screen, three small bodies enter the frame. Like in many of the stills, their heads are chopped off.

Bridget knew the swimsuits, though.

Abigail in blue, Paris, red, Skye, yellow.

The footage is shaky, but there's something deliberate about it. Conversely, the uninhibited way in which the girls move suggests they're unaware they're being filmed.

Suddenly the camera tilts downwards, as if it's slipped out of the operator's hand. The screen goes black, only the muffled sound of conversation to indicate the video hasn't ended.

Then an arc of water: the sprinkler. Giggles. The show's stars have returned. Still minus their heads, this time they're naked.

Bridget identified them by body parts.

Abigail's freckly arms. Paris's round brown belly. Skye's stick-person legs.

They run through the water. Back and forth, and, each time they re-enter the frame, the camera zeroes in. Zeroes in, and lingers. Lingers on their little-girl genitalia.

Again and again, while in the background someone breathes and the crickets sing on.

'Are you all right, hon?' asked Greg as she pushed past him down the steps. 'You're as white as a sheet.'

Bridget thrust the iPad at him. She needed him to tell her it was nothing, that she was over-reacting.

He looked at her questioningly. She hit play. Watched as his expression, so sunny a moment ago, turned.

'What do you think it means?' she asked him.

'I don't know but we're going to find out.'

'Jackson, come here, please.'

At his father's tone, Jackson, who had been slumped across a beanbag, jumped up.

'Whose iPad is this?'

'Dunno.'

'Well, who made this video?'

On third viewing, Bridget is more aware of the details; is convinced she can hear the breathing grow laboured.

'Dunno.'

Jackson won't look either of them in the eye.

'Who does this belong to?'

Greg is standing now. He has spoken very loudly and clearly and the sound cuts through the thick humidity like an icicle.

He held the iPad out in front of him. Disdainfully, thought Bridget, like something dirty. She also thought: so, this is it. The storm is upon us.

At first no one said anything. And then Lucy, as if emerging from a trance, spoke.

'That's ours.'

'Then I think you need to see this.'

Bridget stared, transfixed, as Greg's long legs ate up the lawn. Too late, she thought. We're too late.

He passed Lucy the device. Tristan moved to stand beside her but Roz beat him to it.

The two women watched.

'What the fuck!'

Roz's voice, the grimmest Bridget had heard it in a long time, reminded her of a younger, angrier Roz. *Cunt. My little cunt. Even the good parents can't always protect their kids.*

'Earl!'

Like Jackson, Earl denied all knowledge.

Willow started to cry.

'Let's all calm down a minute, eh,' said Jono. 'I'm sure there's no harm done.'

'No harm,' Roz lashed. 'It's a fucking pornographic video featuring our daughter.'

Bridget looked over to where Zachariah sat under the mānuka tree; perfectly unruffled, only his eyes betraying any interest as they tracked the action.

Don't, Bridget told herself. *Don't.*

But how could she not?

'It was you, wasn't it? You made it, didn't you, Zachariah? You made the video.'

He smiled.

'Stop smiling!'

There was a sudden pain in her forearm. She looked down. Lucy's nails were digging in, hard.

'I think *you're* the one who needs to stop, Bridget.'

Tristan had come to stand next to his wife. Bridget attempted to make eye contact with him.

'You know what I'm talking about, don't you? Tell her! Tell her!'

'Tell me what, Bridget?' Lucy's voice was ruinously calm.

'That your precious son is dangerous. A freak. He's always been a frigging little freak.'

Chapter Thirty-nine

October Wednesday

Bridget stood in front of her wardrobe. *What to wear? What to wear?* She pulled on a pair of black jeans. *No.* She held up a linen skirt. *Ugh.* The pile of rejected garments at her feet mounted.

It was only a school trip, for God's sake, why was she expending so much time and headspace?

At breakfast Jackson had asked her not to wear anything embarrassing. Anything like 'those pants that show your thingy', which she'd interpreted to mean active wear, was out. Surely, though, her almost-adolescent son's sartorial opinions were not to account for all this angst?

She could feel the muscles of her chest knitting together. *Enough, already.*

She dragged the jeans back on. Some white trainers. A khaki shirt. Standard school-mum getup. She put a fine gold chain on. Added another. And another. She studied her reflection. Took the necklaces off again. She could never get that layered jewellery thing right. She scraped her hair back into a ponytail. Applied mascara, gloss. Hopefully she would pass muster.

In the kitchen, Jackson and Abigail were dressed; their school bags packed and ready to go. It would be nice if they could be like this all the time. Without the need for the proverbial bloody carrot.

She didn't normally allow screen time before school; apparently it screwed with your synapses, whatever they were. But to give herself a small precious window in which to get ready, she'd promised them fifteen minutes if they did all their jobs first.

'C'mon guys, time to go.'

Not a flicker.

'Jackson? Abigail?'

Mouths slack, eyes glassy; maybe their synapses were already fucked.

'Off. Now.'

Finally, focus still tracking downward, they stood up. She took their iPads — their Pandora's Boxes — from them.

Bridget assumed Abigail had been watching dance videos, Jackson playing a shooting game, or watching some geeky guy in Seattle or Stockholm drone on about how to play said game.

In truth, though, she had no idea. They could be watching anything, communicating with anyone. Some loser in Minneapolis or Manchester masquerading as a kid their age, grooming them to fulfil his sick fantasies.

She must check whether Greg had installed the latest version of that child-safe filter. Technology was his department. She'd tried following this step-by-step guide to protecting your children online, but halfway through had lost the will to live.

The school had sent home a note last term warning parents what to watch out for when stalking their children online. Apparently, 'Do you send?' was code for, 'Are you up for sharing pictures of your naked body with me?' Bridget wasn't too worried about that though, she knew Jackson would sooner chew his arm off than exchange images of his penis with anyone.

There was so much talk about the ills of social media. Sometimes Bridget wondered whether they weren't being overly paranoid, whether it was just the modern-day equivalent of thinking Elvis Presley and his thrusting pelvis would lead 1950s teens straight to the devil.

It was warm, unseasonably so, and while the walk up to school was perfectly pleasant, as they got closer, Bridget could feel her chest constricting again.

Clearly, she was nervous. Nervous about what? About seeing Zachariah, she concluded.

She'd contemplated trying to get out of the museum trip; imagining Lucy signing up as a parent helper, too, and how unbearably awful that would be. But when the email came out confirming the details, she'd checked the list of addressees and Lucy's name hadn't been among them.

Get it together, Bridget. You're a middle-aged woman, for God's sake, and now you're scared of a flipping kid!

The buses that would take the senior classes to the museum were already lined up outside the school; Miss Smythe was waiting at the gate with a clipboard and an arm festooned with bright sashes.

'There you are,' she said, as if Bridget was somehow holding everything up.

She passed her a sash. Bridget stretched it out in order to decipher what was printed on it: POINT HEED SCHOOL PARENT HELPER. Her heart sank.

'Aren't they neat!' exclaimed a voice behind her.

Jesus. Hi-Vis Mum was actually wearing two of the sashes over the top of her fluorescent vest — one across each shoulder, positioned so the wording was visible front and back. She looked grimly enthusiastic, like a gun-slinging orange highlighter, off to battle.

Miss Smythe smiled approvingly. Her smile soured as Bridget tied her own sash loosely around the strap of her bag.

'Apparently this is how French women wear their scarves,' she explained. 'It gives it a certain *je ne sais quoi*, don't you think?'

She laughed. Miss Smythe nor Hi-Vis Mum did not.

'I've assigned you to Jackson, Sam and Gus,' said Miss Smythe. 'Do you think you can manage that?'

'Of course,' said Bridget, making for the bus she'd seen Jackson getting on.

She was relieved to see Sam and Gus already sitting with Jackson. Their friendship ran hot and cold. Wrangling the three of them would have been no fun if they were having an off week. She cast her eyes over the bus's other occupants. No Zachariah, thankfully.

'Hi, boys,' she said, hovering over the empty place next to Jackson. 'Is this seat taken?'

The expression on Jackson's face was one of unmistakable displeasure. Opposite him, Sam and Gus looked up, then quickly away.

Behind Bridget, children pushed and shoved.

Gathering together the remnants of her pride, she continued down the narrow aisle, wedging herself between a podgy, red-haired boy and a drab-faced girl in a dinosaur onesie on the bench seat at the back. She'd noticed them both around the school. Neither appeared to have any friends. Evidently, she was among kindred spirits.

The bus started with a loud shudder.

Bridget glanced up. There, in one of the seats facing the wrong way, was Zachariah, his face fixed on hers. He cocked his head in her direction; a curiously adult gesture. Blanching, she lifted her hand in a half-wave. *C'mon, Bridget. He's just a kid. Don't let him get to you.*

As the bus pulled out into the traffic, she closed her eyes. It was hot. Stinking hot. She could feel the sun beating down on her, barbequing her thighs in their casing of black denim. She thought regretfully of the linen skirt lying on her bedroom floor.

Bridget inhaled deeply, and wished she hadn't; something smelt bad. She sniffed to her right. No, it wasn't Big Red. Microraptor wriggled, and Bridget was assailed by the odour of unwashed, wee-sy polyester. Ugh, that was it.

By the time they finally drew up outside the museum, Bridget thought she was going to be sick. She elbowed her way through the back doors, gagging loudly as the fresh air hit her throat. A couple of mothers turned around.

'Sorry,' Bridget managed to choke out. 'Don't mind me.'

Too late, she realised one of them was Sina. She gave another of her half-waves. It was becoming her signature greeting. Sina raised her brows in the faintest of acknowledgements.

Spotting her charges hauling themselves up on to a brass statue of a returned soldier, Miss Smythe bearing down on them, Bridget clapped her hands.

'Hey,' she called. 'Get down from there, boys.'

She could sense Miss Smythe's disapproval from the other side of the courtyard. There went another black mark against her name.

Fortunately, just then, the museum educator assigned to their school group asked them to come inside.

Hi-Vis Mum and Ruth, heads bent in earnest discussion, went through the turnstile ahead of her. Ruth was whispering, but the urgent sense of drama with which she spoke ensured her words were largely audible.

' . . . planning a demonstration . . . time to reclaim our neighbourhood. Wrest it back from the paedophiles!'

Bridget cringed. The woman was obviously mad.

Shepherding her wards into the World War Two exhibition area, she ran through the list of who she needed to steer clear of today: Zachariah, Miss Smythe, Hi-Vis Mum, Sina, Ruth.

The educator handed out activity sheets. After several attempts to keep the boys on task, Bridget gave up. What did it matter if they'd rather pretend to kill Nazis than listen to her read out the information panel about the Molotov–Ribbentrop Pact?

Watching the other mothers, who were clustered in small groups, chatting chummily, Bridget experienced a pang of loneliness. She should have cajoled Moana or someone into coming, too. Seeing Microraptor standing over by the life-size tank, playing sadly with the spikes of her tail, she decided to join her.

Bridget heard them before she saw them.

'Say it again! Say it again, you asshole.'

'Get off me!'

Sticking out from underneath the armoured vehicle, three pairs of legs thrashed wildly about. Jackson stood in front of them, clenching and unclenching his fists.

'Jackson,' she said, grabbing him by the arm. 'What's going on?'

Bridget registered the rage in his eyes.

'Tell me,' she demanded. 'Right now!'

'That bastard . . .'

'Who? What are you talking about?'

'Zachariah.'

Without waiting for him to explain, she yanked hard on the legs nearest her.

'Ouch,' complained Sam as she dragged him out.

'Mum,' Jackson protested.

'Don't move,' she instructed Sam.

From under the tank there was a crack, and then a howl.

Zachariah wriggled out feet first and Sam lunged at him.

'Stop it! That's enough!'

Bridget crouched down.

'Are you all right, Gus?'

Gus, his face a mess of snot and tears, peered back at her.

'C'mon,' she said. 'Out you come.'

He inched closer and she moved aside to let him past.

'Who started this nonsense?' asked Miss Smythe, marching over, arms folded menacingly across her meagre bust.

'He did,' said Sam, pointing at Zachariah.

'Is that true?' Miss Smythe asked.

'He said Gus's parents were Nazi-lovers,' said Jackson.

Bridget had forgotten Gus's family was German.

'It was only a joke,' said Zachariah, scuffing at the ground disconsolately.

'Yes, well you can tell Mr Ngata that when we get back to school,' said Miss Smythe. 'See if he thinks it's funny.'

Bridget was surprised to see alarm flare in Zachariah's eyes. And, to her even greater surprise, she found herself feeling almost protective of this boy she had known since birth.

Known and disliked.

Chapter Forty

October Thursday

Bridget manoeuvred her bum closer to the basin. She could almost feel herself melting under the girl's deft strokes. If only she could get comfortable.

She cursed her Pict ancestry. Short-arses!

Still, it could be worse; she could be on a school trip to the museum.

When Bridget had tried to suggest to Miss Smythe on the bus ride back that there might be two sides, Miss Smythe had put a very firm lid on the 'incident'. And when Bridget had raised the school's zero-tolerance bullying policy, she'd said that there was absolutely no point in making a mountain out of a molehill.

Bridget had wondered whether she ought to take it any further, but decided the less said, the less chance there was of Lucy getting involved.

Jackson had shut her down, too. 'Just forget it, okay?' he'd said, slamming his door.

She'd thought she might have more luck this morning, but she'd forgotten what day it was. The only thing the kids had been able to talk about at breakfast was Halloween.

Bridget had been sticking her head in the sand all week about costumes and decorations and trick or bloody treating. In her opinion, America had bestowed more than its fair share of gifts upon the world that should have come with an exchange card: McDonald's, microwave popcorn, Donald

Trump, Hallowfuckenween.

She had tried to broach the subject of age appropriateness with Jackson, whether he might be too old for trick or treating, and he'd looked so devastated she'd wanted to open her big fat mouth and shove the words right back in.

'Can we go to the two-dollar shop after school?' Abigail had pleaded.

'No,' Bridget had said. 'All that plastic. Think about the poor birds and marine life. Not to mention the fossil fuels.'

'I know,' Abigail had said, 'but I really need a bowtie.' And when Bridget had reminded her that she'd got one last year, Abigail had said, yes, but it was yellow; that her friendship group was going as a packet of M&Ms this year, and that she was the orange one.

'So, how are we doing your hair today?'

Bridget looked up. Richard, her hairdresser, hovered behind her, a blow-dryer with a massive diffuser attached to the end of it in one hand, a set of straightening irons in the other. God, it was nice to be asked what *she* wanted for once.

She already looked better, she thought, moving closer to her reflection. The greys at her temples, a recent addition, were no more.

Roz had snorted when Bridget had pointed them out to her. 'Girlfriend,' she'd said, 'that's nothing.'

She mightn't have many, but even that slight dustiness around the edges made Bridget feel washed out, as though she were fading, ebbing away millimetre by millimetre.

'Straight,' she said.

'Good choice,' he said approvingly.

Bridget smiled at him in the mirror.

She'd been coming to Richard for a while now. Unlike previous hairdressers, he never gave the impression he wanted to be friends; never ventured anything about himself. At first it had made her uneasy, his reticence. But she had grown to appreciate it; there were few people in her life who gave her so much and yet demanded so little.

Out on the street a warm breeze blew. Her hair lifted and then resettled, its blunt length grazing her collarbones. Bridget felt new, excited to be going somewhere, doing something adult.

The timing of her hair appointment couldn't have been better.

Amanda was so glamorous these days; on their infrequent lunch dates she was always coming from the airport or dashing off to interview someone extraordinary. Sometimes when Amanda would ask what she'd been doing Bridget found herself making stuff up, not outright lies, just small stretches to make her life sound a little less pedestrian.

As she walked into the restaurant Amanda had proposed, Bridget willed somebody to notice her. Hey, she wanted to shout, check me out! Someone . . . Anyone . . . But her entrance didn't even seem to register with the maître d'.

She waited, unsure what to do.

To imply a sense of ease, she looked around purposefully.

She supposed the aesthetic was what you'd call European bistro. Small round tables, bentwood chairs, a zinc-top bar. The clientele was uniformly late-twenties, uniformly beautiful, and, Bridget realised, running her fingers regretfully through her poker-straight lob, uniformly bed-headed.

So much for the life-changing abilities of a good haircut.

'Bridget!'

Amanda swept in behind her, kissing her on the cheek at the same time as she summonsed the maître d' over.

Before Bridget knew it, they were seated at a table with a view of the courtyard, and a rosé, of the lightest pink, was being poured into a glass in front of her.

Bridget sighed.

'What's that for?'

'Oh, I don't know, I was standing there feeling very middle-aged and slightly foolish and then you arrived, looking so gorgeous, and everyone snapped to attention, and you just made everything seem so easy.'

'Ha! You can talk! Happily married with a beautiful house, two great kids and a successful business. Look at me. Forty next month, and the only thing waiting for me at home is a packet of minestrone soup!'

Bridget laughed. 'It's good to see you.'

Amanda leant across and clinked Bridget's glass with her own. 'Right back at you, sister.'

They went with the waiter's food recommendations, so many dishes arriving in quick succession that they were forced to make room on the rickety table, squeezing the scampi around the burrata.

'Whoever came up with the idea of serving a small plates menu on small tables had to have been stoned,' declared Amanda.

The maître d' overheard and because it was Amanda who'd said it, and because she was so fabulous, he laughed, which made Bridget laugh, too, spraying Amanda with wine.

Mopping her face with a napkin, Amanda said: 'More! We need more wine!'

'Why can't life always be this fun?'

'I thought yours was,' said Amanda. 'All those kids' dinners and book clubs and wild school fundraisers.'

'Save me.'

Over their second bottle, Bridget regaled her with tales of the Real Housewives of Point Heed.

'I mean all I want is four beddies, two bathrooms, two living, a pool, and a garage with internal access. Surely that's not too much to ask,' she mimicked.

'Oh God, that's gold,' said Amanda. 'I have to write it down before I forget.'

'Shit, don't quote me. I'm unpopular enough as it is.'

'What do you mean?'

She told Amanda about the brief in the paper, the hysteria and finger pointing. Her clashes with Ruth and Sina.

'Wow. What a story.'

'Actually, I was hoping you might be able to find out who it is?'

'I'll have a sniff around, but they've really cracked down on suppression orders lately. Even though social media's made it increasingly hard to police.'

'I'd really appreciate it. Roz has been on my case. She thinks I should talk to Darren Peters.'

'I wouldn't if I was you. He hits the turps pretty hard these days. I reckon he's losing the plot.'

On the way home, aware she shouldn't be driving, Bridget called into the supermarket; they needed milk.

Confronted by the vast displays of skeleton cupcakes and candy spiders, she realised she didn't have anything for the trick or treaters. She recalled her quashing of Abigail and Jackson's enthusiasm this morning. *Bad mother!*

On a whim, she got out her phone and composed a group text to a handful of school mothers: 'Sorry for the eleventh-hour invitation, but happy for the kids to use ours as a base tonight. Feel free to come for a drink. Dads welcome, too.'

Bridget hesitated.

What to do about Ivy? She was one of Abigail's best friends.

No, stuff it; Sina had made her feelings very clear.

She pushed send.

Chapter
Forty-one

October
Thursday

Faark!

A queue of girls snaked out the bathroom and down the hall.

'Next,' Bridget called, wielding her good liquid eyeliner like some short-order make-up artist.

When she'd grandly announced the makeover station was open for business, she'd been thinking a slap or two of face paint. She struggled to do a symmetrical flick on herself, let alone four or five sets of small screwed-up eyelids. How the hell did nine-year-olds even know what a cat eye was anyway?

The doorbell rang.

'Can someone get it? Greg? Jackson?'

Out on the deck she could hear the happy hum of adults en route to tipsiness. Jackson's door was closed.

'Don't move,' she said to the red M&M in front of her.

On her porch stood two little girls dressed as fairies. An attractive younger woman with a baby in a front pack waited on the driveway. The baby was wearing one of those headbands with sparkly things erupting out the top of it; the mother sported a pair of glittery pink wings.

'Oh my! What have we here? I'm sure there's a collective noun for a group of fairies.'

The mother looked at her coolly. Bridget recognised her as one of the 'junior Tories' from the meeting last week.

'A herd, that's it. A herd of fairies.'

The two little girls stared at her.

'What do you say?' prompted the mother. 'Ethiopia? Tanzania?'

For a moment Bridget wondered if the woman had lost her mind; spouting random African countries on her doorstep.

'Trick or treat,' said the older girl.

Dear God, these two miniature blonde people were actually named after some of the poorest places on earth. Bridget didn't know whether to laugh or be outraged. She desperately wanted to ask if the baby's name was Uganda.

'Hmm,' she said. 'Let me see. Trick?'

'Where are your lollies?' asked the younger one.

Bridget expected the mother to admonish the girl, but, busy on her phone, she didn't even look up.

She reached for the bowl of treats.

'Uh-uh. Two each,' she chided, as they grabbed fistfuls.

Reluctantly they released their grip and she stepped back into the house, nudging the door shut with her elbow. *Entitled little brats!*

She resumed her post at the bathroom vanity, where, sadly, the line hadn't dispersed.

Her flicks were getting wonkier, and she was contemplating whether or not she needed to redo the eye she'd just outlined particularly badly, when there was another knock.

'Jackson! Greg!'

Nothing.

Faark!

Through the frosted glass she could make out a solitary figure.

Microraptor: still wearing her dinosaur onesie.

'Well, hello again.'

'Hullo,' said the girl sullenly.

'Are you here by yourself? Where are your friends, honey?'

The unmitigated sadness that crossed the girl's face made Bridget wish, for the second time that day, she could eat her words right back up.

She thrust the bowl out in front of her.

While Microraptor's hand danced indecisively back and forth, Bridget studied the girl's fingernails; they were dirty, in need of cutting.

'Take as many as you want, sweetheart.'

Microraptor quickly opened the torn supermarket bag she was clutching and scooped several lollies into it.

'Good luck,' said Bridget. 'Be careful.'

Watching the girl trudge up the drive, an image came to her of Ethiopia and Tanzania with their matching fairy loot bags, all shiny and new like everything else about them.

Bridget rapped lightly on Jackson's door.

Pushing it open, she was assaulted by a fug of almost-adolescence. Three boys lined up on the bed, Jackson at his desk; all four wearing earphones, all glued to their device. None acknowledged her.

She'd invited Sam's and Gus's mothers, but they'd both texted back saying the boys had other plans. She'd wondered whether their refusal had anything to do with the scrap at the museum yesterday. And whether this was something else she should be worried about.

'Hey, c'mon, boys, it's Halloween. If you're going trick or treating you need to get ready.'

'We're just finishing this round,' said Jackson.

'Well, you'd better hurry; the girls are almost ready to go.'

'We're not going with them.'

'I thought that was the plan. You always go together.'

'Nope,' said Patrice, whose little sister, Chloe, was currently waiting to have her eyes done.

'Hmm . . . I think there might need to be some discussion with the parents about that.'

Jackson made a face. A face she translated to mean *please, shut up, you're embarrassing me*.

In the bathroom the girls were having a go themselves, and though Bridget doubted her eyeliner would survive the experience, she decided to leave them to it.

She was heading out to join the adults when there was another knock.

Argh!

Snatching up the lolly bowl, she yanked open the door.

'Oh . . .'

On her doorstep stood Zachariah, in cloak and top hat; two figures, faces hidden behind masks, belts with tails around their waists, hanging back behind him. Bridget presumed the taller of the two, long blonde hair backcombed to resemble a lion's mane, was Skye, and the smaller, grey cardboard trunk almost dragging on the ground, Willow.

'Happy Halloween, Bridget,' said Zachariah.

'Hello,' she said, hoping her voice didn't sound as jittery as she felt. 'Hello, girls. Fancy seeing you here.'

'I'm not a girl,' said Willow. 'I'm an ephalent.'

'So you are,' said Bridget, fighting the overwhelming urge to pick her up like a tube of toothpaste and squeeze some of that cuteness out of her. 'Silly me!'

'Zat's okay.'

'Would you like to see our trick?' asked Zachariah.

No, not really, thought Bridget, nodding enthusiastically.

Willow swung her trunk with a trumpeting sound, while next to her Skye roared and paced.

Zachariah drew out a whip, long and black and lethal.

He brought his hand up, and Bridget shrieked. Flashing through the air with a large crack, it only missed the girls by inches, but they didn't skip a beat, and, obedient as enslaved circus animals, they hunkered down on the ground.

'Oh,' said Bridget. 'Oh . . .'

'Lollies, please,' said Willow.

'Sorry, yes, of course.'

She passed them the bowl.

'Thanks, Bridget,' said Zachariah.

Following them with her eyes as they set off along the road she tore open a packet of Maltesers and upended it into her mouth. She shut the door and reached for another, the spheres of chocolate and malted milk clogging her throat.

'I need wine,' she announced to the deck. 'And you're on door duty,' she informed Greg.

'I thought I was on drinks?'

'We're swapping.'

'What a pleasant idea this is,' said Marcelle, Patrice and Chloe's mother. '*Merci* for the invitation.'

Bridget didn't know Marcelle very well, but she'd been saying for ages they needed to have them over, so she was glad to finally make good on the offer. There was something about her, a kind of effortlessness she found very appealing; not to mention her French accent, which made even the most prosaic of subjects somehow intriguing.

Marcelle was standing with the Shins, who had moved from Seoul the previous year. In spite of the initial language barrier, Jackson had struck up a friendship with their son, Jun-seo, bonding over gaming. The parents both worked in banking. They were very sophisticated and Bridget was a little intimidated by them. She was surprised, yet pleased, they'd come tonight.

'So,' she said, 'apparently the boys are hitting the pavement solo.'

The Shins looked confused.

'They want to go trick or treating alone,' she explained. 'What do you reckon, hon?' she called out to Greg.

He didn't respond.

'Greg,' she prompted him.

'Huh?' He turned to her. 'I was just telling John here, about the importance of creating bee-friendly gardens. They're responsible for pollinating a third of our crops, they're seriously endangered, and what does everyone want me to plant? Fucking succulents!'

Oh God, thought Bridget, *don't let him be in one of those moods*. The Shins appeared even more confused.

'I was talking about whether the boys should be allowed off on their own. It'll be dark soon.'

She checked her watch. 'Well in an hour or so.'

'Of course they should,' said Greg. 'They're practically teenagers.'

'I guess, but given the current situation . . .'

Just then, John's wife, Carol, joined them from the kitchen. She was carrying a bottle of Heineken. Bridget would never have picked her as a beer drinker. She seemed too mumsy.

'Speaking of which,' said Carol, 'John finally got around to putting his name on that Facebook page this morning. I told him if he didn't, it was going to be very embarrassing at Fright Night!'

'What Facebook page?' asked Greg.

'Sorry, honey, I keep meaning to tell you,' said Bridget, quickly explaining the gist of it.

'I guess that makes sense.' Greg took a long draught of beer.

'Did you see that guy with the short trousers isn't on there?' said Carol with a wicked little laugh.

Frank's pants might be flappy, thought Bridget, but bloody Sophie's mouth was flappier.

'Anyway,' Carol went on, 'while there's no denying it's horrible, this is probably their last year trick or treating and I don't want our fears ruining it for them.'

'You're absolutely right,' said Bridget, readjusting her assessment of Carol again. 'Especially if they promise to stick together. I think I've been letting all the hysteria get to me.'

'C'est normal,' said Marcelle. 'But there will always be bad people. How you say it? Bad shit. It is to us to teach them how to live with it.'

'I take it you know what we're talking about?' Bridget asked the Shins.

'I think, yes,' said Jun-seo's father.

'Jun-seo friends tell him about this story,' added his mother. 'This his first Halloween. Maybe just go one hour. Until night?'

'I think that's a good compromise,' said Bridget, wondering if Jackson had been one of the friends to apprise Jun-seo of 'this story'.

They called the boys out.

'One hour,' protested Jackson. 'We're not babies!'

'Jackson, enough!' Greg's voice was stern, and Bridget forgave him his earlier rant.

She suddenly remembered Abigail and her friends. 'It does mean someone's going to have to go with the girls now,' she said. 'I'm not comfortable with them going alone.'

The three other girls' mothers were clustered on the far corner of the deck; their husbands in the opposite corner. Bridget waited for one of them to suggest they would accompany the trick or treaters. But nobody made a move to put down their drink.

'I would like a walk,' said Marcelle.

'Thank you,' said Bridget, smiling at her gratefully. 'That would be great. I'll keep you company.'

'Make sure you hold down the fort here, won't you,' she said to Greg, kissing him lightly on the lips. 'Listen out for trick or treaters at the door.'

Bridget wasn't sure anyone would actually realise they were supposed to be M&Ms, but the girls were beside themselves with the thrill of it, and, as they walked along the street, her heart swelled to see the joy on Abigail's face. Thankfully, she didn't seem to have noticed Ivy wasn't there.

'It's different, n'est-ce pas?' said Marcelle.

'Huh?'

'There's not the same, how you say, vibe, as other years.'

Bridget looked around.

'It's true,' she said.

Where normally hedges were adorned with fake spiderwebs, gory plastic hands poking out of letterboxes, this year most houses were devoid of tat. Even the place on Sainsbury Cres that normally went all out had barely made a token attempt.

With the dark descending earlier than she'd anticipated, somehow the overall effect was even creepier.

Bridget shivered.

The girls were only getting answers to their knocks at every third or fourth house, and, with little sugary reward for their efforts, enthusiasm was starting to wane.

'I'm cold,' said Abigail.

'How about we pack it in then, eh?' suggested Bridget.

Marcelle, who was rubbing her arms, nodded her head vigorously.

Bridget could see the girls wavering.

'If there're any lollies left at home you can divvy them up between yourselves.'

Happily, the lure seemed to work.

'When I was a child,' said Marcelle as they turned onto their street, 'my best friend live nearby and one day I visit for, you know, play, and her father come to the door, naked. *Complètement*.

'He tell me she not home and then he just stand there, never acknowledge he has no clothes on. I run home and when I describe to my mother what happen, she say, "*C'est rien*. It's nothing." It stay with me my whole life. That feeling of something being wrong. Of something being wrong but not being able to say anything. You are right to be careful.'

Bridget was taken aback. Their conversation until now had covered off everything from where to find the best baguettes to the slackness of the girls' dance teacher, but they hadn't touched on anything even remotely serious.

She was trying to work out how to reply to Marcelle's disclosure when the boys came around the corner. A couple of them were wearing scary masks. Jackson's nod to fancy dress was a dressing gown cord tied around his neck, noose-like. Bridget tried not to read anything into this.

'Hey,' she said. 'Good timing. Was it fun?'

'Turns out paedophiles don't drive round in white vans,' said Jackson.

'Nah,' said Patrice. 'More like buses.'

They high-fived.

'What are you talking about?' Bridget asked, but they'd already taken off.

Marcelle raised an eyebrow. She appeared equally nonplussed.

Following them down the hallway, Bridget could feel the excitement coming off them like an electrical charge.

'What did you mean, Jackson?'

'Nothing.'

Out on the deck she sensed the level of drunkenness had gone up a notch or two, everyone mingling more than when they'd left.

'Patrice, *explique-nous ce qui c'est passé, s'il te plaît*.'

Bridget wasn't sure what Marcelle had just said, but evidently Patrice had as little intention of elucidating his mother as Jackson.

In the end it was Jun-seo who owned up.

'Everyone thinks we don't know the story, that we're stupid.'

'What story?' asked Greg.

'About the paedophile. We know a paedophile is here in Point Heed and at the same time we see that bus arrive.'

The Shins were staring at their son with a kind of horrified wonderment.

'Bus,' said Bridget. 'What bus?'

'The Roach Coach,' said Jackson. 'I knew you and Dad didn't want me asking about it.'

'Yeah,' said Gabriel, looking at Carol and John, 'I heard you guys talking about it, too.'

'I don't get it, though, what's the connection between them?' asked Carol.

'After school the other day,' said Jackson, 'we saw this old guy through the window.'

'And he, like, waved at us,' added Patrice.

'Yeah, it was real weird,' said Gabriel.

'And,' prompted Bridget, still unsure where this was going. She was conscious of Abigail's friends' parents listening, spellbound.

'So, we decided to do something about it,' said Jackson.

'What?' asked Greg. 'What did you do?'

The boys all looked at each other.

Again, it was Jun-seo to speak. 'We paint over words.'

Bridget had the distinct sensation her stomach was in her shoes. 'Tell me, Jackson,' she said. 'Tell me what you wrote, this instant!'

He met her gaze, and, in his expression, she saw a new defiance.

'The Pedo Limo. We wrote: The Pedo Limo.'

Chapter
Forty-two

November
Friday

She couldn't hold it in a second more.

Lifting the covers, Bridget slipped out of bed. The air was frigid and her nipples contracted with the sharp shock of it.

She clutched at her crotch, her touch painfully cold.

Oh God, she'd waited too long.

She could feel the urine welling around her cupped palm, the smallest trickle spilling over and down her leg.

Sitting on the toilet, she tore off a length of toilet paper and wiped between her thighs. *Waste not, want not*, she thought, folding the wet part of the paper in on itself and drying the floor.

Easing back under the duvet, her mind whirled with the events of the night before.

All the parents had been on the same page: to atone the boys would go and see the owner of the house bus, apologise for their actions, ask how they could make amends.

Bridget brought her knees up to her chest, tentatively placing an icy foot on the small of Greg's back.

'Argh! What are you doing?'

Before he could roll over, she slotted herself into the hollow between his arm and torso.

'That was pretty intense, hey? Especially with the others standing there, taking it all in. You'd think they would have read the room, made themselves scarce. It just goes to prove my theory.'

Greg groaned. 'What time is it?'

'Almost six. Things always come apart at the seams when the adults sit around drinking while the kids are left to run free. It's like on Hine's.'

'Hmmm . . .'

'Oh God, the poor Shins.'

'Huh?'

'They just looked so flummoxed by the whole thing.'

'Bridget,' said Greg, pushing her gently but firmly back on to her side of the bed, 'I'm sure kids do dumb shit in Korea, too.'

'I know. But I felt embarrassed somehow.'

'What about?'

'I don't know. Paedophilia. Point Heed. Our son . . .'

Laughing, Greg grabbed her in a kind of headlock and pulled her into his belly.

'What are you like?!'

'Help, I can't breathe!'

Bridget wriggled out of his grasp; she knew what this was a prelude to and there was something she needed to do.

'I'm going for a quick jog, before the kids get up.'

She pretended not to notice the way the sheet tented over his groin.

Out on the street she turned left for Alders Ave. She wanted to see the bus.

There was no bus, though.

Maybe she'd got the spot wrong? She ran on.

At the top of Alders she stopped, looked back down the street.

Nope, definitely no bus.

She breathed out a sigh of relief and despised herself for it.

Taking the long way home, she kept her eyes peeled. While plenty of late-model SUVs and European cars lined the streets of Point Heed, it was as if that ominous old house bus had merely been a figment of their collective imagination.

She decided she wouldn't tell Jackson straight away, that she'd let him suffer a little longer.

But at breakfast, she changed her mind. No doubt he'd find out soon enough; it was probably better it came from her.

'You're incredibly lucky, Jackson. I got up early to see for myself exactly how much damage you and your friends had done and the bus has gone.'

As if her words were a soothing balm, the black cloud that had been hanging above him since all the drama last night seemed to magically float away.

'Of course,' she said, passing him his smoothie, 'this doesn't mean you get away with it scot-free. Dad and I are still going to need to come up with an appropriate punishment.'

Her phone rang.

Amanda.

'Hello! You beat me to it. I've been meaning to text. I so enjoyed lunch.'

'Me too. It's crazy we left it so long. Hey, I don't have much time to talk; I'm due on a job and the photographer's making evil eyes at me. But I just wanted to tell you what I found out.'

'You don't muck around!'

'Well, funnily enough, I ended up at The Inkpot last night, and who did I bump into but bloody old Darren Peters. I know I told you I avoid him like the plague these days, but he was semi-sober, so I decided to have a bit of a dig, see what he knew.

'At first, he was quite forthcoming. There were a few pretty young journos hanging about and I think he was showing off, but when I pushed him for specifics, he got a little cagey. Wanted to know why I was asking. Probably worried I was trying to muscle in on his round.

'Anyway, I don't have a name for you; however, I did manage to establish the exact nature of what the guy was caught with.'

'Oh God, is it as bad as the rumours?'

'It depends on how you define bad. I interviewed a senior detective in the online child exploitation unit last year, and she said there's an increasing trend towards younger victims and greater brutality. She described it as being this ocean of material, constantly changing and swelling, with only the resources of a tiny fishing boat to master it.'

'Imagine the abhorrent stuff they must be exposed to. I don't know how you'd go home and switch off.'

'I know. There's no way I could do it, that's for sure. I take my hat off to them. Anyway, they caught your friendly neighbourhood perv through a tip-off from their counterparts in the UK. Earlier this year he uploaded several files containing the sexual exploitation of children to one of those instant messenger platforms. They monitor those things much more carefully now and the company was able to provide the police here with IP addresses for the images as well as the username and email address of two social media accounts allegedly used to distribute the images. And GPS data showed several of the recordings were made at the guy's residential address. Dummy! Shit, Steve's looking like he wants to throttle me now. I'd better go.'

'Wait, what were they? What were the images actually of?'

'Oh, right, well that's the weird thing. They were all pretty much the same. Video after video of these close-ups of wee fannies. Apparently, you can't see their faces. Right, gotta go. Lots of love. Talk soon.'

Bridget put down the phone.

An ugly little thought she couldn't yet articulate began to worm its way through her brain.

Chapter
Forty-three

November
Friday

'Sorry?'

Bridget couldn't focus on what Moana was saying amidst the chaos.

Around her children screamed, waving glow sticks in the night air like tiny ravers. Adults yelled to make themselves heard above Mike the Mobile DJ. Sweat shining on his bald head, Mike was pumping out a steady stream of kid-friendly pop with all the gravity of a man playing to a crowd of thousands on Ibiza. A middle-aged woman in Ugg boots, who Bridget assumed was Mike's partner, danced wildly in front of his booth.

Bridget forced herself to look away.

'I said, do you think they're swingers?'

'Who?'

'Mike and fan girl there.'

'Eww! God, do you think so? I know I'm being awful, but the thought of either of them naked, let alone bonking, makes me feel faintly nauseous. What on earth makes you say that?'

'Everyone seems to be these days. Haven't you heard about those two couples in the junior school?'

'No. Which couples?'

'I'm not sure exactly who they are, but supposedly they've got an "arrangement".'

'Wow. That makes me feel very old and very dull.'

'Yeah, me too. Ben reckons this guy he works with is in an open relationship. It's kind of bizarre because I've got quite friendly with his wife. I know what people get up to in the privacy of their own bedroom isn't anyone else's business, but it's like this elephant in the room now. Like it's stopping us from becoming better friends.'

'Because you don't approve?'

'No, it's not that, well, maybe a little, if I'm being completely honest. But, no, it's more that it's strange being friends with someone when you feel like they're withholding something so major from you.'

'Well, I can definitely relate to that.'

'I get the impression Ben's quite titillated by it.'

'People's fantasies are often fuelled by the thought of others' sex lives.'

'Yeah, I said he can fantasise all he likes, but he'll have to content himself with living vicariously through them.'

'Hey, isn't that Frank, Mr Flappy Pants that Sophie thought could be the culprit?'

Moana turned to look where Bridget was pointing.

'Oh yeah, didn't you hear? Apparently, he'd been away for work. Hadn't heard about what was going on. He's added his name now.'

Bridget snorted. 'So much for Sophie's suspicions!'

'Yeah. And get this, turns out he works for a children's book publisher, hence the interest in encouraging kids to read.'

'God, gossip can be dangerous. Imagine . . .'

Bridget felt a tug on the belt of her leather jacket.

'Mum, I need more money. Please, pretty please.'

'I already gave you all my gold coins, Abigail.'

'But there's this stand over there. Snakes in a tree. It's so cool. They blindfold you and you get one minute to eat as many snake lollies as you can. They're hanging from this cardboard tree and . . .'

'You'll have to go find Dad, honey. See if he's got any change left.'

'But I don't know where he is.'

Abigail gave her most pitiful look. Bridget sighed.

'Sorry, Moana.'

'That's okay. I know what it's like.'

Grabbing Bridget's hand, Abigail dragged her straight across the middle of the dance floor.

'Abigail,' Bridget protested, almost taking out a father doing the floss in unison with a small girl in a *Frozen* costume. 'Couldn't we have gone around the outside?'

'Last time I saw Dad he was over by the sausage sizzle.'

'Hmm, figures.'

By the shaved-ice cart, she spotted Sina, deep in conversation with a mother sporting devil horns.

'I think I saw Dad heading this way,' she said, steering Abigail in the opposite direction.

She hated feeling like she had to avoid someone, but she hated awkward exchanges even more. She wondered whether she ought to be feeling more nervous she might bump into Lucy tonight.

Since that first fateful morning, she'd seen no sign of her, or Tristan for that matter, no indication they were participating in any real way in school life.

Mind you, she thought, a sunken feeling in her stomach, if her suspicions were correct, it wasn't surprising Lucy was laying low.

'C'mon,' she said. 'I'll get some more money out.'

Abigail beamed. 'You're the best, Mum.'

There was quite a crowd at the cash table. Ruth was at the back of the queue and Bridget gestured to a man wearing a Freddy Krueger mask to go in front of her. She wasn't quick enough, though.

'Bridget,' proclaimed Ruth.

'Ruth,' Bridget nodded.

She braced herself for another set-to over zombie wrestling. She'd worked on the stand earlier in the evening, selling tickets, and while the numbers were a little down on previous years, most parents had seemed happy enough to let their offspring have a tussle.

'I suppose you've heard school camp is going ahead?'

Evidently Ruth had moved on to fresh outrage.

'I wasn't aware there was any talk of it not happening.'

'It's unbelievable. Unless we've been informed of his identity by then, there's absolutely zero chance Joshua is going. I mean what if he was your kids' cabin dad?'

'I don't think that's very likely,' said Freddy Krueger.

'And why is that?' asked Ruth.

'He'll have got home detention.'

'Nonsense,' said Ruth. 'The papers are full of crooks getting off with a slap on the wrist.'

'Actually,' said Freddy Krueger, 'I'm a criminal defence lawyer. And from what I understand about the case, as long as he didn't have any priors, that's exactly what he would have been sentenced to. But, regardless, schools are so careful about all that stuff now, there's no way he'd get through the vetting process.'

You'd think this would have been music to Ruth's ears, but her expression was one of such disappointment, Bridget almost wished she could take a photo to show Roz.

As soon as Abigail had her money, she took off to find Chloe. Bridget decided to continue her search for Greg. She wanted to remind him he had the last zombie-wrestling shift.

After helping a small, tearful boy in a Harry Potter costume with a fruitless search for his wand, and stepping on a piece of salmon and avocado sushi that squelched up and over her white trainers, she finally spotted him; standing next to the pop-up wine bar, chatting to Jono and an attractive redhead she didn't recognise.

'Hey,' said Bridget, feeling weirdly like an interloper.

'Hey,' said Greg, 'we were just discussing your favourite subject.'

'Really. What's that?'

'Porn.' He laughed.

'Hi,' Bridget said, offering her hand to the attractive redhead when it became apparent no one was going to introduce her. 'I'm Bridget.'

'Sorry,' said Greg. 'Bridget, this is Kate, my client. Kate, this is my wife, Bridget.'

'Nice to meet you,' said Kate, smiling warmly.

'You too. Hey, Jono.' Bridget gave him a kiss. 'Not child pornography, I hope. I feel like I can't get away from it!'

'We were talking more in general,' said Kate.

'I was saying how I never used to mind it,' said Greg. 'But when we had Abigail, well I guess I realised those women I'd been ogling were all somebody's daughter.'

Bridget looked over at Jono. He appeared distinctly ill at ease.

'So,' she said to Kate, 'which class . . .'

Just then a handsome man came up behind Kate; grabbing her around the waist, he rested his chin on her hair.

'Hi, Greg.'

'Evening, Brett. This is my wife, Bridget. And my good mate, Jono.'

'Actually, we just met,' Brett said, grinning at Bridget.

'Did we?' Bridget looked at him blankly.

Brett reached into his pocket and drew out a Freddy Krueger mask.

'Oh, right,' she said, laughing. 'The lawyer. You guys live on Spur Street. It's all falling into place now.'

'I saw your name on that Facebook page, Brett. Good call, mate. I posted mine this morning. You need to get yours on there, Jono. Safety in numbers, eh?' Greg winked.

'Thank God,' said a loud, familiar voice. 'Some sane adult company at last! First, my beastly children force me to do the Macarena, not once, but twice. What kind of a crap DJ plays that bloody song in the first place? And then I get cornered by fucking Ruth.'

'Us too,' said Bridget, trying to catch Brett's eye, but both he and Kate were staring, wide-eyed, at Roz.

While most parents had only made the most minimal of efforts on the costume front, Roz had crammed her generous curves into a full latex Catwoman bodysuit.

Following another round of introductions, the talk moved on to some big game happening that weekend and Bridget took the opportunity to draw Roz aside.

'What's up, doll?'

She told Roz about her lunch with Amanda and how this morning Amanda had rung with what she'd gleaned from Darren Peters.

'I told you, you should have rung him,' Roz interrupted, the shiny triangle ears on top of her head all aquiver.

'Yes, you were right, but listen, he didn't have, or wouldn't give her, a name. I'm not sure which. It's what he told her the guy was caught with, though. I can't stop thinking about it.'

Roz looked at her expectantly.

'Ugh . . . I don't know how to say it.'

'Spit it out, Bridge.'

'It's been gnawing away at me all day.'

'You're killing me here.'

'I think it's Tristan.' The words spilled out of Bridget, as damaging and astonishing as a flash flood.

'What? What are you talking about?'

'That video on Hine's. The one we assumed one of the kids had made. That I accused Zachariah of. Well, it sounds exactly like what the guy was putting on the internet. All this footage zooming in on little girls' vulvas. All these little girls with their heads cut off.'

'Jesus, are you sure?'

'Yes, no. Oh God, I don't know.'

'That fucker. I'm going to kill him.'

'Slow down, Roz.'

'It all makes sense now, doesn't it? Zachariah and Skye probably moved schools because they found out at their last one. And it explains why Lucy looks such a wreck. We need to tell Greg and Jono. The four of us should go round there. Tonight. Confront them.'

Bridget had known Roz would thirst for action, but she'd forgotten what a hothead she could be. She thought about her mother's advice. About her promise to Lucy: srough sick and sin.

'No,' she said. 'I need to talk to Lucy. Please, Roz, promise me you won't say or do anything. Not yet.'

Chapter
Forty-four

November
Saturday

Bridget considered her reflection, puzzling how her features could be both so doughy, and yet so small, so tight with sleep. It wasn't just that her eyes hadn't fully opened; it was as if everything — nose, mouth, cheeks — had converged at her face's centre point.

Like one of those stress balls, she thought, *that's what I look like: a mauled sphere of latex foam, missing only the company logo.*

She turned on the cold tap, cupping her hands under the stream of water before bringing them quickly to her face. The hand towel almost crunched on contact with her skin. She rubbed roughly.

As good as an exfoliating treatment. A teenage Lucy popped into her head, reading out loud from *Cosmo* magazine. *It says you can make a purifying mask with rolled oats. Gross, face porridge!*

Lucy, oh God, Lucy. What to do?

In the face of Roz's anger last night, Bridget had felt such clarity. Lucy had been her friend first; she had been the recipient of the information; it was for her to deal with.

It was easy to be brave with a few wines in you, though.

She was mindful, too, that she hadn't yet shared her suspicions with Greg. It hadn't been a deliberate decision. She'd wanted to talk to him about it in person, but he'd finished work late and the kids had been amping to get to Fright Night. And then when they got home something had made her hold back.

Keen not to wake the rest of the household, she slipped out the door.

Opening the letterbox to grab the Saturday paper, the only day they still bothered getting it delivered, her eyes strayed to the lavender growing there.

She picked one and ran it under her nose.

Again, she was reminded of Lucy, how she had always insisted on stopping whenever they passed a bush of the purple flower in order to appreciate its scent. *Mmmm . . . like Provence.* Even though, back then, Lucy had yet to step foot out of the country.

In the kitchen, Bridget made herself a cup of English breakfast tea, turning off the kettle just before its shrill whistle kicked in. She sat down at the table with the newspaper, pulling out the glossy magazine and putting it aside to read later.

She wondered if Amanda's feature on the real estate bubble would run today. Recalling how freely she had skewered Point Heed's residents, her neighbours, Bridget's stomach did a little flip. She prayed Amanda would have fudged any identifying details.

Skimming through the latest news, a headline at the top of page five leapt out at her: 'Leafy suburb ablaze over local paedophile'.

Fuck!

Bridget checked the byline: Darren Peters.

Double fuck!

She read the stand first: 'The affluent inner-east community of Point Heed is up in arms a resident caught sharing child pornography online has had his name suppressed.'

Fuck! Fuck! Fuck!

There was Mr Ngata, saying how difficult it was to run a school when there was so much fear among the parent body. There was Ruth, covering off every hysterical theory Bridget had heard her spout the past ten days.

Darren Peters had evidently done his work.

Bridget felt a rush of irrational anger. At herself for asking Amanda, at Amanda for alerting Darren to the story's potential, at Darren for being such a bloody newshound. And, underneath her anger, something else:

an urgent need to warn Lucy, to somehow protect her from the shit storm Bridget felt sure was coming her way.

Before she could chicken out, she picked up her phone, scrolling through the contacts list until she reached L.

She knew Lucy wouldn't answer, but she would leave a message, asking her to please call, that it was important.

She counted the rings: three, four, five. *C'mon*, she urged, *click over*. In her head she practised what she would say.

'Hello, Bridget.'

'Oh . . . hi! I wasn't expecting you to pick up.' Bridget filled the silence with a nervous laugh. 'How are you?'

'Fine.'

She waited for Lucy to return the question, but again there was only silence.

'So, I, ah . . . I see Zachariah and Skye have enrolled at Point Heed.'

'Yes.'

Jesus, she wasn't making this easy.

'I wanted to apologise, actually. For . . . for what happened on Hine's. For blaming Zachariah like that. It wasn't fair of me.'

'Is that why you rang?'

'Kind of. Well, not exactly. The thing is, I know. At least I think I do.'

'Know what?'

'That . . . Oh God, there's no easy way to say this.'

Big girls' pants, Bridget, big girls' pants.

'It was Tristan, wasn't it? Who made the video on Hine's? He's the child pornographer. The one in the papers. It's him, isn't it?'

Bridget was prepared for Lucy's fierce denial, for her to slam down the phone, but her cool, detached manner didn't change.

'I can't talk about this right now.'

'Sorry . . . yes, I mean, no, of course not. I was thinking maybe we could have a coffee soon?'

'No, I'll meet you at the beach in twenty.'

Lucy hung up and, for a moment, Bridget stood there staring at her phone. She hadn't even asked whether it suited her.

In their room Greg was propped up in bed, watching something on his laptop, a pair of headphones on. Bridget waved her hand in front of his face.

'What's up?' he asked, uncovering an ear.

'I have to go out. To meet Lucy.'

'Wha . . .?'

'You'll need to get the kids ready for soccer. I'll explain later.'

They arrived at the same time, both instinctively making for their old spot, at the city end of the beach, underneath the rock they'd nicknamed 'The Doughnut' because of the hole at its centre.

Unsure what to do, Bridget put her arms out. They had always greeted each other with a hug. 'No,' Lucy used to say if she judged Bridget had withdrawn too fast, 'a proper hug.'

But Lucy ducked her embrace and Bridget stumbled. She caught herself on the cliff wall, struggling to appear casual.

She tried to smile. 'Well, this is odd.'

Odd: such a short, sapless word, and yet for Bridget it held the weight of everything that had gone wrong between them in its three little letters.

'Yes, sorry about that,' Lucy said.

There were so many things Lucy could apologise for; Bridget waited for her to elaborate, a flicker of hope in her chest.

'It was impossible to talk at home.'

'No worries,' said Bridget, annoyed she was foolish enough to expect more from Lucy. 'I'm sorry that I just called, out of the blue like that.'

'That's okay. It's important we get things straight.'

Again, Bridget's heart lurched. Lucy did care.

And then, her eyes ablaze with defiance, Lucy said: 'It's not like he actually touched them.'

Crazy, Bridget would reflect later, how, in spite of the horror coming out of Lucy's mouth, all she could think about was how well she knew that face. As well as her own. Perhaps better.

'Look,' said Lucy, passing her something.

A phone. A video.

The screen was quite dark, but Bridget could just make out the wrought iron beds, the toy chest; Skye and Willow's bedroom.

And there they were: two little girls, obviously asleep, nighties bunched up around necks and over faces, private parts exposed.

'See, it's not as bad as you think. No one's being hurt. They weren't hurt.'

While the camera operator wasn't visible, you were conscious of them. Of someone breathing.

Bridget thrust the phone at Lucy, reaching behind with her other hand, seeking something solid, grazing her knuckles on the unforgiving rockface.

His own daughters!

She recalled Tristan's erection, poised above Lucy's open lips, his lily of the valley wings.

God, how could she have fancied him? Disgust swept through her and she could almost taste it. On her tongue, down her throat, choking her.

It's sticking to your face and it's in your mouth, and something is watching you, smiling.

Abigail's description of her bad dream came back to her, as loathsome and unwelcome as a cockroach scuttling out from under the fridge. Someone not *something*.

No, please no. Not her daughter, too.

'Do you see?' asked Lucy.

And with the utmost clarity, Bridget did.

So she did the only thing she could think to do. She ran.

Away from Lucy and her sordid tale.

Towards home. Towards Greg and the kids.

Chapter Forty-five

November Saturday

There was a weird kind of symmetry, thought Bridget, slowing to catch her breath.

It had been Lucy to run off on Hine's. Well not run exactly — they'd been on an island after all.

Refusing to even look at the rest of them, she'd instructed Tristan and the kids to pack their bags.

Initially, Bridget hadn't believed they would actually leave. For starters, they were reliant on Greg to transport them. Greg, who, despite Bridget's pleas to *do something,* had chosen to remove himself from the situation, stowing away behind the filleting station with Jono.

At a loss as to what to do, Bridget had torn around gathering up their stray belongings, placing them in front of Lucy and Tristan's closed bedroom door, too scared to knock.

'Stop,' Roz had said eventually. 'Enough!'

And somehow the solemnity of her tone had penetrated Bridget's frenzy.

She wasn't sure whether money had talked, or Lucy had appealed to Don's sense of compassion, but about an hour later he'd pulled into their little bay in a boat not much bigger than a dinghy with an outboard on the stern. Helping Tristan load the gear on board, Don had lifted an uncertain hand in Roz and Bridget's direction.

As the overloaded vessel started to motor away, Abigail had suddenly appeared from the house.

'Skye, Skye,' she'd called, small legs pumping, Skye's American Girl doll, Kendall, bouncing rigidly in her arms.

Skye looked up as Abigail launched Kendall through the air, but didn't reach out to catch her, and there was a thud as the doll smacked into the side of the boat.

It was Zachariah who'd fished her out.

Holding the soaking wet toy on his lap, he'd locked eyes with Bridget, and even when the boat was but a speck on the horizon, she'd been sure she could still feel the burn of his gaze.

'Hello,' Bridget called as she opened her front door.

'Greg?'

Moving through the empty spaces, she sensed she had only just missed them.

They were nowhere and yet everywhere: in the shoehorn discarded on the hall floor that Jackson used to put his soccer boots on, in the sugary milk puddling in the bottom of the cereal bowl, in the brush netted with Abigail's hair, a scrunchie wound around its handle.

She ached for them ferociously. A ferocity she recognised had more to do with her encounter on the beach with Lucy than the short period of time since last she'd seen them. It was the comfort, the very unconditionality of them, she hankered after.

She wondered if her parents still yearned for her, for each other, like this, or if like most appetites, this, too, waned with age?

Thinking of her mother, Bridget was reminded of what she'd said: Lucy did compartmentalise. How else to explain her willingness to rationalise Tristan's behaviour? Her capacity to live with the knowledge her husband was turned on by little girls, by their own daughters?

As for the rest of them and their shared blindness, well, they had put their own children at risk.

What to do, what to do?

Forcing herself to stack the dishwasher, all Bridget could think was that she needed to talk to Greg, seek his wise counsel. She didn't know why she hadn't told him.

When, finally, she heard them clattering through the door, it took everything she had to remain in place, to wait for them to come to her.

'Mum, Mum!' Abigail raced into the kitchen.

Bridget clutched the table; she felt faint.

'We won, we won!'

'That's fantastic, darling. Congratulations. How about you, Jackson, honey?'

'S'all right. 3–1.'

'To?'

'The other side.'

'All right? Our boy scored the most amazing goal. Straight down the middle!'

Greg ruffled Jackson's hair and, in spite of his adolescent taciturnity, Bridget could tell he was chuffed.

Greg looked at her and his eyes widened with concern. She must appear a sight.

'How about cheese toasties?' he suggested. 'And then you can both give your mum and I some peace and quiet, eh? Go chill out in your rooms for a bit?'

Watching Greg butter bread, Bridget had the impression she was observing this domestic scene from above, from outside her body.

Sandwiches grilled, children dispatched, Greg turned to her.

'Tell me.'

Now that she had him to herself, Bridget found she was unable to wrangle her thoughts, concentrating, instead, on cleaning the grease from between the ridges of the toastie machine.

'Leave that, Bridget. Sit down.'

He was patient while she told him about the suspicion Amanda had inadvertently planted, and about Roz's fury. In her distress, though, she had only really considered what it all meant for her, for her relationship with Lucy. When she revealed to Greg what she'd learnt about Tristan, it was like watching her husband fragment in front of her eyes. As if he was not, as she had always believed, cast from the inexorability of granite, but something far more fragile.

And when she mentioned Abigail's dreams, raised the horrendous possibility their daughter had featured in one of Tristan's videos, her innocence misappropriated and sent out into the big wide world, she saw he could not cope. That it was too much.

'No,' he groaned. 'You're wrong! The paper said it was a father of two. Tristan has three kids.'

'Not in the eyes of the law he doesn't. They always used to talk about Tristan adopting Zachariah, but they never got around to it. Greg, we have to face facts. Lucy as good as admitted to me it was him.'

Bridget felt cruel when she saw how swiftly the hope that had flared in his eyes fizzled out.

All afternoon long they drifted about the house, overcome by a terrible kind of dullness.

At one point her phone rang: Roz. And though Bridget knew Roz would be desperate to find out whether she'd spoken to Lucy, she couldn't bring herself to pick up.

What to do, what to do?

Rather than providing Bridget with any kind of an answer, Greg had simply joined her in her unspoken, helpless refrain. In the end it was Bridget who got it together, who made dinner and sorted the kids. Who decided they would sleep on it. Make a decision in the morning.

That night Greg clasped her to him and she buried her face in the safety of his neck. Tensing when she felt the familiar hardness against her tummy, she placed the palm of her hand flat on his chest.

'Shush,' he said, though she hadn't made a sound.

So, she let him enter her, quietly astonished how, in spite of everything, her body could still respond with such pleasure.

And when Greg began to pant, she forcibly pushed the memory of the quickening of another's breath from her mind.

Chapter
Forty-six

November
Sunday

Bridget dreamt there was a tiny mouse nibbling on her ear. She burrowed further under the duvet.

It was taking small bites now.

Ouch!

She opened her eyes to find Jackson pulling insistently on her lobe. Hauling the sheet up over her bare breasts, she turned on the reading light.

'What the hell?' Greg grumbled, grinding at his face with calloused hands.

'Jackson,' Bridget said. 'Is everything okay, honey? You gave me such a fright, waking me like that. What time is it anyway?'

'Dunno. Four-thirty, maybe.'

'It's Sunday bloody morning, Jackson. The day most normal people sleep in. What's going on?'

'Hush,' she said to Greg, shifting her hips sideways to make room on the bed. 'Here, sit down, honey.'

'I couldn't sleep,' said Jackson.

'Why not, honey?'

'I heard you and Dad.'

For a moment, Bridget thought he'd overheard them having sex.

Jackson's shoulders heaved.

'Oh, honey. What is it?'

'It was me,' he sobbed.

'What are you talking about, Jackson?'

Greg's voice was sharp, too sharp, and she pinched his thigh between her forefinger and thumb.

'What, baby? What was you?'

'The video. I made the video.'

'What video, Jackson?'

Bridget was aware now she was the one sounding harsh.

'On Hine's. The one you accused Zachariah of making.'

Bridget had the awful feeling someone had grasped hold of the corner of this metaphorical rug she was standing on and was pulling it slowly but surely towards them.

'No, Jackson, I was wrong. It wasn't Zachariah. We know who made it now. That's why Dad and I were so upset.'

'I didn't want to tell you.'

'Tell us what?'

'About what was going on.'

No, not a rug; wrong analogy. Too soft. It was more like a bomb. Like a bomb had gone off beneath her. Rubble, limbs, craters; ruin every which way she turned.

'Are you saying it wasn't Tristan who filmed the girls?' Greg demanded.

Bridget shook herself. They weren't approaching this the right way. Her neck clicked.

'Try starting at the beginning, honey,' she said in her most soothing voice.

'That first night we got there . . .'

'Go on.' She stroked his back. 'We're listening.'

'Earl said he had something to show us. You were all sitting around outside. Getting drunk. He got his dad's phone.'

Oh God.

'It's all right, darling. Carry on.'

'And there was some, you know, porn.'

'What was it, Jackson? What kind?'

'I can't remember.'

'You need to try, baby. It's important.'

'It was, you know . . .'

'Was it . . .' Bridget knew what she needed to ask, but couldn't force the words out.

'Lesbians,' Jackson said eventually.

Bridget let out a ragged breath, a breath she hadn't even realised she'd been holding.

'Yeah, these two naked girls like doing stuff to each other.'

'Girls?' Bridget's chest constricted. 'How old were they?'

'I dunno. Old, like twenty-five maybe.'

'Okaaay . . .' said Greg, the tiniest hint of a laugh. 'So, you watched this video and then what happened?'

'The next morning, you know, when Abigail got stung by a bee and we met Don?'

He looked at Bridget. She nodded.

'Yes, I remember.'

'Well, it was Zachariah's idea that we get the girls to go for a walk.'

'Why?'

'To get them away from the house.'

'Yes, but what for?'

'So that he could take their American Girl dolls.'

'What did he want them for?'

It was a rhetorical question; Bridget knew where this was heading.

'To make a porno.'

'Right. That's what he was doing behind the farmhouse . . . But, hang on, does that mean it was Zachariah who videoed the girls in their togs? That I *was* correct after all?'

Jackson went quiet again. This time they both waited him out.

'You know how we went to Don's place? And then we met you at Mermaids' Cove? Don had these special stone things. You could light a fire with them.'

'Flint,' said Greg.

'Yeah, I guess. I don't know why, but I put one in my pocket. And Zachariah saw me. He said I was a thief. That he'd tell on me unless I did what he said.'

'Did what?'

'Made a porno. A real one. Not dolls. He wanted me to video the girls when they were asleep. You know, their thingies. I knew . . . I knew it wasn't right, though.'

'So, you videoed them in their togs?'

'Yeah, but I stopped when they took them off.'

Jackson looked at them, his face stricken.

'You have to believe me!'

Bridget contorted her mouth into what she hoped was a reassuring smile.

'He said I was a wuss, and he took the iPad off me and kept filming them himself.'

'Why didn't you tell us, Jackson?'

'I felt bad for taking Don's stone. I thought this way you wouldn't find out. And you couldn't really see nothing or anything, not in the bit I filmed.'

Bridget sank back down onto the bed.

Jesus. Was no one blameless?

Chapter
Forty-seven

November
Sunday

'We need to talk. Come to the beach. ASAP. I'll wait for you.'

Bridget pushed send. Where yesterday there had been hesitation, now she felt only decisiveness.

She hadn't gone back to sleep. How could she have? Not after what Jackson had told them. She'd lain there, Jackson in between them, his man-child limbs flung across her, trying to shepherd her thoughts.

Pornography: she'd been right about that. About it being like a line of dominoes, with one leading to another, which in turn led to another.

And Zachariah, she'd been right all along about him, too.

But what else? Of what else could she be certain?

There was a connection between what had transpired on Hine's and what Tristan had been done for. There had to be. But what? Had Tristan somehow been grooming Zachariah? Was that it?

And was there . . . she could scarcely bring herself to go there . . . was there some link between this heinous train wreck and her baby girl's nightmares?

It was as if her house was built of sand. No, not sand, something even more tenuous. Dust, her entire fucking house was made of dust. Shifting and swirling around her.

Lucy was clearly deluded; she had to talk to her again. Yesterday had obviously just been a charade; a steaming heap of trickery and half-truths.

Oh God, how was she going to tell Roz? Tell her it was Jono, *her husband*, and his dirty habit, his dirty, *careless* habit, that had been the first domino to topple?

Text sent, Bridget wriggled out of bed. As quietly as possible, she rummaged for a sports bra in her underwear drawer. There was a pair of half-worn leggings and a T-shirt hanging off the hook on the back of the door. She grabbed some socks and trainers. Pressing the bundle to her chest, she eased the door closed behind her.

She didn't bother with the bathroom light, dressing as quickly as she could, sitting on the toilet to lace her shoes. She brushed her teeth, splashed water on her face, swiped deodorant under her arms. Tiptoeing down the hall, she dragged her hair into a ponytail.

About to open the front door, she changed her mind, poking her head into Abigail's room. She smoothed her sleeping daughter's hair off her warm little forehead.

'Love you, my darling,' she whispered.

Outside, the morning air greeted her bitingly.

Bridget began to run.

With no cars about, she was conscious of every sound she made. Breath: *huff, puff*. Heart: *clunk, tunk*. Feet: *smack, thwack*.

She felt as if she could run forever; on and on and on.

The beach was inky and still, the distant traffic glittering kaleidoscopically; city stars.

Curiously, Bridget had no doubts about whether or not Lucy would come. She recalled Lucy's need to show her the video yesterday, as if she sought her approval, her absolution, and she felt strangely powerful.

Normally it would have frightened Bridget to be alone on the beach like this, in the dark, but she had no fear.

She considered what it was she wanted out of this meeting she'd demanded of her former best friend. Answers to her questions, yes. But what of their friendship? Could they resurrect it? With everything that had taken place, did she even want to be friends?

Whatever the outcome, she knew she couldn't live with a watered-down version of what they'd once had.

'Over here.'

Bridget started. She glanced at her wrist. It was only just gone six.

'I didn't expect you to get here so quickly.'

'I don't sleep much these days.'

'I couldn't sleep either . . .' Bridget cleared her throat. 'I'm sorry I left like that yesterday.'

Fuck. She wasn't here to apologise.

Lucy didn't respond.

'Actually, the reason I'm up so early is because Jackson woke us. Very upset. About what really happened on Hine's.'

Still nothing.

'I guess you know it was Jackson who made the video?'

Lucy inclined her head ever so slightly.

'Except, it wasn't just him. Zachariah put him up to it. Threatened him, in fact. And carried it on when Jackson tried to stop. I know I got it wrong before, but I'm pretty certain he's telling the truth.

'He also told us about Jono's smutty video. That Earl showed it to them. That it gave Zachariah the idea. Something doesn't add up, though. I keep running over it in my head. The boys are exposed to porn, which is fucked, but I guess inevitable these days. Anyway, they make their own video, which I find and lose my rag, and then you disappear out of our lives. Until you suddenly resurface, at the same time everyone is going into meltdown over a local child pornographer. So, I put two and two together and maybe I made five, but yesterday you more or less confirmed my suspicions. That Tristan's the child pornographer. And yet I'm missing something. I know there's something I'm not seeing here.'

When Lucy wasn't forthcoming with an explanation, or even an attempt at one, Bridget erupted.

'You act as if whatever the hell is going on in your family didn't, doesn't, affect the rest of us. But did you know Abigail has been having these recurring nightmares?

'No, you didn't, I mean, how could you? You've refused to speak to me for nine months, you don't know anything about my life. But my daughter screams in the night because she thinks something's smothering her. And since you showed me that video on your phone all I can think is that your husband, your fucking husband, maybe he . . . maybe he filmed my daughter, too.'

Bridget's words had come out in a sort of strangled sob.

'No.'

Lucy raised her hand and, for a moment, Bridget thought she was going to slap her.

'No, what?'

'No, he didn't.' Lucy looked at her hand as if she, herself, wasn't sure of her intentions.

'How do you know, Lucy?'

'Because I know he didn't.'

'Oh, c'mon, Lucy. You're the one who showed me that video. What's wrong with you? I thought I knew you, really knew you. But no friend of mine would stay with a man who got off on his own daughters. And what about Zachariah? How do you explain his behaviour? It has to have been learned somewhere. Jackson and Earl didn't watch Jono's girl-on-girl action and suddenly get the idea to go make a video. Jackson said Zachariah wanted him to film the girls at night, while they were asleep. Which sounds awfully like what you showed me on your phone. And I'm sorry, but I don't buy that a grown man got the idea from his step-son. More like he taught him. Planted the seed. Has Tristan been abusing Zachariah? All these years is that why Zachariah's been acting up?'

'No! He didn't do any of those things. He's not like that.'

'What the fuck, Lucy? It's like you're in lala land. He's on home detention. He got caught with child pornography.'

'Yes, he is. But it wasn't him.'

'I don't understand.'

'No, but then you never did. You've never got him.'

'I've never got Tristan? What are you talking about? You guys were our best friends.'

'Not Tristan. Zachariah.'

'Zachariah? What are you talking about?'

'I know you've always thought he was unusual. But ever since he was a little boy, he's had this kind of creative genius. I always thought if only I could just tap into it . . . It's like life bores him. Like he's on a different plane to the rest of us. Where none of the social mores we get bogged down with matter. And he's always had this kind of sensuality; gets it from me, I guess.'

Lucy gave a proud little laugh.

'You remember how I was always grinding up against poles and things when I was a kid? He was the same. Rubbing himself on anything he could find.

'Anyhow, I guess he got the idea on Hine's. All those sticky nights. The kids all in the bunkroom. And you know what little girls are like, tossing and turning so their nighties ride up. Of course, I would have nipped it in the bud if I'd known. But I've always tried to be respectful of his privacy.

'Then, after we got back from Hine's, he was so down. I mean we all were, but he was moping around the house all the time. And I was worried, you know, so I suggested Tristan take him back to that gaming place. Anyway, apparently some of the older guys were talking about the dark web, how there was money to be made. How people would pay for photos of feet, used undies, that kind of thing. So, Zachariah starts making the videos and distributing them through his gaming contacts. It was quite entrepreneurial, actually. He didn't get that from me!'

That same little laugh again.

Bridget felt nauseous.

'So where does Tristan come in to all this?'

'When the police started sniffing around and we realised what he'd been up to, I knew I had to convince Tristan to say he'd made the videos. I couldn't have it coming out. Zachariah's still so young. It would have ruined his life.'

'But what about Tristan's life? Why would he agree?'

'Because he loves me.'

'How could you, Lucy?'

'How could I not? He's my only son. My first-born. And . . . oh, I don't know, I suppose if I'm being completely honest, I've always viewed him through a prism of guilt.'

'Guilt? You've given that child everything. Often at the expense of your girls.'

'All that alcohol, though, all those drugs I was doing when he was conceived.'

'That's because your mother had just died, Lucy. You stopped when you found out you were pregnant.'

'That's what I always let you think, Bridget, but I didn't actually stop. Not straight away. Oh, I did eventually, but at first it was like I couldn't fathom I was having a baby. I was selfish, I guess. Young and selfish.'

A breeze blew in off the sea and Bridget shivered.

'You were trapped in a self-destructive spiral,' she said. 'Probably depressed.'

'Was I? At the time it felt like I was having fun. Plus, there's the fact I have no idea who his father is. Tristan's done his best, but a boy needs his father, his real father. I know Zachariah's different. That he's a square peg trying to fit into a round hole. But I guess I've always held on to what you said to me once.'

'What? What did I say?'

'That as mothers we're only ever as happy as our unhappiest child. Well, he was my unhappiest, always was. And I was so tired. I just wanted him to be happy for once. Thought if he was happy, then maybe I finally would be, too.'

For the first time, Lucy looked at her directly.

'You'd do anything for your kids. Don't tell me you don't get it, Bridget.'

'Of course, I get it. I'd like to think, though, that if one of my children was behaving anti-socially, I'd address it. Seek expert help. But I'll tell you what I don't get, Lucy. I don't get how you could have done that to Tristan. To Skye and to Willow. I've never trusted Zachariah, always been fearful of what he was capable of. But I trusted you, and because of that I chose to trust you knew your son. I trusted you, Lucy, and for that I'll never forgive myself.'

Bridget looked at her oldest friend's beautiful face. Behind Lucy the morning sun had blunted the city stars. Would she ever know the whole story? Did she even really want to know? Perhaps ignorance was sweeter.

The only thing of which she could be absolutely sure was that in some shape or form, in some small way, they were all to blame. Culpable, at the very least, of looking in all the wrong places.

Chapter Forty-eight

December
Monday

It was the ball she noticed first. Or rather, it was the absence of that sad, pink deflated orb. No more *Hola! Soy Dora*.

Maybe Swiper swiped it?

Bridget almost laughed. But didn't. Not when she saw the large, black, shiny Audi parked in the carport. The large, black stone planters flanking the front steps.

No more dusty jumble of gumboots, running shoes, jandals, no more broken Nerf gun; a dull kind of a pain hollowed out her belly. It was as if they had all been erased, not only the mismatched footwear, the broken toys, but their owners, too.

A teenage boy stepped out onto the driveway, dunking a basketball into the hoop attached to the garage wall. That hoop was shiny and new, too.

Zachariah hadn't played basketball. Zachariah hadn't played any sports.

'Nice shot!'

Grinning, he waved in the direction of the open window.

The woman's voice hovered there in the warm summer air.

Bridget pictured her, this unknown, unseen woman, pausing momentarily at the kitchen bench to admire her handsome, athletic son.

No, they hadn't been erased, but swapped out, traded in: for a better model.

Turning back to his game, the boy spotted Bridget standing on the footpath, watching. Embarrassed, she raised a hand in greeting. He looked at her questioningly.

'Sorry, I didn't mean to stare. It's just . . . well, I knew the family who used to live here. I didn't realise they were selling.'

'Yeah, we moved in last week.'

'It must have been a quick sale.'

'I guess.'

'You don't happen to know where they went, do you?'

'Dunno. Think my parents said something about the country.'

He resumed his dribbling.

Walking away from Lucy's old house, Bridget thought about how wholesome this replacement Zachariah seemed, how easily he inhabited his skin, and she was filled with a sense of both loss and regret.

Not for the friendship they'd had, that felt sullied now, shameful almost, but for what they could have had.

If only Bridget had forced the issue of Zachariah with Lucy. Forced her to address his aberrant ways years ago.

If only she hadn't always been so eager to keep her on the pedestal she'd placed her on, so ready to see the best in her.

Then maybe . . .

Maybe what? Maybe she could have protected them? Saved them?

Idiot!

They had each made their own morally ambiguous choices. And Lucy, Lucy with her wilful myopia regarding Zachariah, her willingness to exploit those who adored her, well Lucy more than any of them had made her bed. Made her bed and soiled it, too.

Bridget turned left onto Point Heed Road.

The country!

They were gone. All of them. Lucy. Tristan. Zachariah. The girls. Goneski.

And as she thought this, Bridget became aware of a new feeling fluttering around the edges of her consciousness.

Relief.

For seven weeks, ever since their final encounter on the beach, she had seesawed wildly about how to deal with what Lucy had told her.

She'd felt burdened by it. Had worn its weight like a woollen shawl embroidered with lead bearing down upon her shoulders, chafing at her.

She'd wake up, determined to go to the police. All full of puff and steam. And then by lunchtime she would have changed her mind.

Changed her mind . . . or chickened out?

There was a part of her, Bridget knew, that was scared. Scared of being on the receiving end of Lucy's unpredictable wrath. Scared of jettisoning, once and for all, any memory of love between them.

Sometimes, when she was feeling kinder to herself, she would put her reluctance to report Zachariah down to some weirdly misplaced sense of loyalty. To what exactly, she wasn't clear. Certainly, it wasn't to that little creep.

She'd wondered whether, perhaps, it was to herself, to her former self.

Dobbing in Zachariah meant outing Lucy, and somehow that felt like she was casting doubt upon her own judgement. Like it made a mockery of all those years of friendship; rendered their shared history worthless.

Her initial instinct had been to warn the school, and she'd marched up there that first Monday with every intention of going straight to Mr Ngata. But she'd spotted Miss Smythe deep in conversation with Ruth and Hi-Vis Mum at the school gate, and she'd imagined the field day they would have. She'd imagined Sina, crowing about Bridget having had the audacity to besmirch her husband's name, when all along she should have been paying more attention to her own flock. And she'd backed away.

Then, later that same day, as she was dropping the kids to their various extracurricular activities, Jackson had mentioned Zachariah hadn't been at school. 'Yeah,' Abigail had said, 'neither was Skye.'

And when there was still no sign of them two weeks later, Bridget had started to think maybe they weren't coming back.

Yet while this had reduced the likelihood of crossing paths with Lucy, it hadn't resolved the bigger issue of whether she should be taking the matter further.

Greg hadn't exactly helped.

He'd cried when she'd told him it wasn't Tristan. Hot, fat tears.

And then he'd done what he always did; he'd moved on. If she brought it up, he said they should just put it behind them. That life was too short to expend any more energy on it.

Some days she'd succeed. Succeed at briefly fooling herself all was well in her world.

But how did you *just* put such an agonising situation behind you? How did you *just* move on from all the lies and uncertainties?

Telling Roz had been the worst bit.

She'd expected Roz to explode, to bash down Lucy and Tristan's front door in rage, but, instead, it was as if she imploded. As if the discovery Jono's proclivities had unwittingly triggered the whole ugly mess had quietly but surely destroyed something in her. Some small yet essential part.

Bridget kept trying to reach out to her but, unusually for Roz, she'd gone to ground.

According to Greg, things were pretty rocky on the home front.

'Oh Roz,' Bridget had said on one of the rare times Roz had actually picked up her phone, 'you're not going to leave him, are you? We can't lose you guys, too.'

'Nah,' Roz had said, 'I'll get over it. It just fucks me off, though, you know. No matter how far behind you think you've left it all, that shit will still get you; still bite you on the fucking arse.'

She hadn't been sure if Roz was talking about Jono's porn or her past abuse. It probably didn't matter; for Roz they seemed to have converged.

The only real ray of light these past few weeks had been Abigail's bad dreams. Bridget had been on the brink of making an appointment with a child psychologist, when the dreams had stopped.

And without the nightmares tormenting Abigail, Bridget had decided there was little point in tormenting herself. Even if she were to find proof of a connection to the videos, it wouldn't change anything, would only lead to more pain.

No, she concluded, she had two great kids. She would stop looking for sinister endings to their mostly happy stories.

As she passed the Point Heed Dairy, almost a spring in her step, Bridget noticed the stack of newspapers sitting neatly folded on their stand, and she was struck by an image.

Of herself, one day in the future, blithely flicking through a paper, and stumbling across Zachariah's name.

Not among the 'In Briefs'.

Not two paltry lines.

But a full-page feature: Zachariah, guilty of some vile crime.

And she would wonder whether maybe, if only she'd been more courageous, less conflicted, whether maybe, just maybe, she could have stopped him.

Acknowledgements

I took my sweet, sweet time to write this book. My excuses were copious; the number of people who coached, coaxed and coerced me across the finish line even greater. None more so, however, than my publisher and dear friend, Miff Hurley. It was she who forced me to settle on which story I would tell, and she who pushed and shoved me to eventually complete it. Thank you, Miffy, for being quite the loveliest of taskmasters.

As a journalist I learnt the importance of working under an editor you respected and trusted. As a fledgling author I consider myself extraordinarily fortunate my book was placed in the steady, discerning, kind and cheery hands of Emma Neale.

If someone had told me all those decades ago when I used to girl crush on Joanna Grochowicz in the corridors of the Auckland University Faculty of Arts that one day not only would we both be published writers, but I would consider her a close friend, I never would have believed it. Thank you, Joanna, for the countless pep talks and ever-ready ear.

One of my earliest readers was my wise and loving friend, Jodi Wiltshire, who has more of a writer's way of thinking than she gives herself credit for.

To Geoff Walker, who probably can't even recall reading it, but whose advice about my first chapter sent me off in a superior direction.

By what has sometimes felt like sheer fluke, I count myself lucky enough to be a fully paid-up member of the Tulips, a group of the most successful, clever and ambitious women I know. Deborah, Miriyana, Caro, Sarah, Kim, Michelle: thank you for not giving up on me when I walked away from the media to write a novel. You never failed to inspire me.

Some of my most productive writing was done in the homes of others. Deborah and Carl, Michelle and Campbell, you were the most generous hosts an aspiring writer could hope for.

My utmost gratitude to Richard Upton, who provided me with excellent (and free!) legal advice not once but twice. I'm sorry the book isn't dedicated to you, Richard, as you hinted might be a nice thing to do, but hopefully this acknowledgement goes some way to alleviating your disappointment!

To Babiche Martens, who in the face of my reluctance as a subject and the most unbelievable wind, was not only unfailingly patient, but managed to take a photo of me I actually like.

Many, many thanks to Leonie Freeman, Rebecca Simpson, Jenny Hellen, Courtney Smith, Tessa King, Tracey Wogan, Sandy Cull, Kate Barraclough, Melanie Laville-Moore and all the sales team at Allen & Unwin. While the words on these pages are mine, the fact people can walk into a bookstore and actually buy them is down to your skill and expertise.

I'm so grateful to Stacey Morrison, Charity Norman, Claire Mabey, Jacqueline Bublitz, Kim Knight and Frances Morton, who were kind enough to take the time out of their busy lives to read an advance copy.

To Dov Phillips, who let me see my anxiety was getting in the way of writing the bloody thing!

To my book club - Deb, Deb, Trish, Emma, Trudy, Clarity, Karyn, Kim, Sarah - thank you for teaching me how to read through another's eyes (and that font size is really, really important!).

Thank you to Kim, Sarah, Lynne, Jan, Deb, Karyn, Nicki, Jodi, who helped me to narrow down my vast list of working titles. Your insights made it a far more illuminating experience than expected.

To Kathryn Burnett and my friends in the Writing Room, in particular Sally, Scott, Fiona, Susy and Justine, thank you for all your valuable feedback and shared empathy along the lonely writing road.

To my father, John, who taught me the importance of a sense of discipline and dedication when it comes to your creative practice. If only I had a fraction of yours, Dad.

I dedicated this book to my mother, Lynne, and my other mother, Jan, because their endless loving pride has made me braver and better. If only all daughters were so fortunate.

While it's true children can be the greatest zappers of the thing every writer most hankers after, the time to write, I am eternally grateful to my own children, Archie and Peggy, who were only little when I first began this book, and are now practically grown-ups. Thank you, dearest hearts, for being such a never-ending well of inspiration. I love knowing how proud you are of me. I hope you always know I couldn't be prouder of you.

And finally, George, my very own patron of the arts. Your generosity, as both a human and a husband, leaves me breathless. Thank you, my darling, for enabling me to follow my dream.

About the author

Thrice nominated for New Zealand's columnist of the year, Megan Nicol Reed spent seven long years mining her life for a column that originally ran in the *Sunday Star Times* and then *The New Zealand Herald*'s *Canvas* magazine. Loved and hated in equal measure, the former journalist's weekly words never failed to provoke a reaction among readers. She became particularly known for her gentle skewering of the middle classes. Megan lives in Auckland with her husband, two teenage children and dog. *One of Those Mothers* is her first novel.